Coronation Summer

Margaret Pemberton is the bestselling author of over thirty novels in many different genres, some of which are contemporary in setting and some historical.

She has served as Chairman of the Romantic Novelists' Association and has three times served as a committee member of the Crime Writers' Association. Born in Bradford, she is married to a Londoner, has five children and two dogs and lives in Whitstable, Kent. Apart from writing, her passions are tango, travel, English history and the English countryside.

Coronation Summer

Margaret Pemberton

*MARGARET
PEMBERTON*

PAN BOOKS

First published 1997 by Transworld

This edition published 2015 by Pan Books
an imprint of Pan Macmillan
20 New Wharf Road, London N1 9RR
Associated companies throughout the world
www.panmacmillan.com

ISBN 978-1-4472-6234-3

3 5 7 9 8 6 4 2

A CIP catalogue record for this book is available from the British Library.

Typeset by Ellipsis Digital Limited, Glasgow
Printed and bound by CPI Group (UK) Ltd, Croydon, CR0 4YY

For my youngest daughter, Natasha Christina.
With a grandfather, James Alfred Edward Pemberton,
who boxed professionally in the 20s as 'Stoker'
Pemberton, and a father who also boxed, this book
is very specially for you.

Author's Note

I hope those that know and love the high, grassy green triangle of south-east London that is home to Magnolia Square will forgive the liberties I have taken with their local geography. Magnolia Square, Magnolia Terrace and Magnolia Hill are all fictitious, though Blackheath Village and heath, Greenwich Park and Lewisham and its High Street, are most decidedly not. It is an area I have lived in for nearly all my adult life. I hope I have done it justice.

Chapter One

'So I shall be wearing red, white and blue for the coronation, just as I did for VE Day,' Mavis Lomax said breezily to her younger sister. They were in Lewisham High Street.

Carrie, five years Mavis's junior, was behind the family's fruit and vegetable stall, polishing up a fresh delivery of apples on the corner of her gaily patterned, wrap-around overall. 'You'll look ridiculous,' she said bluntly, placing a nicely gleaming Cox's at the centre of her apple display. 'You looked ridiculous on VE Day, and you were only in your thirties then. As I remember it, your red skirt was split halfway to your thighs and your blue-and-white spotted blouse had a cleavage so low, it nearly met it. Now you're in your forties you should show a bit of sense.'

'I'm forty,' Mavis said with emphasis and a toss of her bottled-blonde, poodle-cut curls, 'not forty-two or forty-four or 'alfway to fifty, and I shall wear wot I bloomin' well like.' She was visiting the stall as a customer and she transferred a wicker shopping basket laden with potatoes and carrots and a couple of pounds of the apples Carrie had polished earlier from one scarlet-nailed hand to the other. 'You should try taking a leaf out of my book and tart yourself up a bit. You're getting to look quite frumpy. Next thing you know you'll be like our mum, wearing curlers all day and only taking your pinny off when you go to bed.'

I

She stood with her weight resting on one leg, the curve of her hips lushly voluptuous beneath the tightness of her caramel-coloured pencil skirt. 'Me and Ted are off down The Bricklayer's Arms tonight,' she continued, noticing for the first time that Carrie, usually so buoyant and ready for a laugh, looked as fed-up as she sounded. 'Why don't you and Danny come with us? We could have a bit of a knees-up, just like the old days.'

Carrie shook her head. 'Thanks, but no thanks,' she said, grudgingly appreciating the spirit in which the offer had been made. 'Danny's coaching at the club tonight, and I don't want Rose sitting in on her own.'

Mavis was about to suggest that Carrie bring her fourteen-year-old daughter with her but then decided against it. She and Carrie were as different as chalk and cheese and, whereas she had quite happily often taken her two youngsters for a drink when they were still under age, it wasn't something Carrie was ever likely to do. 'See yer then,' she said, about to turn on her heel and begin the walk home. A thought occurred to her and she paused. ''Ave yer seen the new boxer the club's signed up? Our Beryl says he's a smasher – tall, blond and 'andsome, with shoulders on him as wide as a street.'

Carrie suppressed a spurt of irritation. Despite her long and apparently happy marriage, Mavis had always been an outrageous flirt and – if the rumours were true – worse, and turning forty hadn't cured her.

'If he is, he'll be fifteen years too young for you,' she said unkindly.

Mavis chuckled, laughter lines crinkling the corners of cat-green eyes. 'That's what you think, our Carrie. If he's twenty-five, I think he'll be just the right age!' Still chuckling throatily, she walked off down the High Street, not the focus of quite as many masculine, head-turning glances as she had once been, but still the object of a good many.

Carrie shook her head in despair. How Ted, her quiet-spoken brother-in-law, endured his rackety home life, Carrie couldn't even begin to imagine.

'Three pahnds o' carrots, dearie, and 'alf a stone o' spuds,' a customer said, opening her shopping bag so that Carrie could tip the veg straight into it off the scales. 'Was that your Mavis I saw you chatting to a minute or so ago? What's she done with 'er 'air? Permed it? I've never seen so many curls on a grown woman before. She'll be able to play Goldilocks in the next Christmas panto, won't she!'

With an effort, Carrie summoned a laugh and agreed with her. She didn't truly feel like laughing, though. Mavis couldn't possibly have known it, but her remark about her becoming frumpy had hit home very hard. That morning, for the first time ever, her husband Danny had addressed her as if she wasn't his wife but his mother. It was something lots of south-east London men did, of course, but usually only after they were well into middle age. Her own father nearly always referred to her mother as 'Ma', rarely as Miriam. 'Put the kettle on, Ma,' he would say lovingly to her. 'Me stomach finks me froat's bin cut.' Daniel Collins, her father-in-law, was just the same. 'I'm off down to The Swan for a couple of jars, Ma,' he would say to Hettie in his breezy, genial manner. 'Do you want me to bring some fish and chips in on my way home?'

Until now, Carrie had never really given it much thought. Her mother and Hettie were both well in their sixties, and somehow their husbands referring to them by the all encompassing 'Ma' didn't seem odd. But she wasn't in her sixties! And she didn't want her husband referring to her as if all sexuality had gone out of their relationship and only loving matey-ness remained. Across the pavement from the Jennings' family fruit and vegetable stall were the large plate-glass windows of

Marks & Spencer's, and, as the stream of pedestrians passing up and down lulled, Carrie could see her reflection quite clearly. She chewed the corner of her lip. Was she beginning to look like her mother? She was big, certainly, but then she'd always been big, and the capacious leather cash-bag she wore for her daily stint at the stall didn't help. Tied around her waist, it was so bulky it would have made a ballerina look as ungainly as an elephant. 'But at least you're not fat, Carrie,' her best friend, Kate Emmerson, always said to her whenever she bemoaned her size. 'You're just splendidly Junoesque.' Carrie folded her arms and, with her head a little to one side, studied her reflection. It was quite true that she wasn't fat in the way many contemporaries of hers and Kate's had suddenly become fat, but then she hadn't had the number of children most of their old schoolfriends had had. A nasty miscarriage some years after Rose was born had ensured there'd been no more babies, though she had dearly wanted more.

A light May breeze tugged at her hair. Coal-dark and thick, with a strong wave to it, she wore it as she had worn it ever since she was a young girl, untidily loose and jaw-length. Sometimes she clipped it back, but only rarely, and she certainly never experimented with it the way Mavis did hers, following every hair fashion that came out and, in-between times, copying the style of whoever was her favourite film star.

'I said, a bunch o' radishes and two boxes o' cress,' a customer said irately, rattling her carrier bag for Carrie's attention. 'Cor blimey, gel, but you ain' 'alf wool-gathering! An' if those lettuces are fresh an' there's no slugs in 'em, I'll take two.'

For the rest of the day, until her father came to pack up the stall at five-thirty and to clear up all the debris that had accumulated around it, Carrie did her best to rise above the depression she was feeling. People didn't come shopping down the market to be served by someone with a long face. They came not only for cheap, fresh produce, but for a smile and a cheery word as well.

'Yer can tell Danny I'll be dahn the club tonight to watch this new bloke spar,' Albert Jennings said, relieving her of the day's takings and paying her handsomely out of them, as he always did. 'It'll be interestin' to see 'ow 'e shapes up. Jack seems to think 'e's got 'imself a real winner.'

Jack was Jack Robson, local rogue; owner of Lewisham's Embassy Boxing Club; Danny's boss; their neighbour and, ever since she and Danny were school kids, their friend.

'Well, if Jack thinks he's the bee's knees, he probably is,' Carrie said, not overly interested. She picked up her raspberry-pink swing-back coat from off a stool, slipped it on and kissed Albert on his leathery cheek. 'See you in the morning, Dad,' she said, grateful that it was he, not her, who trekked up to Covent Garden in the early hours for produce and who always set the stall up. 'Ta-ra.'

As she walked off down the High Street towards the clock tower, she wondered if her lack of enthusiasm about what was going on at the club wasn't, perhaps, part of her problem. To Danny, the club was his whole life. He was both manager and coach and had been ever since the day the club had first opened its doors. It meant that not only did he spend most of every day there, but nearly every evening, too.

'Cheer up, Petal,' a familiar voice shouted from the opposite side of the road. 'It might never 'appen!'

Carrie grinned and waved to old Charlie Robson, Jack Robson's dad.

'Are yer goin' up town next month for the coronation or watching it on me and 'Arriet's new telly?' he persisted, bawling across the road like a town-crier, his gnarled thumbs hooked behind his braces as he stood on the edge of the pavement, making no effort to close the gap between them. 'Only we'll need ter be knowin' 'cos I fink we're goin' to 'ave an 'ouse full and 'Arriet'll need to know 'ow many sausage rolls to make.'

'I'm going up town on Coronation Day, Charlie,' Carrie called back, beginning to cross the road towards him. She stood still for a moment to let a Ford Anglia nip past her and then sprinted to safety.

'Yer won't see all of it like you will if yer watch it on the telly,' Charlie said, put out. He was proud of his and Harriet's new telly and wanted to show it off. 'Yer'll be able to see everyfink wot's 'appening inside the Abbey, as well as outside, on the telly.'

'Yes, I know,' Carrie was unhappily aware that she was disappointing him, 'but the atmosphere won't be the same, will it? And I want to see the colours of the uniforms and regalia and flags and . . . oh, I don't know, Charlie . . . I just want to be a part of it all.'

''Avin' to sleep on a pavement the night afore to get a place to see ain't wot I'd call atmosphere an' colour,' Charlie grumbled good-naturedly, 'but if that's wot you want, Petal, then I 'ope you enjoy every minute of it.'

'Ta, Charlie.' Carrie grinned at him affectionately. Like most of the neighbours in the square where she lived, Charlie was part and parcel of her life, and had been ever since she could remember.

'An' tell your Danny I'll be dahn the club ternight to see this boy wonder my lad's signed up. If 'e's anything like this Rocky Marciano bloke the Yanks 'ave, we'll all be on our way to a tidy fortune.'

Carrie's grin died. She knew that, apart from the legal fights Jack promoted, there were also other fights which didn't get talked about quite so publicly. Fights where large sums of money were placed. Fights where what should have been her housekeeping money from Danny often went down the Swannee.

Thoughtfully she watched Charlie amble away from her. Even in old age he was a bear of a man, and there were lots of stories locally about how, when he was young and in his prime, he'd been a criminal *par excellence*, the bane of every police constabulary for miles around.

She began walking again, continuing on down the High Street until she reached the point where it ended, at the foot of Magnolia Hill. Was Jack Robson a chip off the old block? Did Jack also run outside the law and, if he did so, did he sometimes take her Danny with him? It was a disturbing thought and it wasn't the first time it had occurred to her. She turned right into Magnolia Hill. Usually she enjoyed her walk home towards Blackheath, for the houses in Magnolia Hill were all elegant, nicely kept Edwardian houses with nearly every garden boasting one of the magnolia trees that had given the hill its name. The problem was, she reflected as she walked on, that she and Danny rarely had serious talks about anything any more, and bringing up a subject as touchy as whether or not all Jack's business dealings were strictly kosher wouldn't be easy. She wondered whether she should speak to Kate about her worries. Kate's husband, Leon, though not employed at the club, was nearly as involved in it as Danny. He was a black ex-seaman, and during his naval days he had won medals galore for competitive boxing. And one thing was certain: Leon Emmerson wouldn't be involved in any shady dealing. He was as straight as the proverbial arrow.

She paused at the top of the hill, at the point where it opened onto a spacious square, debating with herself whether to go immediately home or to call in at Kate's. From where she was now standing, her home was only yards away, the first house on the left-hand side of the square's junction with the hill. The house on the immediate bottom right of the square was the house she was born in, and her mother and father and elderly gran still lived there. The first house going up the square on the right-hand side was Mavis and Ted's house, conspicuous for its lack of paint and air of general dilapidation. Next to that was an empty gap where a house had been bombed to smithereens in the war. Then there was Jack Robson's house. Like herself, he was born in Magnolia Square, and, despite the fact that he was obviously now doing very well for himself, he showed no signs of wanting to move away. There were then another three houses before, at the top end of the square, the houses changed character, becoming almost as large and gracious as those in Magnolia Hill. It was in one of these houses that the Emmersons lived.

Carrie dithered for just one second longer and then made her decision. Rose would be home from school and well into her homework by now, but Danny would be home, too, waiting for her to come in and begin making him something to eat before he began his evening stint at the club. Carrie resolutely began walking past her old home. Tonight, if Danny wanted something to eat, he'd jolly well have to stop behaving like a man with two broken arms and make it for himself.

There came the sound of an upstairs window being rapped, and Carrie looked upwards to see her gran waving at her. She waved back, mouthing and signalling that she hadn't time to come in, that she was on her way to see Kate, but that she'd call by on her way home. Leah Singer made a typically Jewish, typically disparaging gesture. Carrie grinned. Her gran was bed-bound and, despite the constant visits of neighbours and grandchildren, always behaved as if she were a neglected prisoner in a medieval tower. It didn't stop her getting to know all the gossip, though, and she would now be wanting to know all the latest about Jack Robson's new boxer.

Carrie glanced across the square, made elegant by the small Anglican church that graced its grassy centre island, to the house where Jack's new protégé was going to take up lodgings. There was no sign of activity there, no youngsters hanging around, so presumably he hadn't arrived yet. She gave a wry smile, aware that she was probably the only person in the square so uninterested, for the Embassy Boxing Club was viewed with affection and pride by Magnolia Square residents. Nearly all of them had helped Jack to get it off the ground in the early days after the war.

Leon had volunteered all his considerable expertise, Danny had done likewise, on a cash basis. Elisha Deakin, landlord of The Swan, had offered Jack the use of empty rooms above the pub. Her mother, Miriam, who cleaned St Mark's Church twice a week, even though she said she was now too old to stand on her feet all day at the market, kept the new-found premises spick and span. Her mother-in-law and father-in-law, Daniel and Hettie Collins, had put a sizeable amount of their hard-earned life savings into it, as had Jack's ultra-respectable, elderly stepmother. St Mark's vicar, the Reverend Bob Giles, had given the club his blessing by saying he hoped it would be the means of keeping a lot of local tearaways off the streets and out of trouble, and the young doctor who had moved his practice into number seven in the spring of 1950 had offered his services to Jack free of charge.

She turned in through Kate and Leon's gateway. A *magnolia sieboldii* graced the small front garden and was in full flower, its delicate blush-coloured flowers heart-stoppingly beautiful. Like all the houses in the top half of the square, a flight of wide, shallow stone steps led up to the front door. At the side of each step was a small pot thick with lavender, rosemary or thyme, and the air was heavy with fragrance and the hum of bees. She didn't bother to knock on the door. She'd been walking in and out of number four as if it were her own home ever since she'd been a toddler.

9

'Hello there!' she called out as she stepped into the hallway, adding unnecessarily, 'It's me, Carrie!'

Kate Emmerson came down the stairs with a squirming child tucked under one arm, a large tin toy truck caked with garden dirt under the other. She didn't look remotely harassed. Her hair was a deep natural gold and she wore it plaited and coiled into a bun. Instead of making her look older than her thirty-five years, the unfashionable style only served to emphasize her innate elegance and gracefulness. 'I left him playing with it in the garden,' she said wryly, obviously referring to the truck as the dusky-skinned, curly headed 'him' in question continued to struggle furiously, 'and the next thing I know there's a trail of dirt all the way up to my bedroom.'

'Gawage!' her youngest son bellowed indignantly as she at last deposited him on his feet. 'Not a bedwoom, a gawage!'

'I don't know how you cope,' Carrie said, secretly wishing she had the same problem and trying not to feel envious. 'Is it true a policeman caught Luke playing in the disused prefabs on Wednesday?'

Luke was the present culprit's eleven-year-old brother: an engaging rascal who looked as if butter wouldn't melt in his mouth and yet was never out of trouble.

Kate put the truck down on to a floor of highly polished linoleum and led the way into the kitchen. 'Yes, it is true, and yes, Luke knew the prefabs were off-limits.' She grinned ruefully as she began filling a kettle with water. 'That was the attraction, I suppose. Honestly, Carrie, you'd never believe the difference there is between bringing up a child who lives at home and goes to a local school and gets into mischief every second your back is turned, and one who is safely parked at prep school.'

Despite the dejection that had brought her to Kate's, Carrie grinned back at her. There weren't many people who would be quite as aware of the difference as Kate, but then, there weren't many people who had such a socially and racially mixed bunch of children.

Daisy, Kate's eldest child, was adopted and, if her pale creamy skin, dark blue eyes and dark hair were anything to go by, had a generous amount of Celtic blood in her veins. Matthew, twelve years old and three years younger than Daisy, was born illegitimately after his fighter pilot father's heroic death at Dunkirk. Matthew's father had come from a wealthy family and Matthew, at his father's family's expense, had always enjoyed a privileged education, going away at seven years old to the same exclusive preparatory school his father had gone to.

Luke, her first child by Leon Emmerson, was born a little over a year after Matthew and was nearly as dark-skinned as his half West Indian father, and then, four years later, Jilly was born, and another four years later, Johnny.

'Want a gawage!' Johnny said now, exasperatedly. 'Twucks need gawages!'

'Why don't you use the garden shed, pet lamb?' Kate suggested, putting the kettle on to boil and then taking two cups and two saucers down from a nearby cupboard. 'After all, trucks can't go upstairs, can they? So the bedroom really wasn't a suitable place. And if you garage the truck in the garden shed, you'll be able to wash it down in there, just like the men do in real garages.'

Johnny, a strap of his home-made dungarees slipping off his shoulder, regarded her thoughtfully for a long, silent moment. 'A hose,' he said at last in the tone of one who knows he's pushing his luck but thinks there's an outside chance he might just get away with it. 'Can I use Daddy's hose, Mummy?'

'Not unless Daddy's with you,' Kate said imperturbably. 'Now have a chocolate biscuit and go and play and let me have a quiet couple of minutes with Carrie.'

The thought of playing with both water and his truck engaged Johnny's attention. He might not be able to play with the garden hose on his own, but he could fill the watering-can from the garden tap and play with water that way. And it wouldn't be naughty because his mummy didn't say anything about not playing with taps and watering-cans. He accepted the biscuit Kate was proffering him and trotted obediently outside, a little angel bent on mischief.

'So what's brought you round at this time of day?' Kate asked her lifelong friend as they waited for the kettle to boil. 'Danny'll be waiting for his tea, won't he?'

Carrie slipped off her coat and threw it over the back of a kitchen chair. 'Most likely,' she said uncaringly, sitting down. 'And as far as I'm concerned, he can blooming well wait. Or make it for himself.'

Kate giggled. Coming from Carrie this was real fighting talk, for she waited on Danny hand and foot, and Kate doubted if Danny would even know where to find a saucepan or a frying-pan, let alone know how to put them to good use. 'What's the matter?' she asked sympathetically. 'Is he driving you mad, talking about nothing else but this new boxer Jack's signed up?'

Carrie propped her chin in her hands, her elbows on the table. 'No,' she said morosely, 'I wish it was that simple.' She chewed the corner of her lip, looking across at her serenely happy friend. How did Kate do it? She never seemed disillusioned or disappointed. But then Kate was married to a man who would never, in a million years, refer to her as 'Ma', and she had not just one child, but a houseful of them. 'Don't you ever get browned-off, Kate?' she asked bluntly. 'I mean, it's not much fun being thirty-five, is it? For me, all there seems to be is working on Dad's stall, coming home to more work of a different kind, washing and cleaning and putting meals on the table and clearing them away again, on and on, *ad infinitum*.'

'That's a long word for this time of day.' Kate's teasing tone of voice was at odds with the very real concern showing in her eyes. She took the kettle off the boil and poured a little into the teapot, rinsing it round to warm it. She knew there were times when Carrie's marriage was under strain, and she knew that the fault invariably lay with Danny. He was such a know-all, and so cocky with it, she doubted if even his best mates would think him an easy bloke to live with. To make it worse, his mother had always doted on him and run round after him, and Danny expected the same kind of slavish attention from Carrie.

'It's just . . .' Carrie began, and paused. She'd always been a spirited, jolly person, not much given to thoughtful intro-spection, but all of a sudden she saw her life as an outsider might see it, and with a stab of shock she realized how lustre-less it had become.

Kate, devotedly in love with a man who loved her with all his heart, mind and soul, glowed with inner happiness no matter how trying her children might be or how tedious her daily chores. But she, Carrie, didn't glow, and it wasn't because she didn't love Danny, for she did. It was simply that they never seemed to talk to each other properly any more, or go out together any more. And when they were together at home, there was never an ounce of romance in the air. ''Ow about it, gel?' was about the most romantic Danny ever got, and this invita-tion was usually only ever issued when he'd had a couple of pints down The Swan.

'It's just that Danny and I never seem to have any fun together any more,' she finished inadequately, not wanting to sink to utter disloyalty by revealing to Kate how lacking in the love-making department Danny was. 'The club takes up all his time. He's round there whether he's supposed to be or not.'

Kate brewed the tea. She, too, often wished the Embassy

Boxing Club to the ends of the earth, for Leon was nearly as bad, acting as a back-up coach at weekends whenever needed, and taking nearly as much interest in the welfare and progress of some of the youngsters who attended the club as he did of their own children. 'Why don't you spend more time down there yourself, Carrie?' she suggested, carrying the teapot over to the table. 'It isn't as if you have to have a babysitter these days, is it? And it certainly isn't as if you wouldn't be made welcome. After all, the club's practically a family business.'

'The club's Jack's business,' Carrie corrected darkly. 'And quite frankly, Kate, I don't know that I'm too happy about the way Jack conducts his business affairs.'

'Well, Jack's always sailed a bit close to the wind,' Kate agreed, wondering if Carrie knew something she didn't. 'But the club is all legal and above board.'

'I'm not sure all of the—' Carrie began and was interrupted by the sound of loud, authoritative knocking on Kate's front door.

'That's a policeman's knock.' Kate's face paled. 'Leon was ferrying a load of combustibles from Gravesend to Rotherhithe this morning!' With visions of there having been a terrible accident on the Thames, she ran from the kitchen.

Carrie hesitated for a moment and then followed her. She had been about to share her worry over whether all the fights Jack arranged were strictly legal, but when she saw that Kate was right, and that her visitor was a policeman, she was glad she hadn't done so. Kate obviously had other troubles at the moment. With fierce intensity, she hoped they wouldn't be serious and that no one had been hurt.

'No one's been hurt, Madam,' the policeman was saying to Kate reassuringly, 'only there's been a bit of bother at your lad's school.'

Kate's shoulders slumped in relief. Luke was always in 'a

bit of bother' at school, though it was coming to something when his headmaster began sending a policeman round to her door. It wasn't as if Luke's misdemeanours were ever of the bullying kind for, like his father, he didn't have a vicious bone in his body.

'Does his headmaster want to see me?' she asked, wondering if Carrie would keep an eye on Johnny for her. 'Because if he does, I'll just get my jacket.'

The policeman's bushy eyebrows rose so high they disappeared completely beneath his helmet. 'You'll have a bit of a journey, Madam, if you don't mind my saying so. Somerset is a tidy step even in this day and age.'

'Somerset?' Kate stared at him as if he'd taken leave of his senses. 'You've made some kind of a mistake, Constable. It's my eldest son who is at school in Somerset, not Luke.'

The policeman sighed. She was a stunning-looking woman but obviously not over-bright in the brainbox department. 'It isn't a Luke I'm here about,' he said, with saintly patience. He looked down at his notepad. 'It's a Master Matthew Harvey, twelve years of age.'

'Matthew?' Kate bunked. What kind of trouble could Matthew be in? Matthew was never in trouble. Intelligent, well-spoken, well-mannered, he was as near to perfection as any boy his age possibly could be. But then, the policeman hadn't said her son was in trouble. He'd said there had been a bit of bother at the school. Fresh fear seized her. 'Has there been a fire?' she asked urgently. 'An outbreak of sickness . . . ?'

'I told you before, Madam, no one's been hurt and they aren't sick or injured either. Your lad has, however, absconded. Now, boys being boys, he'll no doubt be back at school by tonight, safely tucked up and—'

'Absconded? You mean Matthew's run away?'

Kate felt dizzily disorientated. Matthew had been a pupil at

St Osyth's ever since he was seven years old. He liked St Osyth's. He always did well in exams and excelled at games. Somehow, somewhere, there had obviously been a mistake.

'If I could just come in for a moment, Mrs Harvey?' the policeman asked, aware that he wasn't, as yet, making much headway.

'Mrs Emmerson,' Kate corrected automatically, stepping back to let him in and bumping into Carrie as she did so.

The policeman didn't move. Emmerson. So there had been a mistake after all. 'The young lad who's gone missing is named Harvey,' he said ponderously. 'Matthew Harvey. I thought perhaps he was related to the local Harvey Construction Company family, him attending a nob public school like St Osyth's. However . . .' he looked towards Carrie, resplendent in her street-trading pinny, 'I see I've made a mistake and I'm sorry to have—'

'You haven't made a mistake,' Kate said impatiently, hating, as she always did, having to explain Matthew's parentage. Without getting involved in the fact that Matthew had been born illegitimately and that, though adopted by the man she later married, she had come to an arrangement with Matthew's deceased father's family that Matthew would be known by his father's surname, she said merely, 'My surname is Emmerson, my son's surname is Harvey.' She led the way into the house, her mind racing. Where on earth could Matthew be? Had he run away because he was being bullied? He'd never complained of being bullied, but perhaps he was amongst a different set of boys now he was no longer in the prep department, but in the Lower School.

She hurried into the sitting-room, making straight for the fireplace and the many framed photographs on the mantel-piece. 'This is a recent photograph of Matthew,' she said, handing one of them to the policeman, wondering how long it would take Matthew to get to London from Somerset; wondering if he had any money and, if he had, whether it was enough for the train fare home. 'When did my son go missing?' she asked, trying to work out how long it would take Matthew, travelling by train, to reach home.

'I'm not rightly sure, Madam.' The policeman took the photograph out of its frame and studied it. The boy in question was a good-looking boy, Nordically blond like his mother, and with her distinctive high cheekbones and generous, full-lipped mouth. He'd certainly be easily recognizable, and that was half the battle in runaway cases. 'It appears the young gent wasn't present at assembly this morning,' he continued, slipping the photograph into his notebook. 'So he could have been missing since last night.'

Kate's eyes flew in horror to Carrie's. If Matthew had caught a train he would have been home by now. Was he trying to thumb a lift? Dear Lord, was he perhaps even trying to walk home?

There came the faint sound of the front gate creaking back on its hinges and Kate darted past the policeman and Carrie, running out into the hallway and towards her still half-open front door, calling out urgently, 'Matthew? Is that you, Matthew?'

Seconds later the policeman, striding at a dignified pace in her wake, saw her hurtle down the steps fronting her door, not towards a young, white, public schoolboy, but a muscular, middle-aged man of West Indian origin.

'What on earth would Matthew be doing here, love?' the man asked in mystified concern, as, to the policeman's stupefaction, she ran headlong into his arms.

'Matthew's run away from school! He very probably ran away last night!' Relief that Leon was now with her overwhelmed her and suddenly, ridiculously, she felt like crying.

'Well, if that's all, love, it isn't the end of the world,' Leon said, concealing the alarm he felt and reassuring her as best he could. He looked towards the policeman. 'Can you give me some details, Constable?' he asked, his arm still around Kate. 'Did my son speak to any of the other boys, saying why he was running away and where he was going to run to?'

The policeman blinked. His son? Who did the darkie think he was kidding? 'Now look here . . .' he began warningly, and was stopped in mid-tracks by a passer-by.

'I wouldn't waste time chin-wagging with Mrs Emmerson, Constable!' Lettie Deakin, Elisha Deakin's wife, called out with relish. 'Not when her back garden is nearly a foot under water! I'd phone for the ruddy Fire Brigade – or the Lifeboat Service!'

Chapter Two

By the time Carrie left number four it was way too late for her
to honour her promise to call in and have a chat with her gran.
Rose would be wondering where she was and perhaps beginning to worry, and Danny would very probably have already
left for the club. In order not to have to walk past number
eighteen, she cut across the square, walking hurriedly down
the left-hand side of it.

'What's all the ter-do up at the Emmersons?' Nellie Miller,
her gargantuan next door neighbour, called out. 'There's been
a bobby at the 'ouse for nearly an 'our. 'As young Luke been
up to mischief again?' Nellie's twenty stone was crammed into
a sagging armchair that took up all her open doorway. From
there, like a pasha on a throne, she kept tabs on all the comings
and goings in the square, doing so with even more meticu-
lousness than Carrie's gran.

'It was young Johnny this time,' Carrie said, knowing Nellie
wouldn't be fobbed off without a smidgen of the truth. 'He
took the hose off the garden tap and turned the tap full on.
Then he couldn't turn it off again. Kate's back garden looks
like Blackheath pond.'

'Silly little bleeder,' Nellie said with affection. 'Tell 'im I've
a bag of sweeties waitin' 'ere for 'im next time yer see 'im.'

Hurrying up her own front path, Carrie promised to do so.
It was half past six. With a pang of guilt, she wondered if

Danny had left for work without having anything hot to eat. There were two lamb chops under the net in the larder, but he wouldn't have thought to pop them in a frying-pan. Her door was ajar as it always was on warm sunny evenings, and she pushed it wider, calling out defiantly as if she were still down the market, 'If yer still 'ere and yer still 'aven't eaten, it's yer own fault, Danny! Yer shouldn't behave as if you need a map to find the bloomin' kitchen!'

'Blimey,' an unfamiliar masculine voice said in amusement, 'that's a right old greeting for the old man and no mistake.'

Carrie came to a shocked dead halt in the middle of her narrow hallway. There was a man standing in her kitchen doorway. A man she had never seen before. A man who looked more like a film star than a burglar. Tall, broad-shouldered, lean-hipped, with a shock of corn-gold hair, he was leaning laconically against the door jamb. With his arms easily folded, one leg negligently crossing the other at the ankle, he looked for all the world as if he was the one on home turf and she was the intruder.

Carrie's eyes flew to her sitting-room door. It was half open, the room obviously empty, and a strange jacket was hanging on the doorknob. 'Where's Danny?' she demanded and then, an edge of panic in her voice, 'Where's Rose? And who the hell are you and what are you doing in my house?'

The stranger grinned. Unfolding his arms and easing himself away from the door jamb, he said with careless self-assurance, 'Danny's at the club. Rose has gone to see her great-gran. I'm Zac Hemingway. I've moved into the square to be nearer the club. I presume you're Carrie. Danny said you'd soon be home.'

'And he left you here to welcome me?' Carrie shrugged herself furiously out of her coat. When she got hold of Danny she'd give him a rollicking he wouldn't soon forget. How dare he leave a stranger alone in their house? She wanted to march straight into her kitchen in order to bang some pots and pans around and let off some steam, but she couldn't very well do so while Zac bloody Hemingway was near as dammit barring her way. She flung her coat over the newel post, saying witheringly, 'And so you're the new boxer? You're lodging with Queenie Tillet, not me. She's only four doors away,' she added pointedly, 'at number nine, so you'll not have far to walk.'

Zac Hemingway's grin deepened. He didn't have dimples, but he did have a very attractive cleft in his chin. Despite her fury at his cavalier attitude, Carrie couldn't help wondering if anyone ever told him he was a dead ringer for Kirk Douglas, the American film star. She shoved her work-roughened hands deep into the capacious pockets of her wrap-around apron, wishing she wasn't wearing it but not liking to take it off in case he took it as an invitation to make himself even more at home than he already had done.

'Queenie will be expecting you,' she said tartly as he made no sign of moving, 'and I've got things to do. A dinner to cook—'

'If you had the lamb chops in mind, I'm afraid I have a confession to make,' he said, beginning to walk down the passageway towards her. He moved with the well-knit, springy precision of a born athlete, and Carrie stepped hastily up onto the bottom step of her stairs in order that he wouldn't have to squeeze past her to reach the front door.

'And what's that?' she asked, trying to keep her mind on the conversation and, as he drew abreast of her on the other side of the banisters, finding it infuriatingly difficult.

Even though his hands were now plunged carelessly in his trouser pockets, his biceps bulged magnificently, and from beneath his open-necked cotton shirt was a glimpse of a chest so deep and powerfully muscled she couldn't help wildly wondering what he would look like semi-naked in a boxing ring.

'Danny said, as I hadn't eaten, I could help myself to anything I found,' he continued, not looking at all abashed by the admission he was making, 'and the chops were too inviting to ignore.'

She grasped hold of the coat-covered newel post, gaping at him incredulously. 'You ate my Danny's dinner?' She couldn't believe it. 'You helped yourself to my lamb chops?'

He gave a slight, almost Gallic shrug of his massive shoulders. He was so near now that she could see the colour of his eyes. They weren't blue, as she had expected. They were grey, very clear and light and violently alive. 'It seemed like a good idea at the time,' he said with disarming honesty. 'Danny didn't want them. He said he was going to call in at the jellied eel shop for some pie and mash.'

Carrie gritted her teeth. That bloomin' husband of hers! If he'd been within hitting distance she'd have swatted him with the nearest heavy object. 'Well . . . as you weren't to know any differently . . .' she began stiffly, feeling as if she had somehow been wrong-footed and not quite knowing how.

'That's very understanding of you.' He sounded soberly sincere but there was a gleam in his eyes that belied the tone of his voice, and a muscle was twitching at the side of his mouth.

He was laughing at her. Carrie knew he was laughing at her. In stony silence she watched as he picked up the jacket that was hanging on the sitting-room doorknob.

He hooked it with his thumb, swinging it over his shoulder, saying, 'Seeing as how you're Danny's missus, I wouldn't want to have got off on the wrong foot with you.'

Carrie remained frozen-faced, pointedly waiting for him to

leave. With another slight shrug of his shoulders he turned away from her, walking to the front door. It was still wide open and as he stepped out onto her scrubbed, white-stoned doorstep he paused, turning towards her, saying reflectively, 'Just as a matter of interest, when you've got such a lovely voice why did you speak like a fishwife when you first came in the house and you thought only Danny was home?' Not waiting for a reply, which was just as well because Carrie was speechless with disbelief, he flashed her his wide, dazzling smile, gave her a wink, and strode off down the garden path and the square towards number nine.

Very slowly, with legs like jelly, Carrie sat down on her stairs. The impertinence of the man. The bare-faced, insolent impertinence! And he hadn't only been impertinent: unless she was very much mistaken, Zac Hemingway, who could be no more than twenty-seven or twenty-eight, had been flirting with her. She pushed her untidy, deeply waving hair back away from her face, aware that her cheeks were flying scarlet banners. What on earth would Danny say when she told him? Would he even believe her? From her viewpoint opposite the open door she saw a lithe, dearly loved figure approaching her gate. Seconds later her precious daughter was rushing into the house, saying with breathless concern, 'Gosh, Mum! What are you doing sitting on the stairs with your face all red! You're not having a hot flush, are you?'

'No, I'm not!' Carrie said indignantly, rising to her feet. 'I'm thirty-five, you cheeky young madam, not forty-five!' She led the way into the kitchen, crossly aware that, for the first time in her life, she had sounded a lot like Mavis. She filled the kettle for a cup of tea. Zac Hemingway had a lot to answer for, by crikey he had!

*

The Embassy Boxing Club was humming with activity. 'So when's this new bloke going to put in an appearance?' Danny Collins asked his boss. 'It's half past seven. The natives are getting restless.'

The natives were the youngsters from St Mark's Church Scout Group, nearly all of them in shorts and boxing gloves; a hefty proportion of Magnolia Square's elderly and female residents, all perched on whatever rickety chairs or benches The Swan's landlord had thoughtfully provided; and the hard core of bruisingly fit young men who were fast making the club a force to be reckoned with.

'He'll put in an appearance in his own good time,' Jack Robson said easily, 'or he will if he hasn't fallen asleep on your sofa. What did you make of him when you met him?'

They were talking in the small partitioned-off booth in the corner of the gym that served Jack as an office. Danny, dressed in a singlet and shabby flannels with a grubby towel slung around his shoulders, was a man whose physical strength lay in tough wiriness, not physical bulk. His slightly faded mahogany-red hair was cropped close to his head, giving him the look of an ex-jailbird which, more by luck than management, he wasn't.

Jack Robson was a very different kettle of fish. He wasn't overly tall, but the sense of barely reined-in power he exuded made most people think he was well over six foot. All through the war he had fought in the Commandos, and though he had allowed the peak of physical fitness he had reached in his commando days to ebb slightly, he was still, for a man only four years away from forty, unnervingly hard-muscled. Wearing one of the slick suits he was so fond of, with a straight, handsome mouth and with dark curly hair still untouched by grey, he was also devastatingly attractive – and, if appearances were anything to go by, happily married. It was a combination that drove many of the young women who frequented the club wild.

Danny rubbed his chin thoughtfully, saying, 'I dunno really, Jack. 'E certainly looks as if 'e could lift a double-decker bus with 'is tiny finger, but 'e's a bit on the pretty side. If 'e's such dynamite in the ring, 'ow come 'e ain't got a broken nose or a cauliflower ear?'

Jack grinned and adjusted the framed photograph that graced the battered table that served as his desk. 'Because he is dynamite in the ring. He's as fast as greased lightning and so light on his feet you'd think he was bantam-weight, not heavy-weight.' His eyes lingered on the photograph. It had been taken on the promenade at Margate last summer. The sea breeze was tugging at Christina's cloud of smoke-dark, shoulder-length hair, but she didn't have her head thrown back, laughing with full-throated enjoyment as most south-east London girls did when having a good time at the seaside. Instead, her head was slightly to one side, her heavy-lashed eyes unreadable, her slight smile as tantalizing and as enigmatic as that of the *Mona Lisa*.

''E'll 'ave to be light on 'is bloody feet if 'e's goin' to fight unlicensed as well as legit,' Danny was saying.

Jack dragged his thoughts away from Christina, wishing she would come down to the club, if only occasionally; wishing her reason for not doing so wasn't because she was sitting at home reading or sewing, but because she was minding a houseful of kids. 'I've seen him work out, I've seen him fight, and he's gold, Danny, pure gold,' he said, ramming the pain of his and Christina's childlessness to the back of his mind. 'But until he turns up let's keep our visitors happy, shall we? Get Big Jumbo sparring with Tommy. That should keep the old biddies and girls quiet for a bit.'

Danny grinned and turned to go, walking smack into Mavis as he did so.

'Steady on, I've only got the one chest and I don't want you squashing it flat,' Mavis said, stepping back from the encounter and tugging a skin-tight scarlet sweater down over her hips as if, somehow, it had become disarranged.

'It'd be easier to flatten two ferrets in a sack than to flatten your chest, Mavis gal,' Danny said with the easy familiarity that came of his being her brother-in-law and of his having known her ever since he could walk.

'Sod off,' Mavis retorted amicably and then, as he obligingly did so, transferring her attention to Jack. 'So where's the boy wonder?' she asked, hoisting her tight skirt up a little so that she could perch on the corner of his desk. 'Everyone thought he'd be doin' a bit of training tonight.'

'I reckon he will be.' His mouth tugged into a smile. 'He's not on a ball and chain, you know.'

'Lucky old him.' Mavis looked directly into his eyes. 'I wish everyone I knew could say the same.'

Jack's smile died. He looked suddenly every one of his thirty-six years. 'Leave off, love,' he said wearily. 'There's no point and well you know it.'

'There could be.' There was no mistaking the depth of emotion in Mavis's voice. 'We're not kids any more, Jack. It's not as if we don't know what we're about. You've known ever since we were at school how I bloomin' well feel about you, and—'

'Sorry to interrupt,' Danny said cheerily, putting his head round the corner of the booth, 'only Zac's arrived, Jack. Thought you'd like to know.'

'Thanks Danny.' Jack touched Mavis briefly on the shoulder and walked out into the noisy mayhem of his gym.

Danny hesitated before following him. 'Ain't yer coming to cast yer mince-pies over the new arrival, Mavis?'

Mavis didn't move from where she was sitting on the corner of the makeshift desk. 'Is he worth it?' she asked desultorily.

Danny grinned. 'From your point of view I reckon 'e is.'

Mavis looked at the photograph Jack had been toying with. Christina's black-lashed eyes, in a face unmistakably foreign and undeniably beautiful, met hers, their expression as unrevealing as those of a sphinx.

'I suppose I might as well,' she said bleakly. 'I'm certainly not making any headway anywhere else.'

'I can't go to the club to see the new boxer spar,' fifteen-year-old Daisy Emmerson said to twenty-one-year-old Billy Lomax as they stood on the pavement outside number sixteen. 'Not when we've got such trouble on at home.' Daisy hadn't been born an Emmerson. Bombed out in the war, her family killed, she'd been taken in by Kate and, when Kate married Leon, had been adopted by them. From that moment on she had very rightly considered herself to be every inch an Emmerson, and anyone foolish enough to point out that Leon Emmerson couldn't possibly be her dad, his skin colour being so very different to her own, received very short shrift indeed. He was her legal dad and he loved her and cherished her, and if that wasn't enough to make him her dad in the fullest sense of the word, then Daisy didn't know what was.

'But it isn't real trouble, is it?' Billy said reasonably. 'Matthew's only run away from school. Crikey, if my mum thought she'd 'ad real trouble on 'er 'ands every time I ran away from school, she'd 'ave grey hair by now!'

At the thought of Mavis with grey hair a smile twitched at the corners of Daisy's mouth. Mavis Lomax would have to be in a box six feet under before she allowed her hair to go grey!

'Things aren't quite the same at our house as they are at yours,' she said, pointing out the obvious in the kindest way possible. Her house was ordered, welcoming and full of laughter, with very rarely any crossness and never any shouting. Billy's house was welcoming too, in a ramshackle way, but it was far from being ordered, and shouting and laughter followed so bewilderingly hard on each other's heels that Daisy often felt quite dizzy. 'Matthew's school isn't exactly a local school that's just around the corner,' she continued. 'Somerset is miles away, and Matthew's been missing for twenty-four hours now. Mum and Dad are frantic.'

For Daisy's sake, Billy tried to understand what seemed to him to be an unnecessary over-reaction. ''E's probably just scarpered off with a mate for a bit of a good time,' he said, well aware that if he had ever had access to the kind of money Matthew probably had access to, he would most definitely have scarpered off, and done so regularly and on a right royal basis! He dug his hands as deep in the pockets of his tight-fitting trousers as they would go, which wasn't far, wondering just how much money Matthew had inherited a few years ago when his great-grandfather died. It would have been a packet, he knew that. Old man Harvey, of the Harvey Construction Company, had been stinking rich, and as his son had been killed in the First World War and his grandson in the Second World War, young Matthew had come in for the lot.

The money hadn't made any difference to the way the Emmersons lived, though. 'Why should it?' Daisy said to him when he once brought the subject up. 'It's Matthew's money, not Mum and Dad's. His school fees come out of it, but I don't think anything else does. There's executors and trustees, and he has to be educated as his great-grandfather wanted and he has to keep in touch with his Harvey relations. There's a great-aunt in Somerset and another aunt here in London, in Kensington. It's all very complicated. It's not simple, like winning the pools.'

She said now, 'Matthew wouldn't run off just for a bit of fun. Not when he'd know how Mum and Dad would worry.'

Seeing the anxiety in her eyes and hearing it in her voice stabbed his heart something rotten. He took hold of her hand, drawing her a little closer towards him. 'I'll walk you back 'ome,' he said gruffly, for all the world as if number four was a good mile away. 'Mebbe there'll be some news. Mebbe 'e's already back at school.'

She squeezed his hand gratefully and his heart soared. He was potty about Daisy Emmerson. She was so dainty and neat, with her cap of shiny blue-black hair and flawless, creamy skin. It just wasn't possible to imagine Daisy having spots, or unpolished shoes, or grubby marks on her skirt. 'Band-box fresh' was how he'd heard one of their elderly neighbours describe her, and it was a phrase he had never forgotten. Even as a young hooligan, he always knew she would one day be his girl. For years she'd been too young for him to have done anything about it, but she wasn't too young now. She was fifteen and he had every intention of putting their long-term friendship on another, more satisfactory footing just as soon as he possibly could.

The trouble was, he brooded to himself as they walked up the square past the twilight-shrouded church, a girl like Daisy had to be treated with respect. She wasn't the sort of girl that could be taken round the back of the local bike shed for a kiss and a cuddle and, if he were lucky, something more. Nor did he want her to be. What he wanted from his relationship with Daisy was something so special he daren't put it into words, not even to himself.

As they turned in at her garden gate they saw that the front door was open and that eleven-year-old Luke was seated unhappily at the top of the short flight of steps leading up to it, his elbows on his knees, his chin in his hands.

'There's no news,' he said to them glumly as they walked up the steps towards him. 'Mr Giles is here now. Dad wants to go to Somerset to look for Matthew, but Mr Giles doesn't think it's a good idea. He doesn't think Matthew will still be in Somerset. He thinks he'll be on his way to London.'

He was a good-looking boy, his skin colour a dusky coffee, his hair a tightly curling mop, his eyes, like his father's, brown and gold-flecked. His finely modelled cheekbones and well-shaped mouth were, however, carbon copies of his mother's cheekbones and mouth, and the combination, in the eyes of the girls in his class at school, was sensationally distinctive.

He said now, as Billy and Daisy sat down on either side of him, Daisy reluctant to go into the house when the vicar was with her mum and dad, Billy reluctant to leave Daisy until he absolutely had to, 'I don't understand it. Matthew never does anything wrong. And he liked school, I dunno why, but he did.'

'Mebbe he's got a new teacher 'e doesn't like,' Billy suggested helpfully. 'A new teacher can't 'alf make life miserable.'

Luke, who'd never had any trouble getting on with his teachers, despite his lack of enthusiasm for schoolwork, remained silent. He knew Billy was trying to be helpful but Billy didn't know Matthew the way he and Daisy knew Matthew. And he and Daisy knew that even if Matthew wasn't getting on with a teacher, he wouldn't simply have run away. He'd have spoken to their dad about it. Their dad would soon have sorted it out. Their dad might be black and only a Thames waterman, but he wasn't frightened of anyone, not even of the snobby teachers at Matthew's posh school.

There came the sound of someone walking down the hall towards the open doorway and Luke turned his head, expecting to see Mr Giles, but it wasn't Mr Giles, it was his dad.

'I thought I heard Billy's voice,' Leon said as Billy rose hurriedly to his feet. 'How are you, Billy? Is the business doing all right?'

Billy's business was a scrap-metal yard that Jack Robson had loaned him the money to buy, and it was typical of Leon that, despite his frantic anxiety over Matthew, he took time to ask Billy how business was doing.

'It's doing great,' Billy replied truthfully. 'I've just made a deal with the council for all the piping from the old prefabs. They're starting demolition next week.'

Daisy also rose to her feet and slipped her hand into her dad's. His face, always so attractive and genial, had a crumpled, weary look, and she knew that it was because of his anxiety over Matthew. With a stab of shock she noticed for the first time that, at his temples, there were tiny flecks of grey in his crinkly black hair. Her dad was only thirty-eight or thirty-nine. Did people go grey at that age? Or was he only turning grey because he was so very, very worried about Matthew?

'I'm glad you've called by,' he was saying to Billy. 'Will you do me a favour and call in at the club and tell Jack that Matthew's run away from school? He'll know then why I'm not down there tonight to see the new chap go through his paces.'

'Yeah, 'course I will,' Billy said obligingly. Over Leon's shoulder he saw the unmistakable gleam of Mr Giles's dog-collar as the vicar stepped into the hallway from the sitting-room, and knew it was time he was on his way. He liked the vicar, but not so much that he wanted to be waylaid by him. 'Cheerio,' he said, encompassing all three Emmersons in his farewell, but his eyes on Daisy alone. 'I'll see yer tomorrer. I 'ope you 'ave good news by then.'

'So do I,' Leon said with deep feeling.

'Oh dear,' Mr Giles said seconds later. 'I've just missed Billy, have I? What a pity. I've been trying to have a chat with him for ages. He'd make a wonderful youth leader if he'd only put his mind to it.'

Daisy squeezed her dad's hand tightly, knowing that if it wasn't for anxiety over Matthew she would have been in fits of giggles. Even as a youngster, Billy had adamantly refused to be coerced into any of St Mark's Church youth activities.

'I've told the police they can ring me at any time of the day or night and I'll pass on to you whatever information they have,' Bob Giles was now saying to Leon. Acting as the courier of urgent telephone messages was something he was long accustomed to. Very few of his parishioners were on the telephone and, in Magnolia Square, only Jack Robson and his wife had the benefit of such a luxury.

As a grave-faced Bob Giles went on his way and Leon slid his free hand around Luke's shoulders, Luke felt real fear for the first time in his life. Perhaps Matthew hadn't just run away from school. Perhaps he'd had an accident and was lying hurt and bleeding somewhere. Another even more terrible thought occurred to him, and his heart felt as if it was going to stop. What if Matthew had been hurt *by* someone? What if Matthew had been murdered?

Fifty yards or so away, as he stood at the corner of Magnolia Square and Magnolia Hill, looking down towards the foot of the hill and The Swan pub, Billy's heart was also nearly failing him. In the gathering dusk he could see a big black Humber parked outside The Swan and a group of thick-set, spivvily suited men standing nearby, deep in conversation.

Billy knew the car and he knew the men, though only by sight and reputation. They were mobsters – members of a south-London gang of hardened criminals notorious for their vicious extortion and protection activities. If they had now hit on the Embassy Boxing Club as being a future source of protection money, then Jack Robson and everyone who worked for him at the club, or who trained at it, were looking deep trouble in the face. Very deep trouble indeed.

Chapter Three

With his hands tucked in his trouser pockets and whistling tunelessly to give himself an air of nonchalance – a nonchalance he was very far from feeling – Billy sauntered past the knot of men and into the side doorway of the pub. Two flights of creaking wooden stairs led up to the gym, the distempered walls plastered with pictures of fighters: Rocky Marciano, Joe Louis, Freddie Mills, Randolph Turpin, and placards on which were written such homilies as '*Head Down, Hands Up*', '*When in Doubt, Jab Out*', and '*To Rest is to Rust*'.

Once safely out of earshot of anyone in the street, he broke into a sprint up the stairs, barging breathlessly into the gym, intent on finding and warning Jack in the fastest time possible. The gym was packed, not only with the young kids from St Mark's Scout Troop and pukka club members, but with a motley gathering of visitors. He could see his mum, wearing a sizzling red sweater, and his gran and grandad, his gran's steel-grey hair in tight sausage curls, his grandad in a collarless shirt, braces stretched over his magnificent paunch. He could also see elderly Hettie and Daniel Collins, Danny Collins's mum and dad. Hettie was, as always, smartly dressed, a black cloth coat buttoned up to her chin despite the warmth of the evening and the fug of the gym, a black straw hat decorated with artificial cherries set at a rakish angle on her tightly permed hair.

He looked around wildly for Jack. All attention was centred

on a bloke he had never seen before, a bloke who was power-fully hitting the heavy-bag. He was presumably the new boxer Jack was so cock-a-hoop about, and Billy's fleeting glance told him he was a fighter big enough and well-muscled enough to knock a building down.

Danny was overseeing the new guy's workout, and Billy was well-versed enough in Danny's methods to know that there must have already been some loosening-up exercises and stretches. Then would have come a round of shadow boxing. Then a round of boxing. And another round of shadow boxing. The heavy-bag work would be the length of two rounds, followed by more shadow boxing, then skip rope and speed-ball work and, finally, callisthenics.

'Where's Jack?' he urgently asked the nearest spectator who happened to be Jack's dad, old Charlie. 'I need to see him! He's going to get a visit from Archie Duke's boys any minute now!'

Charlie blinked. 'Archie Dook! Wot's a gangster like Archie Dook want wiv Jack?'

Protection money was Billy's educated guess, but he didn't have time to tell Charlie that. 'Where the 'ell's Jack?' he demanded again, knowing the confab on the pavement couldn't go on for much longer.

''E's gorn to get a new speed-ball from the back room,' Charlie said, frowning unhappily. ''Ere, you don't fink Archie's goin' to try and pin Jack fer protection, do yer?'

Billy wasn't listening. Squeezing his way between knots of young, aspiring boxers from St Mark's Scout Troop, he ran towards the back room. Behind him, raucous encouraging comments were being made as Jack's new protégé obligingly moved from heavy-bag work to shadow boxing again.

'When you goin' to put 'im in the ring with Big Jumbo?' he could hear his gran calling out to Danny. 'Big Jumbo won't 'alf 'ave to shift around fer once, won't 'e?'

Jack sauntered out of the back room, a speed-ball in his arms. Billy raced up to him, saying tersely and breathlessly, 'Archie Duke's mob are outside the side door. I reckon they'll be up 'ere any minute. I thought you'd like a bit of warning!'

Jack stood still for a moment. Archie and his boys were trouble, and he didn't want trouble tonight, not with the new bloke and half of Magnolia Square on the premises. 'Is Archie there as well?' he asked, hazel eyes flicking towards the door leading to the stairs.

'I dunno.' Billy had gone to a lot of effort to avoid any eye-to-eye contact when he walked past them all. ''E might be. They were in pretty deep conversation. I don't think they're over this way just for the hell of it.'

Jack grunted, in full agreement with him. The Swan was a low-key local pub, not the sort of pub Archie and his boys frequented when out for a good time. There came the sound of several pairs of heavy feet mounting the stairs. Jack threw the speed-ball to Billy. 'Take this to Danny. Give him the whisper as to who's just arrived and tell him if I need him, I'll shout for him. Otherwise, I want him to carry on as he is doing, with everyone's attention staying on Hemingway. Got it?'

Billy, adrenalin pumping furiously through his veins, nodded. Ever since he was a youngster, Jack had been his hero. Archie Duke's boys wouldn't intimidate Jack. If anything, it would be the other way round!

A big, middle-aged man, his shoulders thrust backwards in order to increase his chest size, swaggered into the gym, four younger men in his wake. All of them looked unpleasant pieces of work. One had a deeply uneven facial scar that looked as if it had been caused by a broken glass or bottle. Another had stubby fingers so misshapen they looked as if someone had, at some time, systematically broken them all.

Jack strolled over to meet them. 'To what do I owe this

pleasure, Archie?' he asked drily. 'It's a bit late for your boys
to want to learn how to hit cleanly with their fists, isn't it?'

Archie Duke smiled thinly. 'My boys aren't in need of any
of your kind of lessons, Jack, and well you know it.'

Both men stood for a moment, eyeing each other up. Though
they had greeted each other on Christian name terms, it was
the first time they had met. Everyone in south-east London
knew Archie by sight, and Archie knew very well from the way
Jack had greeted him, that he was Jack Robson, the club's boss.

'Well, if you want to have a few words, come into my office,'
Jack said, not wanting Archie and his coterie wandering over
to where half of Magnolia Square's elderly residents were happily
clustered, watching Zac Hemingway work out.

As he led the way to his booth, one of Archie's henchmen
nodded his head in the direction of the training area, saying,
'What's going on? You got something special on this evening?'

Jack grinned as if a joke had been cracked. 'No way. Can't
you see all the kids? They're just being given a demonstration
of how to move and throw a good stiff jab, that's all.'

'And the old biddies and the old geezers?' Archie asked,
pausing at the doorway to Jack's booth and looking across the
gym speculatively. 'Why are they here? It looks more like a
Darby and Joan Club than a bleedin' boxing club.'

'They're here for the company and because, unlike downstairs, they don't have to fork out for a half of mild or a port
and lemon,' Jack said easily, sliding into his chair and pulling
one knee up so that the sole of his suede-shod foot was pressing
against the near edge of the table. It was the position of a man
totally at ease, and the ease wasn't merely affected. During the
first few seconds when he stood eyeball to eyeball with him,
Archie Duke knew he was in the presence of a man who wasn't
the slightest bit nervous of him, a man it would be very, very
hard to frighten.

'Now, as you don't want the services of my trainer,' Jack said musingly, 'what is it you're hoping I can do for you, Archie?'

Archie eased himself into the only other chair the office possessed, his henchmen squeezed in a semicircle behind it. 'Well, it's like this, Jack,' he said confidingly, resting a gleamingly shod left foot akimbo on his right knee in a pose quite as relaxed as Jack's and reaching in his inside pocket for a cigar. 'You seem to be a man with a pronounced business flair, very pronounced indeed. This little boxing club of yours has got itself a good reputation, and then there are your other business interests.' He paused, snipping off the end of his cigar and lighting it.

Jack waited, not an ounce of nervous tension showing. He knew very well what was coming and, despite his imperturbability, didn't yet know how he was going to handle it, at least not in the long term. One thing he did know, however, was that he couldn't risk any violence now. Archie's boys had a reputation for not caring too much about the sex or age of the people they hurt, and he had not only Mavis and her mum and dad in the club, but Danny's mum and dad and his own eighty-year-old dad, as well.

'And what other business interests are those, Archie?' he asked, giving an impression of mild amusement.

Archie grinned. His teeth weren't at all well cared for. With genuine amusement Jack realized that Archie was scared of the dentist.

'A certain afternoon drinking club in Soho,' Archie said, blowing a ring of fragrant blue smoke into the air. 'Now, as this is your first venture into such an enterprise and as I have a certain experience where clubs of this nature are concerned, I thought it only right and proper that I should give you the benefit of some friendly advice.' He paused again.

Jack didn't bother to prompt him. All through the conversation he had been listening with half an ear to what was going on at the far end of the gym. Danny had obviously fitted the new speed-ball into the stand, for the sound of Zac Hemingway drumming it violently at lightning speed could clearly be heard. When the speed-ball work came to an end, the workout would be nearly over. People would then begin spilling all over the gym, wanting to see him to tell him what they thought of his new acquisition, and coming face to face with Archie and his boys when they did so.

'You see, Jack,' Archie continued, speaking in an almost fatherly tone, 'some very nasty characters frequent out-of-hours drinking clubs, and owners and staff have to be protected—'

'And you're offering to do the protecting?' Jack asked drily, knowing that time was fast running out if Archie was to be off the premises before Zac Hemingway's workout came to an end.

Archie rolled his cigar around in his mouth and then clamped it between his teeth, grinning yet again. 'For a price, Jack. For a price.'

Jack used his foot to push himself and the chair he was sitting on away from the desk, and stood up. 'I rather fancy I can look after my own safety and the safety of my staff without any help, Archie,' he said blandly. 'But thanks for the offer.'

Archie heaved himself to his feet. 'You're being hasty, Jack,' he said, the glint in his eyes at odds with his apparent mildness. 'You might like to reconsider in a few days' time. If you do, you'll find me in The Horse and Ferret, Deptford.' He turned, walking out of the cramped booth and across to the door leading to the stairs, his entourage in his wake.

Jack held his breath. The speed-ball had stopped drumming. Zac would now be winding down with callisthenics and callisthenics weren't as attention-holding as shadow-boxing or bag-work. If anyone should see Archie and call out to him . . .

The stair door creaked open and then, seconds later, banged shut. Jack let out a deep unsteady breath and sank back down onto his chair. Had he just been threatened? And if so, what was he going to do about it? At least, for the moment, Archie was gone, and for that he was profoundly grateful. But Archie and his cohorts would be back, of that he hadn't a moment's doubt.

He heard the sound of Danny's plimsolled feet scurrying across the gym. Seconds later he was rounding the booth's doorway, saying urgently, 'You all right, Jack?'

Jack gave him a grim smile. 'For the moment. Archie's after protection money. I told him I wasn't in need of protection and he said I might like to reconsider my decision in a few days' time, which might just mean that, in the duration, he's going to take some kind of action to make me change my mind.'

'Bleedin' 'ell!' Danny sank down on the straight-backed chair that Archie had just vacated. 'I thought at first 'e was 'ere 'cos 'e'd 'eard about 'Emingway. I thought 'e was goin' to try an' poach 'im. I never thought 'e'd be wantin' protection for the club.'

'It isn't this club he's primarily interested in,' Jack said, his eyes flicking to the doorway to make sure no one was approaching. 'It's The 21 he's interested in.'

Understanding dawned in Danny's eyes. Jack had bought The 21, a small Soho drinking club, a mere couple of weeks ago. Like many of Jack's more dubious business forays, it was one that wasn't common knowledge in the square. Danny doubted that Jack had even told Christina about it, for he never told her anything which would cause her even the slightest disquiet. Where Christina was concerned, Jack was ultra, ultra protective.

'We knew it would happen, of course,' Jack said wryly. 'I'm just surprised how soon it's happened. The club hasn't even opened its doors under my management yet.'

Danny, who was privy to all Jack's business dealings, legit-imate as well as not quite so legitimate, said, 'I thought you might 'ave got off the 'ook where protection was concerned, seeing as 'ow the club was up for grabs with ten months of a valid drinking licence still to run.'

Jack shot him a lop-sided grin. 'That wouldn't fool Archie, Danny. He'll know we'll be running it as a gambling club.'

Danny didn't grin back. He was trying to work out which would be the more unpleasant – a police raid on the club, or a raid by Archie and his boys.

Jack read Danny's thoughts as clearly as if he'd spoken them out loud. 'A police raid would be a picnic compared to a raid by Archie and his cronies,' he said drily and then, as Billy put his head around the door, 'as it is, I'm glad we've nothing to worry about where Zac is concerned. His track record speaks for itself of course . . .'

'Eh?' Danny's bewilderment, until Billy spoke from behind him, was almost comic.

'Is everything OK, Jack?' Billy asked anxiously. 'If you've got trouble I'll be only too 'appy to give you an 'and.'

'There's no trouble,' Jack lied, flashing Billy a warm smile. 'Archie was just being nosey, that's all.'

Relief and disappointment fought for supremacy on Billy's personable face. He didn't want Jack to be facing trouble from one of London's most notorious underworld gangs, but on the other hand the adrenalin that had surged along his veins at the prospect of such trouble, and of taking an active part in deflecting it, was dizzyingly exhilarating.

Jack, well aware of how willing Billy was to enter the lists on his behalf, gave an inward sigh of relief at his not having had to do so. He'd known young Billy since the day he was born and the last thing he wanted was to involve him in any underworld ugliness. Billy was the kid brother he never had. If Billy were to get himself glassed or knifed in a fracas with Archie and his boys, Mavis would never forgive him. Even worse, he would never forgive himself.

He rose to his feet. 'Did Zac keep his audience happy?' he asked, walking over to Billy and, sliding an arm around Billy's shoulders, strolling out of the office with him.

Billy, who had been far too on edge wondering what was happening between Jack and Archie to take much notice of Zac Hemingway's workout, said, 'I reckon so. I think they'd 'ave preferred it, though, if Danny 'ad 'ad 'im sparring with Jumbo.'

'That'll save for another night,' Jack said easily as they walked across to where Zac was towelling down, surrounded by a cluster of boy scouts.

''Ow do yer manage to 'it and not get 'it, when yer in the ring?' one of them was asking.

Zac tossed his towel to one side and began pulling on a pair of trousers over his training shorts. Showering facilities were meagre at the Embassy and he'd be in Queenie Tillet's peeling, claw-footed bath in two shakes of a lamb's tail. 'You move your head after you punch,' he said, showing no signs of impatience to be on his way. 'If you're down here Friday night I'll give you a few tips on how to do it.'

'Will yer?' The youngster's face glowed. Wait till he told the kids at school! His teachers could stick their sums and English compositions where the monkey stuck its nuts. He was going to be a boxer when he grew up. He was going to be a world champ!

Jack observed the little interchange, bemused. If Zac Hemingway was going to be good with the kids who hung out

at the gym it would definitely be to the club's benefit. It was
a bit of a turn-up for the books, though. When he'd been tipped
off by a mate of his, a PT instructor at Parkhurst Prison, that
a red-hot boxing prospect was due for release, he certainly
hadn't anticipated the jailbird in question being an asset where
the club's youngsters were concerned. But then he hadn't anticipated Hemingway being so likeable and easy to get on with.
He continued to watch Zac exchanging repartee with the
admiring youngsters and Miriam and Hettie, both of whom
were always over-generous with advice to anyone and everyone.
Without knowing Zac's history, it would be impossible to guess
at it, and it would have been easy to come to the conclusion
that, no matter how good he was in the gym, he didn't have
the innate meanness necessary for the professional ring. It would
have been easy but, as he alone knew, very, very wrong.

'Queenie ain't much of a dab 'and in the kitchen,' Miriam
was saying as Zac shrugged his way into a short-sleeved vest.
'If yer need somethin' a bit more 'ot and fillin' than she puts
on the table, pop in to our 'ouse. I'll soon knock up somethin'
to put 'airs on yer chest!'

'Any hairs on my chest'd be so blond they'd look like fuzz
on a baby's bottom,' Zac said with a good-humoured grin.

Mavis was standing within earshot and though her eyes were
on Jack, she heard Zac's response to her mother and chuckled
throatily. In her books, a man without a mat of sweaty chest
hair was far preferable to one with – especially if his chest was
as magnificently muscled as Zac Hemingway's.

''Ave yer met me sister-in-law?' Danny, who had darted ahead
of Jack and Billy and was now at Zac's side, asked him. 'Any
match yer 'ave with Mavis at the ringside and 'ollering in yer
corner is as good as won.'

Zac picked up his leather bomber jacket and, hooking it with his thumb, slung it over his shoulder. 'Nice to meet you,' he said, concealing his surprise.

If Danny hadn't told him, he'd never have guessed that the bottled-blonde now standing in front of him, her weight resting provocatively on one hip, a saucy gleam in her eyes, was Danny's wife's sister. Carrie Collins's hair was as untidy as a gypsy's and as smoke-dark. She also possessed a rosy-cheeked freshness that would have done credit to a country girl. There was nothing countrified about Mavis's scarlet-painted lips and nails. Despite her age, which he judged to be nearer forty than thirty, she looked every inch a West End good-time girl.

'Nice to meet you as well,' Mavis said, putting on a show of flirtatiousness in front of Jack that she was far from feeling. As she put her hand in Zac Hemingway's big paw she reflected wryly that at least she wasn't having to try overly hard to be flirtatious. Zac Hemingway was the most gorgeous-looking man she'd ever set eyes on in her life. If it wasn't that her heart was breaking for Jack, she'd have been well and truly smitten.

'Come on you two, don't make a meal of it,' Danny said crudely, making an assumption that was far from correct. 'I need to get these kids off 'ome and I want an early night fer once.' In truth he wanted the club emptied so that he could have a proper discussion with Jack about Archie Duke. If Archie had swaggered into The 21 with his unwanted offer of protection he wouldn't have felt quite so jumpy. Like Jack, he felt that Archie in Soho was one thing and that Archie in Magnolia Hill was quite another. 'Not that an early night with my old woman is much of a pleasure,' he added, playing it for a laugh as the kids in question began trooping towards the stairs. 'She's so big she doesn't so much take 'er clothes off, as strike camp!'

Big Jumbo, Zac's prospective sparring partner, tittered. It was an oddly unpleasant sound coming from such a gigantic mound of a man. Danny's parents and his parents-in-law, well used to what they regarded as his harmless cracks at Carrie's expense, merely grinned. Zac didn't grin, though. He looked across at Danny with such an odd expression on his face that Mavis wondered if Danny had said or done something to rile him during his training workout. If he had, Jack wouldn't be very pleased. Jack liked a happy ship. He said it made for an easy life.

Later that night as he lay in bed, watching Carrie slip a sensible but very pretty sprigged cotton nightie over her head, Danny said bluntly, 'We 'ad unwelcome visitors at the club ternight, pet.' Unlike Jack, it was never Danny's way to shield his other half from worries or unpleasantness. In Danny's book, a worry shared was a worry halved.

Carrie sat down on the edge of the high, brass-headed bed, her back towards him, and slipped off the slippers she had been wearing all evening. It had nearly killed her, but ever since he returned home she had fought the temptation to ask him how the evening had gone; especially how the evening had gone where Zac Hemingway was concerned.

'Who?' she asked, swinging her legs into bed and looking towards him. 'Was Nellie there, being as disruptive as usual?'

'Nah,' Danny was contemptuously dismissive. What was Carrie thinking of, imagining he'd get his knickers in a twist over Nellie? 'Nellie can't get up the stairs to the gym any more,' he added, wondering just how much he could safely tell Carrie. 'She needs two strong men just to get 'er over 'er doorstep!'

Carrie gave her feather pillow a shake and settled back against it. 'Who, then?' she asked with mild curiosity. 'Wilfred Sharkey?'

Wilfred Sharkey was a local religious maniac who made a nuisance of himself everywhere, especially outside the clock tower in Lewisham High Street.

'Nah.' Danny laced his hands behind his head. He wanted

45

to tell Carrie about The 21 but he knew she'd immediately think of the kind of girls that would frequent it and that she'd go off the deep end. She might, God forbid, even tell Christina. 'The visitors were Archie Duke and his boys,' he said, deciding how much he could safely tell to shed some of his burden of worry. It meant fudging the details a little, but the basic problem remained the same. 'He's after protection money from Jack.'

Carrie shot upright against her pillows so suddenly her hair tumbled forward all over her face. 'Archie Duke? You're joking, Danny! Dear God, please tell me you're joking!'

If Danny had had any doubts at all as to the potential ugliness of the situation, Carrie's reaction dispelled them. Carrie didn't worry over trifles. 'I'm not joking, pet,' he said unhappily. 'He swaggered in this evening, four of his boys in tow, and put it to Jack straight. He wants protection money for the club.'

'For the Embassy?' Carrie stared at him in incredulity. 'But the Embassy's as much a youth club as it is a hard-nosed boxing gym! Why would a big fish like Archie Duke bother with a small-time boxing gym?'

'Hey, 'ang on!' Danny unlaced his hands, deeply aggrieved. 'We ain't that small-time! Especially not now we 'ave Zac Hemingway.'

Carrie's eyes opened even wider. 'Is that why Archie paid the club a visit? Because he's interested in Zac Hemingway?'

'Nah, he don't know nuffink about Zac. Zac was doing a workout when Archie came in and 'e didn't even wander over to take a decko at 'im. He just wants protection money fer the club, that's all. And before you ask why he wants it, 'e wants it because 'e likes to be the big man with a finger in every pie – and because 'e's a greedy git.'

Carrie slid slowly down against her pillows. Archie Duke taking an interest in the Embassy Boxing Club. It didn't bear thinking about – and nor did young Matthew's disappearance. Of the two worries, her greatest anxiety was for Matthew. Jack would, somehow or other, solve the problem of Archie. But what would happen if Matthew didn't soon return either home or to his school? He'd been missing for over twenty-four hours. Where on earth could he be? And how on earth was Kate managing to remain sane and calm?

Chapter Four

'I shall lose my mind with worry if there isn't news of him soon,' Kate said to Leon.

Even though it was well after midnight, neither of them were in their night-clothes. How could they possibly go to bed and sleep when they didn't know where Matthew was? What if the police called to say Matthew had been found and wanted them to travel to a distant police station to collect him?

'I'll make another cup of cocoa, love.' Leon's dark, attractive face was taut with anxiety. Where the devil had Matthew got to? It wasn't the fact that Matthew had run away from school that worried him so much as the fact that there'd been no word from him since he'd done so. After all, he would only have run away in order to go home. He was only twelve years old. Where else could he possibly run to? He pondered the problem in the kitchen and then, when he returned to the sitting-room with two steaming mugs of milky cocoa, said tentatively, 'You don't think he'll have gone to one of his Harvey aunts, do you?'

Kate sucked in her breath. It was a thought that hadn't occurred to her. Matthew's visits to his Harvey relations were more in the way of duty visits than pleasant trips, and yet . . . it was a possibility. Hope flared in her eyes and then almost immediately died. 'If he'd turned up on either of their doorsteps they'd have contacted us.' She saw Leon's generously shaped

48

mouth tighten. Both Matthew's aunt and his great-aunt would have been carried kicking and screaming into hell before voluntarily contacting Leon. 'Or if they didn't contact us,' she added, well aware of his thoughts, 'they would have contacted the school.'

Their eyes held, other thoughts occurring to them, thoughts neither of them wanted to put into words. Both of Matthew's Harvey aunts kept in regular contact with St Osyth's. It was, after all, the school Matthew's father had gone to, and his father before him, and his aunt and great-aunt had been attending speech days and sports days there for many, many years. They were on exceedingly comfortable terms with Matthew's headmaster, which was more than could be said for their own relationship with him.

From the very first time he met them he was obviously uncomfortable and patronizing. When discussing one of Matthew's early school reports he even went so far as to ask Leon if he was able to read it adequately or if he would like it to be read to him. Even now, years later, the mere memory filled Kate with bitter, burning anger. Leon handled the incident with a quiet dignity that had, in Kate's eyes, put St Osyth's headmaster to shame. It made no difference to their future relations with him, however. Despite the surface courtesy with which he treated them, they both knew how he felt about them: they didn't personally pay Matthew's school fees and so no respect needed to be accorded to them on that score. Kate was a white woman in a mixed-race marriage, and so obviously a woman with little self-respect. As a black seaman who had been allowed to adopt his wife's illegitimate child, a child whose natural father's family were white and upper-middle-class, Leon was obviously a man with ideas far above his station.

As a consequence of his prejudiced views, the headmaster

far preferred discussing Matthew's scholastic progress and welfare with Matthew's aunts rather than with them. Unsaid, but implicit, was his regret that Matthew's aunts were not Matthew's legal guardians, thereby saving him a great deal of social embarrassment.

'Perhaps one of them has,' Leon said slowly. 'Perhaps Matthew *is* with one of his aunts and the school have been informed and are taking the line that it's up to the aunt in question to contact us and to tell us so, not them. And perhaps Matthew thinks his aunt has contacted us. That would explain a lot, love, wouldn't it?'

Kate nodded, her eyes flying to the clock on the mantelpiece. It was twenty to one.

'We can't phone at this time in the morning,' he said gently, reading her thoughts. 'We're going to have to be patient for another six or seven hours, and we might as well try and get a little shut-eye whilst we're doing so.'

Reluctantly she nodded agreement, her arm sliding around his waist as his arm circled her shoulders. Bed, a few hours sleep and then a telephone call that would, hopefully, put an end to the worst of their anxieties. 'I feel a hundred,' she said wryly as, her head resting against his shoulder, she allowed him to lead her to the bottom of the stairs.

He looked down at her, his brandy-dark eyes full of love. 'You don't look a day over twenty-five,' he said truthfully and then, aware of just how bone-deep her weariness was, he lifted her into his arms, carrying her up the stairs as he had on the day they married.

Four doors away, at number twelve, Jack Robson sat gently down on the edge of the big double bed he shared with Christina and eased off his shoes. What an evening! He'd anticipated a confrontation with Archie Duke somewhere down the line, but he hadn't thought it would come quite so soon and he certainly hadn't anticipated being confronted on his home turf.

'Is that you, darling?' Christina murmured sleepily, turning over beneath broderie-anglaise-edged sheets and stretching a hand out towards him.

Jack felt his throat tighten with emotion. Christ! He loved Christina so much there was nothing he wouldn't do for her. He remembered the one thing she wanted more than anything else in the world and familiar, bitter frustration swamped him. A baby. It wasn't much to ask for, was it? Other couples had babies at the drop of a hat, whether they wanted them or not. But he and Christina didn't, and they didn't know why.

'Be patient,' Doctor Roberts had said to them before he retired. 'You're both young and fit. A baby will come along eventually, in its own good time.'

'Try to stop worrying about it,' Doctor Roberts's young successor said, when five years had gone by and there was still no sign of the longed-for baby. 'Worry only makes conception more difficult.'

That was three years ago. Nowadays the subject was one they could hardly bring themselves to talk about. Christina was thirty-five. Where babies were concerned, time was ticking by.

He said to her now, ''Course it's me. Who did you think it was? The milkman?'

She smiled in the darkness and opened her eyes. 'You're late,' she said accusingly in the soft, gentle voice that even after eight years of marriage still sent tingles of pleasure down his spine. 'Have you been having a drink with Danny?'

When they first met she had spoken with a slight German accent; now not even a trace of it remained and people ascribed her elusive air of 'foreignness' to the fact that she was Jewish.

'No.' He didn't tell her that Danny had hopped off home at an unusually early hour. Instead, undressing swiftly, he said,

'I've just been pottering about, tidying up some odds and ends of paperwork.' He pulled on a pair of striped cotton pyjama trousers. He never wore a pyjama jacket with them. He always slept bare-chested, even in the depths of winter. 'Zac Hemingway showed up tonight. Danny is as impressed with him as I am.'

She made a small sound which could have meant anything and which he took as meaning that she was pleased for him about Hemingway, and closed her eyes again.

He slid into bed beside her, the feather mattress sinking comfily beneath his weight. 'Don't go back to sleep, sweetheart,' he said huskily, sliding an arm around her, the silky softness of her hair as it brushed his naked flesh increasing his already fierce state of arousal.

There was no response from her and, curbing the urgency of his desire with long-practiced patience, he cupped a full, firm breast in a powerful, careful hand.

'I'm tired, darling,' she murmured as his thumb gently brushed her nipple. Her voice was blurred, as if she was already drifting back into a heavy sleep.

As she moved slightly, turning away from him, a pulse began to pound in the corner of his jaw. He didn't for one minute believe she was almost asleep. She was feigning it, as she often feigned it. Feigning it because she didn't want to hurt his feelings.

The temptation to persist, to simply overcome her disinclination with loving force, nearly overpowered him. For some women such an approach would both be expected and excitingly welcome, but he knew that Christina wasn't one of their number. Christina wasn't remotely like any other woman he had ever known – and in his time he had known a good many. There was an air of frailty about her he found profoundly sexually disturbing; a delicacy and a lady-like refinement he had never been able to bring himself to wilfully violate.

With his hand still cupping her breast, he nuzzled the nape of her neck, his lips hot against the extravagant satin of her hair. 'Come on, sweetheart,' he whispered persuasively, 'you can't be that tired. And I want you. I want to make love to you.'

She covered his hand with hers, making a slight, negating movement with her head, still not speaking. In the darkness her engagement ring gleamed. It was a ring that had been bought during the war – a ring that couldn't possibly have been bought out of army pay. Set in gold, a circlet of tiny diamonds edged with pale mauve amethysts.

She hadn't been overawed by it, like a local-born girl would most likely have been, nor did she query how he could possibly have afforded it, like a local girl would most sensibly have done. But then, Christina wasn't a local girl. Her upbringing had been far different to Kate's and Carrie's and Mavis's, or any of their friends. Her German-Jewish parents had been middle-class professional people and, by Magnolia Square standards, affluent. They would have expected such an engagement ring for their daughter.

Certainly, as far as he was able to tell, it never occurred to Christina that her engagement ring was in any way exceptional – and nor did he want it to. Wheeling and dealing in order to buy it for her had been his pleasure. He wanted her to have the best of everything. It was why, over and above his many other business interests, he was now carving himself a niche as a boxing promoter, why he had bought The 21. He wanted to make money, big money, in order to spoil and cosset her and to somehow compensate her for all she had suffered when, as a young girl, she had endured the nightmare of being Jewish in Hitler's Germany.

He gritted his teeth, hardly able to contain his physical disappointment. She was breathing rhythmically and deeply now, but he didn't believe she was asleep. She was simply pretending. Reluctantly, admitting defeat, he removed his hand from her breast, rolling away from her onto his back, staring up bleakly into the darkness. On the increasingly rare occasions when they did now make love, did she pretend then as well? Had she, where lovemaking was concerned, always pretended? It was a crucifying thought.

As he sensed her falling into genuine sleep he folded his hands behind his head. Sex had never been a problem for him. Ever since he was in his teens there'd always been more than enough girls willing and eager to accommodate him, and he knew enough about himself to know that now, in his mid-thirties, he was both an accomplished and a considerate lover. He also knew that no one who knew him would believe he was going short where sexual satisfaction was concerned. But he *was* going short, and had been for a long time.

Not for the first time, it occurred to him that his present level of physical frustration was totally unnecessary, especially when he knew from experience that nearly every girl he gave the wink to would be interested. And then there was Mavis. He and Mavis went back a long way. For a man enduring the kinds of problems in his marriage that he was, Mavis was a serious temptation. He sighed heavily, longing for a smoke. Knowing that if he lit a cigarette he would disturb Christina he tried, instead, to sleep. But sleep was a long, long time in coming.

The next morning, as soon as he felt he could decently wake Bob Giles, Leon Emmerson strode swiftly across the top right-hand corner of Magnolia Square towards the vicarage. It wasn't long after dawn, and the sky was a rich, ripe apricot, promising a day of glorious sun. In the wide shallow garden of the double-fronted vicarage, a pair of blue tits, bright as butter-

54

flies, flew wrangling into a bush of golden broom. Ruth Giles, the vicar's wife, was a passionate gardener, and there were deep drowned-purple pansies and vivid-eyed pale pink phlox massed next to the broom and, nearby, clusters of late-flowering, sharply yellow tulips.

Oblivious of the garden's dew-wet beauty and of the jogging figure who had just entered the square from the short terrace that led from it on to Blackheath's heath, Leon turned swiftly in at the gate, sprinting the last few yards up the pathway to the front door, knocking on its pristine paintwork with tense urgency.

Zac came to a halt, standing with his hands on his hips, breathing deeply. He was on his way back to his lodgings after a six-mile circuit over the heath. He always followed the same routine when it came to roadwork, walking fast for half a mile, jogging for a mile, sprinting at full belt for a good half mile and then walking once again.

The heath was splendidly close for such workouts, and there was also nearby Royal Greenwich Park for when he wanted to ring the changes. All in all, he was well satisfied with his new digs and their location. Though the steeply sloping street opening out of the bottom end of Magnolia Square led down to Lewisham and its busy street market, the tree-shaded top end of the square, and the heath and nearby Blackheath Village, were pretty enough to be almost rural, which made the sight of a man obviously West Indian, or of West Indian extraction, even more unexpected than it would normally have been.

He watched with interest as a dressing-gown-clad male figure opened the vicarage door and, without preamble, ushered the early morning visitor inside. He continued on down the uneven numbered side of the square. The man was obviously known to whoever had opened the door to him, and Zac wondered if he was a local. If he were he would be used to people being taken by surprise when they first saw him, for Lewisham and Blackheath were too far from the docks for there to be many black sailors about, and the days when black GIs had been a novel sight on the streets were long past.

He slowed to a saunter as he neared his lodgings. There were only another three houses before the bottom corner of the square, and the house on the bottom side of the square was the Collins's. If Carrie Collins worked on a stall in Lewisham market she would surely be up and about by now. He halted at Queenie Tillet's gateway. Though the Collins's downstairs curtains were drawn back, the curtains at the bedroom windows were still drawn. Was that because Danny liked as much shut-eye as he could possibly get in the mornings? Or was Carrie, too, still in bed?

'Morning,' a cheery female voice with a northern intonation called out to him from the other side of the square. 'Are you Queenie's new lodger? She usually only takes in theatricals. If you don't watch your step you'll find yourself calling everyone "Ducky" and mincing like a nancy-boy!'

Zac grinned. 'That'll be the day,' he rejoindered good-temperedly.

Yorkshire-born Lettie Deakin went on her way, chuckling, her dog enjoying its early morning walk, gambolling happily at her heels. Lettie liked a well set-up young man, especially when he had a pleasant disposition. She wondered if Mavis Lomax had laid eyes on their new neighbour yet. It'd be cradle-snatching, of course, for Queenie's lodger could only be in his mid-twenties, but if everything she'd heard about Mavis was true, Mavis wouldn't let that deter her. And the young man in question was a lovely-looking young man. As they would say in her home town of Bradford, he was a reet bit o' right!

*

'Who was it at the door?' Ruth Giles asked, scrambling into sensible underclothes.

'Leon.' Bob Giles paused at their bedroom door. 'There's no need for you to come downstairs, dear. He's making a telephone call to Matthew's school. He seems to think Matthew may be at the home of one of his Harvey relations, and that, if they'd been informed he was there, the school might have been lax in letting him and Kate know.'

Ruth, nearly twenty years her husband's junior, stepped into a tweed skirt and zipped it up over still slim hips. 'But why on earth should he think a thing like that?' she asked, keeping her voice low so that it wouldn't carry down the stairs and into the hall where Leon was, presumably, now speaking to either the secretary or the headmaster of St Osyth's school. 'He's Matthew's father. If the school had any information about Matthew, he's the first person they would contact.'

'He's Matthew's adoptive father,' Bob said, his voice as low as hers as he tried to keep half an ear on what was happening in the hall. If there was good news he would surely be able to tell by the tone of Leon's voice. 'And though that shouldn't make an iota of difference, in the case of Matthew and Leon it does. Or it does where Matthew's school is concerned.'

Ruth pulled a raspberry-coloured jumper over her head and stared at him, her curly brown hair framing her face like a tumbled halo. 'Because Leon's a lovely dusky dark shade and Matthew isn't?'

Despite the gravity of the situation a smile twitched at the corners of Bob's mouth. 'Because it is so patently obvious that Leon isn't Matthew's natural father, and couldn't possibly be his natural father, yes,' he said, overcome by a rush of love for her. 'And because St Osyth's is one of the oldest public schools in the country and distinctly snobbish.' He paused, listening to see if Leon was still on the telephone or not. He was, and sounded as if he might be for some time.

'If Matthew were Leon's natural son, and Leon were an African king or prince, I shouldn't think Leon's colour would matter an iota to Matthew's headmaster,' he continued, deciding he probably had time to dress hurriedly before going back downstairs to commiserate with Leon, or to advise him. 'But he's not. He's a Thames waterman.'

'Thames watermen are princes of the Thames. Matthew's headmaster should think himself lucky he has a waterman amongst his pupils' parents!'

Bob clipped his dog-collar around his neck. Ruth was spot-on, as always. He shrugged himself into a dark jacket, sending a mental prayer heavenwards in gratitude for her love and for her endearing way of seeing things. 'I think Leon has come off the telephone,' he said, instinct telling him that whatever Leon had been told, the news wasn't good.

She read his mind with practised ease. 'I'll come downstairs with you and make a cup of tea for us all. How long is it now that Matthew has been missing?'

'Thirty-six hours.'

Silently she followed him from the bedroom. Thirty-six hours! Where on earth could Matthew be? Her heart felt tight within her chest. When Matthew was a tiny baby and temporarily in his Great-Grandfather Harvey's care, she had been his nanny. Indirectly it was because of Matthew, and her consequent friendship with Kate and the visits she then made to Magnolia Square, that she had met Bob. He was a widower and, over tea and ginger biscuits in the Jennings's kitchen, she fell in love with him almost at first sight.

'Matthew isn't with either of his aunts,' Leon said abruptly, standing near the hall table, despair in his voice. 'The school notified them of Matthew's disappearance even before they notified us via the police, and they've kept in constant touch with them.'

Ruth, who never intruded when her husband was acting in his professional capacity as shepherd of his flock, slipped into the kitchen. It was so out of character for Matthew to be behaving in a way that would cause his parents such anxiety. He wasn't remotely a young tearaway. No matter what the personal faults of St Osyth's headmaster, the school itself was one which inculcated the virtues of good manners and courtesy and, unlike some boys his age she could mention, Matthew was a courteous and sensitive child.

She filled the kettle at the sink. Out in her back garden a blackbird was happily rooting for worms. If Matthew wasn't with either of his Harvey aunts, and he hadn't returned home, where else would he have gone? She put the kettle on the gas stove, waiting for it to boil, thinking as hard as she could.

'There isn't anywhere else,' Leon was saying to Bob. 'The only other family Matthew has, apart from his aunts, is his Grandad Voigt, and Kate walked down to Greenwich yesterday afternoon to break the news to him. He and Ellen haven't seen Matthew, or heard from him.'

Ellen was Kate's stepmother, a kindly, chronically shy woman, who had never had children of her own and who adored all five of her step-grandchildren.

'Was it the headmaster you spoke to, or the school secretary?'

'The headmaster.' A spasm of bitter frustration passed across Leon's usually good-humoured face. The headmaster had spoken to him as he always did, as if he'd just emerged from a jungle thicket and was way too inferior to be spoken to civilly.

Bob registered the expression and was able to make an accurate guess as to what had caused it. Long ago, when he talked to Leon and Kate before marrying them, he warned them that not everyone would look with favour on their mixed-race marriage and that they would have to be prepared not only for the difficulties that beset every marriage but for other, more specific, difficulties, also.

He said now, 'Was the headmaster able to throw any light as to why Matthew should have run away? Has he spoken to Matthew's friends? To his various teachers?'

Leon ran a hand over his crinkly hair. 'Yes, he has, but Matthew doesn't seem to have confided in anyone. According to his teachers he seemed perfectly normal on the day he disappeared. There was a games lesson in the morning followed by a double period of history. His games master said Matthew had bowled beautifully and that he was looking forward to playing in an inter-school match scheduled for the end of next week.' He paused as Ruth came out of the kitchen, a mug of steaming tea in either hand. 'His history master said Matthew's class were studying Napoleon's retreat from Moscow and that Matthew, as usual, showed lively interest,' he continued, taking one of the mugs from her as Bob relieved her of the other one. 'In the afternoon he had a music lesson, which isn't one of his favourite lessons, but which he doesn't dislike enough to explain his running away that evening, then he had an English class and then the school's career officer gave a talk on careers the boys might like to consider.'

Bob raised his eyebrows slightly. 'A careers talk is a little premature for a class of twelve-year-olds, isn't it?'

Leon shrugged. St Osyth's was a public school so many worlds removed from his own state schooling that nothing in its curriculum surprised him. 'I don't know about that,' he said truthfully. 'All I know is that it doesn't account for Matthew's running away from school some time that evening, or, if he didn't go that evening, running away early next morning.' He sipped at his tea, not really tasting it, dreading the thought of returning home. Kate had such fierce hopes where Matthew's aunts were concerned. When he told her Matthew wasn't with either of them she was going to be devastated. 'I suppose,' he said reluctantly, 'I suppose I should telephone the aunts and speak to them myself, shouldn't I?'

Bob nodded.

Leon sighed. Speaking to Matthew's aunts was going to be even more of a nightmare than speaking to his headmaster. They both spoke with such plummy accents it was nearly impossible for him to understand what they were saying, and he knew that both of them would somehow blame him for Matthew's disappearance.

'I'll be in the kitchen with Ruth,' Bob said, knowing that though one of Matthew's aunts lived in London, in Kensington, the other lived in Somerset. It would take quite some time for the telephone connection to be made between London and Somerset and, when it finally was made, Leon would want to be able to talk in privacy. 'I'll have a fresh cup of tea waiting for you when you come off the telephone,' he added, aware that the day ahead was going to be both long and fraught, 'and I think we'd better have some toast with it. Kate won't be wanting to make you a breakfast this morning. She's going to have too much on her mind.'

Chapter Five

'Kate must be worried out of her mind,' Christina said, appalled.

Billy, who was pretty appalled himself when he woke up that morning to the realization that he still hadn't told Jack about Matthew's disappearance, said, 'She doesn't look to be in a flap about it, but then Kate never flaps, does she?' He was seated at the table in the Robson's roomy kitchen, his hands around a pint mug of steaming tea.

Jack, who'd been in the middle of shaving when Billy's early morning knock had rudely disturbed him, was still only half-dressed, his trousers sitting low on his hips, his belt buckle glinting against firm, olive-toned flesh. 'What are the police doing about it?' he asked, a frown furrowing his brow.

Billy shrugged. 'I dunno. I 'spect they'll be keeping a look-out for him, but what else can they do? It isn't as if he's only a nipper, is it? He's twelve years old. When I was twelve I was always making myself scarce. Whenever the circus moved off from its bank holiday pitch on the heath, I always went with it for a few days. I know Rochester and Gravesend even better than I do Woolwich and Greenwich. Mum must have gone spare with worry but it would've never occurred to her to put the coppers on to me.'

This was undoubtedly the truth, but Jack was well aware that now, with Christina present, was not the time to reminisce about Mavis's slapdash attitude to the responsibilities of motherhood. Billy wasn't to know it, but in the Robson house any mention of Mavis was strictly *verboten*.

'Me neither.' There was more than an edge of irony in his voice. When he was young Matthew's age, his dad, Charlie, had been a gelly-man, blowing bank safes open the length and breadth of the country. There'd have been as much chance of Charlie walking into a police station to report him missing as there would have been of pigs flying.

Christina turned the light down under a pan of tomatoes and mushrooms and poured tea into a china cup with forget-me-nots painted on its rim and, after placing it on a matching saucer, carried it to the table. Despite his having Mavis for a mother, she had a soft spot for Billy. In many ways he was a younger, less tough, less blatantly sexual, version of Jack, the Jack of pre-war, pre-Commando days. The Jack that Mavis had known, and she had not.

'As soon as we've had breakfast I'll go and see Kate, and see if there's anything I can do to help,' she said, her voice and face betraying no hint of her turbulent thoughts. 'Perhaps I'll be able to look after Johnny for her, or take Jilly to school.'

'I reckon Daisy'll be taking Jilly to school,' Billy said, wondering if he might be lucky enough to accidentally-on-purpose bump into her as she did so. By the time Daisy usually walked across the heath to Blackheath Village and her own school – posh Blackheath High School for Girls – where she and his cousin Rose were scholarship girls, he'd been at his scrap-metal yard in Greenwich for a good hour. This morning was different, though. This morning he'd had to pass Leon's now-belated message on to Jack.

Christina suppressed a spasm of disappointment. She would have liked to take seven-year-old Jilly to school. As Jilly trotted along at her side, her hand in hers, she could have pretended that Jilly was her little girl – hers and Jack's – and that the walk was one the two of them took every day. She could have pretended that her days weren't empty and pointless but were, instead, filled with the deeply satisfying tasks of mothering and cherishing.

'Then I'll ask if I can look after Johnny,' she said, carefully avoiding Jack's eyes, not wanting to see the expression she was sure would be in them. 'Are you going to stay for breakfast? The tomatoes and mushrooms are nearly cooked, and the eggs will only take a couple of minutes.'

'No, but thanks all the same.' Billy rose to his feet. He'd have liked to talk to Jack about Archie Duke but, as it was clearly impossible to do so, he didn't fancy hanging around. He had a business to run for one thing, and for another, he just couldn't feel comfortable in Christina's presence. She was too self-contained. Too reserved. There was no south-east London buoyancy or fizz to her. Instead, there was an elegance so cool and sleek, it was unnerving.

Take this morning, for instance. Any other woman, woken so early by an unexpected visitor, would be dressed in a comfortably shabby dressing-gown and slippers. Christina wasn't wearing a dressing-gown of any description, nor was she wearing one of the floral-patterned, sleeveless, wrap-around aprons that most south-east London women wore when at home, doing their chores. Instead she was wearing wedge-heeled sandals with a pair of grey flannel slacks, a white shirt and a big, soft grey Shetland sweater. A sweater that must have cost a small fortune. With her satin-dark shoulder-length hair held away from either side of her face with ivory combs, she looked more like a Hollywood film star than a south-east London house-wife. She didn't look like an American-born Hollywood film star, though. There was something too foreign about her for that; something too disturbing and elusive.

He paused as he stood on the doorstep after letting himself

out of the house. It was ten past eight. If he dawdled for another few minutes he might well see Daisy and Jilly leaving number four on their way to their respective schools. If he did, he could give them a lift in his little run-about lorry. It would be a bit of a squeeze for the two of them up front in the cab, but Daisy and Jilly wouldn't mind. He took a dog-end out of his jacket pocket and lit it, leaning against the Robson's gate to wait for them.

Twenty minutes later, Christina left the house, doing so even before Jack had left it, walking up the square towards number four, the sun on her face already warm, the air fragrant with the scent of magnolia blossom. There were magnolias every-where in Magnolia Square, though why there were so many and who had originally begun planting them, no one had been able to tell her. On the island in the centre of the square, at the doorway of St Mark's Church, there was an old and magnifi-cent magnolia tree, its branches aching with snowy, rose-tinted blossom. In the garden of number six was a magnolia bush, its star-shaped flowers a flawless white, and in Kate's garden was a glorious *magnolia sieboldii*, all of ten foot high and five foot wide, its pendulous creamy flowers cradling stamens the colour of jewelled wine.

'Mornin'!' Hettie Collins called out to her from the far side of the square as she set off for a morning's shopping down Lewisham market, her black coat buttoned up to her throat despite the May sunshine, a black straw hat crammed over her iron-grey curls. 'Is there trouble at the Emmersons? Leon was banging on the vicarage door at six o'clock this morning. I know, because I saw him when I was letting the cat in.'

Hettie wasn't a street trader, but her voice was loud enough for one. Christina, unsure of whether Matthew's disappearance was common knowledge and, if it wasn't, if Kate wanted to keep it that way, gave a slight shrug of her shoulders. 'I can't stop to chat, Hettie!' she called back to her. 'I'm in a hurry! 'Bye!' and before Hettie could make a response, she turned her back on her, walking at a brisk pace up Kate's black-and-white diamond-tiled pathway.

Hettie gritted her teeth, staring after her malevolently. She didn't want a friendly chat. She wanted a straight answer to a straight question. Squaring her shoulders and thereby shifting her ample bosom into a more comfortable position beneath the strained buttons of her coat, she stomped off in the direction of Magnolia Hill and Lewisham. She'd never liked Christina Robson. In the days when Christina had been Christina Frank, a Jewish refugee everyone had felt sorry for, she'd felt sorry for her, too, but she'd never liked her. Why Jack Robson should have married her, when he could have married a nice and jolly south-east London girl, she didn't for the life of her know. She'd put good money on one thing, though. The day would come when he'd regret the choice he'd made. She was as sure of that as she was of her own name.

Christina knocked on Kate's lemon-painted front door and, without waiting for the door to be opened for her, opened it and stepped into the hallway beyond, calling out in time-honoured Magnolia Square fashion, 'Cooee! It's me! Christina!'

The Emmerson house was Edwardian and the hall and the hallway beyond it, leading past the foot of the stairs towards the back of the house and the kitchen, was high-ceilinged and spaciously wide.

''Lo, Auntie Cwistina!' a little voice carolled back from behind a kitchen door half-panelled in panes of coloured glass.

Seconds later the door was wide open and Johnny was charging down the hallway towards her, one strap of his dungarees still unfastened, his unbrushed mop of hair a riot of tangled curls. 'I'm not staying at home today!' he informed her gleefully as he ran into her arms. 'I'm going to Auntie Cawwie's. Have you come to take me to Auntie Cawwie's? Are we going to the park? Are we going to feed the deer?'

'Come through,' Kate said to her a trifle breathlessly from the kitchen doorway, the heavy braid of hair she usually wore coiled in a bun swinging over her shoulder. It was waist-length, and with her un-powdered face and unlipsticked mouth, she looked scarcely old enough to be Johnny's mother, let alone the mother of a twelve-year-old boy and the adoptive mother of a child even older.

'I assume Jack's told you the news?' she said, as Christina walked into the kitchen, Johnny in her arms and straddling her hip. 'I'm just getting Johnny ready to take over to Carrie's. She's going to look after him for me today while I go down to Somerset by train. I want to talk to Matthew's headmaster face to face.' In the light of the sunshine streaming through the window, her face was ivory pale and there were blue-shadowed circles of sleeplessness and anxiety carved beneath her eyes.

Christina's heart plummeted. Not only had she been denied the pleasure of taking Jilly to school, but it looked as if she was also going to be denied the pleasure of looking after Johnny. 'But won't Carrie be working down the market?' she asked. 'Won't it be difficult for her? It might be easier if I looked after him for you.' Her voice was so studiedly casual it would have taken someone with a lot less on her mind than Kate to realize the passionate plea lying behind it.

Kate swung her braid back over her shoulder and, taking Johnny from Christina's arms, sat him on her draining-board.

'It's kind of you to offer,' she said, beginning to brush his hair in such swift haste that Johnny yelped in protest, 'but Carrie's already told her dad she won't be serving on the stall today, and her mum's going to stand in for her.' With Johnny's riot of silk curls as neat as she had time to make them, she speedily adjusted his dungarees strap. 'I want to try and catch the ten-thirty train from Paddington to Taunton, so it means being at Blackheath Station by nine-fifteen at the latest.' Scooping her still-complaining child from the draining-board, she set him back on his feet. 'Will you take him to Carrie's for me?' she asked, sweeping her braid into a neat coil in the nape of her neck. 'That will save me at least five minutes.'

'Is Leon going with you?' Christina had already lifted Johnny back up into her arms. She hadn't seen sight or sound of Leon since entering the house, but it was possible he was at the vicarage, making telephone calls.

Kate began taking hairpins out of the pocket of her turquoise cotton skirt, anchoring the heavy weight of her corn-gold hair with swift expertise. 'No.' She gave a hasty look towards her kitchen clock. 'He's gone to work. He doesn't know I'm going. I only decided I ought to do so a half hour ago. I'll be back by late tonight, though, and I've left him a note.' She touched her wrist, realized she hadn't put her watch on, and whirled out of the kitchen in order to find it.

Christina hugged Johnny close. Kate and Leon had obviously judged he was too young to be told about Matthew's disappearance because he was giggling, his dusky cheeks winsomely chubby, his toffee-brown eyes dancing with high spirits. Her throat tightened. Why was it so easy for some women to have children and so hard, often impossible, for others to have them? There simply seemed no logic to it. Carrie, for instance, had conceived and carried Rose without even thinking about it, but when a second baby came along, she had miscarried at six months and there had been no babies since. As for Kate . . .

Christina looked around her friend's cheery kitchen. Kate had never had any trouble in conceiving and carrying babies.

Or of adopting them. On the open-shelved dresser, propped against a collection of prettily patterned plates, were school photographs of Daisy and Matthew, Luke and Jilly. On the wall near the window was pinned a splodgily painted picture of an unrecognizable object, presumably painted by Johnny. A little above it was a crayoned picture of a slightly fleshed-out stick figure, its head crowned with a mass of squiggles to indicate tight curly hair. A balloon was coming out of a smiling mouth with the word 'HELLO' printed inside it. Underneath the figure was the proud and very carefully printed caption, 'MY DADDY' and, in the bottom right-hand corner, the childish signature, 'Daisy, aged 10'. Daisy's love for Leon and Kate, and theirs for her, was obvious. Why, then, if she and Jack adopted a child, should it be any different? Why was Jack so adamant that an adopted child would not at all be like having a child of their own? Why was he so violently opposed to the very idea of their adopting a baby?

Kate burst into the kitchen, a cream-coloured jacket over one arm, her handbag in the other. 'Right! Let's be off! I might just make the next train to Charing Cross if I run all the way to the station!'

Seconds later Christina and Johnny were standing on the pavement outside number four, watching Kate run fleet-footedly across the top right-hand corner of the square, past the vicarage and into Magnolia Terrace.

Johnny's sunny expression changed to one of sudden uncertainty. 'Is Mummy coming back?' he asked, looking up at her as he stood by her side, his hand in hers.

'Yes, Johnny, of course she is.'

There wasn't a shadow of doubt in Christina's voice, and Johnny's fears vanished. 'Mummy should have made me sandwiches, shouldn't she?' he said chattily as she began to walk him across the square. 'Sandwiches like Daddy's sandwiches.

Sandwiches *so* big.' With his free hand he stretched his thumb and forefinger as wide apart as they would go.

Christina smiled down at him, wondering what Carrie's reaction would be if she suggested to her that she looked after Johnny for her. She could make a picnic lunch and they could spend the day in Greenwich Park and perhaps go for a walk down by the river . . .

'Who that man?' Johnny asked as they walked past St Mark's towards the bottom left-hand corner of the square. He pointed to the top step of number nine where Zac Hemingway was sitting in the sunshine, watching the world go by.

'I've no idea.' A quick glance in Zac's direction told her he was most likely Jack's new protégé, but she didn't want him to overhear her talking about him. He would no doubt hear enough people doing that without her joining their ranks – and anyway, she could easily be wrong in her assumption. Queenie Tillet took all kinds of people in as lodgers, many of them, such as visiting circus or fairground folk, on a very temporary basis. The young man on Queenie's top step, a white T-shirt stretched across his bulging chest muscles, a pair of jeans snug on his hips, could very easily be a circus strongman, or an exhibition wrestler, or . . .

'Good morning,' he said pleasantly as they reached Queenie's gateway. 'Lovely day, isn't it?'

With reserved politeness and avoiding direct eye contact with him, Christina agreed that it was, indeed, a lovely day.

Zac grinned to himself as she quickened her pace, the toddler at her side having to break into a trot to keep up with her. Despite the harmlessness of his few friendly words, she hadn't liked him speaking to her. He wondered how she reacted when wolf-whistled at, in no doubt at all that it was something that happened with great regularity. His grin deepened. The blokes in question wouldn't get very far, that was for sure. The toddler

at her side had obviously been fathered by the darkie he'd seen
entering the vicarage in such haste a few hours earlier. He
wondered if she was the kiddy's mother, or if the Scandinavian-
looking girl who came out of number four with her, and who
then sprinted off in the direction of the heath, was his mother.
Either way, the chap in question was exceedingly lucky. Both
women, in very different ways, were stunning head-turners.
With deepening interest, he saw the classily turned-out young
woman walk up the Collins's front path. So she was a friend
of Carrie Collins, was she? He rose to his feet, hooking his
thumbs in the pockets of his Levi's. They were about as dis-
similar as two dark-haired women could be, one possessing an
air of silk-smooth, understated elegance and aloofness; the other
slapdash and aflame with gypsy vibrancy. Of the two, he knew
who appealed to him most. It wasn't only the father of the little
boy now skipping across the doorstep of number seventeen
who was lucky. Danny Collins was lucky too – though he didn't
seem to know it.

Daisy stood in assembly, the majestic cadences of William Blake's
'Jerusalem' resounding around her. It was her favourite hymn
and she usually sang it with great enjoyment. But not this morning. This morning she didn't want to sing. This morning she
didn't even want to be at school. Three rows in front of her
she could see Rose's distinctive head of mahogany-red curls.
She knew that Rose would know of Matthew's disappearance,
because her mother would have told her of it when she explained
that she was looking after Johnny for the day.

'Bring me my bo . . . w of burning go . . . ld,' chorused her
fellow pupils, with little respect for tune.

Daisy caught Miss Bumby, her form-mistress, looking at her
disapprovingly, and unenthusiastically joined in on 'Bring me
my arrows of desire.'

71

It was typical of Rose's mum that she wouldn't think twice about giving up a day's work in order to help her own mum out. Her mum and Rose's mum had been best friends since they were toddlers, just as she and Rose had always been best friends. All the same, there was no need for Johnny to be spending the day at the Collins's. *She* could have stayed home from school and looked after him. That way, she would have been on the spot if there was news of Matthew. As it was, she was stuck in school and, even if Matthew were found, she wouldn't know about it until she got back home, at teatime.

'Bring me my spea . . . r, O clouds unfo . . . ld,' sang Blackheath High en masse. 'Bring me my chario . . . t of fi . . . re.'

She hadn't yet had a chance to talk with Rose, and wouldn't have until lunchtime, because Rose was a year younger and in a different form, but she knew how worried Rose would be, for Rose knew that Matthew wasn't like some local boys, happy to play truant just for the hell of it. He didn't have the disposition of a tearaway. He was too naturally solemn, too introspective.

'I will not cea . . . se from mental flight, Nor shall my sword sleep in my ha . . . nd,' warbled her classmates at full throttle as the end of the hymn came in sight. 'Till we have built Je . . . ru . . . sa . . . lem, In Eng . . . land's green and pleasant land!'

As the hymn came to a rousing conclusion, Rose turned her head, her eyes meeting Daisy's, the urgent query in them unmistakable. Daisy lifted her shoulders in an expressive, negative shrug and then, under Miss Bumby's eagle eye, was obliged to turn, filing out of the hall with the rest of her classmates in a crocodile that would have done credit to a military parade-ground.

At the classroom door, Miss Bumby detained her. 'A few words Daisy, if you please,' she said peremptorily.

Daisy stepped from the crocodile, her heart leaping. Was there news? Had her mother telephoned the school from the vicarage, asking that a message be passed on to her? 'Please God,' she prayed inwardly. 'Please, please . . .'

'I saw your arrival at school this morning,' Miss Bumby continued crisply, crushing her hopes instantly. 'It was highly undignified. The school entrance is not suitably sited for lorries – especially lorries loaded with rusting old ovens and laundry coppers—'

'Scrap-metal,' Daisy said in a taut, tight voice. 'The lorry was loaded with scrap-metal.'

Miss Bumby, unaccustomed to being interrupted in such a manner, breathed in sharply, her thin nostrils whitening. Daisy Emmerson was a bright girl – undoubtedly university material – but she'd never gain a university place if she began neglecting her studies for such an unsuitable boyfriend while still in the fifth form. A scrap-metal-collecting lorry-driver indeed! Why, the young man was no different to a rag-and-bone-man or a street totter!

'May I remind you that fifth- and sixth-formers are not encouraged to have boyfriends,' she said acidly. 'They interfere with a girl's schoolwork, and your schoolwork, though of an exceptionally high standard, must remain at a high standard if you are to gain a place at university.'

Daisy's cheeks flushed scarlet in a mixture of anger, frustration and embarrassment. She wanted very much to put Miss Bumby in her place by truthfully stating that Billy wasn't her boyfriend, but knowing how very much Billy hoped that one day he would be, couldn't bring herself to do so. 'The friend in question is a family friend,' she said stiffly. 'I had to take my younger sister to her junior school this morning and, so

73

that doing so wouldn't make me late, he very kindly gave both me and her a lift.'

Miss Bumby had a long enough experience of teenage girls to know when one of them was telling her the truth. She gave a satisfied nod. 'Then the subject is closed,' she said, scrupulously fair as always and also mightily relieved.

As she turned and led the way into the classroom, Daisy followed her, unhappily aware that, for herself, the subject was far from closed. For nearly a year now Billy had wanted to put their relationship on a different, more intimate, footing. 'Yer fifteen now,' he had said exasperatedly when she had been reluctant to follow through from hand-holding to kissing. 'Girls get married at sixteen! Yer can't tell me they don't do so without 'aving done any kissing and petting before'and!'

Daisy was sure he was right in his assumptions.

She knew from her schoolfriends, many of whom broke school regulations with great brazenness when not within sight of the school-gates, that long kissing sessions on the back seats of local cinemas were considered a quite normal activity. But not for her. At least not yet.

Miss Bumby began marking the class register, calling out names in her dry, clipped voice. Daisy's thoughts continued to dwell on Billy. The problem was, her schoolfriends' boyfriends were schoolboys from nearby St Joseph's or St Dunstan's. They weren't mature twenty-one-year-olds, running a business of their own, having served two years in uniform doing their national service. Billy, she knew, was serious about her. In no time at all he would be wanting to put an engagement ring on her finger, and though in many ways that would make her the happiest person in the world, it would also mean an end to all her dreams of an Oxford university education.

'. . . Daisy Emmerson . . .' Miss Bumby called out without looking up from her registration book.

'Here, Miss,' Daisy replied automatically. If only Billy were a few years younger, she mused, and still at school, then things would be so much simpler. She became aware of stifled giggling coming from behind her.

'Any old iron?' the class comedian was singing rag-and-bone-man style under her breath. 'Any old iron, junk or lum . . . ber?'

As all the girls within hearing distance collapsed into stifled giggles, Daisy flushed scarlet, not in embarrassment, but in angry indignation. How dare her classmates make fun of Billy? He was twice the young man any of their wimpish grammar-school or public-school brothers or boyfriends would ever be.

As Miss Bumby, hearing only the giggles and not their cause, glared and rapped on her desk with a ruler for order, Daisy opened her geography textbook in readiness for the first lesson of the day. One thing was for sure: when the time was right for her to become Billy's girlfriend, she wouldn't let any snide remarks about his occupation stand in her way – and she certainly wouldn't let them do so if, as a university graduate, she became his fiancée!

Chapter Six

Carrie waved Christina goodbye, as oblivious as Kate had been to the need that lay behind Christina's words when she offered to look after Johnny for her. 'Well now,' she said, looking down at him as he stood in the centre of her kitchen, 'what shall we do today? Shall we visit the donkey-man on the heath, or go to the pond, or to—'

'Yer can collect me boots from the menders, Ma,' Danny said, sitting unshaven at the kitchen table as he studied the racing column in the *Daily Express*, a steaming pint pot of tea cradled in his hands. 'And yer can get me some dubbin while yer about it,' he added, wondering whether he dare risk a quid on Little Italy in the two o'clock at Haydock or if, considering what he'd already parted with at the bookies that week, he should keep his hand in his pocket instead. 'And I'm out o' wintergreen. The new liniment Jack's bin tryin' out ain't 'alf as good.'

Carrie, who had been bending down to speak to Johnny, straightened up. 'What did your last slave die of?' she asked with such unexpected and out-of-character tartness that Danny abandoned his scrutiny of the day's runners and stared at her in bewildered amazement.

'Blimey, pet, what's got into you?' he asked, deeply aggrieved. 'I only asked fer some dubbin and some—'

'I know very well what you asked for!' Carrie was filled with

such a rush of resentment and frustration that if Johnny hadn't
been present, she would have clouted him around both ears.
'But did you have to ask for them as if I'd nothing else to do
all day? And did you have to speak to me as if I was your
blooming mother?'

Danny blinked, totally at sea.

'My name's *Carrie*,' she said, aware of his incomprehension
and suddenly, ridiculously, feeling as if she wanted to cry. 'And
I'd like to be called Carrie.'

'Well, 'course you do, pet,' Danny said, blissfully unaware
that he ever called her anything else. 'An' if yer like, if yer
feelin' out o' sorts, I'll get the dubbin and wintergreen misself.'
He abandoned the *Daily Express* and his pint pot and rose to
his feet. 'I'll tell yer wot,' he said, still clueless as to what had
so upset her, but not liking to see her upset, especially when
Kate's little nipper was standing nearby, all eyes and ears. 'Why
don't I make yer a nice fresh cuppa? An' when you and Johnny
'ave finished visitin' the donkeys or the pond, why don't yer
visit the gym?' As he walked past Johnny en route to the kettle
and the sink, he ruffled Johnny's mop of silky curls. 'You'd like
that, wouldn't yer mate?' he asked, grinning down at him. 'Yer'd
like to 'ave a go on one of the punch-bags, wouldn't yer?' Danny
liked nippers. When Carrie, six months pregnant, had lost their
own little nipper and the doctor advised them she shouldn't
become pregnant again, he was devastated. He was also pragmatically realistic. After all, it wasn't as if they didn't have a
kiddie. They had Rose, and Rose was a kiddie in a million. She
was a little gem. And if trying for another baby meant putting
Carrie's health at risk, then as far as he was concerned, there
was no contest. He'd settle for what he already had, thank you
very much, and be grateful for it.

'How is he going to reach a punch-bag?' Carrie asked,
resignedly aware that the present moment was not the time and

that nor, with Johnny present, was it the place, for a proper argie-bargie with Danny.

'I'll lift 'im up.' He began filling the kettle at the sink tap. 'Which'll be a darn sight easier than lifting you up, pet,' he said, grinning broadly. 'If we ever 'ave a fire I could get our mahogany wardrobe dahn the dancers quicker'n I could get you dahn 'em!'

Carrie walked Johnny over the heath to the donkeyman. His pitch was just opposite the top entrance to Greenwich Park, and he had been there for as long as Carrie could remember, his half a dozen donkeys giving placid rides to small children. Still smarting over Danny's wise-crack about her weight, she paid the donkey-man sixpence and then stood by as he hoisted a radiant-faced Johnny astride the donkey of his choice. She didn't know exactly how much she weighed, because she hadn't been on a set of weighing-scales since a day trip last summer to Margate when, as well as a slip of paper with her weight on, she had received another slip of paper.

'*You will have a lucky life and live in exciting times*' it had said. She was unimpressed. The war years had been exciting, but she certainly didn't want to live through anything like them ever again. The slip of paper with her weight on had stated that she was twelve stone eight pounds. Was she perhaps thirteen stone now? Down at the market she'd have to sell a hell of a lot of potatoes to sell thirteen stones' worth!

'I'm a cowboy, Auntie Cawwie!' Johnny shouted to her from the back of his placidly plodding donkey. 'I'm chasing Indians!'

Carrie laughed and waved acknowledgement, but inside she wasn't laughing. Thirteen stone. That was probably what her mother and her mother-in-law weighed. Common sense told her that she didn't look like her mother or mother-in-law. Big she might be, but she still curved in and out at all the right places and nothing wobbled where it shouldn't.

Johnny, once again on terra firma, was beaming up at her, saying, 'Can we go to see Uncie Danny at the gym now, Auntie Cawwie? I've been there with Daddy and I like it.'

Carrie thought of the all-pervading smell of heatrub and liniment, and winced. She'd do a lot to keep Johnny happy, but she didn't want to spend a precious day away from the family fruit and veg stall watching her other half putting sweating boxers, and aspiring boxers, through their paces, and besides, Zac Hemingway would no doubt be at the gym and she didn't want to run into him again in a hurry. She'd had quite enough male aggravation for one day without letting herself in for more.

'Why don't we have tea and toasted tea-cakes in Chieseman's?' she suggested, knowing it would be a temptation Johnny would find hard to resist. 'If you're especially good, we'll have ice-cream sundaes afterwards.'

Johnny beamed, his eyes shining. A visit to Chieseman's, the big department store opposite Lewisham's clock tower, was always a very special treat. It had the biggest toy department for miles around and a cafe that, as well as selling toasted teacakes and ice-cream sundaes, also sold cream cakes and deliciously sticky iced buns.

'And can we visit your market stall?' he asked eagerly as she took hold of his hand and began walking him towards the nearest bus stop. 'Can I help polish apples and take owanges out of their boxes?'

Carrie gave a deep, defeated sigh. Not only had she let herself in for a buttered toasted tea-cake that would do her hips no favours whatsover, but she'd also let herself in for a jaunt down the High Street on the one day when she thought she'd escaped from it! 'All right,' she said, knowing when she was beaten. 'But we're not going to stay there long, pet lamb. I see quite enough of the market, working in it, without paying it unnecessary social calls!'

Johnny giggled. He liked his Auntie Carrie, though she wasn't his real auntie, of course. Johnny wasn't sure, but he didn't think he had a real auntie. His big brother, Matthew, had. Matthew had two aunties, one of them a great-aunt, which meant she was very, very old. Matthew had once had a great-grandad as well, though he and Jilly and Luke and Daisy had never had one. Instead, they had Gran and Grandpa Voigt who lived in Greenwich, and though Matthew's great-grandad hadn't been his, Jilly's and Luke's and Daisy's great-grandad, Grandpa Voigt was also Matthew's grandad. It was all very complicated, but he didn't worry about it because his mummy had told him it was nothing for him to worry about and that he'd understand everything much better when he was a little older.

'Has Mummy gone to see Maffew at his school?' he asked chattily as they began to re-cross the heath, walking towards the hill that led the short distance down into Lewisham.

Carrie, aware that Kate hadn't told Johnny about Matthew's disappearance from school, squeezed his hand and nodded. After all, Kate *had* gone to Matthew's school, and so she wasn't completely misleading him. Much to her relief, he didn't ask any more questions as to why he was spending the day with her. Once in Lewisham they went into Chieseman's and had tea and toasted tea-cakes in the cafe. Johnny also had an ice-cream sundae, and Carrie exercised great will-power by not ordering one for herself, and not ordering a selection of cream cakes either.

It was scarcely fifty yards from Chieseman's to her dad's market stall, but it might just as well have been five hundred. First of all they ran into Christina Robson's mother, Eva. Like her daughter, Eva was a German Jewess, but unlike her daughter and despite having been married for three years to a Greenwich butcher, her English was heavily accented.

'So vat are you doing not working today?' she asked Carrie cheerily, her near-white hair elegantly styled, an emerald chiffon scarf adding panache to a classically elegant, but inexpensive, beige pleated skirt and cream-coloured blouse. 'I buy tomatoes from your *Mutter* and she says you haff other fish today to fry.'

'Did she?' Carrie suppressed a surge of annoyance. It was a relief to know her mother wasn't broadcasting to all and sundry the reason why she was manning the stall, but there was no need for her to make it sound as if Carrie had taken the day off for no very good reason.

Eva fumbled in her handbag and then, taking out a toffee, bent down and offered it to Johnny. 'There, *Liebling,*' she said, beaming fondly at him. 'A toffee for a little boy *sehr, sehr gut.*'

Carrie felt a lump come into her throat. With her first husband and her only son murdered by the Nazis, and with the war years spent not knowing if Christina had escaped the same fate, Eva had suffered more than her fair share of grief. What she longed for now, in some way to compensate her for all she had lost, was a grandchild – and it was beginning to look as if she would never have one.

With a polite 'fank you' Johnny took the toffee and popped it into his mouth. Mindful of the giant sundae he had just eaten, Carrie regarded him with some misgivings, hoping he wasn't going to make himself sick. 'We're just on our way to see my mum now,' she said, not wanting to stay chatting any longer in case Eva proffered Johnny another toffee 'for later'.

'*Schade.*' Eva hid her disappointment stoically. '*Auf Wiedersehen*, cheerio for now.'

'*Auf Wiedersehen,*' little Johnny said, much to Carrie's surprise. Then, as they began crossing the High Street, she remembered. Kate's father was German, and though it was very seldom anyone heard him speak his native language, he had obviously troubled to teach his grandson a few simple phrases.

'Cooee there!' Lettie Deakin called out, carrier bags bursting with vegetables in either hand. 'Won't it be grand if the weather stays like this for the coronation?'

'It'll be smashing,' Carrie agreed, thinking how strange it was that so many of her friends and neighbours were German. Not that anyone really thought of Christina or her mother as being German. 'Jewish refugees' was how they were described by the few people who bothered to describe them at all. Carl Voigt, Kate's father, wasn't Jewish, and so came into a different category. He'd been taken a prisoner during the First World War and, when the war was over, he hadn't returned to Germany but had married a south-east London girl and settled in Magnolia Square. Widowed far too soon, he had only moved away from the square and to nearby Greenwich when, shortly after the end of the Second World War, he had married his middle-aged lady-friend.

'Skiving, Carrie, are we?' the pot-bellied gent manning the first fruit and veg stall they came to called out to her genially. 'Wish I could take a day off whenever I felt like it!'

'You might as well, the amount of trade you do!' Carrie riposted with a grin.

He grinned back. A bit of friendly rivalry and joshing never did anyone any harm, and he liked Carrie Jennings. She never had a bad word to say about anyone, was always cheery and, like her father, was as honest as the day was long.

From where they now were, Carrie could see her mother weighing out carrots for a regular customer and not looking any too happy about it. Knowing very well that once her mother caught sight of her she was going to complain loud and long about standing in for her, she took a deep, steadying breath.

She took it a second too soon, for instead of the next person she spoke to being her mother, it was her niece, Beryl.

''Lo, Auntie Carrie,' nineteen-year-old Beryl said, pushing her way through the mid-morning crowd thronging the High Street and using the childhood diminutive with happy unself-consciousness. 'I know why you're looking after Johnny today, so you don't have to do any explaining in front of little ears.'

'That's a relief.' There was no sarcasm in Carrie's voice, only sincerity. If Johnny learnt that Matthew was missing from school and that the police were searching for him, he'd be both bewildered and distressed, and his distress would only make things even more difficult for Kate. 'What are you doing out of the office so early? It isn't lunchtime yet, is it?'

'I've been to the Post Office for the office-boy. He's got a heavy cold and shouldn't really be at work,' she added, just in case her aunt should think her errand a demeaning one for a fully fledged shorthand typist. 'And I thought on my way back I'd have a word with Gran. She doesn't really like working on the stall any more, does she? She says it makes her legs ache.'

Carrie made a sound that could have meant anything, and in this case meant that Beryl was being far too gullible and soft-hearted. Miriam's legs only ached when she was doing something she didn't want to do. At other times they would carry her for miles.

'I've been into Woollies for a new lipstick as well,' Beryl continued, fishing the item in question out of her cardigan pocket. 'What do you think of it?' She twisted the plastic barrel and regarded the cerise-coloured contents doubtfully.

Carrie didn't blame her for being unsure about it. It was far too hard and bright a colour for a girl as young and as un-sophisticated as Beryl. 'It'll make you look as if you have a spoonful of jam in the middle of your face,' she said truthfully, but without the least hint of unkindness. 'I know you don't believe me, love, but you actually look better without make-up than with it.'

Beryl didn't believe her. She was a tall, firmly fleshed girl with straight, mousy hair and a face other people found shiningly and endearingly trusting and without guile, and which she was convinced was unredeemingly plain. 'I thought it might make me look a little less like a Sunday School teacher,' she said wistfully, shoving the offending article back into her cardy pocket.

Carrie regarded her in loving bemusement. 'But you *are* a Sunday School teacher, love.'

'I know.' Beryl grinned sheepishly. 'I just don't want to look like one. Especially not tonight. I'm going to the gym tonight and the new boxer will be there and he's absolutely wonderful, Aunt Carrie. He's—' she stopped short, the blood draining from her face.

He was walking towards them; there was no way he could avoid them – and here she was, in an everyday cotton dress and cardigan, and without even the saving grace of a dusting of powder on her nose! She turned her back swiftly, praying he would simply walk past without seeing her. She wanted to look special when he first spoke to her. She'd already ironed a lace-collared blouse to perfection and starched the petticoats she wore beneath her best summer circular skirt, all in readiness for wearing to the club that evening. She had a face pack, too, that she intended using, and if he stopped and spoke to them now, none of the effort she took would be any use whatever. His first impression of her would be that she wasn't worth a second glance, and then he might never, ever, *give* her a second glance!

'Please God,' she prayed inwardly. 'Please let him not know Aunt Carrie yet! Please let him not stop and speak to her!' Shifting her stance so that her back was placed firmly towards him, she waited with a fiercely beating heart for him to draw abreast of them, for him to walk on past them.

He drew abreast, but he didn't walk past. Instead he slowed to a halt, his shadow falling over them as he said to Carrie in easy, teasing familiarity, 'I expected to see you behind your dad's market stall this morning, not in front of it.'

Carrie sucked in her breath in what sounded like exasperation. What her facial expression was, Beryl didn't know. With her cheeks no longer pale, but brilliant scarlet, she was staring down at the pavement in an agony of self-conscious shyness.

'I'm child-minding,' Carrie said in what, for her, was a quite cross voice. 'And I don't have to account to you for how I spend my time, do I?'

'Not unless you want to,' Zac said affably. 'Whose is the little nipper? I saw him earlier this morning, but wasn't sure if it was his mum he was with.'

'If she was blonde and her hair was in a plaited bun, it was his mum.'

'Then it wasn't.' He knew now which of the two extraordinarily attractive women he saw coming out of number four was married to the darkie, but he still didn't know who the other one was and nor, it seemed, was Carrie going to tell him. One thing was for certain, though. His new neighbours were proving to be an interesting bunch. He glanced across at Carrie's companion, wondering whereabouts she fitted into the picture.

Carrie saw the glance and, knowing how fervently interested in him Beryl was, said with grudging politeness, 'I don't think you two have met yet, have you? Beryl, Zac Hemingway, Jack's new boxer.' She hesitated for a moment. She couldn't now say, 'Mr Hemingway, my niece Beryl.' It would be too ridiculously formal, seeing as how they were all neighbours. Well aware that once she had referred to him by his Christian name there would be no going back, she said even more grudgingly, 'Zac, my niece Beryl.'

Wishing herself a thousand miles away and vowing never again to leave the office without benefit of powder and lipstick, Beryl reluctantly raised her head. Zac saw a pleasant-looking girl who, beneath her furious blushes, had an amazingly good skin, but whose unpowdered nose was a little too large for her ever to be described as conventionally pretty.

'I met your cousin Billy last night at the gym,' he said, trying to put her at her ease.

'Billy isn't my cousin, he's my brother.' Beryl's blushes were beginning to ebb, but only slowly. Close to, Zac Hemingway's physique was even more spectacular than it was at a distance. It was a blazingly hot day and he was wearing American Levi's and a white T-shirt that was straining over a chest so broad and deep it would have put Charles Atlas to shame.

Zac's eyes glazed slightly. This fresh-faced, wholesome-looking girl was Mavis's daughter? His disbelief was almost as deep as when he discovered that Mavis and Carrie were sisters. 'Have I met all the family now?' he asked, disguising his disbelief with a grin that turned Beryl's knees to water. 'That's your gran at the fruit and veg stall, isn't it? She was at the club last night with your grandad and your mother and your brother. I've met your uncle Danny, of course. He's my trainer. And I've met your cousin Rose.'

'Then you've met all of us, apart from my dad.' There was pride in her voice as she mentioned her dad. Her dad was a quiet bloke who didn't look like a hero, but undoubtedly was one. In the war, under enemy fire, he had saved the lives of several men and had been awarded a medal for bravery.

'We have to be on our way,' Carrie said before Beryl could begin telling Zac about her dad's distinguished war record and they found themselves talking to Zac Hemingway for half the morning. 'I've promised Johnny he can help on the stall for a little while and—'

'Come on then, let's have a word with Carrie's mum,' Zac said, transferring his attention to Johnny who, his hand still in Carrie's, had been waiting for such a move with admirable patience.

This wasn't at all what Carrie had intended, but she could hardly say so, not with Johnny beaming up at Zac, and her mother now looking towards them and beckoning furiously in a way that quite obviously meant she wanted him bringing across so that she, too, could have a chat with him. She looked across at Beryl, saw that she was quite seriously wondering if she dare stay away from her office for a further ten or fifteen minutes and said, 'You'd better be getting back to work, Beryl love. Your boss will be wondering where on earth you've got to.'

It was a statement there was really no arguing with. As reluctant now to say goodbye to Zac Hemingway as she had been to say hello to him, Beryl nerved herself into meeting his eyes properly. Blushing yet again, she said ingenuously, 'Will you be at the gym this evening? I'm going to be there and I expect my grandad will be there as well.'

'That'll be champion, your grandad makes a very supportive audience,' Zac said, while Carrie regarded her niece thoughtfully. If Beryl was always so transparent when trying to make headway with someone she fancied, then it was time she was advised not to be.

'Are yer comin' over fer a chat, or are yer not bloomin' comin' over fer a chat?' Miriam bellowed, standing behind an impressive display of leeks and cabbages with her cotton-gloved hands deep in the leather cash-bag tied around her waist.

'Coming!' Carrie shouted back.

''Bye,' Beryl said, speaking really only to Zac.

'Now I see where you get the mouth on you, when you give your old man a blasting,' Zac said under his breath to Carrie.

There was no opportunity for Carrie to give him a set-down. They were now face to face with her mother, and her mother was saying belligerently, 'What's our Beryl doin' skivin' off work at this time o' day? 'Er boss'll be givin' 'er the old 'eave-'o if she doesn't sharpen 'er ideas up. And what are you doin' down 'ere when you're supposed to be child-mindin'?'

'Johnny wanted to pay you a visit,' Carrie said as Johnny made a dive for the front, lowest level of the stall, and began eagerly rearranging apples and oranges.

'Then you might just as well 'ave worked 'ere as normal an' let me save my legs.' She turned her attention to Zac. 'I've got chronic legs, they're always lettin' me dahn,' she confided, conjuring up a picture that had Zac's mouth twitching in a grin he could hardly contain. 'Not that anyone cares, mind,' she added darkly and, as Carrie never ceased running around for her, unfairly. 'What I need is a pair o' legs like yours, young man. I bet they never let yer dahn, do they?'

Zac, his thumbs hooked in the pockets of his jeans, agreed that they hadn't done so yet.

'What, not even in the ring?' Carrie asked, feigning surprise. 'I thought being knocked down and knocked out was all part of a boxer's repertoire.'

'Not this boxer's,' he said, amused by her efforts to rile him.

'I should think not,' Miriam averred stoutly. 'Not with those legs. I said to Albert last night, "with those legs 'e'll go ten rounds an' never notice the first bell's gone."'

Zac made no response to this flattering remark, because he was no longer looking at, or listening to her. He was looking at Carrie. She was wearing a scoop-necked, white-belted scarlet dress that looked as if it had been punished in the wash, for the seams were strained around her hips. Her only jewellery, apart from her wedding ring, was a fine gold chain from which a heart-shaped locket hung. As her eyes met his, very bright and very green, he couldn't help but be aware that the locket was lying snug between the full, rich curves of her breasts. He felt a rising in his crotch. With her square-jawed, high cheek-boned face and mass of untidy dark hair, she attracted him more than he'd been attracted by any woman for a long, long time and with sudden, overpowering certainty, he knew that he wanted to make love to her. The irony of his realization wasn't lost on him. After two years enforced celibacy at Her Majesty's pleasure, he'd not only fallen for a married woman, but a woman he was quite certain had never been unfaithful in her life.

'And so you'll be comin' with us all then, when we go up town to watch the coronation procession?' Miriam was saying to him, more as a statement of fact than a query. 'If we want a good pavement spot to see everythin' from, we'll have to bagsy it the night before. Malcolm Lewis, Mr Giles's scout-master, says we can take a couple of 'is troops' groundsheets with us. That should stop the cold strikin' through to our you-know-whats.'

Carrie raised her eye to heaven in mock despair at her mother's free-and-easy vulgarity. Johnny, a half-eaten apple in one hand, an orange he was saving for later in the other, scrambled out from under the front of the stall. 'Will me and Mummy and Daddy and Jilly and Luke and Daisy be going with you?' he asked, toffee-dark eyes ablaze with anticipation at the very thought. 'Will we be sleeping out on a pavement as well? And Maffew,' he added. 'Will Maffew be coming home for the cowonation?'

There was a sudden tension that bewildered Zac. Carrie lost her look of mock despair and instead looked seriously concerned.

Miriam's eyes had suddenly filled as if she was about to burst into tears.

'I'm not too sure if Matthew will be allowed home from school for the coronation,' Carrie said at last, her voice strained. 'I expect he, and everyone else in his class, will watch it on the television.'

Johnny, accustomed to Matthew only being home in proper school holiday time, found nothing odd about such a possibility. Zac did, though. He wondered if perhaps Matthew, who was obviously one of Johnny's older brothers, was a young delinquent in an approved school somewhere, perhaps a borstal. It was the only reason he could think of for him being educated at what was a residential school far from home.

A little later, walking back down the High Street in the direction of the clock tower, Johnny straddling his shoulders, and Carrie resigned to the fact that she wasn't going to be able to shake him off no matter what she did, walking alongside him, Zac said, 'Is the certain person who isn't likely to be home on Coronation Day in an approved school then?'

At any other time Carrie would have choked with laughter and said that Matthew's school was highly approved, though not in the sense Zac meant. Instead she said soberly, 'No. The person in question has never been in any kind of trouble whatsoever. He's educated differently to . . . to . . .' She hesitated, glancing upwards at Johnny to see if he was listening in on the conversation or not. He wasn't. He was clinging on to Zac's hair, giggling with joy at being so dizzyingly high and trying to attract as much attention to himself as possible. 'He's educated differently to the other children in the family,' she continued as they crossed the busy main road towards Chieseman's, 'because he had a different father, and his father's family were monied and wanted him to receive the kind of education his father had.'

'Then he goes to a nob's school? A public school?'

Carrie nodded.

Zac was intrigued, especially considering the unconventional nature of Johnny's mother's present marriage. 'You said "had" a different father,' he said as Johnny shouted out to someone he knew. 'Does that mean that the gent in question is dead?'

Carrie nodded. She wasn't betraying any secrets. Everyone in Magnolia Square knew Kate's history. 'He died twelve years ago, piloting a Spitfire at Dunkirk.'

Neither of them spoke for a little while. Carrie, because she was thinking back to the far-away days of the war; days that now seemed to belong to another world, and Zac, because he was realizing that when Carrie and her friend Kate were old enough to be having love affairs and babies, he was a wet-behind-the-ears, fourteen-year-old schoolboy. He glanced across at her. The knowledge that she was six or seven years older than him didn't make any difference to the way he felt about her. She possessed a combination of gypsyish sensuousness and radiant wholesomeness that he found deeply erotic.

'And all those other names Johnny mentioned – Jilly, Luke and Daisy – are those all Johnny's other brothers and sisters?'

Despite her renewed concern over Matthew, a smile curved Carrie's mouth. 'Yes,' she said, having nó intention of elaborating, because to do so would just take too long, 'they're all Kate's children.'

'Blimey!' Zac was profoundly impressed. Five children and, if his calculations were correct, she wasn't a day over thirty-two and looked more like twenty-two.

They turned the corner into Magnolia Hill, with Carrie reflecting that never before had she been the object of so much female envy. All the way down the High Street, admiring eyes were turned in Zac's direction. Once or twice she had glanced covertly across at him to see what his reaction was to so much blatant attention. He seemed totally unaware of it. He certainly wasn't preening himself, and the attractive swagger in his walk was the loose-limbed grace of natural-born athleticism, not cock-of-the-walk male vanity. Even in much quieter Magnolia Hill, the girls and women they passed, no matter what their ages, all eyed him with undisguised interest. Carrie couldn't really blame them. He was what film magazines described as 'a gorgeous hunk of beef-cake', and even she had to admit that he possessed other qualities, too, which were decidedly attractive. The way he was carrying Johnny home on his shoulders, for instance, and the way he'd chatted to her mum. A lot of young men she knew simply wouldn't have taken the trouble.

As they neared the square, she wondered if he had a girlfriend. If he hadn't, he was going to find himself inundated with offers, especially as he was boarding with Queenie. Queenie's boarders were nearly all theatricals, and her Edwardian house, one of the largest in the square, was home to a constant stream of pretty young actresses and dancers. She frowned slightly. With rivals such as those, she didn't think Beryl was going to be in with too much of a chance, which was a pity for Zac Hemingway as well as for Beryl, because Zac Hemingway would have a long, long way to go before he found another girl as unspoilt and as tender-hearted.

'Will you be coming down the gym tonight?' he asked as they rounded the left-hand corner of the square and came to a halt outside her front gate.

Carrie's well-marked eyebrows nearly flew into her hair. 'Me?' she gurgled with laughter. 'Not bloomin' likely! I get enough of the smell of wintergreen living with Danny, without seeking out more!'

With a shaft of disappointment, Zac swung Johnny down from his shoulders. It seemed that everyone in Magnolia Square, from school-kids to old age pensioners, were keen on coming to the gym to watch him work out and that the only person who wasn't was the one person he would have liked to have had there.

'Uncle Danny! Uncle Danny! I've been on a donkey and helped Auntie Cawwie's mum on her market stall!' Johnny yelled, racing up the garden path as the front door opened and Danny, leaving the house for his afternoon stint at the gym, waved affably in Zac's direction.

''Ave yer, young fellow?' Danny said, grinning down fondly at him. 'An' I 'ope yer 'ad a bite to eat as well.' He strolled down the path, Johnny scampering at his heels, saying in a disgruntled tone of voice to Carrie, 'Which is more than I did, seein' as you weren't 'ome in time to make me anything.'

Carrie had had far too pleasant a morning to take exception to what was, coming from her nearest and dearest, a quite unexceptional and, in the circumstances, almost a reasonable remark. 'Never mind, love,' she said consolingly. 'I'll bring you a plate of something hot down to the gym.'

Their little marital exchange of words was quite beyond Zac's understanding. Was Danny seriously put out that Carrie hadn't been home to make him something to eat, or not? And if he were seriously put out, what was a spirited woman like Carrie doing, reacting to such a remark in such an apologetic manner? It wasn't the first time he'd been confused by similar, overheard snippets of conversation between husbands and wives. If he'd ever had a home life he would, he supposed, have known instinctively what was affectionate banter between a married couple and what was not, but he'd been an orphan, and in the Dr Barnardo's home he was brought up in there had been care and concern, but no marital role models whatsoever.

''Bye,' Carrie said to him cheerily, turning away from him and walking up her front path towards the door Danny had so conveniently left wide open.

'What time will I be seein' yer dahn the gym?' Danny asked him.

Zac didn't reply. He was watching Carrie as she stepped into the house to make a plate of something hot for her other half. Whatever the state of the Collins's marriage, one thing was for sure. He fancied Carrie Collins. He fancied her something rotten.

Chapter Seven

Jack surveyed his new premises with satisfaction. Above a strip club, in the heart of Soho, it was a tidy little drinking club and he reckoned he was going to do very well with it. There was a mirror-backed bar, a couple of full-sized snooker tables for shooting craps, several smaller tables for rummy and poker and Kalooki, and room for a minuscule dance floor. He'd bought it with a drinking licence that still had another ten months to run, and was confident that, helped by his many contacts in the boxing world, its present, rather staid membership of mainly ex-officers and ex-NCOs, would soon be much increased and vastly enlivened.

All he now needed, before the club opened under his management, was the right kind of bar staff. Previously, the bar had been tended by a wing-commander type sporting a handle-bar moustache and a manner to match. He was ideal for a club catering primarily for ex-servicemen, bored and dissatisfied by peace-time monotony, but he wasn't ideal for the kind of club that would soon, Jack hoped, be full of boxers and fringe show-biz personalities. He shot the right cuff of his well-cut suit jacket and glanced at his ostentatious gold watch. It was nearly two o'clock, and at two o'clock he was interviewing a string of girls in the hope of finding a couple who could efficiently, and glamorously, tend the bar, and a third with enough management ability to be able to oversee the running of it.

Two hours later, he knew he had a problem. The girls were all experienced where bar-work was concerned, and were all glamorously tarted up – too glamorously tarted up. When he concluded each interview by saying that the club was a straight, afternoon drinking and gambling club and that he didn't want bar staff making arrangements with customers for after-hours sexual services, he was greeted by looks of incredulity.

'No way, Mister,' one after another of them said. 'This is Soho and we're either barmaids that are also hostesses, with everything hostessing means, or we ain't barmaids at all. Sorry.'

Jack had appreciated their frankness and began to wonder if he'd been a little hasty in dispensing with the services of the ex-RAF barman. He wanted a raffish atmosphere in The 21, but no blatant sleaze, and it was beginning to look as if such an ideal was going to be very difficult to achieve. Musingly, he locked up and walked down the stairs into Dean Street, turning left to call in at the nearby Jewish bakery in order to take home a little something for Christina's mother. As he neared the entrance he heard a laugh coming from inside the shop that he'd have recognized anywhere.

'So vy not bring your gran back here at tea-time on Coronation Day?' elderly Edie Levy was asking Mavis as she served her with a dozen freshly baked bagels and a giant-sized cake. 'So long it is since ve have seen her. Vy she never come up town no more? Vy she pretend she is old?'

Mavis gave an infectious, deep-throated chuckle. 'She ain't pretending, Edie. Gran can give you fifteen years easily. She must be at least eighty-two!'

'Eighty-three,' Jack corrected as he stepped up beside her at the counter. 'I happen to know because she's the same age, and her birthday's in the same month, as Christina's gran, and it was Jacoba's eighty-third birthday in April.'

Mavis's eyes danced. She always loved running into Jack unexpectedly, but running into him when they were far from Magnolia Square and its eagle-eyed busybodies was a real treat. 'And what are you doing at lunchtime in the middle of Soho?' she asked saucily. 'You've not been visiting a strip club, 'ave you?'

Jack grinned. 'Not that I know of,' he said, deciding there and then that though he intended keeping his ownership of The 21 a secret from the majority of his Magnolia Square neighbours, there would be something offensive about keeping it a secret from Mavis. 'I've just been visiting a club I'm about to open.'

Mavis picked up her bagful of bagels, her green cat eyes widening. 'You mean a club you've bought?' she asked, knowing that Jack never, but never, worked for anyone but himself.

He nodded, saying to Edie, 'An apple-strudel, Edie love,' and then, to Mavis, 'Do you fancy having a look at it? It's only round the corner.'

'Not 'alf!' Mavis's enthusiasm was unbounded. Fancy Jack buying into a little bit of naughty Soho! She wondered who else knew, and was pretty sure that, apart perhaps from Danny, no one did.

'An unofficial ex-service club it used to be,' said Edie, who had been selling Jewish speciality cakes via Mavis to her old friend Leah Singer ever since Leah had found the journey up town too much for her, and who had been serving them to Jack ever since Jack had married Christina, adding her two-penny-worth with easy familiarity. 'Always it was full of middle-aged ex-servicemen, drinking pink gins and telling stories about their RAF and Army days.'

'Blimey!' Mavis pulled an expressive face. 'It doesn't sound as if it was too lively! I 'ope you're going to put a bit of fizz into it, Jack.'

'Oh, I think I'm going to be able to do that,' Jack said nonchalantly, his mind already made up as to how this was to be achieved. He picked up his boxed cake. 'Ta-ra for now, Edie. Be good.'

'At my age, you tell me that?' Edie made as if to throw something at him, cackling with laughter as she did so. It was good he would be doing business only a stone's throw away. He was the kind of man who brought a bit of spice and sparkle to life.

Mavis, who would have been in complete agreement with Edie's opinion if she had known of it, tucked her hand into the crook of his arm.

He looked across at her, flashing her a smile that had her heart doing cartwheels. 'And now you know what I'm doing in Soho, what are you doing?' he asked teasingly. 'Not swinging the old handbag, I hope.'

'Course not, cheeky bugger.' Mavis wasn't at all put out at the suggestion that she might be doing a bit of street-walking. In Mavis's eyes street-walkers were working girls, and though she'd never been a member of their ranks, she certainly wasn't contemptuous of them. 'I'm up here because it's a lovely day and I'm bored,' she said as they turned the corner into Dean Street, her dizzyingly high heels rat-tatting on the pavement. Her shoes were suede and the same cornflower blue as her costume. The lightweight cloth skirt was tight, with skittish side splits, and the nip-waisted jacket had a flounced peplum that drew much male attention to the lush curves of her hips and her effortlessly seductive wiggle. 'I'm supposed to be doing an afternoon stint at the biscuit factory,' she added as they came to a halt outside a doorway squeezed between the entrance to a strip club and a dubious-looking bookshop, 'but they're going to have to do without me.'

With his free hand, Jack took a key from his trouser pocket and opened the door. 'You're wasted packing biscuits,' he said truthfully, leading the way upstairs. 'I thought you were barmaiding at The Anchor in Greenwich?'

'I am, but that's at weekends. Mid-week afternoons I'm at the biscuit factory.'

There was resignation in Mavis's voice. Not since the war, when she'd been a motor-cycle messenger with the ARP, had she had an occupation with any zip to it. For a while she'd been a bus conductress. For a little while longer she'd been a cinema usherette. Occasionally she stood in for Carrie at their dad's market stall, and occasionally she helped Elisha and Lettie Deakin out at The Swan. The excitement factor, whatever she did, seemed to be nil, and there were times when she positively ached for the heady, adrenalin-packed days when she'd ridden Ted's motorbike through streets either blacked-out, or bombed and burning.

'Crikey!' she said now as he crossed a relatively spacious landing and flung open a door. 'What a smashing little spieler!'

'It is, isn't it?' Jack didn't often give his feelings away, but there was no way he could keep the satisfaction from his voice. 'I'm hoping to attract the boxing crowd. Jack Solomons has his office only a lick and a spit away and hopefully I'll be having quite a few dealings with him.'

Jack Solomons was the biggest, most successful boxing promoter in the country, and Mavis was duly impressed. 'You mean dealings with him where Zac Hemingway is concerned?' she asked, wandering over the red-carpeted floor in the direction of the mirror-backed bar.

Jack nodded, leaning back against the door, watching her with deep affection. Even at forty years old, and with laughter lines crinkling the corners of her carefully made-up eyes, she was still quite a girl. He reckoned she always would be, for her sexual attraction stemmed as much from her bubbly effervescent zest for life as it did from her blowsy good looks.

'How about it then?' he asked as she ran scarlet-tipped nails along the polished surface of the bar.

She sucked in her breath, the scarlet-tipped nails coming to an instant halt, and he cursed himself for being so foolish as to have worded his invitation in a way that could be interpreted sexually.

'The club,' he said lightly, easing himself away from the door. 'How would you like to manage it for me? Five afternoons a week, no evenings.'

She breathed out unsteadily, her disappointment that he was not, at long last, propositioning her, savage. Then realization as to what he *was* propositioning dawned. If she were to be managing it, it would be her club, near as dammit! And unless she was very much mistaken, Christina would never know about it – and their mutual sharing of one secret from Christina could, surely, very easily lead to others.

'You're on, Jack love!' Euphorically she rounded the bar. A job up in town among the bright lights, necessitating constant contact with the one man in the world she'd happily lie down and die for! Of course he was on. It was the best offer she'd had in a long, long while. Hell's bells, it was the best offer she'd had *ever*!

As she whirled towards him in happy delight, he broke out laughing, holding his arms wide in order to catch hold of her and swing her around. From now on The 21 would have all the zest and fizz it could possibly cope with, and all without the slightest hint of sleaze. 'We're going to make a great team, Mavis love,' he said, still laughing as she nearly knocked him off his feet.

Mavis's heels kicked the air gleefully. Of course they were going to make a great team. And not just a great business team. Not if she had her way! 'Let's open a bottle of bubbly, Jack love,' she said breathlessly as he finally set her back down on her feet. 'Let's drink a toast to a bloomin' wonderful future!'

'Things don't look too good I'm afraid,' Matthew's headmaster said sombrely to Kate. 'None of the boys or the masters have been able to shed any light on the mystery as to why Matthew should have run away – that is, if he *has* run away.'

Kate didn't need to ask him to explain what he meant by his last remark. She'd arrived at St Osyth's after first visiting the local police station and had already been told that Matthew's disappearance was now being treated as a possible abduction. She said now, as she had said earlier to a kindly detective-sergeant, 'But who would have abducted him? It isn't as if Matthew is a small boy who would have gone off with a stranger if he'd been offered sweets. And anyway, he disappeared from *school*. It isn't as if he disappeared during free time and was in the village, or in Taunton.'

With his elbows resting on his desk, the headmaster steepled his fingers, pursing his lips as he did so. In many ways it would be much to his, and the school's, advantage if Matthew Harvey had been abducted. It was, after all, far preferable for a pupil to be missing involuntarily, rather than voluntarily. Yet, as Matthew's mother so rightly pointed out, Matthew would have had to break very strict school rules to be outside the school grounds at any time after his last lesson of the day and the time when his absence had first been noted. And with no track record of ever being unruly or disobedient, such behaviour on his part would only deepen the mystery, not clarify it, which, as far as the headmaster was concerned, brought him back to the one aspect of Matthew's life which might be held accountable for his having run away. His bizarre domestic situation.

He cleared his throat, wondering how best to broach such a delicate subject, wondering what Matthew's father, who, as a former pupil, he remembered well, would have thought if he had known the day would come when his son would have a black man for a stepfather. 'As no reason has been found within the school to account for Matthew's disappearance,' he began, feeling, oddly enough, as if he were conducting an interview with one of his upper-middle-class parents and not a working-class housewife with a very dubious home life, 'and as there can be no reason to suspect an abduction such as kidnapping, perhaps it behoves us to look elsewhere for a motive for his disappearance.'

Kate's gentian-blue eyes steadily held his. Why didn't the man use simple English? Did he think, perhaps, she wouldn't know what the word 'behove' meant? If so, and if he were trying to emphasize what he obviously felt was the social and educational gap between them, he was failing badly. Her father had been a grammar-school teacher and she knew just as many little-used words as anyone else – and she certainly didn't feel his, or anyone else's, inferior.

'I'm not sure I follow you,' she said, wondering if he was aware of something she was not. 'Matthew would only have run away if he were unhappy—'

'Which, as far as school was concerned, he was not.' The interruption was made with such heavy emphasis that warning bells suddenly started clanging in Kate's brain. What on earth was this pompous, unlikeable man suggesting? He leaned forward across his massive mahogany desk, resting his weight on clasped hands. 'Is it possible, perhaps, that Matthew is unsettled in mind where your domestic arrangements are concerned, Mrs Emmerson? It is often difficult for a boy to come to terms with a parent's—' he had been about to say 'remarriage', and then, remembering that Matthew's great-aunt, Miss Deborah Harvey, had bluntly informed him that Matthew's mother had never been married to her nephew, he stopped himself in time, 'changed circumstances,' he finished a little inadequately.

Kate rose to her feet, her fingers, with their almond-shaped, unpolished nails, tightening around the strap of her shoulder-bag. She knew exactly what was being insinuated, and her rage was so intense she could barely trust herself to speak. 'Matthew's domestic circumstances haven't changed since he was adopted eight years ago when he was little more than a toddler,' she said in a voice throbbing with such passion the headmaster could hardly believe it was coming from such a Nordically cool-looking woman. 'Matthew's father is his *father*. He isn't his stepfather; he isn't a so-called "uncle"; he isn't a passing *boyfriend* of mine!'

The headmaster rose to his feet to face her, reminding himself that only women of a regrettable type indulged in sexual congress with black men and that he needn't feel as if he had behaved with loutish bad manners towards a lady.

'You're speaking from a position of complete ignorance!' Kate blazed, wishing she were a man and that she could deflate his insufferable smugness with a smart punch to his jaw. 'If Matthew is unsettled, the very first person he would turn to would be his father!' She could feel tears of anger and utter frustration pricking her eyelids and blinked them back furiously, not wanting them to be mistaken for tears of weakness. Why were some people so crassly prejudiced? Why couldn't they judge Leon by the kind of man he was, and not by his skin colour? And why, why, why couldn't they understand that Leon and Matthew's relationship was as close as that of any other loving father and son?

'Matthew's father has never let him down, *never*!' She was trembling with the force of her anger. 'Whatever the reason for his disappearance, it isn't because of unhappiness at home, and the sooner you and the police get that into your heads, the better! And now that that's understood, I'd like to speak to Matthew's classmates.'

'The police have already carried out that task.' The headmaster's voice was glacial. He wasn't accustomed to being spoken to with such lack of deference and, especially coming from such a source, he didn't like it. He didn't like it one little bit. He hooked his thumbs into the folds of his gown, thrusting out his chest as he did so.

Kate was unimpressed. She wasn't leaving the school until she had spoken to Matthew's classmates, and that was that. 'I'm aware the police have interviewed several boys,' she said, her anger now fully under control, her voice clipped and curt, 'and now *I* would like to speak with them. So if you please . . .'

The headmaster didn't please, but knew he couldn't possibly say so. With no other option, he walked from around his desk, fuming at how well-spoken she was. A south-east London working-class woman, who had had at least one child out of wedlock and who bedded with a black man, had no business speaking in a voice that would have been happily at home at a polite dinner or garden party. It was too unnerving, too deeply unsettling. Severely discomposed, he swept off in the direction of class one alpha, taking savage delight in the fact that Mrs Emmerson had to keep breaking into a run to keep up with him.

'And so what did Matthew's friends say?' Ruth Giles asked Kate, several hours later. They were seated at a large pine table in the vicarage kitchen. Kate hadn't yet collected Johnny from Carrie's, or gone home, even though she knew Daisy, Luke and Jilly would all be home from school by now, and that Leon would most probably be home from work.

'They said nothing more or less than they said when the police talked to them.' The skin seemed to be stretched tight over her cheekbones, and there were blue shadows of weariness and desperate tension beneath her eyes. 'The last lesson on the day he disappeared was given in what was normally a free period, and was more of a talk and discussion than a lesson proper.'

'About careers?' Ruth prompted, who knew a talk on careers had been given to Matthew's class because Leon had told her and Bob so, the previous morning.

Kate nodded, pressing her fingers against her temples. 'Nothing out of the ordinary was said.' Her voice was thick with fatigue from sleeplessness, her head hurting as she tried to make sense of it all, tried to think what could have happened to Matthew; where he could possibly be. 'The careers master discussed some professions he thought the boys should be thinking about. Apparently a lot of St Osyth boys become lawyers and barristers, and most of the period was given over to a discussion as to which subjects they should be concentrating on if they wanted to follow school tradition.' Her voice cracked, breaking completely. 'Where on earth can he be, Ruth?' Tears streamed down her face. 'If he had run away he would have run home. I know he would have run home!'

Ruth rose from the table and crossed the kitchen, lifting her kettle from the hob. Kate was crying properly now, and she had no intention of trying to stop her. Not for a little while, anyway. Knowing Kate as she did, she knew that at home Kate would have fought back her tears so as not to alarm and bewilder Johnny and Jilly, who were still in happy ignorance as to Matthew's disappearance. A cry now, when such considerations didn't have to be taken into account, would do her the world of good. She filled the kettle at the sink and then placed it back on the hob. The law as a profession. If that was what Matthew eventually decided on, it would certainly be a first where Magnolia Square was concerned. Most local boys either worked in one of the area's many street markets or got themselves jobs in the docks or on the river. Leon Emmerson was a Thames waterman, for instance, and in normal circumstances it would have been customary for Matthew to follow in his footsteps and to embark on a formal apprenticeship so that one day he, too, would be judged fit to navigate a barge under oars anywhere on the Thames's seventy miles of tributaries, creeks and water-ways.

She waited patiently for the kettle to boil, aware that, even where circumstances were normal, not all boys followed auto-matically in their father's footsteps. Young Billy Lomax, for instance, hadn't become a docker like his dad, Ted. Instead, with Jack Robson's help, he had set up in his teens as a scrap-metal merchant. As the kettle began to puff spurts of steam and she took it off the hob, she reflected that Billy's enterprise had also been a first where the square was concerned. She brewed the tea, a slight frown puckering her brows. There was an awfully big difference between becoming a scrap-metal merchant and becoming a lawyer.

'Is the law something Matthew is interested in?' she asked curiously as she set the teapot on the kitchen table. 'It isn't something I've ever heard him mention.'

Kate gave a slight shrug of her shoulders, her tears still staining her cheeks. 'I don't know,' she said, not finding the subject relevant to the crucial subject of where Matthew could be. 'He's only twelve. I don't suppose he knows what he wants to be yet. I s'ppose that was why the careers master was giving a talk. To give Matthew and the other boys some ideas.'

Ruth sat down and poured fresh cups of tea. For a moment or two neither of them spoke. Kate was thinking about Leon, knowing that now another day had passed without news of Matthew, his anxiety, like hers, would be spiralling into panic. Ruth was thinking how odd it must be for Matthew, away at school for most of the year amongst boys who would probably live their entire lives without socially meeting a docker or a Thames lighterman, and then coming home in the school holidays and spending each day, all day, with Leon on the Thames as he ferried wood, or grain, or coal, or whatever other freight he happened to be handling.

'I've always thought of Matthew as being happiest on the river,' she said musingly. 'I remember in the first months after the war, when Leon was back home and he and the older children were getting to know each other again, it was always Matthew, not Luke, who was his shadow whenever he went down to the river.'

Despite the sick dread by now almost swamping her, Kate managed a shaky smile of reminiscence. 'Yes, I remember too. He used to live in an old jersey he thought looked like a proper seaman's jersey, and a pair of battered little wellingtons. Leon's barge, then, was the *Tansy* and I'd send them both off in the morning with sandwiches and never see them again until dusk. I remember him once saying to me he thought Greenland Dock was just like Blackheath fair on a bank holiday!'

'Well, I suppose it would be, to a small boy. All those barges and launches and tugs and ships.' Ruth pushed the sleeves of her raspberry-coloured cardigan a little higher up her arms. It was part of one of her many twin-sets, all of which she wore with gently gored skirts of grey flannel or softly muted, heathery-flecked tweeds. Today's skirt was all hazy mauves and purples and looked as if it had been hand-woven in a croft on the Outer Hebrides; not for the first time, Kate thought her friend would have been far more at home in a manse in a small Scottish village than she was in a vicarage in a boisterous south-east London square.

Ruth, who had never been to Scotland in her life and would

have been very surprised if she'd known the kind of impression she gave, said now, 'A love of the Thames is something that gets into people's blood, isn't it? I can't imagine Leon, for instance, happy working anywhere else but on the Thames.'

'No.' Kate's shaky smile of happy reminiscence faded. Leon. He would be wondering where she was. She hadn't told him, when he had left for work that morning, that she was going to go down to Somerset, to St Osyth's. Daisy would have done so, of course, when he came home, or if not Daisy, then Carrie would have told him where she had gone. 'I must go, Ruth.' She rose to her feet, her fresh cup of tea untouched. 'Leon doesn't know where I've been and there may have been some news whilst I've been away.'

If there had been, the vicarage would have been one of the first places to have heard about it, but Ruth didn't say so. What she did say was, 'I don't think you've really been listening to what I've been trying to say, Kate. I've been thinking and thinking all day about why Matthew should run away, and I think the talk the careers master gave did have something to do with it.'

Kate stared at her.

Ruth pushed her chair away from the table, rising to her feet, her voice urgent. 'Don't you think it's possible that a talk on careers, where it's taken absolutely for granted that the only kind of careers to be contemplated are the professions – law or medicine or something equally prestigious – might have seriously distressed him if what he really wants to be is a Thames waterman, like Leon?'

Kate continued to stare at her, this time in bewilderment. 'But one of the reasons Matthew attends St Osyth's is so that he can have more choice in life than Leon had—'

'But what if Matthew doesn't want more choice?' Ruth's gentle face was fierce. 'He'll know very well the hopes his Harvey aunts have for him, and he probably knows that you, too, have similar hopes. And what if those hopes are totally opposed to what *he* wants from life? What if what Matthew wants to be is a Thames waterman? What would his Harvey aunts say to that? I don't suppose they'd like it very much, would they?'

Kate sucked in her breath unsteadily. For the first time she was listening to a suggestion that made a glimmer of sense. Matthew's aunt and great-aunt would most certainly not like the idea of him following in Leon's footsteps! And Matthew would know that and . . .

'Mrs Giles! Is Mum with you?' The voice was Luke's and it was coming from the direction of the vicarage's ever-open front door.

'She's with me in the kitchen!' Ruth shouted back, certain by the urgency in Luke's voice that Matthew had been found.

'Oh God!' Kate stumbled towards the kitchen door and the hall beyond, feeling as if her heart had stopped beating. Had there been news? And if so, what news?

Luke stood on the doorstep, his face flooded with relief at having tracked her down. 'You'd better come home quick, Mum,' he said, dashing her hopes in an instant. 'Matthew's aunts are at the house, and there's bloomin' ructions going on!'

Chapter Eight

'So what we goin' to do 'bout Jack Robson, Archie?' Ginger, Archie Duke's chief henchman, asked him. Along with Archie's other 'boys', he paid Archie dutiful attention.

Archie was holding court in a corner of the Horse and Ferret in Deptford. It was his favourite pub. The landlord was in his pocket, the regular barmaid was obliging in more ways than one, and the regulars were all pleasingly deferential. He grinned, his fat rump centred firmly on a bar stool, his legs splayed in order to balance the weight of his beer belly, his massive hams straining beneath trousers hand-tailored in a loud, Prince of Wales check, his highly polished shoes shining like twin suns.

'What we goin' to do about 'im?' he asked rhetorically, grinning. 'I'll tell you what we're goin' to do about 'im, old son.' He stabbed the air with his cigar. 'We're goin' to teach the cheeky bleeder a lesson he won't forget in a hurry, that's what we're goin' to do about him!'

There were appreciative chuckles all round. No one Archie lit on as a prospective benefactor ever escaped scot-free if they refused to play ball, but there'd been a rather curious atmosphere when they accompanied Archie on his visit to Jack Robson's boxing club, and some of the boys had wondered if Robson was going to score a first in the walking away scot-free department.

'What we waitin' for then?' Pongo, a recent recruit to Archie's inner circle asked glibly. 'We're all tooled up, let's give him and his club a goin' over now.'

'He ain't opened its doors yet, bird-brain,' a powerfully built, much younger man said contemptuously. 'We can't frighten off the customers if there ain't no customers to frighten, can we?'

Pongo cast a swift look around the circle to try and read what his reaction to such contempt should be. Five pairs of interested eyes met his. Reading aright that everyone present would like to see him have a go with the big-shouldered big-mouth and that this could only mean it was unusual for anyone to do so, and with good reason, the recruit wisely kept his lips buttoned. Archie, who always enjoyed seeing someone bested, sniggered.

Ginger, now he knew how Archie was going to play the Robson card, said with high satisfaction, 'We'll wait till Robson's opening-night thrash and then we'll give him and his punters a night to remember.'

As the 'boys' – all of them, with the exception of the big-shouldered big-mouth, well into middle-age – savoured this prospect, the pub doors opened and a heftily built navvy strolled in.

Like everyone else who had entered the Horse and Ferret that evening, he paused for a moment before approaching the bar and then, on registering Archie's presence, walked over to Archie's sacrosanct corner.

''Lo, Mr Duke,' he said, coming to a halt a deferential couple of feet away. 'What can I get you?'

'A brandy-chaser,' Archie said, not recognizing the navvy even by sight, and not caring. It was enough that the navvy had recognized *him* and, like everyone else who stepped through the pub doors, had immediately acknowledged his presence in a suitable manner. Everyone kowtowed to Archie. It was the way he liked it. It was what being a hard man and a grafter was all about.

'I thought word was out Robson was going to be putting up against us in a dog-fight,' a rather thoughtful-looking, long-time crony of Archie's ventured. 'Won't blitzing his club put the kibosh on such a fixture?'

'A dog-fight? What's a dog-fight?' Pongo asked his nearest neighbour out of the corner of his mouth.

His neighbour wiped a foaming line of best bitter from his upper lip and, as the question that had been put to the group but that everyone knew had really been put to Archie alone, remained unanswered, said, 'It's an illegit boxing-match, stupid. Don't yer know nuffink? Arnie fights reg'lar for Archie in 'em. Yer can put a packet on 'im every time, an' even if it isn't a carve-up you'll still be quids in.'

Arnie was the big-shouldered big-mouth, and Pongo was grateful he'd had the sense not to tangle with him. He opened his mouth to ask what a carve-up was and then thought better of it. It didn't do to look too stupid, and, anyway, what else could it be but a fight that was fixed?

Archie was looking seriously nonplussed and, in order to help him out, Ginger said scornfully, 'Robson couldn't put any-one up against Arnie! The boxers at 'is club are all kids. Yer saw 'em for yerself the other night. Nippers, most of 'em. Even Jack Solomons wouldn't pull a crowd billing one of them in a fight!'

'The bloke knocking 'ell out o' the speed-ball wasn't a nipper,' Pongo said, glad of the opportunity of making a statement no-one could argue with. ''E looked like a bloke who knew 'is business.'

No one responded. Unlike Pongo, they hadn't taken any notice of the bloke working out. They'd been too intent on giving Archie the kind of swaggering Mafiosi back-up he expected on such occasions. It was the boxer amongst them who set the record straight. 'No bloke who knew his business would be working out in front of an audience of kids and old dears,' he said with reasoned scorn. 'In a proper ring he'd be down in less time than it takes to boil an egg.'

Archie's familiar snigger reassured everyone that a gaffe hadn't been made. If Jack Robson was going to be daft enough to put one of his fighters up against Arnie in a dog-fight, then doing over his spieler was going to be neither here nor there. The silly bugger was simply going to lose out every which way there was.

'Where the 'ell's the barmaid with your brandy-chaser, Archie?' Ginger asked solicitously. 'Don't she know you're not a man to be kept waiting? Some people just don't know when they should spring to it, do they?'

'Spring to it? *Spring to it*? How dare you walk in our house like the Wicked Witch of the North and speak to my little sister like that?' Daisy stormed at Deborah Harvey. 'If you want a cup of tea, you can jolly well wait until one is offered to you!'

'Why is she saying Matthew's runned away?' Jilly was demanding, tugging hard on Daisy's hand. 'Why is she here? Why is Daddy putting Johnny to bed when we haven't had our supper yet? Where's Mummy?'

'Do you think I should take Jilly home with me whilst Leon sorts this little lot out?' Carrie, who had deposited Johnny home only five minutes earlier, was yelling to Billy above the din.

Billy, in the house ostensibly to see if there was any news about Matthew, but really in order to see Daisy, lifted his shoulders in a helpless gesture. He was damned if he knew what anyone should do. He'd never known Daisy lose her temper in such a way before. Hell's bells! He never knew she *had* such a temper before!

'Want to stay up, Daddy!' Johnny was yelling from somewhere at the top of the stairs. 'Want to see the nasty witch lady!'

Kate raced up her front path, Luke at her heels.

'Trouble, dear?' Lettie Deakin, who was always in the offing when least wanted, asked with animated interest as she drew near the gate, her little dog skittering around her feet.

Neither Kate nor Luke looked over their shoulders to reply.

'Dad had to let Miss Harvey in!' Luke panted as Lettie came to an interested halt at the bottom of their path and Kate took the shallow flight of steps leading to their front door, two at a time. 'He couldn't leave her out on the doorstep, could he?'

Kate didn't know what Leon could have done. What she did know, though, was that in another five minutes half the square would be privy to what was going on. Elderly Harriet Robson, who lived next door at number two, was already shuttering up a bedroom window to see what all the kerfuffle was about, and Mr Nibbs, who lived on the other side of her, was standing on his top step, pretending to be enjoying the evening air as he listened avidly to the shouts and counter-shouts.

'How *dare* you speak to me like that, you ill-bred young woman!' Deborah Harvey thundered at Daisy.

'Want Mummy!' Jilly hollered tearfully to anyone who would listen.

'Want downstairs!' Johnny shouted, pummelling Leon's shoulders in frustrated rage as Leon hastily deposited him in his bedroom.

'Don't you dare call Daisy ill-bred!' Carrie erupted, facing Miss Deborah Harvey, her hands on her hips, her eyes flashing fire. 'You're the one who's out of order, accusing Leon of being responsible for Matthew having run away, and talking to Daisy as if she's a skivvy!'

'If, before, I had had the slightest doubt as to the regrettable quality of my great-nephew's home life, I have so no longer!' eighty-year-old Deborah Harvey fumed, so resplendent in funereal purple and a matching, be-feathered toque hat, that Jilly believed Queen Mary was throwing a fit of fury in their kitchen. 'Never have I been in such a disorganized, ill-mannered, uncouth household!'

Leon's footsteps thudded at a run down the stairs. Kate, her agonized eyes meeting his, sprinted into the hallway.

'There's only one of them here!' Leon said breathlessly to her unspoken question as, together, they hared down the hall towards the kitchen. 'The older one. The first thing she said was that she doesn't like Blacks, Irish or Roman Catholics, and that nothing but concern for Matthew's welfare would have persuaded her to step foot across the threshold.'

'She left out Germans and Jews,' Kate said bitterly, reaching the kitchen first and making a head-turning entrance.

'Mummy!' Jilly ran towards her, throwing her arms thankfully around her waist.

'Thank God you're here, Kate!' Carrie said in vast relief.

'This nasty, *nasty* woman says everything is Daddy's fault and that he should never have been allowed to adopt Matthew!' Daisy blazed, determined that her mother should know exactly how out-of-order Matthew's great-aunt had been.

'That's enough, Daisy.' Kate's pleasantly modulated voice didn't rise by so much as a decibel, but the room was instantly brought to order. 'Would you put the kettle on now, love, and make us all a cup of tea? Jilly . . .' gently she unwound Jilly's arms from around her waist, '. . . would you go upstairs and read a story to Johnny for me, pet?'

Daisy and Jilly both reluctantly did as they were asked, and Kate finally addressed her attention to Matthew's great-aunt. 'I'm sorry I wasn't in when you arrived,' she said civilly. 'Would you sit down and have a cup of tea? Then perhaps we can pool our thoughts as to why Matthew might have run away.'

Deborah Harvey breathed in hard through rocking-horse nostrils. 'The reason for my great-nephew having run away is blatant, Mrs Emmerson,' she said icily, tugging a net glove more tightly over the back of an arthritic hand by its frilled cuff. 'My nephew's child should never have been adopted by a . . . a . . .'

For an appalled moment Carrie thought Deborah Harvey was going to say 'nigger'.

'By a man of colour,' Deborah Harvey said with more restraint than she usually showed when referring to Matthew's adoptive father. Steadfastly refusing to even look in Leon's direction, she continued fiercely, 'Such an arrangement is a deliberate flouting of nature and has never been in my great-nephew's best interests.'

Kate sucked in her breath, the skin tight across her cheek-bones.

Leon said, 'Let me deal with this, love,' in a voice so quiet, Carrie's scalp prickled.

Billy cleared his throat, thinking it high time he took his leave. 'I fink I'd best be off . . .' he began, trying to catch Daisy's eye, hoping she would leave the house with him.

Kate cut him short, her eyes glinting fire as, speaking to Leon but staring at Deborah Harvey, she said categorically, 'No, Leon. I think this is something I should handle.'

It was Carrie who saw Leon's body freeze with a completely new kind of tension and who realized that the hideous scene had taken on a whole new dimension. 'Blimey,' she thought to herself, deciding, like Billy, that she, too, should be taking her leave, 'Kate and Leon are going to be falling out next if Kate isn't careful. Why on earth did she override him like that? He's more than capable of handling Miss High and Mighty Harvey, and he's the one that's being got at, after all.' Aloud she said, 'I'm off. 'Bye Kate. 'Bye Leon.' She didn't say goodbye to Deborah Harvey. She knew what Deborah Harvey's opinion of market traders was. Heavy-hearted at all the problems Kate was having to deal with, she let herself out of the house, fairly sure that Billy would soon be following her example.

It was deep dusk now, and St Mark's spire was dark against a sky pin-pointed with faint stars. She hesitated at Kate's gate. Danny would be at the boxing club and Rose would be doing her homework. If she didn't return straight home she certainly wouldn't be missed. Glad that she'd bothered to slip her swagger-coat on for the short walk from her house to Kate's, she turned up its collar against the now cool air and set off in deep depression in the direction of Magnolia Terrace and the heath.

Beryl gave herself a last look in the mirror of her kidney-shaped dressing-table and then ran eagerly down the stairs. She'd had a long, lingering bath, lying with a face-pack on amongst as many bubbles as she could coax from a packet of Hollywood-style foam bath. She'd rinsed her hair with lemon-juice when she washed it, ironed and re-ironed her lace-collared blouse and yellow circular skirt and now, with mascara on her eyelashes and California Poppy perfume dabbed on the insides of her wrists, she was ready for the world. Or, more precisely, for the Embassy Boxing Club.

'Where you goin' love?' her dad asked as, with no sight or sound of Mavis, he sat listening to the radio, the plate of doorstep, corned-beef sandwiches he'd made for himself balanced on the arm of his armchair, a steaming pint pot of tea by his feet.

'The boxing club.' Beryl hesitated. She loved her dad dearly and under normal circumstances, seeing as how her mum wasn't home and he was in on his own, she would have asked if he fancied going to the club with her. Tonight wasn't normal circumstances, though. Tonight she wanted Zac Hemingway to notice her, really notice her, and she'd be too self-conscious to help him do so if her dad were with her.

'The club?' Ted Lomax's eyebrows rose high. 'What on earth is the attraction there, pet?'

Beryl had never fibbed to him in her life, and didn't do so now. 'There's someone there I like, Dad,' she said, blushing.

Ted Lomax's interest in where she was going, and why, which until then had merely been cursory, instantly deepened. He pushed his plate of sandwiches a little to one side, turning in his chair so that he was facing her properly. 'A boy? One of the older scouts?'

Beryl's blush deepened. 'No, Dad. He's a boxer, a proper boxer. He's ever so nice, honest. You can ask Aunt Carrie if you like. She likes him, and so does Gran.'

Ted wasn't sure that his mother-in-law's opinion counted for much. If Miriam was asked who'd written Shakespeare's plays, she'd have been stuck for an answer. Carrie, though, was another matter. Carrie had a sensible head on her shoulders. Even so, when it came to Beryl's welfare he didn't intend trusting anyone's judgement but his own. He eyed his plate of sand-wiches and pot of tea regretfully. He'd been looking forward to enjoying them while listening in to a football match. However, if he was going to go down to the club to check out the young man Beryl was interested in, he might as well walk down there with her.

'Just a mo, pet,' he said, rising to his feet, 'and I'll get my jacket.'

'There's no need for you to come with me, Dad!' Beryl's cheeks were scarlet with mortification. What if her dad be-gan grilling Zac Hemingway as if it were an understood thing that Zac was interested in her? She'd die! She would just die! And anyway, if her dad's idea of a suitable boyfriend for her was a boy scout, he'd have ten pink fits when he laid eyes on Zac!

'Don't be silly, love,' Ted said with what he thought was sweet reason. 'If you've got your eye on a chap, I want to make sure he isn't a wrong 'un, don't I? I can't have my best girl bein' messed about.'

'But he doesn't know I've got my eye on him!' Beryl protested, certain other people's fathers didn't behave so ultra-protectively. She certainly couldn't imagine her Uncle Danny taking such a line with Rose, and she knew that though Daisy Emmerson was the apple of her dad's eye, Leon Emmerson would never, but never, embarrass her.

Ted, not for the first time, was in a quandary. If she didn't want him to go with her, then he didn't want to force his company on her; on the other hand, if there was a bloke in the offing, it was his fatherly duty to make sure he was the right kind of a bloke. 'I'll only pop in the gym for five minutes, pet,' he said, trying to find a compromise, 'then I'll go downstairs for a drink. Your grandad will be in The Swan, I expect. I haven't seen him for a chat all week.'

The elation and sense of anticipation that had been singing along her veins a few minutes earlier was now almost completely gone. And then, faintly, but growing louder with every second, Beryl heard the familiar rat-a-tat-tat of her mother's high-heeled shoes ringing out on the pavement.

'Mum's coming!' she said with a relief as vast as if Mavis were a troop of cavalry. 'Mum's met Zac! She'll tell you he's all right!' and not waiting to find out his response she dashed out of the house, narrowly avoiding running full tilt into her mother as she did so.

'Steady on, love!' Mavis said in high good humour. 'Anyone would think there was a fire!'

Beryl ignored this remark. 'Dad's in,' she said breathlessly.

'I think he's a bit lonesome.' And with this telling bit of information she ran off in the direction of Magnolia Hill, her yellow skirt swirling like a banner in the thickening dusk.

Mavis bit the corner of her lip. She could have done without Ted being in and waiting for her. She'd had a glorious afternoon and now came the hard part. She'd have to tell Ted about it. 'Hello love, I'm home,' she said unnecessarily as she stepped over the doorstep, wondering just what his reaction was going to be when she told him she was going to be working in Soho – and especially what it was going to be when she told him the identity of her new guv'nor!

''Ello gal,' Albert Jennings said to his favourite granddaughter as she paused to get her breath at the top of the stairs leading into the gym. ''Ow are you today, my pretty?'

'I'm fine, Grandad,' Beryl said truthfully, her eyes on the open doorway behind him. The speed-ball was being hammered, but she couldn't see by whom and there were several regulars working out with weights and skipping ropes. None of them, however, had a shock of barley-gold hair or laughing grey eyes. 'Are you just arriving, or leaving?' she asked, knowing that it didn't matter which, for her grandad wouldn't make her feel self-conscious in front of Zac Hemingway. He wouldn't know how.

'I'm leavin' now all the excitement's over,' Albert said, fumbling in a pocket of his baggy trousers for a packet of tiger nuts. 'Though I'm only leavin' as far as the public bar.' He proffered the bag of nuts. It was an offer Beryl, mindful of her new lipstick, declined. 'I'll be safe in there ternight,' he confided with a conspiratorial wink. 'Yer gran worked the stall today an' she doesn't 'ave enough energy left to follow me over 'ere.'

Normally Beryl would have been amused by her grandad's attempts to make himself out to be henpecked and hard-done-by, but now all she was aware of was that he wouldn't be leaving the gym if Zac were there, nor would he be leaving if there was still hope Zac was going to put in an appearance. 'What excitement, Grandad?' she asked, her heart beginning to pound in sick dread. 'Jack's new boxer hasn't been and gone, has he? I haven't missed seeing him work out, have I?'

'Blimey, pet!' Albert rocked back on his heels slightly, genuinely startled. 'Since when 'ave you bin interested in boxin'?'

Beryl flushed. 'I'm not really.' It was true. It wasn't boxing she was interested in. It was just one particular boxer.

Albert chuckled and fumbled in his pocket for another handful of tiger nuts. 'Then it's just as well you missed all the excitement, because I don't fink you'd 'ave liked it. Poor old Jumbo is flat out and yer Uncle Danny is raisin' the roof. 'E says 'e only wanted Zac to spar with Jumbo, not knock 'im sideways into the middle of next week!'

'Then Zac's gone?' Disappointment roared through her, so intense she was almost on the verge of tears.

'Wasn't much fer 'im to stay for,' Albert said cheerily. 'Not with Big Jumbo well an' truly out of it an' Jack nowhere to be found.' He popped a tiger nut in his mouth. 'Leon wasn't 'ere, either. 'E's got problems at 'ome I expect, young Matthew still not 'avin bin found. An' Charlie and Daniel weren't 'ere. Daniel'll be listenin' to the football on the wireless. Gawd knows what's kept Charlie 'ome, but whatever it is, 'e chose the wrong night fer it! 'Emingway stopped Jumbo dead in 'is tracks in a way I've never seen before in my life. A couple of rounds of Fancy Dan classy punching and nifty footwork and then, wham! A left 'ook from out of nowhere that 'ad killer instinct written all over it. It 'it Jumbo square on the chin and that was it . . . Jumbo was down on the canvas, out cold fer the first time ever, and your Uncle Danny was throwin' a pink fit.'

Miserably Beryl thrust her hands deep in her cardigan

pockets. With hardly anyone else in the gym, save for her uncle and her grandad, she'd missed a perfect opportunity of bringing herself to Zac Hemingway's attention. 'Do you think he'll come back, Grandad?' she asked, a small flame of hope spurting into life. 'It's not very late yet, is it? He might come back in the hope Jack will have turned up. Or he might come back to make sure Big Jumbo is all right, because I'm sure he didn't mean to hurt him.'

Albert regarded his soft-hearted granddaughter fondly. What she was doing in a boxing gymnasium, he couldn't for the life of him think. She certainly didn't have the first clue as to what boxing was about. 'Why don't yer come downstairs with me, pet, an' 'ave a ginger ale?' he suggested companionably. 'Yer'll know if Zac 'Emingway does come back, because the Snug door opens out on to the stairs an' it's always ajar.' He tucked her arm into his. 'An' yer can tell your old grandad when yer goin' to start to do a bit o' courtin'. Me an' yer gran 'ad bin married a year when we were your age. No sense in messing abaht, I said to 'er. If you don't snap me up sharpish, someone else will!'

Beryl hesitated for a second. From inside the gym she could hear her Uncle Danny shouting to a schoolboy bantam-weight. 'When the right lands, yer weight should be shifted to yer left foot!'

She sighed. There was no sense in staying in the gym if Zac wasn't there. 'All right, Grandad,' she said, kissing him affectionately on his leathery cheek. 'Let's have a drink together and you can tell me about all the ladies who took such a shine to you before Gran got you safely up the aisle.'

Carrie walked aimlessly over the tussocky grass of the heath. The moon was high and though there were no street lights other than the distantly flickering gas lights of Blackheath Village, she had no difficulty in avoiding the many clumps of gorse that grew on the eastern side of the heath, or the occasional gravel-pits roughly filled with war debris. She lifted her face to the night breeze. In the eighteenth and early nineteenth centuries, the heath had been the haunt of highwaymen who had used the gravel-pits to hide out in, making sorties from them to rob stage-coaches making their laborious way up Shooters Hill, then the main route out of London towards Dover and the coast. One cottage, half-hidden in one of the heath's many dells, was reputed to have been the home of the infamous Dick Turpin. Carrie wondered wryly if there had been a Mrs Turpin and, if there had, if her life, too, had been an unexciting round of washing, cleaning, cooking – and being taken for granted.

She sighed, changing direction slightly to avoid the dark shape of someone taking a dog for a walk. She knew why she was feeling so down-in-the-mouth, for she and Kate had always reacted to each other's worries as if they were their own, and at this precise moment in time there was certainly plenty to worry about. Even when Matthew was found, as God willing, he soon would be, she knew her friend's problems wouldn't be over. She would always have to cope with barbed, ignorant, racially prejudiced remarks – and with the ongoing difficulty of having a child who enjoyed an education and, for most of the year, lifestyle, far more privileged than that enjoyed by his brothers and sisters. He would also, when he was twenty-one, inherit the fortune bequeathed to him by his Harvey great-grandfather. It was a potentially very divisive situation within their family, one that could very easily lead to jealousies on the other childrens' parts, and Carrie knew that such a prospect caused both Kate and Leon much concern.

The yellow gas lights were no longer so distant now. The dark outline of St Michael's and All Saints Church, sited on the edge of the heath at the village's top corner, was clearly visible, as were the black silhouettes of the trees clustering around the nearest of the heath's many ponds. She paused. There wasn't much point in continuing on into the village, for she couldn't very well go into one of its many pubs when she was on her own. She pushed her hands deeper into the pockets of her coat and headed, instead, for the inky-blackness of the trees.

The Hare and Billet public house faced out onto the heath and from where he was standing, a few yards from its brightly lit, open doorway, Zac watched Carrie's approach with a perplexed frown. When, instead of walking off the heath and into the village, she changed direction, heading instead towards the black belt of trees and the pond, his perplexity turned to concern. What the devil was she playing at? The open heath at night was no place for a woman on her own. At first, when he recognized her in the darkness by her distinctive build and walk, he assumed she was taking a dog for a late evening stroll, and then, when he realized there was no dog, that she was on her way to visit, or to meet, someone in the village. Now he didn't know what to think.

''Night, me old shiner!' a Hare and Billet regular said, stepping out of the pub and walking a little unsteadily past him. 'Next time you fight, let me know an' I'll be there, cheerin' you on!'

Zac made a suitable response and bade his well-wisher goodnight. It hadn't taken him long to establish friendly relations in the pubs of his choice. Everyone in The Swan, of course, knew him already, but he had no intention of drinking only in The Swan. It was too local. The Hare and Billet was just far enough away from Magnolia Square to be a pleasant walk and to provide drinking companions who weren't also neighbours.

As his recently made acquaintance weaved his way unsteadily

homeward, Zac continued to stare broodingly across the narrow road towards the heath and the pond. He could no longer see Carrie, which meant she must have come to a halt within cover of the trees. There was a burst of laughter behind him as more people erupted out of the pub and into the now chill night air. Zac ignored them. When he'd stepped out of the pub a few minutes ago he'd intended making his way to the gym for a word with Jack Robson. Now, instead, he turned up his jacket collar and strode across the road and on to the rough grass of the heath.

Carrie stared down into the dark, glimmering water overcome by an overwhelming sense of futility. Was there never going to be any more to life than the present tedium of household chores and long days spent manning her dad's market stall in Lewisham High Street? And why, suddenly, did it seem so tedious? It never had before. Was it because she was now thirty-five, and the doors leading to choices in life, doors she could once have opened with ease if she had so desired, were fast being bolted and barred against her?

Certainly the door of choice leading to a large family was one that was no longer open to her. Once she had thought she would have as many children as Kate; perhaps, as Danny loved kids just as much as she did, even more. Now she knew there would only be Rose, and Rose was fast growing into a young woman and no longer needed the same, all-consuming kind of mothering and cherishing that she had when she was small.

There was a cracking of twigs behind her and she turned, unalarmed, expecting to see a late-night walker exercising his dog, or a Hare and Billet customer about to embark on a short cut home across the heath. Instead she saw a by now familiar figure, tall and broad-shouldered, his blond hair glistening in the moonlight as pale as barley in September.

He didn't speak. He couldn't. He was too overcome with relief. She hadn't entered the darkness of the trees to meet someone clandestinely. He could have told immediately, by the expression on her face and in her eyes, if, when she had turned at his approach, it had been in the expectation of greeting a lover. Carrie didn't speak either. Her heart was beating too lightly and rapidly somewhere up in her throat for her to be able to do so. His face in the moonlight was all deeply shadowed angles. She was vividly aware of the razor-sharp slanting of his cheekbones and the faint hollow beneath them; the hard, exciting cut of his mouth; the tough chin, its slight cleft emphasizing the forcefulness of his face.

As she stood in silence a yard or so away from him, the dark opaque water at her back, a blackly swaying canopy of leaves above her head, she was aware that something very strange was happening to her; something that had never happened to her before. It was as if, at any moment, she was about to step off a precipice into infinite space.

A mere twenty yards or so away light still spilled from the Hare and Billet's windows and open door, and the noise of laughter and shouted goodnights could clearly be heard. Was heard and ignored.

'Carrie?' His voice was thick and low, with an urgent undertone that sent the blood fizzing in tumult along her veins.

She was on the very edge of the precipice now, so confounded by desire for him she could hardly stand.

'Carrie?' He moved towards her and she knew that now, *now*, she must move swiftly away from him; must ask cheerily what he was doing in the village when he had said he would be at the gym; must claw her way back to normality; back into the safe world she had been inhabiting until a few seconds ago.

She couldn't do it. He was no more than twenty-seven or twenty-eight and she was thirty-five. She had never in her life been unfaithful to Danny, not even in thought, not even during the long war years when he was a prisoner of the Italians. And still she couldn't move or speak. He was only inches away from her now and when he reached out for her, she forgot all about the age difference between them; forgot all about Danny; forgot all about the sane, sensible person she once had been. With a small, primeval cry she swayed against him and, as his mouth came down on hers in swift, unfumbled contact, her hands slid up around his neck and into his hair, her lips parting willingly beneath his, her capitulation total.

Chapter Nine

'Rubbish! Balderdash! Absolute stuff and nonsense!' Deborah Harvey said with the kind of rough-shod certainty that had once helped Britain gain an empire. She was seated, ramrod-straight, on one of the Emmerson's kitchen chairs. Daisy had left the house with Billy, the other children were all in bed, the only people facing her, ranged at either side of the kitchen table, were Kate and Leon.

'It isn't rubbish,' Kate said, striving to keep her voice as non-confrontational as possible. 'Matthew has always loved the river; whenever he's home from school he always spends every minute he can on it.'

'That's true.' Leon wasn't really talking to Deborah Harvey. What was the point? She wouldn't have taken the slightest notice of anything he said. He was looking across the table at Kate, hope fierce in his eyes and his voice for the first time in forty-eight hours.

If Matthew ran away because he suddenly realized the kind of future that was being envisaged for him, a university education followed by a career in the law, or some other profession he wanted no truck with, then it meant they knew what they were dealing with. Matthew hadn't been abducted. He hadn't come to harm. He had simply been overwhelmed by the realization that what was expected of him by his Harvey aunts, his school and, for all he knew, his parents, was worlds away from what *he* wanted. And he had done what many boys his age did when confronted with situations they didn't know how to face or handle: he had run away.

Deborah Harvey's arthritic, net-gloved hands tightened on the silver knob of her old-fashioned walking cane. The news that Matthew had been in the habit of spending all his time, when home from St Osyth's, sailing the Thames like a tinker, didn't surprise her in the slightest. It did, however, appal her. Illegitimate or not, Matthew was a Harvey, and his mother had no business allowing him to run wild like a slum child. As for her suggesting Matthew had run away from St Osyth's because he had suddenly realized the kind of profession he was being educated for there, when what he wanted to be was a Thames waterman, words failed her.

Leon Emmerson might have Thames water in his veins, and so might the dark-skinned children he had fathered, but her great-nephew didn't – and if Kate Emmerson thought otherwise, then she was a fool. She didn't look a fool, though. Grudgingly Deborah had to admit that if she'd known nothing more about Matthew's mother other than of her being Toby's fiancée at the time of his death, she would most likely have thought highly of her. For one thing, unlike so many modern young women, she wasn't noisy or brazen or flashy. There was an inner radiance and a tranquillity about her that was both soothing and deeply attractive – and she was well-spoken and intelligent. Even the fact that she had allowed herself to become pregnant out of wedlock could have been forgiven her, considering that it had been war-time and that, if she hadn't done so, the Harvey line would now be at a complete end. What couldn't be forgiven, though, was her marriage to a half-caste ex-sailor. And then, as if that hadn't been madness enough, she had announced that he was going to adopt Matthew and the courts had allowed him to!

It was an outrage neither she nor her niece had ever come to terms with, or ever would come to terms with, and the result was now obvious for all to see. Matthew had run away and she, Deborah, didn't blame him. She didn't blame him in the slightest.

'I'll begin looking for him down by the river at first light,' Leon Emmerson was now saying with passionate intensity. 'That's where he'll be. I'm sure of it.'

Struggling hard not to betray the tiredness she now felt, Deborah rose to her feet. It was after midnight. She hadn't been out of bed so late for over twenty years. 'You may be right,' she said tightly, speaking to Leon but not looking towards him. 'But if my great-nephew *is* down by the river, I am quite certain his reason for being there is not the one that has been suggested.' She turned to make an abrupt exit, bumped into the chair she had just vacated and staggered. Leon stepped forward swiftly, steadying her by her arm. Deborah froze. Leon dropped his hand, his face tightening. Did she think his colour would rub off? Would she have preferred to fall rather than him make physical contact with her?

'I'll walk you to the front door, Miss Harvey,' Kate said swiftly, smoothing the moment over. 'If we find Matthew tomorrow I'll telephone you immediately.'

'There'll be no need.' Deborah's voice was tighter than ever. The moment when Leon Emmerson took hold of her elbow was over, but it had profoundly shaken her. 'I shall have my chauffeur take me to wherever it is thought Matthew might be.'

'Wherever he's sleeping at night, and I reckon it'll be in an unused barge, he'll be spending the days on the towpaths or the piers,' Leon said, civil despite the provocation to be otherwise. 'First thing in the morning I intend rounding up as many of my neighbours as possible and we'll make a start on the

Surrey Canal towpath. He used to love tiddlering there when he was small.'

Deborah didn't know what tiddlering was and, assuming it to be a working-class pastime, didn't ask. She had all the information she required and now she needed her bed. 'Good night,' she said briefly to Kate at the door. 'There's no need to accompany me further. My chauffeur will assist me.'

Kate didn't protest. With her stomach muscles in knots of tension, she merely stood in the lighted doorway as the uniformed figure hurried up the path to respectfully lend an arm to his employer, all her thoughts on the coming morning. Would they find Matthew? Would he, please God, be down by the river, as near to home as he could get without having to face the music of his running away?

'Course I'll help,' Jack said at first light next morning as, still in his pyjama bottoms, he stood on his front doorstep having answered Leon's knock. 'Just give me a sec to get some kit on and I'll be right with you.'

'Blimey, Leon. You're up early, ain't yer?' old Charlie said a few minutes later as, bleary-eyed, he stood at his open front door. 'I ain't bin knocked up so early since the rozzers copped me for the Catford bank job just before the war.'

'Goodness gracious me, Leon. Whatever is to do?' retired Mr Nibbs asked, splendid in a burgundy wool dressing-gown. 'Help you look for young Matthew? Well, of course, dear chap. I'll just make myself a Thermos. It could be a long morning, couldn't it?'

'Crikey, mate! Yer startin' off a bit early, ain't yer?' Danny grumbled good-naturedly as he leaned with his head out of his bedroom window. 'The pigeons 'aven't piddled yet!'

As he ducked his head back into the room, Carrie pushed herself up against the pillows, saying anxiously, 'What is it? What's happened?'

Danny scratched an armpit and looked around for his clothes. 'Leon thinks young Matthew may be 'iding out down by the river. He wants a bit of help in lookin' for 'im. 'Ave yer seen what I've done with me trousers, pet? They've vanished into thin bloody air!'

'Perhaps you left them in the bathroom.' Carrie could hardly believe they were carrying on such a normal conversation. Couldn't he tell, just by looking at her, that something cataclysmic had happened to her? Couldn't he sense it? Guilt washed over in huge drowning waves. Had she really spent an idyllic age in Zac Hemingway's arms last night? Had he really told her she was beautiful? The most beautiful woman he had seen in years?

As Danny ambled out of the bedroom towards the bathroom, she waited for shame to suffuse her. It didn't. Instead, hard on the heels of her guilt, came deep, indescribable joy. She felt alive. More alive than she'd felt in years and years and years. Realization rocked through her. She felt alive because, from the moment she had entered Zac Hemingway's arms, perhaps even before she had entered his arms, she had fallen instantaneously and irrevocably and dizzyingly head over heels in love with him.

'A mug o' tea would go dahn a treat, gel,' Danny said, re-entering the bedroom and zipping his flies up as he did so. 'I ain't used ter turnin' out this early on a mornin'. Gawd knows 'ow dockers do it. I don't.'

Carrie stared at him. Unshaven and, as yet, unwashed, he was very far from being the answer to a maiden's prayer, but he was the man she had loved and lived with all her adult life. He *was* her life. Her real life. What happened the previous evening wasn't real. It had been too wonderful, too magical, too unbelievable to be real. And it couldn't be allowed to happen again. For if it happened again—

'I said "a mug o' tea would go dahn a treat",' Danny said, aggrieved. 'Cor blimey, girl, what are yer waitin' for? Christmas?'

'But I *want* to come with you.' Christina swung her long legs from the brass-headed double bed to the carpeted floor. 'I've nothing else to do, have I?'

'Christ Almighty, sweetheart, you make it sound like a complaint.' Knowing they would be searching boats and tow-paths and piers and docks, Jack reached for a pair of Levi's instead of one of his many pairs of hand-tailored suit trousers, adding with barely suppressed irritation, 'My ma and my grans would have given their eye-teeth to have had nothing to do all day!'

Christina raised her arms, lifting her lace-edged night-dress up and over her head. They were on the verge of having another of their ever more frequent rows. What was the use of pointing out that she wasn't his mother, or one of his grandmothers? That she was, instead, a woman who had lost dearly loved members of her family in the Holocaust and who wanted to create another family? And if she couldn't do so by having babies of her own, then surely they could adopt some?

She stepped into a pair of silk cami-knickers and reached for a matching underslip, saying in a sudden rush, knowing it was the wrong time to be bringing up the subject, but unable to help herself, 'I want us to visit an adoption agency, Jack! I know you don't like the idea *Liebling*, but if we don't adopt we're never going to have children and I'm not getting any younger! I'm thirty-five. When my grandmother was thirty-five she'd had half a dozen children . . .' That she had slipped into German, even though it was only for an endearment, was a measure of her inner turmoil.

The word grated on Jack as if it had been a swear word. Why, with her history, would she still even think in German? It didn't make sense to him, but then lots of things about his dearly loved wife didn't make sense to him. This baby lark, for instance. No one wanted kids more than he did. But he wanted *his* kids, not someone else's! He was a man who had never settled for second-best, and he certainly didn't intend doing so when it came to something as all-important as kids.

'No, sweetheart,' he said as gently as possible. 'You know how I feel. How the hell would we know what we were getting? The kiddie in question could have inherited all sorts of nasty characteristics – and not just characteristics. What if it turned out to be epileptic, or asthmatic, or what if there was a history of insanity in its family?'

'But everyone has to take chances when they have a baby!' Her smoke-dark hair, usually so smooth and glossy, tumbled unbrushed to her shoulders in disarray. She was still half naked, her skin a pale, pale olive, her waist fragilely narrow, her breasts full and firm, the nipples wine-dark.

He felt a rising in his crotch. Dear God in heaven, how was he supposed to argue with her when all he wanted to do was to make love to her? He dropped the T-shirt he had been about to wear onto the bed. 'Tina . . .' His voice was husky with desire. There was time, before he joined in the search for Matthew, for them to make love.

She read the intention in his eyes and was having none of it. She grabbed for her bra, putting it on with trembling hands, saying in a cracked, passionate voice, 'Do you know how like the Nazis you sound, Jack? *They* couldn't abide the thought of non-perfect babies either!'

'Christ Almighty! That's the most ridiculous . . . most outrageous—'

'Is it?' Her amethyst eyes flashed fire as she snatched a blouse from the wardrobe clothes-rail. 'I don't see the difference, Jack. I really don't!'

It was the worst, ugliest row they had ever had. He wanted to put a stop to it; he wanted to go back in time so that when she mentioned going to an adoption agency he gave her a less unequivocal response. It was impossible to do so, and it was also impossible to apologize. Why should he, for Christ's sake? He hadn't done the Nazi name-calling. If there was any apologizing to be done, *she* was the one who should be doing it.

'We're on our way, Jack!' Leon Emmerson's voice shouted up from the square. 'We'll meet you down on the Surrey Canal towpath!'

Jack strode swiftly to the open window, sticking his head out, shouting down in response, 'There's no need, Leon. I'm going to be right with you mate!' He rattled the window down on its sash cords, turning round, saying in a voice almost as raw with emotion as hers had been, 'We'll finish this conversation some other time. What matters right now is finding young Matthew. If you want to do something useful today, why don't you keep Kate company? She must be at her wits' end.'

It was as near to putting things right as he could get. It did at least give him the excuse to walk out of the house in the hope that when he returned to it, she would be her normal self again.

Pulling his T-shirt on over his head, he clattered down the stairs. By rights he had plenty of other things to do today other than search for a missing child. He was due to meet with Jack Solomons to fix a fight with him for Zac, and he was due to meet with an illegit promoter as well, in order to fix a pirate fight. Kate Emmerson was, however, one of his closest friends, and finding young Matthew for her had priority.

He slammed out of the house, breaking into a run in order to catch up with Leon and the other friends and neighbours Leon had rounded up to help in the search. A Nazi! Had Christina really, near as dammit, called him a Nazi? Now that sexual temptation was out of his way, outraged indignation began to give way to anger. He hadn't fought the Germans the length and breadth of war-torn Italy and Greece to be called a Nazi by his wife, by hell he hadn't!

'Don't look so fierce, old chum,' Elisha Deakin said to him as he caught up with him and the others. 'We're going to find the little perisher. You want to be glad you and your missus don't have any nippers. The little buggers are nothing but trouble!'

'Your mum and dad are goin' to go crackers when they find out you've scarpered off school,' Billy said, deeply concerned.

'No they won't.' There was no doubt at all in Daisy's voice. 'They're far too worried about Matthew to care if I skip school for a day, and I have to. I have to help look for Matthew. Mum and Dad are now certain he's down by the river somewhere, and I think they're right. Matthew's always been potty about the river. When he was only four or five he would spend all day on the river with Dad. It's so obvious he has a fever to follow Dad afloat that I can't imagine why we didn't realize it before.'

They were standing on the riverside path in front of Greenwich Naval College.

'And do you say your dad and his mates are starting their search off down Surrey Canal way?'

Daisy nodded, her neat cap of shiny dark hair cut in a demure bob. 'Matthew used to spend a lot of time there when he was smaller. If they don't find him there then I 'spect they'll start on the docks.'

Billy tried to put his hands in the pockets of his trousers but they were cut so tight it was impossible. He let them fall to his sides, wishing he had the nerve to take hold of Daisy's hand, or to put an arm around her shoulders. If it had been evening, he would have. It was easier to do things like that on an evening. It seemed more natural and she very rarely rebuffed him. He reckoned she'd rebuff him if he tried it on now, though, at nine o'clock in the morning. Especially when her mind was on her missing young brother.

'Your dad doesn't sail the *Tansy* now, does he?' he asked, looking down at his suede shoes and seeing, with a pang of grief, that the dried mud on the riverside path was doing them no favours whatsoever.

Daisy shook her head and he couldn't help noticing that her shoes were as immaculate as when she had left home. He didn't know how she did it. Even as a small girl in the middle of the Blitz, she'd never had a hair out of place. 'I don't think she's river-worthy any longer,' she said, staring out over the river, frowning as she tried to decide where they should begin their search. 'She's moored somewhere up in Barking Creek, serving as shelter for ducks.'

Billy felt his heart lurch to a standstill. The *Tansy* was the barge on which Leon Emmerson had served his apprenticeship as a lighterman, in the days before the war. After the war, when he had returned to Civvy Street, the *Tansy* had been waiting for him and he often took Matthew, and Luke, too, out on her for the day, sculling down to Gravesend, or up to the Greenland Dock in Rotherhithe or the more colourfully named Deadman's Dock at Deptford, or Execution Dock at Wapping. In those days, before he'd been sent away at seven years old to

St Osyth's Preparatory Department, the *Tansy* had been Matthew's second home.

'I bet the *Tansy's* givin' shelter to more than ducks!' he said in high elation, forgetting his fear that if he took hold of her hand she might rebuff him, and seizing hold of it anyway. 'I bet it's giving shelter to Matthew as well!'

Daisy stared at him, her cornflower-blue eyes widening to the size of saucers. 'Oh my Lord . . .' she said in whispered realization. 'Of course!' Her fingers interlocked tightly with his. 'Of course that's where he'll be! Why on earth did no one think of it before!'

Billy's heart soared, and for more reasons than one. 'Then let's reccy it out. 'Ow do we get there?'

She began leading him at a run back along the towpath, saying breathlessly, 'First of all we go back to your lorry, then we drive through the Blackwall Tunnel and out on to the East India Dock Road.'

'Where to after that?' he panted as, still hand in hand, they veered off the end of the footpath on to pavement.

She laughed, the first time she had laughed in days. 'We head straight out to Barking. From there we might have to park up and walk out to the creek. I don't suppose there'll be any proper roads.'

As they raced to where he had parked his lorry, it occurred to Billy that it might have been easiest simply to go in search of her dad and tell him where they thought Matthew was. Leon would then have rowed his present barge upriver to Barking for a look-see and he, Billy, wouldn't be about to ruin his precious blue suede shoes by ploughing through creek-side marsh and mud.

'Daisy, do you fink—' he gasped doubtfully as they came to a winded halt.

'I think we should hurry,' Daisy said, eyes glowing, impatient for him to open the high cab door and to give her a leg up. 'Traffic can be dreadfully heavy in the tunnel. It might take us ages to get to the other side of the river!'

Billy slicked his quiff back with his free hand, knowing he was beaten. He'd simply have to buy another pair of shoes, that was all. He grinned as he gave her a hand up into his cab. What were a pair of shoes when he'd have Daisy to himself for most of the morning? With a bit of luck it might take them an age to find the *Tansy*. It might even take them all day!

'We've bin 'ere an hour now and we've searched the canal banks both sides,' Danny said to Zac Hemingway in the cosy fug of Bert's Dining Rooms where he, and most of the other searchers, were taking stock over pints of steaming tea and, in Danny's case, a plate of eggs, sausage and mash, as well. 'Who let on ter yer wot was 'appening?'

'Jack Robson's ma.' Zac pulled out a battered wooden chair from a nearby table and straddled it. 'She said I'd be wasting my time going into the gym for a morning workout. That you and Jack, and nearly everyone else in the square, were down Surrey Canal way, looking for the Emmerson kiddie.'

Danny grinned and dunked a piece of crusty bread into his egg. 'Yer'd better start understandin' who's who, mate, or yer goin' to come a right old cropper,' he said affably. 'Fer starters, the lady with the pleasure o' bein' Mrs Robson senior ain't Jack's ma, an' if 'e 'eard yer refer to 'er as 'is ma, 'e'd 'ave a pink fit!' He reached for a bottle of brown sauce and shook it liberally over his sausages. 'Jack's ma died when 'e and 'is twin brother were nippers. 'Arriet is Charlie's second wife – an' before she took leave of 'er senses, givin' up dignified spinster'ood to marry Charlie, she used to be Jack's 'eadmistress!'

Despite being faced with the rather off-putting sight of Danny shovelling away sausage and mash on an upturned fork, Zac grinned. He didn't know much about the stresses and strains of family life, never having had a family, but he could well imagine that to have your dad marry your headmistress might be a bit much to take.

'I didn't know Jack had a twin,' he said, interested. 'Does he live local?'

Danny laid his fork down, his freckled face suddenly sombre. ''E's dead,' he said briefly. ''E went off to fight with the International Brigade in the Spanish Civil War.' He fell silent, remembering. He and Jerry Robson had been good mates. They'd gone all through school together and, when they left, he signed on in the army and Jerry went to Spain. A month later he was killed; one of hundreds of disarmed militiamen rounded up by the Nationalists and executed in a bullring in a town called Badajoz.

At a nearby table, Leon and Nibbo, and Jack and his dad, were deep in earnest conversation. 'If he's down the Greenland Dock it'll be like looking for a needle in a haystack,' Jack was saying pragmatically. 'You can't see water there for barges and launches and tugs and ships.'

'Jack very rarely talks about Jerry.' Danny pushed his plate away, his appetite gone. 'But he finks about 'im a lot. An' so do I.'

'There aren't any schoolchildren down here, though,' Nibbo was saying, a battered Panama hat pushed to the back of his head. 'Surely a boy of Matthew's age would be easily spotted amongst all those dockers and stevedores and crane-drivers and truckers?'

'There's only one way to tell.' Leon pushed his chair away from the table and rose to his feet. 'Come on. We'll do the Greenland first and then the King George and King Albert.'

Danny was still staring into the middle distance, lost in thought. Zac rose to his feet and pressed his hand lightly on

Danny's shoulder. 'Come on,' he said gruffly. 'Pay for your grub. We're off down the Greenland Dock.' As he fell in behind Jack and the massive, shambolic figure of Jack's dad, he was aware of a spurt of intense irritation. He'd started off not being too keen on Danny. Now he was beginning to like him. And liking Danny when he was so rapidly falling in love with Danny's wife was something he hadn't bargained for.

Chapter Ten

'Course I'm not mistaken,' Lettie Deakin said indignantly to Mavis as they stood on Lewisham clock-tower's traffic island, Lettie en route to Chieseman's department store, which stood on the north-west side of the High Street, Mavis heading in the opposite direction, towards Woolworths and the market. 'We were slack at the pub last night and I slipped out to get a bit of fresh air. It was late, near closing time, and I took the dog up to the heath for a bit of a run.'

'If it was dark, and if they were in a clinch, how the hell could you recognize them?' Mavis asked scathingly, finding Lettie's latest scandalmongering so ridiculous she wasn't even angry at it. Carrie enjoying an illicit late-night rendezvous on the heath with Zac Hemingway, indeed! Lettie might just as well have said that Bob Giles was having an affair with Princess Margaret, or that the Pope was a Protestant.

Lettie, well aware of Mavis's contemptuous disbelief, put her shopping basket down at her feet and folded her arms across her ample chest. 'Now just you look 'ere Mavis Lomax,' she said confrontationally, 'I ain't blind and I ain't 'alf-witted. I saw what I saw, and what I saw was your married sister and Zac Hemingway, kissing as if there was going to be no blinkin' tomorrer!'

Mavis's eyes narrowed into slits. Silly beyond belief though Lettie's story was, if she persisted in spreading it, some silly

142

bugger would believe it – and the silly bugger in question just might be Danny. 'You're a liar, Lettie Deakin,' she said through gritted teeth. 'And if I hear you repeating your cock-and-bull story to anyone else, I'll have your teeth down the back of your throat, so help me I will!'

Lettie was a Northerner and not intimidated easily. 'You and who else's army?' she demanded, outraged at being called a liar when she was telling the God's own truth.

''Morning, ladies!' With a beaming smile Daniel Collins hopped nippily onto the traffic island out of the way of a number 21 bus. 'Lovely day for a friendly gossip, isn't it?'

Lettie's eyes held Mavis's, bright with malicious satisfaction. Daniel was Carrie's father-in-law. 'Lovely,' she agreed, picking up her basket. 'Are you on your way back to the square, Daniel? Because if you are, I'll keep you company as far as The Swan.'

'Where the flaming hell's our Carrie?' Mavis demanded of her mother three minutes later, marching up to the family market stall at top speed.

Miriam, standing in for Carrie for the second time in a week, was in no mood to be pleasant. 'She's 'elpin' Kate keep sane while Leon an' your dad an' 'alf the square look for that little perisher, Matthew,' she said bad-temperedly, arranging the best of a freshly opened crate of tomatoes on the front of the stall so that the previous batch, fit only for frying, weren't so conspicuous. 'And as far as I'm concerned, she's takin' liberties.'

'Are Carrie and Kate looking for Matthew as well? And if they are, where are they looking for him?' It wasn't often Mavis felt an edge of panic, but she was feeling one now. Lettie was a silly cow and quite capable, under the guise of 'only speaking out for the best', of repeating her barmy story to Daniel. Daniel was too sensible a man to believe it, but he would be deeply disturbed that such a rumour was circulating about his daughter-in-law, and if he shared his concern with his wife, all hell would be let loose. Hettie would be convinced that Carrie must have done something to spark off the rumour, and Carrie's life would be a misery for months.

''Ow the 'ell do I know where they are?' Miriam was fed up to the back teeth. Just because one of the Emmerson kids had hopped the wag from school, people were behaving as if the world was coming to an end. Albert had abandoned their other market stall at Catford and gone charging off with Jack and Charlie and Nibbo, and God only knew who else, looking for him. Carrie had breezily announced that she was going to be spending the day with Kate, even though they'd both seen Christina going into number four with obviously the same intention. And she, Miriam, was manning the perishin' market stall again!

'Nice, firm tomatoes!' she shouted in a voice that could have brought ships ashore in the thickest of fogs. 'Get your lovely toms 'ere!'

Mavis, aware that she had got from her mother all the information she was going to get, said tartly, 'The toms you're hiding underneath ain't nice and firm. If Dad knew you were trying to clear fryers at salad prices, he'd have a pink fit.'

'Well yer dad ain't 'ere, and it aint 'im that's selling 'em,' Miriam retorted with spirit, 'though he bloomin' well should be! Come on ladies! Buy your lovely salad tomatoes 'ere! Pick o' the crop! Hard and sweet!'

'He's a sweetheart, Great-Gran, really he is.' Beryl had nipped back to Magnolia Square in her lunch hour in order to spend it with her bedridden great-grandmother. It was something she often did, for her great-gran loved company and gossip, and could never get enough of it.

'A boxer?' Leah Singer, eyes fiercely bright despite her frail frame, looked doubtful. 'Why for do you want a boxer as a boyfriend? And ain't boxers *shvartzers*? Leon Emmerson is, and he used to be a boxer. And that Sugar Ray Robinson is. Why for don't you find a nice Jewish boy, Dolly?'

'Because I don't think of myself as being Jewish, and I don't know any Jewish boys,' Beryl said reasonably, shifting her position on the edge of the bed so that she wouldn't squash the sleeping lump beneath the covers that was Boots, her great-gran's Pekinese. 'Grandad's family isn't Jewish, and Gran never behaves Jewish, not like you – and so Mum certainly hasn't. And my dad's a Catholic, or had you forgotten?'

Leah raised age-mottled hands upwards in a despairing gesture. Albert, her good-natured *goy* son-in-law, had a lot to answer for. At least when Jack Robson had married a Jewish girl he went to a Rabbi once a week for a year, taking the time and trouble to understand her religion. In the far-off days before the First World War, when Albert married Miriam, he'd made no such similar gesture. The only Jewish things Albert had been interested in were salt beef sandwiches and apple dumplings.

'And Zac isn't black, Great-Gran,' Beryl continued, trying to set her mind at rest. 'Though I don't see why it should matter if he was.' Beneath the bedclothes Boots wriggled peevishly and Beryl obligingly shifted her position yet again. 'He's blond. As blond as Kate Emmerson. And he's ever so nice.'

Leah was unimpressed. Nice he might be. Jewish he wasn't. 'Of course he's nice,' she said querulously, 'he ain't got his feet under your table yet, *nu*.'

At the thought of Zac Hemingway having his feet under her table, Beryl blushed. She'd had crushes before, but this one was different. This one was serious. 'And he doesn't have a girlfriend, Great-Gran,' she said, eager that Leah should be aware of everything in Zac's favour. 'I know, because he's lodging with Queenie Tillet, and she told me he hasn't.'

Leah rolled her eyes expressively upwards. So young and innocent was this great-granddaughter of hers. If this blond *shaygets* hadn't a girlfriend now, living in a lodging-house full of dancers and actresses, he soon would have. 'And your ma?' she asked, not very hopeful of an encouraging answer. 'What does your ma think of this young man of yours?'

Beryl's blush deepened. 'He isn't my young man yet, Great-Gran, and Mum's only seen him at the gym. She hasn't really met him properly. Aunt Carrie has, though, because Uncle Danny is his trainer.'

Until the birth of her great-grandchildren, Carrie, her youngest granddaughter, had always held a special place in Leah's heart because, unlike Mavis, she was at least dark-haired enough to look a little Jewish. And, unlike her elder sister, who seemed incapable of putting anything other than eggs and chips on the family dinner table, she could cook. Carrie's chicken soup was chicken soup to die for.

'Then I'll ask your Aunt Carrie what sort of a young man this young man is. A chancer you don't want. And if he's a boxer . . .' Leah lifted her bed-jacketed shoulders and her hands high, '. . . a boxer sounds like a chancer, Dolly. Trust me. I've been around a long time. I know these things.'

'Kate and Christina and Carrie are out helping search for Matthew,' elderly Harriet Robson said to Mavis in clipped, educated tones. 'I'm looking after Johnny for her. If you'd like a cup of tea . . . ?'

Mavis shook her head. She'd no time for cups of tea, especially with a woman who had once written on all her school reports, '*A bright girl, but slipshod. Could do better.*'

'No thanks, Harriet. I need to find Carrie. You don't know where they're looking for Matthew, do you?'

Harriet tucked an imaginary wisp of hair back into her immaculate bun and stepped further out on to the doorstep, pulling Kate's door behind her a little so that, if Johnny came running into the hallway, he wouldn't overhear what they were saying. 'I'm not sure, Mavis.' She dropped her voice slightly, her face grave. 'Somewhere down by the river. Leon and the men have gone down to the Surrey Canal, and I do know that if they don't find him there, they intend to begin a search of the docks.'

'Blimey!' With a docker for a husband, Mavis was well aware of just how enormous and difficult such a search would be.

'Matthew loves the river.' Harriet was very careful not to slip into the past tense. 'Both Kate and Leon are quite sure that if he *has* run away, and not been abducted, that is where he'll be.'

Mavis's eyes held Harriet's for a long, horrified moment. When Billy was Matthew's age he ran away from school so often that she packed him jam sandwiches for when he got peckish. She was well aware, of course, that Matthew running away from a school he boarded at was a bit more serious, but she hadn't thought of his disappearance as being *seriously* serious. For the first time she realized the kind of fears Kate was living with and understood why Carrie felt she must be with her.

Deep in thought, she made her way back down Kate's lavender-edged pathway. Kate, Christina and Carrie couldn't go roaming around the docks like Leon, a Thames waterman, could, and if Leon and his search-party had already earmarked the Surrey Canal towpath for part of their search, they wouldn't be there either. As the gate clicked shut behind her, she paused. Where else would a young boy go, down by the river? There was the high-tide beach in front of Greenwich Naval College, but that was so close to home it would surely have already been searched. Where else might her friends and her sister have thought of looking? As she gazed across the square she suddenly realized she was staring straight at Hettie and Daniel's front door. It was ajar. Did that mean they had a visitor, and was the visitor Lettie? At the thought of Lettie filling Hettie's head with wicked nonsense about Carrie, Mavis's sense of urgency increased. She needed to find Carrie. Once Carrie knew what was being said about her she would soon put a stop to it and, even more importantly, she would be able to make sure she spoke to Danny before his mother, or any other trouble-maker, did so.

Woolwich. The thought came out of nowhere and brought with it instant certainty. The Woolwich free ferry across the Thames had always been a place truanting boys made for. They could hang over the deck rails all day if they wanted to, watching the spuming water beneath the huge paddles and shouting and waving at the mass of shipping coming up and down river. Luke Emmerson was always being hauled home after spending the day there when he should have been at school. It was one of the first places Kate would look for Matthew and, on a number 54 bus, it was only fifteen minutes or so away.

'Nibbo thought Leon's youngster might be here as well,' Zac said pleasantly, standing on the ferry pier, his thumbs hooked in his jeans pockets. 'And as he didn't fancy being hit on the head by a jib or a hoist, or falling down an open hatchway, he asked me if I'd mind leaving the search on the docks to come out here with him.'

'And?' Mavis asked, looking past him along the pier's narrow gangways to where a ferry, one of three, was ploughing land-wards, a flag emblazoned with London County Council's emblem of a castle and a shield, fluttering gaily at its bow.

'And we've had a look on all three ferries and there's no sign of him,' Zac said, intrigued by the fact that even Mavis cared enough about Matthew Harvey's disappearance to spend time helping in the search for him. This warm, whole-hearted rallying together when a neighbour needed help was something he'd never experienced before. It was as if, beneath the banter and gossip, the people who lived in Magnolia Square really cared about each other.

'Bugger,' Mavis said graphically, the river breeze tugging at her Betty Grable curls. She withdrew her attention from the approaching ferry and the sight of Nibbo's distinctive Panama as he stood amid a crowd of shift-workers waiting to disembark, making direct eye contact with Zac for the first time. Her tummy somersaulted as if she was on a fairground ride. He was a good-looker, all right. She wasn't remotely surprised her Beryl was crackers about him, or that there was already tittle-tattle about his love-life. A man like Zac Hemingway would never be short of female company, that was for sure. That the company in question would be in the bathing-beauty class also went without saying – which only made Lettie's rumour-mongering about Carrie all the more ridiculous.

'You haven't seen Carrie, have you?' she asked, as the ferry's gong clanged and, down-river, a large ship with a Blue Star funnel hove into view.

He didn't answer straight away, merely looked quizzically down at her in a way that made her instantly think he already knew of the rumours and was trying to decide if her question was quite as innocent as it sounded.

'She's with Christina Robson and Kate Emmerson,' she added, wondering how on earth Lettie's rumour-mongering could possibly have reached him and, if it had, who else it had also already reached.

He shook his head, the sunlight glinting his hair to gold. 'No,' he said, his eyes continuing to hold hers, an expression in them she couldn't quite fathom. Knowing there was nowhere else she could now search for Carrie, she gave a resigned shrug of her shoulders. She'd done her best. She couldn't do more.

The black and yellow ferry was now docking, but Nibbo showed no sign of disembarking. Instead he was questioning each new passenger who filed aboard, presumably asking if they had seen a young boy answering Matthew's description.

'Just so you know,' she said off-handedly, seeing no reason why he shouldn't be put in the picture, 'Lettie Deakin is under the fanciful impression that you and our Carrie have got a hot love affair going. It might seem too daft to worry about to you, but Carrie's husband ain't the Brain of Britain and neither is his mother. They might just believe it, and then Carrie's life will be a misery.'

A muscle pulsed at the corner of Zac's jaw. The down-side of a neighbourhood community that rallied together in times of trouble was that it was also bloody nosey! How, in the name of all that was wonderful, had Lettie Deakin cottoned on to his feelings for Carrie! He remembered the dog that was always yapping at Lettie's heels and gave an inward groan. She'd obviously seen him with Carrie while taking the wretched animal for its late-night walk. He chewed the corner of his lip, wondering how he felt about the cat being let out of the bag so early on in the game and decided that, apart from his concern for how it would affect Carrie, he didn't care a jot.

Mavis grinned wryly, anticipating his disbelieving, ridiculing reaction. It didn't come. Instead he frowned slightly, the expression in his eyes decidedly thoughtful. Mavis's grin died. She was an awful lot of things, but she wasn't a fool. For the first time in her life she understood the expression about time standing still. Through the high, protective ironwork of the pier she could see a tug steaming upriver, probably heading for one of the many wharves east of Greenwich. In mid-river, the

Blue Star ship, taking advantage of a high tide, continued to approach. The ferry that had already set off on the crossing from North Woolwich drifted, its paddles still, as it made way for it. The clouds were very high in the sky. The shipping very low in the water.

Her eyes held his. 'It's true!' she said in such stark disbelief, she barely recognized her own voice. 'Sweet Jesus! You and our Carrie really were on the heath and up to no good last night, weren't you?'

If the accusation had come from anyone else Zac would have lied, if only for Carrie's sake. Mavis was Carrie's sister, however, and for some reason he couldn't quite fathom, he didn't want to lie to her. It was as if, by openly acknowledging to her that there was something going on between himself and Carrie, it would make it impossible for Carrie to have second thoughts and to refuse to see him again. 'If we were,' he said with easy nonchalance, 'it's our business and no one else's.'

Mavis stared at him goggle-eyed, too stupefied for speech. This huge blond hunk and Carrie? Carrie who, to the best of her knowledge, had never stepped out of line ever! Carrie, who had never even gone out with another boy before going out with Danny, and who certainly hadn't gone out with anyone else afterwards! It was almost too incredible for belief. Almost, but not quite. They had, after all, been seen. And Zac Hemingway was now brazenly admitting it.

Mavis sucked in her breath. 'You bloody bastard!' she hissed, her fists clenched, her eyes blazing. 'How dare you play fast and loose with my kid sister?'

A middle-aged couple, a young child in tow, were hurrying past them, down to the ferry's boarding point. 'Disgraceful behaviour!' the woman said in loud indignation. 'It shouldn't be allowed, not when there's children about! Someone should do something!'

Mavis had never been deterred by an audience, and wasn't deterred now. 'As for whose business it is!' she stormed, 'I'll bloody show you whose business it is!' Her clenched right fist shot towards his jaw with such venom, speed and accuracy that, if it hadn't been his main object in life to be ready for such attacks, he would have been spread-eagled, sagging-kneed, against the ironwork of the pier's gangway. As it was, he side-stepped with swift expertise, his hands seizing hold of her wrists.

'Now just steady on for a minute,' he said reasonably, an edge of amusement in his voice. 'For one thing, Carrie may be your younger sister but she's hardly a kid any more. She's a mature woman well able to make up her own mind as to her own behaviour. And for another . . .' his hold on her wrists tightened as Mavis swore, struggling to be free, '. . . for another, you don't seem to be taking into account the fact that I may not be playing fast and loose with Carrie, but that I'm deadly serious.'

Mavis stopped struggling and stared at him. 'Serious? *Serious?* Who the bleeding hell do you think you're kidding? Carrie may not be old enough to be your mother, but she's old enough to be your auntie! And she's married and has a family! And I don't believe for one minute that she's your usual type! You're just having a joke at her expense, that's what you're doing Mr oh-so-smooth-and-slimy Hemingway!' and, for good measure, she kicked him on his shin with all the force she was capable of.

Zac's amusement vanished. He'd been entertained by her outrage at behaviour he was certain she indulged in herself, but he wasn't even mildly entertained by her accusation that he was having a joke at Carrie's expense. Just what made Carrie's family so blind to her blazingly vibrant physical attractiveness? Her husband treated her as if she was part of the household furnishing, not a woman with as much sex appeal as an undiscovered Jane Russell, and now here was her sister unwittingly betraying the same kind of opinion.

Not even registering the vicious kick to his shin, he let go of her wrists, seizing hold of her shoulders, shaking her in real anger. 'For Christ's sake, what is it with your family and Carrie? Anyone would think she was a middle-aged frump the way you all talk about her! Can't you see her as she really is? Can't you see how very special she is?'

Mavis's anger fled – to be replaced with something far more terrible. Fear. This head-turningly handsome man had genuinely fallen for Carrie and, as amoral in these matters as she herself tended to be, had not let the fact that Carrie was married stand in his way. In the ordinary way of things, Carrie would be the last person in the world to have her head turned by a man, but Zac Hemingway wasn't ordinary. He wasn't ordinary at all.

'Leave Carrie alone!' There was passionate urgency in her voice. This was serious. Really serious. 'Don't steam into her life, disrupting and disturbing it!'

Aware of her change of mood, he released his hold on her shoulders. 'But she might want it disrupting and disturbing,' he said, once more tucking his hands into the top of his pockets, his stance unknowingly and impudently casual.

Mavis had never rated her brother-in-law very highly, but in her own way she was fond of him. He'd be devastated if he knew of the burgeoning affair between Carrie and Zac, and it could only just be burgeoning because Zac hadn't been in Magnolia Square long enough for it to be anything else. 'Do one thing for me,' she said fiercely, aware that Nibbo was finally making his way ponderously back to them. 'If anyone else asks you about your relationship with Carrie, don't say to them what you've just said to me! At least have the sense and decency to try and put them off the track!'

As he never had the slightest intention of doing anything else, Zac gave a slight, complying nod of his head. He knew what she was after: time in which, as she saw it, to talk sense into Carrie. Well, she wouldn't do so – he'd see to that. He was a man who had never before given his heart to anyone not a parent or a sibling, and certainly not to a woman. But something instantaneous and overwhelming had happened to him when he first confronted Carrie. Not only did he fall hook, line and sinker for her unaffected, gypsyish vibrancy, he'd instinctively sensed her worth. Carrie Collins was genuine through and through, and he'd had a hard enough life to be able to appreciate that quality above all others. If she felt for him what he felt for her, he was damned if he was going to take into account the feelings of a man who treated her with a careless affection more suited to a dog than a woman. He couldn't see Nibbo approaching from behind him, but over Mavis's shoulder he saw other familiar figures approaching: Leon and Jack and Charlie and Danny.

'We have company,' he said, not wanting Mavis to inadvertently blow the gaffe in front of Danny. 'By the look of them, they've had no more success with their search than me and Nibbo.'

Mavis wheeled round, saw in consternation that Danny was nearly upon them, and in vast relief that Jack was hard on his heels.

'We've had no joy, mate!' Zac shouted out to Leon.

'No one's seen any boy of Matthew's description,' Nibbo added as he joined them, a trifle breathless after his walk along the pier gangway. 'I've spoken to the captain and crew on all three ferries. Over the last couple of days they've had the usual one or two boys riding the boats when they should have been in school, but none of them were Matthew's age, or fair-haired.'

Leon's dark-skinned face looked almost grey with worry.

'Then all we can do is to keep searching the docks,' he said, refusing to give up hope and refusing to leave the search for his adopted son in the hands of the police who, as far as he was concerned, seemed to be doing absolutely nothing. 'You don't know where Kate, Christina and Carrie are looking, do you, Mavis?'

Mavis shook her head, acutely aware that Danny was now standing in close proximity to Zac. Was this perhaps how Carrie felt when she saw Jack in Ted's company? For the first time in her life she understood just why Carrie got so angry with her where Jack was concerned. Understood, but was incapable of letting it change anything. 'You couldn't drop out of this search, could you, Jack?' she asked him, so glad to see him it was all she could do not to throw her arms around his neck.

He looked down at her, his eyebrows rising slightly. What could be so important she wanted him to drop out of searching for Matthew? Then he saw the distress in her eyes and his own eyes darkened. 'What the heck's the matter, love?' he asked, concerned. 'What's happened?'

She shook her head swiftly, not wanting Zac Hemingway to overhear. If he did he would assume, when she and Jack went off together, that she was about to tell him everything. That she was very probably going to do so was neither here nor there. She just didn't want Zac Hemingway reading her as if she were an open book. 'Nothing,' she lied, wanting only the comfort of his company. 'Let's find a transport cafe and have a couple of strong mugs of tea.'

He slid his arm around her waist, knowing her too well not to know that she was almost on the brink of tears – and Mavis on the brink of tears was an unheard-of phenomenon. 'Come on, love,' he said affectionately, 'Two mugs of tea it is.' He looked towards the little group they had distanced themselves from. 'I'm off for now!' he called over to them. 'But I'll meet up with you later!'

Accustomed to Jack and Mavis's long-standing and matey friendliness, no odd glances, apart from Zac's, followed them as, in close and easy proximity, they walked off the pier together.

'What gives there, then?' Zac asked Danny, taking care old Charlie didn't overhear him.

'Mavis and Jack?' Danny grinned, his spiky red hair standing straight up on the crown. 'No one knows – which is probably just as well. When it comes to a bit of close-to-home 'anky-panky, what yer don't know yer can't grieve over, can yer?'

Chapter Eleven

Deborah Harvey was seated in the drawing-room of her niece's London town house. From the muslin-draped windows there were magnificent views of Holland Park. Not in view, but agreeably close by, lay Kensington Palace, home of royalty, and Kensington Gardens. It was all a far cry from south-east London and, to Deborah, the offensive gregariousness of Magnolia Square. 'How people live on top of each other like that, I cannot begin to imagine,' she said in genuine bewilderment to her fifty-five-year-old niece. 'Neighbours were in and out of the house all the time I was there. I might just as well have been in Piccadilly Circus. A woman friend of Matthew's mother freely admitted to being a market-trader. Can you imagine? A market-trader, and she's in and out of Matthew's house as if it's her own! There was also a young man there with trousers so tight he must have been sewn into them, and his hair was worn low over his forehead in a most peculiar kind of roll – quite unnatural.'

'Perhaps his trousers had been badly dry-cleaned?' Genevre Harvey suggested tentatively. 'I remember once when I sent a wool skirt to Harrods—'

'I shudder to think of the influence these people must have on Matthew,' Deborah continued, riding rough-shod over an interruption she considered inane. 'No wonder he's run away! He should either be with you during his school vacations, or with me at Tumblers. Tumblers is, after all, his true family home. It is the home he will inherit.'

Genevre Harvey, as thin and angular as her aunt, but possessing a far more malleable manner, crossed to the window, lifting the muslin drapes aside, the better to see the street and the park. 'And do you say people are in and out of the house all day long?' she asked, knowing better than to continue with the story of her dry-cleaning mishap. 'It must be very strange, mustn't it?' There was a hint of wistfulness in her voice, as if, as well as being strange, she also thought it might be pleasant.

'It must be exceedingly inconvenient!' Deborah retorted tartly. 'And it is certainly extremely working-class and not at all a suitable environment for Matthew.'

Genevre remained silent. She was sure Deborah was right, and that Matthew would be much happier spending his school vacations with either Deborah or herself, and yet it had to be admitted that his south-east London home sounded interesting. She had never, of course, seen it for herself. When her grandfather was alive he had deemed any meeting between herself and Kate Emmerson as unnecessary and, after his death, when Deborah became head of the family, she, too, had refused to sanction any such demeaning familiarity.

It meant that the mystery persisted as to why her young brother had become unofficially engaged to a girl who, within months of his death and Matthew's birth, was to embark on a liaison with a half-caste West Indian. Even now, all these years later, she still couldn't quite believe it to be true. It was simply too bizarre; too like the kind of thing one read about in the more lurid Sunday newspapers.

'. . . and so I shall return in order to be on the spot in case this latest assumption, that Matthew is in hiding down by the river, should prove to be correct,' Deborah said, squaring her shoulders in readiness for the ordeal of another trip south of the Thames.

'Would you like me to come with you?' Genevre suddenly wanted to put an end to the mystery. She wanted to meet Kate Emmerson. She wanted to understand.

'Good heavens, no!' Deborah was emphatic. 'There's no need for both of us to slum with market-traders and young hooligans – and it will be a wasted trip, of that I haven't a minute's doubt. It is the police who will find Matthew, not a bunch of rag-tag hoi-polloys. And when the police do find him, I shall make quite sure they understand why he ran away. When I think of the teasing he must have endured at St Osyth's on account of his regrettably unusual home life . . .' She shuddered, words failing her.

Despite her forbidding demeanour and waspish manner, Deborah Harvey had a soft centre. It was one few people glimpsed or even suspected existed, and it was one reserved entirely for her great-nephew. Deborah loved Matthew; she loved him dearly. He was the child and the grandchild she had never had. He was also, as his father was at the same age, a boy to be proud of. And she would not let his disastrously unsatisfactory home life make him wretchedly miserable. She would *not*.

Addressing her as he always did, as if she were the queen, her chauffeur said, 'I'm afraid we have a slow puncture, Ma'am.' It was forty-five minutes later, and the Bentley was turning majestically and slowly into Magnolia Terrace.

'Then see to it, Adams.' Deborah's manner was even testier than usual. She was too discomposed at once again being south of the river, too worried about Matthew, to be bothered with an irritation that was, after all, Adam's concern, not hers.

'Yes, Ma'am.' Adams swung a little bumpily into Magnolia

Square, drawing to a halt outside number four, too accustomed to his employer's irritability to be rattled by it. 'If you're going to be long, Ma'am, I could nip to the garage in Shooter's Hill Road. It'll be easier for me to mend the puncture, or change the wheel, there. A half hour should be long enough and—'

'Yes, yes, yes!' The last thing Deborah wanted to be bothered with were the ins and outs of attending to a punctured tyre. She wanted to speak with Kate Emmerson again, and to do so without the hampering presence of Leon Emmerson.

Adams opened the rear passenger-seat door for her and, the instant she was safely on the pavement, returned to the car. He hadn't felt too good for the past day or so and wasn't relishing the thought of having to tussle with a tyre. The sooner the job was done, the happier he would be.

As he drove away, Deborah breathed in deeply, preparing herself for the ordeal ahead. The Emmerson house would no doubt be full to overflowing with undesirables again, but as she wanted to be on the spot while the day's search for Matthew was taking place, their proximity would just have to be endured. Using a parasol as a walking stick, she made her way up the shallow flight of steps leading to the lemon-painted door, grudgingly noting the pretty and carefully tended pots of herbs lining her way. Lavender. She grew a lot of lavender in her garden at Tumblers. It associated well with rosemary, and there was rosemary here, too, as well as thyme and basil and flamboyant, purple sage.

For a brief second it was almost possible to imagine herself miles away from south-east London, and then a voice called out with offensive familiarity, 'You're wastin' your time callin' on the Emmersons! 'E's down by the river with a party of neighbours, looking for 'is missing lad, and she's with a couple of women friends, doin' the same thing!'

Majestically Deborah turned, looking back towards the pavement.

Lettie Deakin shifted a laden shopping basket from one hand to the other. 'And the older kids are all at school and little Johnny's bein' looked after by the vicar's wife, so you won't get an answer no matter how long you stand there knocking,' she added informatively.

Not by a flicker did Deborah reveal how she felt at this news. She merely made the slightest possible inclining movement with her head, indicating chill gratitude for the unasked-for information. Lettie sniffed, unimpressed. Nobs. They were all the same. None of them had a civilized word for anyone but their own. It would serve the Emmersons' posh visitor right if she had to stand on their doorstep all day waiting for them to come home.

As Lettie continued on her way, muttering beneath her breath, Deborah's lips tightened. She had specifically told the Emmersons she would be returning today to wait for news of Matthew. Or had she? She frowned, trying to remember. Had she, instead, said that her chauffeur would take her down to the area Leon Emmerson intended searching? And just how long was Adams going to be before he returned for her? Had he said half an hour? And if he had, how could she possibly stand in the street for such a length of time? Only common people stood in the street. She looked around for somewhere to sit, but there was only the low wall fronting the garden. Never in her eighty-four years had she sat on a garden wall, and she wasn't about to begin now. She gritted her teeth, her kid-gloved hands tightening on the carved ivory handle of her parasol as she steeled herself to wait for Adams's return.

From her doorway and sagging-bottomed armchair, Nellie Miller watched Deborah Harvey with interest. Her house was at the bottom end of the square, and as the Emmersons' house was at the top end, on the opposite side, and St Mark's Church dominated the centre of the square, she didn't have a totally unrestricted view. She could, however, if she leaned as far as possible to the left, see past the corner of the church to at least a partial view of number four. She had done a lot of leaning to the left in the days during the war, when the Harvey Bentley had first driven into the square, parking outside the Emmersons and setting everyone's eyes out on stalks. Its chauffeured occupant then had been old man Harvey, Matthew's great-grandfather. Now, if the gossip grapevine was to be trusted, it was Deborah Harvey, Matthew's great-aunt.

The ramrod-straight figure wavered slightly and Nellie made a disparaging noise, not remotely surprised. It was a hot day – far too hot to be guyed-up as Deborah Harvey was guyed-up, a mauve toque hat crowning her head, a royal purple coat reaching nearly to her ankles.

Minutes ticked by and still the Bentley, which had edged out of the square a good twenty minutes earlier, didn't return.

'So what are yer goin' to do, ducks?' Nellie asked ruminatively, as if Deborah Harvey was within hearing distance.

What Deborah Harvey did was to move away from the Emmersons' front door and, with increasing unsteadiness, begin descending the steps that led to the pathway. Even before she had reached it, Nellie could no longer see her. As the minutes ticked by and she didn't again come into view, either making her way up the square, or down it, Nellie's concern grew. 'She's come over queer,' she said to herself, knowing the feeling, for with her weight she came over queer with tedious regularity. She sighed heavily and, knowing there was only one thing to be done, she embarked on the mammoth task of heaving herself out of her chair and onto her feet.

Dizzy from the heat and the unaccustomed exhaustion of

standing, Deborah saw a moving mountain lumberingly making its way towards her.

'Ain't the Emmersons in?' the mountain of flesh said a few minutes later, puffing for breath as it came to a halt in front of her.

Appalled at being addressed in public in such a manner, and by such a person, Deborah drew in an affronted breath, about to deliver a suitably crushing reply. None came. She felt too unwell to speak. She felt very unwell indeed.

The absence of an answer to her question didn't faze Nellie, for she didn't need one. Having watched all the many comings and goings in the square since early morning, she knew very well that the Emmersons weren't home. 'Ain't feelin' very chipper, are yer?' she said sympathetically. 'It's them barmy clothes yer wearin'.' She indicated her own massive and mottled unstockinged legs and comfy, cut-at-the-sides-to-make-more-room, slippers. 'Yer need to let the air get to yer flesh in this 'eat. I do. I ain't worn anythin' confinin' fer years.'

'My chauffeur . . . the garage . . .' Deborah swayed giddily. She needed Adams and the Bentley and a swift ride back to Genevre's Kensington flat and a restorative pot of Lapsang Souchong. 'If he could be contacted . . . told I've been taken unwell . . .'

Nellie looked up the square towards Magnolia Terrace and then down the square, towards Magnolia Hill. There was no one about, not even a playing kiddie. 'Yer might 'ave quite a wait till someone who could trot to the garage puts in an appearance,' she said, 'an' I can't go. It's winded me just comin' over to see if yer'd like to sit in my 'ouse for a while and 'ave a cuppa.'

Deborah's eyes took on a glazed expression. Was this vulgar mound of a woman actually suggesting that she, Deborah Harvey, accompany her to her house for a cup of tea? It was so unthinkable a suggestion, so preposterous, it beggared belief.

'Yer don't need to worry about not being able to see yer chauffeur when 'e comes back fer yer,' Nellie said, assuming this to be the reason for the lack of a grateful response. 'If I could see you from my front doorway, we'll be able to see 'im, an' when he comes back we can give 'im a 'olla so 'e'll know where you are.'

Deborah put a gloved hand to her throbbing head, knocking her toque hat awry as she did so. She had thought she was being accosted by a casual passer-by, and it was dawning on her that this was not the case and that the woman had puffed and panted her way across the square purposefully in order to help her. Considering the elephantine state of her legs and the difficulty she had in walking, it was an act of quite extraordinary kindness.

'You'll only get 'otter and dizzier if yer keep on standin' 'ere,' her unlikely Samaritan was now saying. 'Whereas if we 'ang on to each other, we can be back across the square an' in my front room 'avin' a cup o' char in two shakes of a lamb's tail.'

Deborah had never in her life 'hung on' to anyone. Especially not to anyone stockingless, corsetless, and wearing broken-down slippers. A cup of tea, however, sounded wonderful – and if she didn't have a cup of tea, there was the terrible possibility she might faint in the street. 'Thank you,' she said stiffly as small black dots swam across her field of vision. 'That would be . . . most kind.'

'Bugger it being kind,' Nellie gave a coarse cackle, taking hold of Deborah's arm to give her some support, 'I just don't want you passin' out on the pavement and makin' the place look untidy!'

'Crikey,' Billy said, standing in the *Tansy's* cabin hatchway 'Someone's made a right old mess in here.'

There were sheets of newspaper littered everywhere, a pile of what looked like recently gathered wood kindling, several empty tins of food, a tin kettle. Desperately eager to see for herself, Daisy squeezed past him into the cabin. At the sight that met her eyes, she felt a thankfulness so deep she knew she would never forget it. 'It's Matthew's mess!' she gasped exultantly. 'It must be!' With shining eyes she began picking up the newspapers, looking for the date on them, saying as she did so, 'No-one else would camp out here, would they?' She thrust a newspaper towards him. 'Look! It's only a few days old!' Her voice cracked and broke and she began to laugh and cry at the same time. 'Matthew's been here ever since he ran away, Billy! We've found him! *We've found him!*'

Billy's relief was nearly as great as her own. He was old enough to remember the day Matthew was born. He had been nine years old and he and Beryl had made a pint of liquorice-water and bottled it in an old lemonade bottle. He had taken the foul-coloured concoction round to number four as a gift for Matthew and, when Kate had gently explained that babies couldn't drink liquorice-water, had selflessly drunk it himself in order not to waste it.

He said now, stepping cautiously into the cabin, terrified of dislodging the barge from its rusty anchorage, 'What do we do now? Let your mum and dad know or wait 'ere till Matthew comes back from wherever 'e's nipped off to?'

Daisy's hesitation was fractional. It would take ages to get back to Magnolia Square, and even when they did get back there, it was doubtful if her mum and dad would be home. They would still be out, searching. 'We'll wait,' she said, euphoric at the thought of the greeting they would receive when they walked into Magnolia Square with Matthew in tow. 'I'm so happy, Billy! I've never been so happy before!'

In the small and dingy cabin, she was a picture of such

radiant perfection that Billy's heart felt as if it were somer-saulting in his chest. 'Daisy . . .' With a voice just as choked with emotion as hers had been, he began to cross the distance dividing them. Now, while they were out on the lonely creek, and the only person who could possibly disturb them was Matthew, was the time for him to kiss her as he had ached to kiss her for so long. He reached out for her, saying clumsily, 'I love yer, Daisy. I've always loved yer. I love yer so much I don't know how to—'

She didn't let him finish. She danced into his arms, hugging him tight, tears of joy salt-wet on her cheeks. 'You're wonderful, Billy! No one else thought of looking here for Matthew! Not even Dad!' Her budding breasts were pressed hard against his chest like little apples. Her gleaming cap of blue-black hair was as soft against the curve of his jaw as silk. There was a deli-cious fragrance of lemons about her, as if she'd washed with lemon-scented soap or rinsed her hair in lemon-juice. And, overcome by the wonder of their having found Matthew's hiding-place, she wasn't listening to him. She wasn't listening to a single word.

'Daisy . . .' His voice took on a note of rough urgency. He had to make headway with her now, for if he didn't, it might be ages before he had another such opportunity. 'Daisy, listen to me. I'm glad about Matthew, but it ain't Matthew I want to talk about. I want to talk about us.'

She moved within the circle of his arms, looking up at him, her glowing eyes meeting his. Terrified she was also about to step away from him, he held her fast, saying with raw hoarseness, 'I want to kiss yer, Daisy. Yer don't have to kiss me back, if yer don't want, but I want to kiss yer! I *have* to kiss yer!'

Daisy was riding such a wave of ecstatic emotion there was no room for caution. Billy had found Matthew, and when she told him he was wonderful, she had meant it with all her heart. A smile of happy compliance curved her lips. If Billy wanted to kiss her, then she very much wanted to be kissed.

Sensing her reaction, Billy's heart began slamming against his ribcage as if it was going to explode. This was the moment he'd dreamed about for years; this was a moment he would remember for as long as he lived. 'I love yer, Daisy,' he said, the breath catching at the back of his throat as he lowered his head to hers. 'I shall love yer for always.'

Daisy trembled, aware of the solemnity of the promise, and then his mouth was on hers, hot and sweet, and time rocked and stood still, never to be the same again.

Carrie, Christina and Kate sat in rare silence around Carrie's kitchen table. Christina was never overly talkative and Kate was never raucous, but usually when they were together Carrie's infectious exuberance saw to it that they were as gossipy and giggly as schoolgirls. Now, however, after their day-long abortive search for Matthew, all three of them were deep in silent, unshared thoughts.

A baby, Christina was thinking. A baby would make her feel complete and whole. Without a baby, there seemed no point to anything. Without a baby, she and Jack weren't a family. They were just two people with not even nationality or religion in common, who had fallen heedlessly in love and, believing that the differences between them wouldn't matter, had married. Her hands tightened in her lap as she stared at the plate of ginger biscuits which Carrie had placed on the table. The differences between them wouldn't have mattered if there was a baby, or if Jack agreed to adopt a baby. But he hadn't done so. Wouldn't do so. And now, because she could no longer endure lovemaking and the cruel hope, always dashed, that lovemaking brought in its wake, their marriage was becoming crippled – so crippled that even thinking about it made her want to gasp with pain.

Carrie's thoughts didn't make her want to gasp. They were far too mind-shattering for such a straightforward reaction. All day long she had been unable to think of anything but the long, passionate embrace she had shared with Zac Hemingway, one turbulent emotion following hard on the heels of another as she had tried to come to terms with her behaviour. First had come guilt, then disbelief, then the fervent resolve never to even speak to him again. Utter horror at the desolation she would feel if she kept this resolution had then swamped her like a tidal wave. She had to see him again. If she didn't see him again she would die.

This realization had set the whole crazy cycle of reactions into a fresh spin. She was thirty-five years old, for goodness sake, not a love-struck adolescent! Her struggle for common sense had made no difference whatsoever. She felt as if she were an adolescent. She felt young and joyful and alive.

Her hands tightened around her untasted mug of tea. Was this wonderful, dizzying feeling how Kate felt about Leon? How Christina felt about Jack? If it were, there was far, far more lacking in her marriage to Danny than she had ever previously imagined. The question was, what was she going to do about it? She remembered the deep, delicious, giddy joy of being held in Zac's arms, and her cheeks burned a fiery red. She knew what she wanted to do about it – by crikey she did – and it was something no one who knew her would ever believe.

Kate took a sip of her tea, not tasting it, her thoughts full of Matthew. Where was he? What would she do if all the searches failed to find him? If he never returned home again? When she, Carrie and Christina returned to the square a half hour or so ago, Harriet Robson had called out to them that Leon's search party still hadn't returned. 'Don't go into an empty house,' Carrie had said to her, aware of how she must be feeling. 'You and Christina come home with me and I'll make us all a cuppa.' And so here she was, sitting in Carrie's, waiting, as she had waited for three days now, for news of her eldest son. To have done so without also thinking of his dead father would have been an impossibility. Toby Harvey had been her first, and until Leon had come into her life after his death, her only love. His photograph stood in a silver frame on their mantelpiece, his place in her heart special and unique.

Leon had never been jealous, for he had always known he had no reason to be, that though Toby was part of the pattern of her life, and a very special part, it was the love she now shared with him that was its whole. Now, staring down into her tea, her thoughts were of the days before the war, when she and Toby had first met, when everything had seemed golden and full of rosy promise.

'Carrie!' Though the kitchen was at the back of the house, the women heard the front door crash back on its hinges and recognized Mavis's voice. 'Are you in?' she was demanding now as the house reverberated from her noisy entrance. 'I've bin lookin' fer you all bleedin' day!'

Jolted out of her reverie of Zac, Carrie rose speedily to her feet. Mavis in a temper was the last thing she needed when she had Kate and Christina in the house, especially when Kate was so deeply distressed. 'Hang on and I'll be with you!' she yelled back, walking swiftly out of the kitchen in order that the confrontation could take place without an audience. The instant she saw the expression on Mavis's face, she forgot all about sparing Kate and Christina the sight of a sisterly tussle. Mavis wasn't on one of her usual trawls for an enjoyable scrap. Standing in the centre of the hallway, Jack a yard or so behind her, she looked positively ill.

'What's the matter, Mavis?' she asked in alarm, fingers of terror squeezing her heart. 'Is it Matthew? Have they found him . . .'

Mavis saved her from putting the unthinkable into words. 'No, it ain't Matthew, Carrie. It's *you*!'

Carrie blinked. Mavis worrying about her was a rare old turn up for the books. Usually it was the other way around. All her life she had worried about Mavis – and most times with good cause!

'Me? What about me?' She looked from Mavis to Jack in bewilderment, aware that both of them were regarding her with very odd expressions in their eyes.

Mavis put a hand on the polished knob of the banister newel post, as if to steady herself. 'I ran into Lettie Deakin this morning. She told me she saw you and Zac Hemingway up on the heath together last night, and that the two of you were up to no good. I told her she was a lying cow.' She paused, her eyes holding Carrie's while behind her Jack continued to prop the door open. 'Then I ran into Zac bloody Hemingway,' she continued when Carrie made no effort to speak. Couldn't speak. 'And guess what? *He* seems to think he was up on the heath with yer, kissing yer, as well!'

Still Carrie couldn't speak. If Zac had told Mavis, who else had he told? Her head reeled. And why had he told anyone? Dear God, why?

Reading her mind, Jack shifted his weight against the door, his hands deep in his trouser pockets. 'I reckon he told Mavis because she's your sister,' he said, trying to sound objective about it and not feeling at all objective. Christ Almighty! Carrie in a sneaky kiss and cuddle with Zac Hemingway! Carrie? Even though the truth of it was written all over her face, he could still scarcely believe it.

'Zac bloody Hemingway seems to think you and he are at the start of something big,' Mavis continued, her voice as taut as piano wire. 'Though how the hell he can know in such double-quick time, beats me.'

It beat Jack as well. Zac was an ace boxer and quick as lightning in the ring, but, as he had said earlier to Mavis, it didn't mean he had to be an equally fast worker out of it! 'You still haven't told Carrie there's a chance Lettie's also talked to Albert,' he said now, focusing the conversation on what seemed to him to be the most immediately urgent aspect of the affair.

Carrie's cry of anguished dismay brought Kate and Christina hurrying out of the kitchen. The only voice either of them had heard until then had been Mavis's. Now, as Kate ran down the passage to where Carrie was standing in an attitude of utter horror, her hands pressed hard against her mouth, Christina came to an abrupt halt.

Jack was at the open front door, and it was obvious he hadn't just arrived there, but that he had been there for as long as Mavis had been talking to Carrie; that he and Mavis had arrived together and were intending to leave together; that they had probably been together all day.

'Has there been news of Matthew?' Kate was demanding of Carrie and Mavis with fierce urgency.

Jolted by the shock of realizing that Carrie wasn't in the house on her own, Jack's hands were out of his pockets, his instantaneous reaction one of relief that the person visiting Carrie, and who could so easily have overheard Mavis, was Kate and not one of Magnolia Square's gossips or, even worse, Hettie. In the same split second, with the alarm still evident in her eyes, he registered Christina's presence. 'Hello love,' he said easily, hoping she, too, hadn't overheard what Mavis had said to Carrie. It was bad enough that he and Mavis now knew about Carrie's clinch with Zac, without Christina knowing about it as well.

'Why are you here?' Her voice cut across Mavis's as Mavis hastily reassured Kate she had no bad news regarding Matthew. 'You said you were going to be by the river all day with Leon and Danny.' Christina knew she sounded like a shrew but she couldn't help it. She had seen the alarm flash through his eyes and was certain it was because he hadn't wanted her to know that he'd been spending time with Mavis.

'I was, for most of the morning,' he said, trying to keep his temper as she continued to make no move towards him, but to stare at him as challengingly as if he'd just done her a great hurt.

Still Christina didn't move. If he'd been with Leon and Danny for only 'most of the morning', it meant he had probably been with Mavis ever since then, and it was now going on for six o'clock!

'I'm fine, Kate, really I am,' Carrie was saying to Kate, sounding far from fine. 'Mavis just had some news that was a bit of a shock, that's all.' She flashed Kate a pale imitation of her usual sunny grin. 'It's nothing for you to worry about, though. You've got enough on your plate as it is.'

With tremendous effort, Christina forced her thoughts away from Jack's relationship with Mavis – a relationship she was growing more and more convinced was clandestine – too fond of Carrie not to be concerned about her. In all the years she'd known Carrie, she'd never seen her look so distracted.

'What ought I to do?' Carrie was now speaking to Mavis, and it was the first time anyone present had ever heard her ask that question of her elder sister.

'Check whether Lettie's said anythin' to Albert,' Mavis

said bluntly. 'And if she 'asn't, make sure she bleedin' well doesn't!'

Aware that something was seriously amiss and that Carrie didn't need visitors hanging around, Christina reluctantly moved away from the kitchen door, walking down the passageway towards the hall and Jack. As she reached the foot of the stairs where Carrie, Mavis and Kate were standing, she paused and, avoiding all eye contact with Mavis, said to Carrie, 'Whatever's happened, I hope things turn out all right, Carrie.'

Carrie was too choked up to speak. What if Christina knew *why* she was upset? What would she think of her then?

As Christina reached Jack's side, he slid his arm around her waist, ignoring her stiff unresponsiveness. 'We're off then,' he said to the others, and then, as he stepped out onto the pathway, he came to such a sudden halt, Christina stumbled against him. 'Hell's bleeding bloody bells!'

'What is it?'

He didn't answer her. Instead he spun on his heels and hurtled back into the house. In alarm and bewilderment, Christina looked up and down the square. There was nothing to see apart from Nibbo's cat, stretched full out on the pavement as it enjoyed the early evening sun, and Hettie, imitation cherries bobbing on her black straw hat as she marched down the square towards number seventeen, obviously intent on having a few mother-in-law-like words with Carrie.

Chapter Twelve

Zac wasn't in the habit of feeling sorry for people, but as he walked with Leon across the heath towards Magnolia Terrace, he felt sorry for Leon. Despite splitting up their original search party, so that after the abortive search of the ferry boats Danny and old Charlie had returned to Rotherhithe for a further search of the Greenland Dock area, Nibbo and Elisha had headed back to Deptford and he and Leon had covered the wharves in and around Greenwich, no sign of young Matthew had been found.

'I just don't understand it,' Leon said for the thousandth time. 'I know you don't know Matthew, Zac, and so it might be hard for you to believe it, but Matthew isn't a boy with any waywardness in him. For him to have run away like this . . . not letting anyone know where he is or if he's all right or not . . .' Leon ran a hand wearily over his kinky hair, '. . . it's totally out of character, and it doesn't make sense. It doesn't make any sense at all.'

Zac made a noise in his throat that could have meant anything, and that in this case meant he believed every word Leon was telling him. And he did. After a day in Leon's company, if there was one thing he was sure of, it was that Leon would never fudge anything. If he said a thing, that thing would be God's honest truth. He took a packet of ten Weights out of his hip pocket and offered one to Leon, before taking one out for himself. Such blatant integrity was something he'd never subscribed to himself. As far as he was concerned, he couldn't see that it got anyone anywhere. It certainly hadn't done so in Barnardo's. He lit his cigarette and inhaled deeply. Without a bit of fudging and ducking and diving, life in an orphanage would have been utterly impossible.

'Daddy! *Daddy!*'

Even though the voice shouting from some distance behind them was female, and clearly not Matthew's, both Leon and Zac spun round as if shot.

'Matthew's hiding out on the *Tansy*, Daddy!' the very pretty girl running hard to try and catch them up, shouted out. 'It was Billy's idea to look there!'

'Christ Almighty!'

It was a blasphemy Zac was sure Leon rarely gave vent to, and it was uttered as if he'd been pole-axed.

The girl was fleet-footedly closing the distance between them, calling out breathlessly as she did so, 'Billy's still aboard the *Tansy* waiting for Matthew to return to it! I didn't want to come home without him but as time is getting on Billy said one of us should come and let you know so you wouldn't be worrying any more . . .'

Leon tossed aside the cigarette Zac had given him and broke into a sprint. Zac watched in bemusement as the two of them raced over the rough grass towards each other. The girl was obviously the adopted, eldest Emmerson child, though if the pleasing jiggle of her school-blouse-covered breasts were any-thing to go by, she was no longer a child in the real sense of the word. She raced into Leon's arms, hugging him tight, her eyes shining, her face radiant.

'There are newspapers in the *Tansy's* cabin, Daddy! And all of them are only a few days old! And there are empty food tins and fresh wood-kindling!'

Zac grinned, glad the missing kid had been found, vastly amused at the sight of Leon with his eldest daughter. It seemed to him that 'Daddy' was a babyish expression, coming from a girl on the verge of womanhood, but that it was also a rather endearing one.

'But have you *seen* Matthew?' Leon was asking her urgently.

Zac didn't wait to hear her reply. He'd given his entire day up in searching for the Emmerson kid, and he had other things to attend to now. An evening of hard training in preparation for the fight Jack had arranged for him and the little problem of Lettie Deakin and whether she'd dropped him and Carrie right in it by not only telling Mavis she'd seen them kissing, but by telling Carrie's father-in-law also. And then there was Carrie herself. He wasn't going to allow what had happened between them to be a one-off, never-to-be-repeated event. He'd waited a long time to find a woman who aroused in him the deep, complex emotions Carrie aroused in him, and now he'd found her, he wasn't going to lose her.

With long, easy strides he turned into Magnolia Terrace. Perhaps the first thing he should do was to have a word with Lettie. If she hadn't blabbed to Albert Collins, it meant he still had Danny as his trainer. And if she had? If she had, he would simply ask Leon to stand in as his trainer – and he'd do his damnedest to get Carrie to move in with him!

'Course I didn't say owt to your pa-in-law!' Lettie was saying indignantly with Yorkshire bluntness. 'What the heck do you take me for? I only gave Mavis the impression I might do, because she'd been so bloody high-handed with me and got me so bloody riled!'

Carrie could never remember feeling so relieved over anything, not even the end of food rationing. The tizzy she'd been in had, however, made one thing perfectly clear to her.

Whatever her chaotic, tumultuous feelings where Zac was concerned, they couldn't be indulged in. She wasn't cut out to be a faithless wife. It was too wearing on the nerves.

Lettie put the glass she'd been polishing on the bar top and picked up another from out of the sink. 'What I will say though is this. If you're going to play away from home, Carrie, play a bit bloody further than the heath! The world and his brother are up there at night, walking their dogs. You'd get as much bloody privacy canoodling at Lewisham clock tower!'

Carrie refrained from making any comment. Grateful as she was that Lettie hadn't broadcast her juicy tit-bit of scandal any further than Mavis, she wasn't about to make her a confidante. With a return of her natural cheery smile, she turned to go. There had been no customers in The Swan when she had entered it, and there were still no customers, even though it was getting on for six o'clock. Presumably all the regulars were, like Danny, giving Leon a hand in searching for Matthew. As she neared the door, her thoughts turned to Rose. Where on earth was she? She should have been home from school an age ago. Had she, perhaps, met up with Daisy, and were they doing a bit of searching of their own?

She was just about to reach out for the door handle when the door swung abruptly open. This time her cry of shock brought no one running to her side. Lettie Deakin merely put down the glass she had been polishing and settled her generous weight comfortably against the bar in order to enjoy what was obviously going to be a very interesting free show.

'Do you always pop into the pub on your own for an early evening tipple?' Zac asked teasingly, his eyes, as they met Carrie's, flushed with the heat of another, far more disturbing emotion.

'No. Of course not.' Her voice was a croak. Her knees were jelly. Her heart was hammering wildly somewhere up in her throat. With a tremendous effort, she remembered that she was going to have nothing further to do with him and that she was deeply outraged and furiously angry with him. 'I came to have a word with Lettie and, according to Mavis, you know very well why!'

With one hand, he shut the door behind him, with the other he took hold of her arm. There was ownership in his fingers, complete possession. 'Then we're both here for the same reason,' he said, sensing immediately she had convinced herself that the previous evening had been, on her part, a shameful, never-to-be-repeated, aberration. 'And as you've obviously already spoken to Mavis, you'll know that I didn't tell her anything she didn't already know.'

It was on the tip of Carrie's tongue to retort that he most certainly had done! Then she remembered just what it was he had told Mavis and bit the words back, aware she could hardly fling at him that he'd said he believed he and she were at the start of something big!

'And was Mavis right in believing Lettie had told Albert?' he asked, looking across to where Lettie was openly and avidly listening in to everything.

'Course I didn't,' Lettie wasn't remotely abashed at being caught so openly ear-wigging. 'It's no use running a pub and not knowing when to keep your trap shut about who's playing around with who.'

Carrie tried to shake herself free of Zac's hold. She was wearing the same scarlet cotton dress she'd been wearing when she had met him down the market and young Johnny was with her, the sweetheart neckline revealing the full, voluptuous curves of her breasts. 'I hope you're not including me in that last remark, Lettie!' she said explosively, the gold locket on her necklace dancing down into her cleavage, 'because contrary to what you might think, *I'm* not playing around with anyone!'

Lettie pursed her lips. 'Well if you're not, dear, you're making a damn good imitation of it,' she said as, far from allowing her to shake him off, Zac began steering Carrie back towards the bar.

'A tomato juice and a gin and tonic,' he said, pulling a ten-shilling note out of his back jeans pocket with his free hand.

'I don't want a tomato juice!' There was an edge of hysteria in Carrie's voice. It was as if Lettie's seeming acceptance that she was having an affair with Zac meant that she really was having an affair with him!

'I'm not buying you one.' Despite the flare of panic he'd felt when he realized she intended trying to end things before they'd even really started, there was amusement again in his voice. 'The tomato juice is for me. I'm in training, remember?'

With a sharp, determined effort, Carrie wrenched her arm free of his hold. She didn't particularly want to have an audience to what she was now about to say, but she didn't seem to have any option. 'I can't drink with you here, Zac, or anywhere else.' Considering that her whole body was again responding to him in the most flagrant, indecent way imaginable, her voice was commendably level and firm. With an effort she avoided looking him in the eyes and with an even greater effort didn't allow her glance to fall on her arm where he had taken hold of her and where she knew she would see the imprint of his fingers. She had to spell out how things stood between them and leave. She hadn't to marvel at how scorched her skin felt where he had touched her, or to dwell on the mystery as to why, having had time to come to her senses, she still wanted nothing more than to catapult into his arms as if they were the one place she belonged. Bewilderment twisted in a knot deep in the pit of her stomach. It was as if she had become a stranger to herself. As if the old Carrie Collins no longer existed and a new Carrie Collins, frighteningly capable of anything, had taken her place.

Zac gazed at her averted face, his mouth tightening. He'd

known this little scene was going to come but hadn't anticipated it taking place in front of Lettie. Lettie, however, already knew there was something going on between him and Carrie, and he certainly wasn't going to let Carrie say her little prearranged piece and then hurry home to make Danny's dinner! With a lean strong hand he encircled her wrist, holding her fast.

Lettie's eyes glazed. She'd witnessed some interesting scenes in her time, but this one took the biscuit.

'Let me go!' Carrie's voice was no longer steady. She could do what she had determined to do – draw a line under the whole incredible episode – but not if he had hold of her; not when he was so near she could smell the male scent of him; not when she could see the heat in his eyes, smoking them the colour of quartz.

'There's something you have to understand, Carrie.' His voice was low and urgent – so low that Lettie, to her chagrin, was having difficulty in hearing. 'I wasn't just fooling around, last night.' He'd drawn her close, his mouth against the untidy tumble of her hair. 'I've fallen for you hook, line and sinker, Carrie Collins. I've fallen for you in a way I've never fallen for a woman before.'

Carrie gasped in sheer, disbelieving incredulity. He was making love to her again! And this time he was doing so in public! In outraged indignation, she pushed herself violently away from him. This had to stop. It had to stop now. What if Danny walked into the pub? Lord Almighty, what if her *mother* walked in?

'I'm going home!' Her voice shook with passionate intensity. 'I'm going home and I'm never going to be alone with you again, Zac! Not ever!'

In other circumstances Zac would have pointed out that they weren't alone now, not with Lettie listening in to them, glazed-eyed. Instead, aware of just how much was at stake, he said with a fierceness that sent shockwaves tingling down Lettie's spine, 'Just because something happens out of the blue, doesn't mean it wasn't meant to happen! What's happening between us is special, Carrie. You're special! I've trusted my instincts all my life and I'm trusting them now. Don't pretend this isn't happening. Don't—'

The pub door slammed open.

'Evening, all!' Daniel Collins stepped across the threshold, beaming jovially. 'Are you spreading the news about young Matthew, Carrie? It's grand to know he'll soon be home, isn't it?' He walked across to join them, slapping his folded evening paper down on the bar, saying to Lettie as he did every evening between six o'clock and seven o'clock, 'A pint of light and bitter, Lettie, if you please.'

Lettie could cheerfully have throttled him. In another few minutes Zac Hemingway would have been professing undying love to Carrie, and now he couldn't do so! Compared to being a witness to that little scene, the news that Matthew Harvey had been found was very small beer – very small beer indeed!

Carrie grasped at the news as if at a life-line. 'Matthew's been found?' With her eyes holding his, she began to back away, moving on unsteady legs towards the door. She mustn't think of all the things Zac had said to her, or the tone of voice he had said them in! 'That's wonderful news. Kate and Leon must be over the moon with relief.' Even more importantly, she mustn't give way to the all-consuming desire he had aroused in her – desire so intense that in the seconds before her father-in-law's entrance, she'd been on the point of forgetting all about her vow to never, ever be alone again with him. 'Who found him? And where?'

The door was firm at her back now. Another minute – two at the most – and she'd be outside and hurrying home in order to make Danny his dinner, no longer the Carrie that a bruisingly fit, head-turningly handsome young man thought it reasonable to make public love to, but the Carrie rarely to be seen not wearing a street-trader's pinny, the Carrie no one, not even her husband, ever looked at twice.

'Don't you know, pet?' Daniel regarded her fondly. 'I thought Danny must have told you and you'd come in here to spread the news.' He leaned against the bar, waiting for Lettie to finish pulling the beer for his light and bitter, too uncomplicated a man to wonder what other reason Carrie could have for being in The Swan so early on in the evening, especially when Danny wasn't with her. 'Daisy and Billy tracked him down,' he continued as Lettie finally placed a brimming pint glass within his reach. 'They found him aboard the *Tansy*, Leon's old barge. She's out of commission now and berthed somewhere up Barking Creek. Leon hared off over there the minute he heard.'

With her eyes still locked on Daniel's, aware that Zac's eyes hadn't left her face even for a moment, Carrie managed a smile. 'That's smashing – and it'll put that mealy mouthed old aunt of Matthew's in her place. She seemed to think there was as much chance of finding Matthew by the Thames as finding him on the moon.' She half-turned, her hand closing on the door handle. ''Bye,' she said, wondering for how long Lettie would manage to keep her mouth shut, and what would happen when the effort became too much for her.

''Bye, pet.' Daniel's pint was snug in his callused hand. As the door banged shut, he said affably to Zac, glad of the opportunity to have a few friendly words with him, 'How are you settling in?' and then, not waiting for a reply, 'I don't expect you'll be having any problems. We're a friendly bunch in Magnolia Square, aren't we, Lettie?'

Lettie gave an hysterical snort. 'Oh, aye, we're a friendly

bunch all right,' she said when she could at last trust herself
to speak. 'In fact, Daniel, I think you'd be surprised if you
knew just how very friendly to strangers some folks have been!'

'And you've been with her nearly all day? Because she was
upset? And you can't tell me what it was she was upset about?'
Still wearing the burgundy silk shirt and white linen skirt she'd
worn whilst searching for Matthew, Christina stared at Jack
across the width of their immaculately made bed, rigid with
hurt and a whole host of other, far more complex and dark
emotions.

Jack ran a hand through his thick shock of unruly dark hair.
This kind of scene was becoming increasingly frequent – and
tedious. There was no way he could tell Tina why Mavis had
been so upset and, even if he could, he could see no reason
why he should do so. He had come up to the bedroom for a
clean shirt before going over to the gym and she had followed
him upstairs, intent, so it seemed to him, on a quite unnecessary quarrel. 'Let's give it a rest, shall we?' he said with barely
concealed impatience. 'I have to get over to the club to let Zac
know I've arranged a fight for him and—'

'That's all that's important to you, isn't it?' Her usually soft
voice held a hard edge of bitterness. 'The boxing club and the
fight game and the money that can be made from it.' She
thought of the way things should have been; of summer evenings
spent together in the garden as their children laughed and
shrieked and played on swings or in a paddling pool, her resentment so intense it felt as if it were eating her alive.

Jack heard the resentment and completely misconstrued it.
Christina had class. Class that was inbred, not merely assumed.
Class he had always been proud of and that had never threat-
ened to become a divisive issue between them – until now.

'And how would you prefer I earn the money that keeps a

roof over our heads?' he demanded, his voice a whiplash of barely controlled fury, 'By being a test-pilot or a brain surgeon or a university professor? I'm a south-east Londoner, for Christ's sake, not a middle-class, public-school-educated toff!'

It was the first time he had ever spoken to her in such a way and he made not the slightest apology for it. He'd put up with her stand-offishness where the club was concerned for long enough. 'Perhaps if you came down to the club some time . . . took an interest in it . . . you might look at it a little differently!'

The white counterpane-covered bed divided them like a battleground. Christina could feel her knees wanting to buckle against it. The club! She *hated* the club! It smelled of hot liniment and dirty socks and sweaty jock-straps. On the rare occasions she visited it, she felt glaringly out of place. Unlike Carrie, who worked amongst the colourful language and earthly repartee of a street market, she couldn't shrug off the coarse jokiness that most of Jack's boxers indulged in. Mavis, of course, did so with ease. If Mavis was told a risqué joke she was quite capable not only of laughing at it with full-throated enjoyment, but of capping it with a joke of her own. Was that what Jack wanted? A woman who had never shown the slightest interest in home life and who certainly wasn't a caring mother in any conventional sense of the word? Perhaps his real reason for not wanting to adopt children was that, like Mavis, he felt that children were a hindrance when he enjoyed late-night clubs and bright lights so much.

She pushed a long smooth wave of satin-black hair away from her face, saying tautly, 'I don't want to visit the club! I don't want to watch brainless, beefy men training to hammer other equally brainless, beefy men senseless! I don't want—'

'Me. Is that what you're trying to say?' His voice was a hard, raw rasp. Thin white lines edged his mouth and a pulse had begun to throb at his jaw-line. 'You don't want me any more? Is that why you've been giving me the cold shoulder in bed for so long, Tina? Is that why you keep trying to make an issue over my friendship with Mavis? Because you want an excuse to cut and run?'

She gasped, aware that they had crossed a hitherto un-crossed line; that where their personal relationship was concerned they were in strange, never-before visited country. 'Is that what you would like me to do?' Without the hard edge of the bed against her legs she would have fallen. 'Would my cutting and running make everything easier for you? For you and Mavis?'

Something snapped within Jack. He was sick to death of having his words twisted; of bending over backwards trying to understand her moodiness; of being considerate, and damn-near celibate! With panther-like speed he rounded the bed, seizing hold of her shoulders, intent on shaking sense into her. Her response was to freeze into icy rigidity and it was a response that tipped him over the edge. Instead of shaking her, he dragged her down onto the bed, the burgundy silk tearing beneath his fingers as she tried frantically to twist away from him and he imprisoned her beneath him.

'Jack, no! Please! *No!*'

He silenced her with his mouth, pinioning her wrists in an iron hold high above her head as, with his other hand, he pushed her skirt high.

'Course yer not forcin' yerself on me,' Nellie said stoutly to Deborah Harvey. 'I invited yer in for a cuppa, didn't I? It ain't your fault your chauffeur chappie bunked off without so much as a by-yer-leave.'

Despite having now been several hours in Nellie's company, Deborah still had difficulty translating her speech into plain

English. The meaning of 'bunked off' was, however, clear even to her. Where, though, had Adams 'bunked off' to?

'We'd better 'ave another cuppa,' Nellie said practically, heaving herself out of her chair.

Deborah shuddered. She needed the reviving effects of tea, but Nellie's tea was like no tea she had ever come across before. ''Ow do yer take it?' Nellie had asked when they'd first entered the house. 'With milk an' sugar?' 'Just a slice of lemon, if you please,' she had replied, too grateful at having been saved from passing-out in the street to be her usual, autocratic and stand-offish self.

'Lemon? Lemon?' Nellie's eyebrows had shot nearly up into her hair-net. 'It's a cup of tea I'm offerin' yer, Blossom, not a bleedin' gin and tonic!'

Deborah didn't know which had rendered her most speechless, the prospect of a cup of tea without lemon, or being called Blossom. Both shocks paled into insignificance, however, compared to the shock of discovering that the milk she had asked for, as a substitute for lemon, was not milk as she knew it but a sickly sweet substance which came from a tin.

'Gettin' used to the condensed milk now, are yer?' Nellie asked, pausing to get her breath back after the exertion of hauling herself to her feet. 'By the time we've had this cuppa, young Luke will be calling by an' 'e'll be able to tell us if 'is mam and dad are 'ome yet.'

Deborah stiffened, not having the slightest desire of finding herself in the company of one of Matthew's rude and objectionable mixed-race siblings. The prospect was so distasteful that it put all thoughts of the hideousness of condensed milk completely out of her mind.

'There wouldn't 'ave been much laughter an' companionship for Matthew if Leon 'adn't got together with Kate,' she said sagely, deciding it was time her guest was told a few home truths. "E'd 'ave just been an only kid with no real family life at all. As it is, 'e's part of a big, boisterous, loving family. I used to watch 'im when 'e was a little nipper. Always with Leon 'e was, riding on 'is shoulders or trotting along, 'olding 'is 'and. Leon never told 'im to run off or to make 'imself scarce and then, when Leon's own nipper came along, 'e never made 'im a favourite. In fact, 'e always used to seem to be spending more time with Matthew than with Luke, seeing as 'ow it was Matthew who was mad about the river an' always wanting to be aboard a barge.'

Deborah made no response whatsoever. Seated as rigidly upright as it was possible for anyone to sit on one of Nellie's sagging-bottomed armchairs, her purple toque still slightly askew, she remained as impassive as a stone statue.

Nellie shrugged her shoulders, sending rolls of fat quivering and wobbling like a seismic eruption. Not being born yesterday, she could guess the reason for Deborah Harvey's hostility where the Emmersons were concerned, but she couldn't understand it. What did it matter what colour Leon and his kids were? They could be sky-blue or pink with yellow polka-dots for all she cared. What mattered was the kind of people they were – and Leon and his kids were the very best kind, by crikey they were! She continued on her ponderous way into the kitchen, leaving Deborah to face some very unpalatable facts.

The Emmersons hadn't, as she had thought, been feeding her a cock-and-bull story when they told her that Matthew loved to spend time down by the river. It was true. Yet Matthew had never once mentioned the river when he had been with her, at Tumblers. And she was quite sure he had never done so when in Kensington, with Genevre. Did that mean that she and Genevre didn't know Matthew as they had always believed they knew him? It was an appalling thought; almost as appalling as the prospect of Matthew not feeling a misfit in a mixed-race, working-class family!

Through a window prudently bereft of nets, she saw the tousle-haired, dusky-skinned figure of the elder Emmerson boy turn in at Nellie's gate at a run. Her lips tightened into such a thin line they almost disappeared. She wouldn't answer the door to him when he knocked and, with luck, Nellie might not hear him. The satisfaction she was looking forward to, that of seeing him having to go back from wherever it was he had come from, was denied her.

Luke didn't bother to knock. There was no need. Nellie's front door was open as usual, and he simply sprinted straight in, coming almost instantly to an abrupt halt. 'Blimey!' Panting for breath, he stared at her as if she was a Martian just landed from Mars. 'What are you doing here?'

Deborah waited in icy silence for Nellie to lumber into the room and to come to her aid. She didn't do so, and there was nothing for it but for her to answer his question herself.

'I am here, you ill-mannered young man, because . . .' she paused – she couldn't possibly admit to the indignity of having been taken ill in the square – 'because—'

'She 'ad a funny turn after her chauffeur chappie buggered off and didn't come back fer 'er,' Nellie said, manoeuvring her bulk, and a tray, into the room with difficulty, and wondering why doorways weren't as wide as they'd once been. 'Is your mam and dad 'ome, an' if they are, 'as there been news of Matthew?'

Luke's grin nearly split his face in two. 'He's been found!' He took the tray out of her hands and set it down on the nearest available surface, slopping tea as he did so. 'Daisy and Billy found him aboard the *Tansy*, and Dad's gone to get him!'

'Well, ain't that just wonderful news?' If it were physically possible for her to have done so, Nellie would have danced a jig. 'Don't that just beat the band?'

Deborah's relief was so total it betrayed her utterly. With a shuddering gasp she covered her face with her hands, and, to Luke's and Nellie's stupefaction, began to weep, the tears seeping heedlessly between her gnarled, be-ringed fingers.

Chapter Thirteen

'So the fight's definitely been fixed, Archie?' Ginger asked Archie as he and the rest of the 'boys' clustered respectfully around him in the Horse and Ferret. 'And Jack Robson doesn't know his bloke's opponent is going to be Arnie?'

'He hasn't a clue,' Archie said in high satisfaction, cigar smoke wreathing his head. 'Not a bleedin' inkling.'

There were chuckles of laughter all round. As Jack Robson was under threat either to pay protection to Archie or face unpleasant consequences, it was obvious he wouldn't have agreed to the match if he'd known who his fighter was being set against. The mediator who arranged the fight had, however, seen that Archie's name wasn't even mentioned and, as they all knew how superior Arnie was to any fighter Jack Robson might have, they were all looking forward to betting heavily on the outcome and making themselves a nice little packet.

'An' when are we goin' to do his Soho spieler over fer 'im?' Archie's bottle-scarred mobster asked impatiently. 'We ain't seen any fun and games for ages, an' we're lookin' forward to it.'

'Saturday night,' Archie said, shifting his fat rump a little more comfortably on his bar stool. 'That's when he's opening and that's when we'll let him know what happens to people who are given the opportunity of contributing to our business funds and don't take it.'

There were more chuckles. Archie had a wonderful way of putting things. Sometimes he spoke just like a nob.

Jemmy, Archie's longer-serving crony, and a man credited by the others as being something of a thinker, said musingly, 'Do yer reckon Robson will be there when we hit it, or do yer reckon it'll be only bar staff and croupiers and the blowsy piece who's runnin' it fer 'im, that'll be there?'

'Robson's bound to be there,' Ginger said, saving his boss the indignity of having to state the obvious. 'That's what's goin' to make everythin' so much more fun.'

'But if he ain't,' Jemmy persisted, leaning forward a little to stress the point of what he was about to say, 'if he ain't, who is it who's goin' to get hurt? The punters or the staff?'

There was an awkward silence. By 'staff' they knew that Jemmy wasn't referring to bar staff or croupiers but to the blowsy bit of goods who was apparently going to be running things for Robson – and that he was doing so with good reason. Their ace boxing-bet, Arnie, didn't like women, or not unless he was hurting them. It was a kink that had caused them a bit of trouble in the past. Slapping a bit of skirt around was one thing, doing her the kind of injury that could risk a murder charge was quite another, especially when it was a charge they might all be dragged in on.

'Whoever gets in our way,' Archie said easily, flashing Arnie a look of warning, 'but there's to be no going over the edge. Got it?'

There was a tangible sigh of relief from three of Archie's followers. Of the other two, Arnie merely began cracking his knuckles, and Pongo, Archie's newest recruit, was left bewildered. What had the sudden awkward atmosphere been all about? He wasn't thick – he always pulverized anyone who said he was – but sometimes he just couldn't work out what was going on. 'Yer've 'eard about the kid, then?' he said, bringing the conversation round to something that, thanks to drinking sessions in Blackheath's the Hare and Billet, he just happened to know something about. 'The kid that's a Harvey and heir to squillions of Harvey cash?'

Archie's piggy eyes narrowed. He hadn't heard, and he didn't like hearing from a minion. Where minions were concerned *he* did all the imparting of information, thank you very much.

Pongo, happily regardless of this time-honoured tradition, said, 'They thought he'd been found on his darky step-dad's old barge. Some of his gear was there, and his dad and a young scrap-metal dealer bloke waited ages for him but he never showed. Then the coppers were called in and did a proper search and found the kid's fingerprints everywhere, but no kid.'

''E's been kidnapped for the cash 'e'll come into,' Jemmy said, beginning to clean his nails with a penknife. 'It's somethin' we should 'ave thought of doing. There's pots of money in the 'Arvey family. The old gel 'as a mansion in Somerset and always rides around in the back of a bleedin' Bentley.'

'She ain't doin' so at the moment,' Pongo said, eager to be helpful once again. 'Her chauffeur had a heart attack in the garage in Shooters Hill Road. It caused a hell of a ruckus. A mate of mine who drinks in the Hare and Billet is a mechanic there and he told me.'

'And what did the chauffeur have for breakfast then?' Archie asked sarcastically. 'Did your mate tell you that as well?'

Pongo blinked. What did the chauffeur's breakfast have to do with anything? 'I don't know about his breakfast,' he said, hating it when people sniggered and he didn't know what they were sniggering about, 'but I do know the coppers don't think the kid was kidnapped. Now they know he's been on the barge, they think he ran away of his own vol . . . vol . . .'

'Volition,' Jemmy finished for him kindly, wiping his penknife clean and putting it back in his waistcoat pocket.

'And now he ain't there any longer, they think he must have thrown himself in the Thames.'

'What, topped 'imself?' Ginger asked incredulously. 'A kid? What would 'e want to do a bleedin' stupid thing like that for?'

'I 'spect he did it fer the same reason he ran away,' Pongo said with dogged logic, 'and that's not all!'

Everyone waited with interest. Everyone but Archie. This latest recruit to his ranks was turning out to be a right little clever-clogs and was going to have to go.

'Robson's missus has left him and run off to her ma's in Greenwich!'

Archie eyed him balefully. 'Robson's missus is a German-Jewish bint who had all her family snuffed by Hitler. She doesn't have a ma in Greenwich or anywhere else.'

'I think she does, Archie,' Jemmy said with pacifying mildness. 'Like her daughter, she's a classy bit of stuff, looks more French than German, and she married a widowed butcher with a shop down by the *Cutty Sark*.'

Archie wasn't remotely mollified. He glared at the hapless Pongo, wondering how best to be rid of him, saying for starters, 'It's your turn to buy a round and mine's a Remy Martin. A double.'

'So what's the news, Dolly?' Leah Singer asked, propped up in bed by half a dozen pillows, a quite unnecessary stone hot water bottle and Boots.

Beryl shifted the complaining Pekinese to the bottom end of the bed and sat down in the place he had warmed. 'I don't really know where to start, Great-Gran,' she said truthfully. 'There's ever so much trouble on over Matthew.' She took a paper bag of mint imperials out of her cardigan pocket and proffered it to Leah, her voice wobbling as she added reluctantly, 'They think he may be dead.'

'Then they don't think very good.' Leah helped herself to a mint. 'For why would a boy like Matthew do away with himself? It's a *tummel* over nothing. Matthew will soon be home fine and dandy, just see if he ain't.'

Beryl's shiningly plain face remained deeply troubled. She hoped her great-gran was right, she really did, but the police didn't seem to think it was only a *tummel*. The police had told Kate and Leon to prepare themselves for the worst.

'And so what else is happening?' Leah sucked on her mint imperial. 'There's other trouble, ain't there? Just because I can't go downstairs no more don't mean I'm blind and deaf! There's been a ruckus at the Robsons' and no one can tell me there ain't. They only live three doors away and I ain't stupid, *nu*. I know the difference between an ordinary set-to and a nasty set-to.'

Beryl's eyes had grown so round they resembled a marmoset's. Had her great-gran actually heard what had taken place at the Robson's? If so, she was the one who should be doing the gossiping; no one else knew anything other than that Christina had run from the house in tears and that she had a small suitcase with her.

'There was a row, Great-Gran. There must have been. Christina's gone to her mother's. Jack isn't saying anything, and he looks *terrible*.'

Leah's rheumy eyes glinted. She might be in her dotage, but she knew one thing and that was that Jack Robson had never looked truly terrible in his life. How could he, a man with all his *chutzpah* and devilry? 'For why hasn't he gone down to Eva's and brought her back home?' she asked, practically. 'It don't sound like Jack not to have done so. And where is Eva going to sleep her in that little house in Greenwich?'

Beryl's smooth forehead puckered in consternation. This was a problem no one else had thought of. Just as her gran had always had Great-Gran live with her, so Christina's mother had her aged mother living with her – and that meant that in a tiny Georgian terraced house there was no room for unexpected visitors.

'Perhaps she'll share a bed with Jacoba,' she said doubtfully, not truly being able to imagine such a possibility.

Leah snorted. Christina's grandmother, Jacoba Berger, was her own age and an old, old friend. Jacoba wouldn't want to be sharing a bed. Jacoba thought the world of her grandson-in-law and she'd want to know why Christina had been fool enough to have left him. And that Christina had been a fool, Leah wasn't in any doubt. A man like Jack Robson wasn't the kind of man it was wise to leave. There were too many other women eager to warm his bed. Her own grand-daughter, for one. She rolled her mint imperial round on her tongue and eyed Beryl thoughtfully. Was Beryl aware of the undercurrents beneath her mother's relationship with Jack? She was so endearingly naive that Leah doubted it. Mavis and Jack's friendship was of such a long duration it no longer excited comment, and there was no reason why Beryl should suspect that there was more to it than met the eye. She, Leah, wasn't endearingly naive, though. She'd been around a long, long time and she could read her eldest grandchild like a book. Mavis was in love with Jack. She'd always been in love with Jack.

Deciding it was a subject best left alone, she gave Boots a prod to stop him snoring, and said, 'And your gran and grandpa – what have they been barneying about?'

'Tomatoes,' Beryl said, relieved that this time she did at least have a proper answer to her great-gran's question. 'Grandpa caught Gran trying to palm off frying tomatoes as salad tomatoes. Gran says that when she's on the stall by herself she'll do as she bloomin' well likes, and Grandpa says that she'll do so over his dead body. They've been at it for days.'

Leah sniffed, her sympathies, for once, with her daughter. If Miriam could get good prices for poor tomatoes why for shouldn't she do so? 'And Hettie?' she asked, determined not to let Beryl go until she'd had her curiosity satisfied about everyone. 'I saw her stomping down to Carrie's in a high old temper the other day, when I was on my commode. Has my *nebbish* of a grandson-in-law been complaining Aunt Carrie doesn't feed him properly?'

'It wasn't anything to do with Uncle Danny.' Beryl couldn't remember a time when there had been so many squabbles taking place in the square at the same time – squabbles her great-gran seemed to know an indecent lot about. 'She took high umbrage because she'd left a line of washing out when she went down to the shops and, when there was a flash thunderstorm, Carrie didn't take it in for her.'

Leah raised gnarled hands in an age-old gesture of despair. Hettie Collins was a woman never happy unless complaining about something – and a woman with less to complain about never breathed. Hadn't she got a pearl of a husband in Daniel? Hadn't she a daughter-in-law in a million in Carrie? Wasn't Rose the brightest, bonniest grand-daughter imaginable?

Before she could begin a litany of all Hettie's blessings, Beryl offered her another mint imperial. She didn't want to talk to her great-gran about Hettie. She wanted to talk to her about Zac. 'Have you spoken to Aunt Carrie about Zac, Great-Gran?' she asked hopefully. 'Has she told you how nice he is? How he's nice to everyone, even the small boy scouts who plague him for tips on how to box?'

Leah was grateful for her second mint imperial. It meant she could pretend to be having a problem with it while it gave her time to think how best to answer. She *had* spoken to Carrie about Zac Hemingway. As Beryl had taken such a shine to him she wanted to know what kind of a young man he was. That a simple question could have aroused such an extraordinary reaction, Leah still couldn't quite believe. And she still didn't know what to make of it. 'Yes, he's quite nice,' Carrie had said, rummaging in her handbag with such intensity anyone would think she'd mislaid the crown jewels. 'No, he isn't at all a suitable young man for Beryl.' She thought he wasn't going to be staying in Magnolia Square for long. She thought he was too old for Beryl.

'For how can he be too old for her?' she had asked, mystified. 'He's only in his mid-twenties, *nu*!'

Carrie's head had remained bent as she had tossed first one item out of her handbag onto the bed, and then another. 'He's quite possibly older than he looks,' she had said, her hair cascading all over her face so that Leah had had difficulty in hearing her. Distractedly she had begun gathering up all her scattered possessions, stuffing them back from where she had taken them. He wasn't Beryl's type. She didn't want Beryl to be hurt. Boxers were a decidedly dodgy breed. She had to go home and get Danny's dinner on. And then she'd gone, clattering down the stairs as if, unless she got on with Danny's dinner that very instant, she'd be facing a firing squad! It had all been very odd. Too odd for Leah to fathom.

'Your grandpa tells me Zac Hemingway is very patient with the youngsters,' she said, answering Beryl's question as obliquely as possible. 'And he says he's a versatile fighter and that he can knock an opponent out with either hand.'

This wasn't quite the response Beryl was after, but it was better than nothing. At least her great-gran no longer seemed to disapprove of Zac's profession, and at least she was talking to her about him. She certainly hadn't been able to get her mother or her aunt to talk about him. Carrie had clammed up as tight as an oyster when she had asked her if she thought she stood a chance with him. As for her mother . . . Her mother seemed to have taken a quite inexplicable dislike to him, and for someone as easy-going and exuberantly friendly as Mavis, it was very odd behaviour indeed.

'I don't know what's the matter with everyone at the moment, Great-Gran,' she said, mystified. 'Everyone seems to be acting really oddly. I can understand why the Emmersons are on edge, but Mum and Aunt Carrie are nearly as bad. It's as if they've all got a 'flu bug or something.'

Leah screwed her lips as if she'd just sucked a lemon. Whatever was going on in the square, and that something over and above young Matthew's disappearance was going on she'd sensed for some time, it wasn't a 'flu bug. She scratched the top of Boots's head. So what was it? If Beryl didn't know and neither Mavis nor Carrie were prepared to tell her, she'd have to find out some other way. From Nellie, perhaps. Or Lettie. Lettie always knew everything that was going on. She'd get Albert to ask Lettie to visit her, *then* she'd know why Mavis and Carrie were both acting as if they were seriously out of sorts.

'But whatever it is, it ain't 'flu, Dolly,' she said to Beryl who was now on her feet and about to go back to work. 'Though it says in the paper these new immigrants will soon be suffering from it.' She patted the newspaper laying on the bed where a banner headline proclaimed, *Immigration increases from West Indies.* 'It says two hundred and fifty Jamaicans were piped ashore yesterday morning by a ship's band when they landed at Plymouth, and that, even though it was a glorious warm day, they all complained that the weather was cold!'

'Well, I suppose it seemed cold to them,' Beryl said, unclipping the pink plastic hairslide that had slid low in her slippery, poker-straight hair. 'It must be very hot in the West Indies, mustn't it?' She pushed her hair away from her face and re-clipped it, looking down at the accompanying photograph of black, hopeful, smiling faces. 'It must be very strange for them, coming from islands of sun and sea to live in London, in places like Lewisham and Deptford.'

'They'll do what Jewish people have always done, *nu*. They'll adapt,' Leah said, not envying them the task. 'And now that the government is encouraging so many of them to come here to work on the buses and in the hospitals, think of the difference it will make to the Emmersons. With more black faces on the streets, Leon won't get stared at and pointed at so much.'

At such a happy prospect, Beryl beamed, temporarily forget-ting how troubled she had been feeling. Leon never talked about the way some people reacted to his skin colour, but she knew there had been nasty incidents. Once, when he went with her Uncle Danny into the Dartmouth Arms in nearby Forest Hill, the landlord had refused to serve him, or allow him to be served, and another time, when he was with Billy at a football match and Billy had been only a youngster, a gang of hooligans had turned on him, kicking and punching him and yelling that he should get back to where he had come from.

''E comes from Chatham!' Billy had sobbed and shouted, all to no avail. As he said later, when telling her what had happened, 'They didn't care where Leon 'ad come from, Beryl. They only cared that 'e was black.'

'Maybe this news about the immigrants will cheer Leon up a bit,' she said now with typical naive optimism. 'I'll tell him about it when I next see him. It's awful seeing him look so worried. Mum says he's aged ten years this last couple of weeks.'

If Leon had known of Mavis's opinions, he would have disagreed with it. He didn't feel as if he had aged ten years.

He felt as if he had aged twenty. Somehow his brief conviction that Matthew was aboard the *Tansy* and would soon be home again had, when it proved false, made everything even worse than it had been before. Before the search of the *Tansy*, when he found a sweater he identified as being Matthew's, and the police found Matthew's fingerprints and, apart from prints left by himself, Daisy and Billy, Matthew's prints and Matthew's alone, it was possible to believe that Matthew had, perhaps, been abducted. But no longer. No strange abductor would have known of the *Tansy's* existence. Matthew had hidden out on her voluntarily and alone, and then, in a lonely area of the creek, had vanished.

The police questioned both himself and Kate with rigorous thoroughness. They didn't say so, but he knew he had been under suspicion. After all, he had known of the *Tansy's* existence, and hadn't made the suggestion to search her. He knew the police were wondering if, perhaps, he had taken Matthew to the *Tansy*, murdered him and dropped his body into the Thames. Perhaps, if he hadn't had consistent alibis for the period over which Matthew disappeared from school, they would have voiced their suspicions and charged him – though whether they could have charged him with murder, when there was no body, he didn't know. He did know, though, that the very thought that anyone could believe him guilty of harming Matthew filled him with a revulsion crucifying in its intensity. He loved Matthew. He loved all his children, but Matthew was special.

When Kate went into labour with Matthew it was during the war and he was a sailor on sick-leave, lodging with her and already, though she hadn't known it, in love with her. In the aftermath of a bombing raid, no doctor or midwife was able to get to Magnolia Square in time to assist with Matthew's birth. He had acted as Kate's midwife. Single-handedly he brought

Matthew into the world, and the experience was one that had forged an unbreakable bond, not only between himself and Kate, but between himself and Matthew also.

And now Matthew was missing and the words 'juvenile suicide' and 'drowned' were being bandied about by the police with greater and greater frequency. He didn't believe Matthew had drowned himself, though. And, despite all her tears, neither did Kate. But if Matthew had been aboard the *Tansy* and was so no longer, and he hadn't drowned, where was he? It was a puzzle that tormented him day and night and he was far too obsessed with it to be even remotely cheered by Beryl's kindly meant remarks about black immigration.

Later, though, exhausted after another long and abortive day spent searching for Matthew, this time down around the marshes of Erith, he gave the subject a little more thought. The large-scale black immigration now taking place would, surely, be all to the good where racial ignorance was concerned. The people who, at the moment, reacted so violently when faced with the sight of a dark skin weren't likely to continue doing so when dark skins were no longer a rare oddity but became a common sight. There'd even been a slight change in Deborah Harvey's attitude of late, though that was due to Luke.

He rested on the *Tansy's* oars. On the day Deborah Harvey had visited the house, only to find none of them at home and then to find herself stranded by the apparent defection of her chauffeur, Luke had behaved commendably. For one thing, when he ran into her so unexpectedly at Nellie's, he did not refer to her as the Wicked Witch of the North, and for another, when he found out why she was there, he sprinted off to the garage in Shooter's Hill Road to find out what had happened to her chauffeur. By then, of course, Kate had escorted Deborah Harvey back to their own house. The two of them were so euphoric at the belief that at any moment they would be reunited with Matthew, that there were none of the tensions that usually existed between them.

Luke had returned with the news that Adams had suffered a heart-attack and been taken by ambulance to Lewisham Hospital. He suggested that if Malcolm Lewis, Mr Giles's scoutmaster, became Deborah's temporary chauffeur, driving her back to Kensington in the Bentley, it would solve the problem of how she was to return to her niece's home and of what was to happen to her car, all in one go. And, as he had pointed out, there weren't really any other alternatives. The only other car drivers in the square were Billy and Jack. The thought of Billy at the wheel of a Bentley made even Kate shudder, and Jack wasn't the kind of bloke who had time on his hands for such good deeds, at least not for someone he didn't even know.

'Plus,' Luke had said, gold-flecked brown eyes shining at the thought of riding in the Bentley, 'if I go with them, Malcolm Lewis won't be lonely coming back home on the bus!'

Later, of course, by the time Malcolm Lewis did chauffeur Deborah Harvey home, all euphoria had ebbed. Leon returned from the *Tansy* and Matthew was not with him. At that stage, the police had not yet given their grim opinion as to what they thought had happened to Matthew. Nevertheless, Deborah Harvey had crumpled in a way that was shocking in its unexpectedness.

'She gave way at Nellie's, as well,' Luke said to him when out of Deborah's hearing. 'That was with relief, though, when she thought you were bringing Matthew home.' He had frowned, obviously trying to come to terms with something he found difficult, saying, 'I think the Wicked Witch of the North really cares for Matthew, Dad. I think she loves him, just like we do.'

It was a conclusion that Leon had had no option but to agree with. Since that night, a rather odd bond had been struck between Deborah Harvey and Luke. On the pretext that Malcolm would need company on his return journey, he had travelled to Kensington with her. When, exhausted both physically and emotionally, she needed help in negotiating the steps leading into her niece's exclusive block of flats, he had offered it, as he would have offered it to anyone. He also helped her into the old-fashioned, iron-cage lift and, finally, into her niece's flat.

'Though it isn't a flat like the flats in some of the big houses in Magnolia Hill,' he said later, when he finally returned home. 'It's enormous. All the rooms have big doors that fold back on themselves and open out on to other rooms. And it's filled with statues and dried flowers and overstuffed cushions.'

'What was Matthew's other nasty old aunt like?' Jilly asked, intrigued. 'Is she a wicked witch as well?'

Luke hesitated and then shook his head. Matthew's Aunt Genevre had looked a little witch-like, being tall and thin and bony, but she wasn't witch-like in the way Deborah Harvey was. 'She was quite nice,' he said truthfully, 'but she was a bit embarrassing. She kept staring and staring at me as if she couldn't believe her eyes and then she started asking me so many questions that Malcolm got tired of waiting for me and started off back home on his own.'

'What kind of questions?' Jilly was in her nightdress and had, until Luke's return home, been in bed, supposedly asleep. 'Questions about Matthew?'

Luke shook his head. As he told his mother later, some of the questions had been most peculiar. 'She wanted to know what a Thames waterman was and she wanted to know what tiddlering was. Deborah Harvey had told her that Dad said Matthew used to like tiddlering down on the Surrey Canal towpath, and she didn't have a clue what it meant. She even wanted to know if, 'cos Dad's half West Indian, we ate funny food and if, when he was at home with us, Matthew ate funny food as well.'

It was the sort of question Leon had been asked all his life and which never ceased to test his patience. He was at the point where the Roding met the Thames and as the grey-green water slapped and gurgled round her iron sides he shoved on one oar and heaved on the other, bringing her head round up river.

Ever since Matthew had first disappeared, he had taken leave of absence from work, spending all day, every day, in looking for him. As the police had long since finished with their inspection of the *Tansy*, he took to conducting his searches of the Thames and its tributaries aboard her. For one thing, being aboard her made him feel close to Matthew. It was full of memories of the days when Matthew was small and they had spent such a lot of time on her together, and it was the last place that he knew, without doubt, Matthew had been. He looked out over Barking Reach. He'd promised Jack that tonight he'd call in at the gym so that he could give his opinion of how he thought Zac was going to shape up in the pirate fight that had been fixed for him, and to offer any thoughts he had as to fight tactics. At any other time it was a task he would have been looking forward to, but not now; not when Kate was crying herself to sleep every night; not when there wasn't the slightest clue as to Matthew's whereabouts.

When he was safely out of the main shipping lane he again shipped oars, staring sightlessly across to Greenhithe's grey shoreline. Where was his beloved, adopted son? He had to be somewhere, but where? In the name of God, *where*?

Chapter Fourteen

It was a question Matthew could have answered only very approximately. He was somewhere on the North Atlantic, he knew that. And he knew that he was heading for the South Atlantic, but where his final destination was to be, he could only guess. Venezuela? Brazil? The Spanish crew aboard the *Orion* seemed to think it a great joke that he didn't know and teased him unmercifully whenever he asked. 'Perhaps around the world, *amigo*! Perhaps to the south pole!'

He eased himself into a more comfortable position on a heavy coil of rope. He wasn't a willing passenger aboard the *Orion*. He had spent the first few nights after he ran away from St Osyth's aboard the dear old *Tansy*, trying to sort out the complex emotions and anxieties that had suddenly descended on him like a terrifying black cloud. During the day he roamed his old haunts down by the docks, revelling in the familiar sights and sounds and smells, all the time trying to drum up the courage to return home and face up to, and explain, his having run away.

The *Orion* was berthed at Fresh Wharf and was busy unloading when he nipped aboard her for a look around. He found a nice quiet corner far aft and fell asleep and, through all the manoeuvring of the boat as it re-loaded and turned around, its captain eager to be away before lighterage fees dug into the profits, he stayed asleep. By the time he was found and rudely shaken awake, there was a scattering of buoys, the scanning flash of a lighthouse and, in the gathering darkness, no other sign of land. The Spanish captain had refused absolutely to return his ship to the estuary and to hand him over to the Thames river police. His unwelcome passenger wasn't a small child. When he was a similar age, he'd been sailing the seas of the world as a deck-hand, and he saw no reason why, for convenience sake, Matthew shouldn't now gain similar experience.

'We back in Thames four, five weeks,' he said when Matthew had protested, appalled. *'No hay que llorar!* One mustn't cry! No harm done, eh?'

'But no one will know where I am!'

At the thought of the scenes that would now be taking place at both his school and his home, Matthew grew dizzy with horror. When he was aboard the *Tansy*, no one knew where he was either, but that had been different. Then he was in familiar surroundings and only a half an hour away from home. Even more importantly, he'd known he was going to set his mum and dad's minds at rest within hours or, at the most, within another day. But not to be able to let them know for another four or five weeks that he was all right! What on earth would they be thinking? They would be worried sick. They might even think he was dead!

'Can't you radio the Port of London authorities?' he had pleaded. 'Can't you ask them to get a message to my dad telling him where I am and when I'll be back? My dad's a Thames waterman, they won't mind!'

Captain Juarez had shaken his head. 'No,' he had said unequivocally. *'No es posible.'*

He hadn't explained why. If his stowaway couldn't work out for himself that the Port of London authorities would mind very much that a ship's captain had overlooked the presence of a twelve-year-old boy aboard his ship and would want to know why he hadn't immediately taken action to return him to land, then he wasn't going to help him do so. If he docked in Rio within fourteen days he would receive a bonus. If he didn't, and he certainly wouldn't do so if he turned his ship about, he would not receive a bonus. The matter was as simple as that.

'*Lo importante es llegar a tiempo,*' he had said to his crew. 'The important thing is to arrive on time.'

Matthew knew there had been some talk among the men of putting him ashore when they called at Lisbon. 'He could go to the British Embassy,' Jaime, a young crew member who had taken a shine to him, said. 'That would be OK for him, eh?' Matthew didn't know whether to be disappointed or relieved when the general consensus of opinion was that this would not be OK as they, as well as their captain, might fall foul of the law for not having returned to port the instant they became aware they had an unintended passenger aboard. Matthew, too, didn't know how, if he did turn up at the British Embassy, he would be returned to England. Would his parents have to reimburse the cost of his return journey? They wouldn't be able to do so. Only his aunts had that kind of money, and at the thought of his aunts being approached by a government department with a demand for money to cover the cost of his fare from Lisbon to London, his heart nearly failed him. It would be much more straightforward to stay aboard the *Orion* until she returned, in four or five weeks' time, to London. That way, though he would have put people through a lot of worry, at least he wouldn't have put them to any expense.

With that decision made and with the knowledge that there was absolutely nothing he could do about the situation, he resigned himself to enduring it. It wasn't hard. In fact, if it hadn't been for the thought of how his mum and dad would be worrying about him, he would have been in seventh heaven. He loved being afloat. He knew every bend and loop of the

Thames, but he had never been out to open sea. Not until now. Why couldn't people understand that great rivers and seas were magical places? His dad did, of course. His dad had served aboard an escort ship in the war, sailing the very ocean he was now sailing, but doing so across to North America, not curving south as he was now doing, via Madeira and Tenerife. Later on in the war he had served on a ship protecting the Arctic convoys on their Murmansk and Archangel run and, off Norway, had been torpedoed and fished from the sea by the Germans to spend the rest of the War as a POW.

He hugged his knees, looking out over the glittering vastness of the ocean. He loved his dad. He was the best dad in the world. He wasn't his biological dad, though, so he hadn't inherited his love of being afloat from him in the way that people inherited the colour of their eyes or hair.

He clasped his hands around his knees a little tighter. Sometimes he thought things would be simpler if his dad *were* his biological dad and he, like Luke and Jilly and Johnny, was brown-eyed and dusky-skinned. That way he would never have gone to St Osyth's and no one would have expected him to become a lawyer. His dad would simply have taken him down to Waterman's Hall, near Billingsgate Market, and had him bound to him as an apprenticed lighterman. He would have had to vow an oath of loyalty to his 'Sovereign, Present Company, Future Employers and Master' and to promise to 'Dwell and Serve upon the River Thames' and to 'Learn his Art,' and his dad, who would have been his master, would have had to swear to 'Teach, Instruct, Provide Meat, Drink, Apparel and Lodging for him for the next five years'.

He knew all the words, just as if he had already been apprenticed, and he knew lots of other things apprentices had to know, too. All things his dad had taught him. He knew the tide times and phases of the moon, the names of points, reaches, bridges, tidal sets, parts of a barge and how to get to all the different wharves, docks and watermen's stairs. There were lots of other things to learn, too, of course, and he was looking forward to learning them. Ever since his dad had first come into his life, marrying his mum and becoming Daddy-Leon to him, he had wanted nothing more than to be just like him. And being like him meant becoming that most wonderful thing in the world, a prince of the river – a Thames waterman.

The trouble was that his real dad hadn't been a Thames waterman. Until the war had broken out and he had joined the Air Force, his real dad had been destined to take over the family business, the Harvey Construction Company. And that was what his aunts, and his mum and dad, wanted *him* to do, also. They wanted him to become a lawyer first, for, as his great-aunt Deborah once said to him, a good grounding in law was an enormous advantage to a businessman. He hadn't understood then that she meant *he* should obtain a good grounding in law. That realization only came in the lecture given by his school's careers master, and it was so sudden, and so over-powering, he thought he was going to die beneath its weight.

Businessmen wore suits, collars and ties and ate formal lunches with other businessmen and worked indoors in stuffy offices. He didn't want to do those things. He wanted to get up at the crack of dawn and to see, from the Thames, the sun rising over Barrow Deep and Mucking Flats. He wanted to wear a Guernsey and a duffel-coat and knee-high sailing boots. He wanted to eat doorstep-sized fried egg and bacon sandwiches for his breakfast and to have a lunch of boiled beef and carrots, or steak and kidney pudding, or pie and mash, in Sid's Dining Rooms, Stepney.

He raised his face to a sun far hotter than any English sun. Though the Thames couldn't possibly be in his blood and his bones, Harveys having no connection at all with the river and, until she married Leon, his mother having none either, he felt as if it were in his blood and his bones. And it wasn't only this deep, deep feeling and longing. He wasn't clever enough to become a lawyer and to run an international company. His mum and dad and his aunts didn't know that, though, and he lived in dread of the day they would find out. Especially he dreaded the thought of his great-aunt Deborah finding out. So far at school, because he was quiet in class and because he always tried hard, he had been able to bluff things out and hadn't, as yet, received any poor end-of-term reports. Things would change, though, when it came to school-leaving examinations and entry examinations for university.

A familiar feeling of sick helplessness churned in his stomach. He didn't want to let anyone down – and yet, even if he was capable of not doing so, he didn't want to take over his father's family's construction business. He just wanted to do what *he* wanted to do, what he enjoyed doing, what he was capable of doing and could do well. When they had docked in Madeira, Jaime had taken him ashore for an hour or two, to see Funchal. '*Que paisaje tan hermoso!*' he had said, indicating a soaring back-drop of silver-green, silver-tawny, silver-violet splendour, gashed by ravines. 'A beautiful landscape, eh?'

Matthew wondered if his dad had ever been to Madeira and if he, too, had seen gaily painted sledges being pulled up and down the steeply cobbled streets by oxen, and the odd-looking black fish many people carried, its body curled in a loop over their arms, its tail stuck conveniently through its mouth.

By the time the *Orion* called in at Tenerife, he and Jaime had become good friends. When he woke suddenly in the middle of the night to find a deck-hand he barely knew trying half-nakedly to get into his narrow bunk with him, it was Jaime who had woken at his cry of alarm and who shouted and yelled at the man in question, threatening to lay violent hands on him unless he returned to his own bunk, *pronto*.

He squinted his eyes against the sun's glare. There would be no more ports of call now; even though he didn't know which part of South America they were making for, he knew enough about geography to know that. There was an increase in activity at the far end of the deck and he rose to his feet, knowing he was soon going to be asked to pitch in and lend a hand. Not for the first time it occurred to him that the scrape he had got himself into was one that would have been more typical of Luke. Not that Luke had any longings to run away to sea, it was just that if there was any trouble to be found, it was usually Luke who found it. He dug his hands deep in the pockets of his short school trousers, wandering in the direction of his shipmates, wondering why it was that no one in his family seemed to realize it was Luke, not he, who was the clever one. Perhaps it was because Luke didn't do well at school, but that was only because he found everything so easy and got so bored. One thing was certain: it was Luke who should have gone to St Osyth's, not himself. Luke would have enjoyed the prospect and the challenge of studying something complicated like law. His fists clenched in his pockets. Without a shadow of a doubt he knew that he would never do so. Not even to please his mum and dad. A tight knot of determination replaced the feeling of sick helplessness. Not even to please his great-aunt Deborah!

'The cook wants helping peeling potatoes,' Jaime said to him as he approached. 'Sorry, *amigo*.'

Matthew gave a lopsided grin and shrugged. He didn't mind peeling potatoes. If only his mum and dad knew where he was, he wouldn't mind anything. He wondered if, when the *Orion* reached wherever it was she was sailing to, he would be able to go ashore and perhaps, with money borrowed from Jaime, send a cable home. That way he wouldn't be worrying so very, very much about his mum and dad. That way they would, at least, know that he was all right.

Jaime, too, was wondering what was going to happen when the *Orion* sailed into port. Captain Juarez had already made it clear to him that he was not to take Matthew ashore, as he had at Madeira and Tenerife. 'Better if no one knows he ever left England,' he had said practically. 'That way we can be blamed for nothing, eh? Whatever our young friend says when he does return home, it will simply be a fanciful story. A boy's story. A story without corroboration.'

The problem troubling Jaime was one no one else seemed to be worrying about, especially not Captain Juarez. What if, in their home port of Rio de Janeiro, their orders for their next trip were not a return to London? Such things happened. On the kinds of ships they sailed, they happened all the time. What would happen to his young friend then? Would Juarez dump him in Rio or take him with them to Cape Town or Lagos or to wherever else it was they were bound? That his young friend's fate was so very problematical was a very troubling thought, *Jesu-cristo!* It was a very troubling thought indeed!

Chapter Fifteen

Jack's bright yellow Cadillac snarled into life and seconds later was out of the square and haring along Magnolia Terrace towards the heath. Jack usually got a great kick out of his car. There wasn't another one like it in the whole of south-east London and it was a certain attention-getter and head-turner. For all he cared at the moment, however, he could have been driving a battered pre-war Austin. From where he and Christina had started out, how on earth had they reached the situation they were now in? He loved her, for Christ's sake! His hands tightened on the wheel until his knuckles showed white. He loved her, yet he had treated her as if she were a whore. It was no wonder that the instant he released his hold of her she half-scrambled, half-fell off their bed and began flinging hastily grabbed clothes into a suitcase. Mere minutes later, her face still stained by tears of protest and pain, she hurtled out of the house and, hard as he tried, he hadn't seen her since.

He knew where she was, of course. Hell, the entire square knew not only that she had left him, but that she had gone to her mother's in Greenwich. Whether it was Hettie who saw her leave the house with her suitcase and who later spoke to Eva, or some other busybody, he didn't know and didn't care. He swung the Cadillac on to one of the narrow, unpavemented roads that criss-crossed the heath, heading towards Greenwich

213

and the river. He was too dazed with disbelief at his own actions to go after her when she walked out, and, besides, he knew that if he had done so, it would have resulted in a public scene, with heaven only knew who listening in on it. He tried to see her, of course, but when he drove down to Eva's, she refused to come to the door to talk to him and Eva, a protective Jewish mother to the hilt, refused to let him over the doorstep. He was furious with her, furious with Christina, and even more furious with himself. Hadn't he always known that, because of her history, heavy-handed tactics would never get him anywhere with Tina? He groaned and slewed the Cadillac into Croom's Hill, speeding down into Greenwich. Christina's history was vile. As a young girl she saw her father and brother dragged from their home by Nazi thugs and shot dead in the street. What she had suffered at Nazi hands she had never told him – or anyone. She had, though, been scarred emotionally and mentally by her experiences. He knew that from the first moment he met her, and, knowing it, he vowed no one would ever hurt her again.

Uncaring of the local speed restrictions and heavy traffic, he swerved into Greenwich High Street. Well, he'd blown that vow with a vengeance! If it was possible for a woman to be raped by her husband, then he'd raped Tina. And what had been gained by it? Nothing. Absolutely bloody nothing! At high speed he passed Eva's husband's butcher's shop and then three minutes later, after several right and left turns, he screeched to a halt outside a small, trim Georgian terraced house. With luck, this time she'd speak to him and he'd be able to persuade her to return home. That way he would then be able to give other things his attention. The opening of The 21, for instance, and Zac's forthcoming fight, and the little matter of Archie's threats of a show of violence if he, Jack, didn't toe the line.

Grimly, having no intention of toeing Archie's line, or anyone else's, he strode across the pavement and up to the brass-knockered front door.

'*Wie geht's?*' Eva said pleasantly, opening the door to him. 'How are you, Jack? It is not very nice, is it, this situation?'

Jack didn't bother to reply. That the situation was not very nice was self-evident and he was in no mood for meaningless generalities. 'I want to see Christina,' he said bluntly, putting one foot in the doorway so that it couldn't be closed in his face.

Eva obligingly opened it a little wider so that he could easily enter. '*Sie ist nicht hier,*' she said, the ring of truth in her voice. Her eyes held his, deeply troubled. 'Vas is the matter, Jack? Vy are you and Christina no longer happy? Vy does she spend all day out valking by herself, returning vith blue shadows beneath her eyes and not a vord for me, or for George?'

George was Eva's husband, a gentleman his friends thought had fallen well and truly on his feet when he had persuaded Eva to marry him. Jack could well understand why. Even in her mid-fifties, and after enduring the horror of Hitler's Germany, Eva was a strikingly beautiful woman. Like her daughter, it was a beauty that was bone-deep, etched in the fine sculpturing of her cheekbones and jaw, emphasized by flawless skin and eyes the colour of amethysts.

With the door now wide open to him, he didn't bother entering. If Christina wasn't there, there was no point.

Eva touched the eau-de-nil silk scarf that was tied rakishly around her throat, adding elegance to a white, short-sleeved sweater and a straight, kick-pleated, navy skirt. 'Vill you not tell me vat has gone wrong between the two of you?' she asked in deep concern. 'Is it because there is no child—'

'For Christ's sake, Eva!' Jack made no attempt to hide his angry reaction. Things were bad enough without their childlessness being dragged into it. He wondered what Eva would say if he told her it was hardly surprising there was no baby when Christina never wanted him near her in bed any more! Instead he said tautly, 'I'm not sure what the hell it is that's going wrong between me and Tina, Eva, but I'm going to put it right, I promise you that.'

Eva believed him. As she watched him stride back to his distinctive American car, his dark hair as tightly curled in the nape of his neck as a gypsy's, his short-sleeved shirt emphasizing arm muscles of stevedore proportions, she just hoped that he would put things right soon. If he didn't, and if Christina continued with her present inexplicable behaviour, refusing to even see him, then there was no telling where it might all end, except that it would end in tears. With eyes dark with anxiety she watched him slide behind the Cadillac's wheel and gun the engine into life. Though he had been angrily exasperated by the very idea, she was certain the root of the trouble was his and Christina's continuing childlessness. What answer, though, was there to that problem? If God didn't send babies, he didn't send them. With a heavy heart she closed the door and went back into her kitchen. She would bake. Baking always comforted and soothed her. She would make *Apfelkuchen* and *Schokoladenkuchen* – the apple flan because it had been Christina's favourite when she was a child, the chocolate cake because, like all Englishmen, George adored it.

Christina stood beside the tall iron railings that protected the playground of Maze Hill School from the busy pavement. The infant class were out at play, shouting and shrieking with high spirits as they exuberantly let off steam. Some of the little girls had bows in their hair, either at the end of pigtails or anchored with hair-slides and hair-grips. One little girl, whose mother had obviously handmade her red gingham-checked dress, sported an outsize hair ribbon of the same material; another had her cardigan buttoned up wrongly and white ankle socks that half-disappeared beneath her heels.

She wondered how she would dress her little girl, if she had one. Any child she had would be bound to be dark-haired for both she and Jack had dark hair. Bright colours, then, would suit their daughter. And like the mother who had so lovingly made the red gingham dress, she, too, would make all her daughter's clothes herself. Ice-cold fingers of reality squeezed her heart. She was never going to have a little girl to make pretty clothes for. She and Jack were never going to have a child. Bleakly she turned away from the railings, not even sure if she and Jack had a marriage any more. How could they have when he was turning into a frighteningly aggressive stranger?

She began to walk aimlessly in the direction of the river. She'd always known there was a side to Jack she knew very little about. The blatantly roustabout side of him, the side of him that had thrived on the dangers of being a commando in war-torn Italy and Greece. The side of him that loved boxing or, as he always referred to it, 'the fight game'. Though it was never spoken of between them, she knew that some of his business dealings were not always legal. Jack loved a bit of recklessness in life, a bit of danger. In a bizarre way, that was what had attracted her to him. He was so unlike the kind of respectable, middle-class, professional man she would, if it hadn't been for the war, have been expected to marry. And he had sex appeal. He had lots and lots of sex appeal.

She crossed busy Trafalgar Road, heading for the riverside walkway that ran in front of the Royal Naval College. Had their love for each other been a case of opposites attracting? And was that attraction, where Jack was concerned, waning? If so, it would explain why he didn't want them to adopt a baby, and it would explain the amount of time he was now spending with Mavis. She stood by Greenwich Pier, gazing unseeingly across the broad, glittering expanse of the Thames. The brutish way he had taken her on the day she left him – was that the kind of sex Mavis enjoyed? And was that why he had treated her in such a manner? Because he had been thinking of Mavis and wishing it were Mavis he was with?

'Are yer gettin' on the boat dahn to Westminster, or ain't yer?' the man selling tickets asked. ''Cos if you ain't, yer standin' in the way of those that are!'

Christina blinked, feeling oddly disorientated. What was the man saying to her? And why was she on the pier? A feeling of panic bubbled up into her throat. What on earth was happening to her? Was she so unhappy that she was beginning to lose her mind?

'Come on, dear. On the boat or out of the way,' the ticket-collector said, wondering if she was drunk. She didn't look the kind of woman who would be drunk, but these days there was never any telling.

Christina took a hasty step backwards and bumped into a small child. She spun round to apologize, gazing down into an aggrieved little face.

'Are you all right, Judith?' the smartly dressed, middle-aged woman holding the child's hand was asking, though not with much concern. 'Has the lady hurt you?'

'I'm so sorry . . . I'd no idea she was behind me . . .' Christina felt dreadful. The child was only four or five years old, and if they had been standing a little nearer the edge of the pier, she could easily have knocked her into the Thames!

'Oh, don't worry,' the woman said, satisfied no great harm had been done. 'If she hadn't been lagging behind me it wouldn't have happened. It's a nuisance taking her anywhere. She never keeps up. Her other auntie, the one we're visiting today, says exactly the same. There's no pleasure in taking her out. None at all.'

Throughout this diatribe, Christina and Judith had continued to stare at each other. No longer aggrieved, Judith's eyes were big and dark and solemn. Far too solemn for a child her age. There was another expression in them, too. An expression of unhappiness, and stoical acceptance of that unhappiness, that spoke straight to Christina's heart.

'You're her auntie?' she asked the woman, her eyes not leaving Judith's.

Judith's aunt nodded, quite happy to spend a few minutes chatting. 'For my sins,' she said caustically. 'Her mother was my youngest sister. She never had much common sense and when she was eighteen she ran off with a Bermondsey Jew-boy. He left her a year later to scarper off to Israel with a girl of his own faith, and I don't suppose he even knows Babs is dead.' Her mouth tightened, scarlet lipstick seeping into runnels around her lips. 'It was pleurisy that did for her. "Look after Judith, for me," she said before she died and so here I am, having to take her with me everywhere I go.' She waited for the sympathetic noises this little speech usually met with, but none came.

Christina didn't even make a commiserating clicking noise with her tongue. Instead she said, 'You don't have to take Judith with you today, if you don't want to. You could leave her with me. You could leave her with me every day.'

The woman's jaw dropped and alarm flashed through her eyes. 'How could I do that? I don't know you!' She yanked Judith closer to her, as if frightened Christina was going to make off with her then and there.

There was interest mixed with her alarm, though, and, seeing it, Christina knew that if she could ease the woman's conscience she'd be only too glad to have her look after Judith for her. She concealed the fierce urgency she was feeling in order not to alarm the woman more, saying persuasively, 'I'm Christina

Robson. I live in Magnolia Square, just off the heath.' She hesitated for a second and then said, 'My husband, Jack, has a boxing gym in Magnolia Hill, above The Swan public house.'

The alarm was fast fading from the woman's face. 'The Jack Robson who drives a big yellow American car?'

Christina nodded and held her breath. It was a gamble, mentioning Jack's name. She'd done so because he was such a well-known local figure it was possible the woman would know of him, but whether, if she did so, she would regard him as being respectable enough to serve as a reference was quite another matter.

'Well then, that's all right,' the woman said. 'He was in Italy in 1944, wasn't he? My brother took part in the Allied assault on Monte Cassino and I remember him saying Jack Robson had been out there.'

'Yer ferry's comin' in!' the ticket-collector called out.

The woman looked towards the boat that had just docked and then back at Christina and finally down at Judith.

Reading her mind, trying to put the last of her doubts at rest, Christina said persuasively, 'Tell me how long you're going to be and we'll meet up with you at the jellied eel shop.' The jellied eel shop was just across the road from the pier. If she and Judith arrived there before Judith's aunt, they could have a cup of tea whilst waiting for her to arrive.

'I don't know,' the woman said, obviously sorely tempted. 'She is my responsibility after all and—'

'Don't want to go to Auntie Flo's,' a little voice suddenly said, deciding the matter for her. 'Want to stay with the lady.' And to prove her point, Judith moved from her aunt's side and, standing beside Christina, slipped her hand into hers.

It was a moment Christina knew she would never forget. Joy

surged along her veins. It was as if, in that one moment, her old childless life had come to an end and she now stood on the brink of a whole new existence.

'Oh, well then,' the woman said, shrugging her shoulders dismissively, 'if that's the way Judith wants it . . .'

'What time at the jellied eel shop?' Christina could barely force her voice to be steady. She and Judith were going to have a wonderful time together, and there would be lots of other wonderful times, too, for Judith's aunt obviously found her an encumbrance she could well do without. Perhaps she would be able to look after Judith every day. Perhaps, one day, she might even . . .

Before she could even finish formulating her last dizzying thought, Judith's aunt was giving Judith a perfunctory kiss and telling her to be a good girl. 'And don't be cheeky to Mrs Robson and don't wee-wee your knickers,' she added and then, transferring her attention to Christina, she said, 'Not that she's likely to be cheeky – she's too moody and sulky for that kind of behaviour. I'll be back four o'clockish if that's all right with you.'

Christina nodded, her hand tightly clasping Judith's, marvelling at how little her aunt knew her. Judith wasn't moody or sulky. She was unhappy, and no wonder, when her father had deserted her and her mother had died. She remembered her own deep pain when, through the war years and with her father and brother dead, she had been separated from her mother and grandmother, not knowing where they were or even if they were still alive.

'I don't know your name,' she said now as Judith's aunt turned to go, 'and we should exchange addresses in case one of us has an accident and can't meet up at four o'clock.'

'Madge Dracup,' Judith's aunt said over her shoulder, not wanting to dally and miss the ferry and clearly not remotely interested in Christina's address, 'and I live at fifty-six New Hyland Street.'

'My name isn't Dracup,' Judith said, her face upturned trustingly to Christina's. 'My name is Levy, but auntie doesn't like it.' Christina looked down into an elfin face framed by hair as dark and as satin-smooth as her own. '*I* like it,' she said, feeling as if her heart were going to burst. 'Levy is a pretty name. It's a Jewish name and lots of Jewish names are pretty.'

In happy companionship they began to walk from the pier towards the short road that led to Greenwich Park.

'Do you know other Jewish names?' Judith asked, intrigued. She had heard the word 'Jewish' spoken many times by her Auntie Madge and Auntie Flo, but never in a nice way; never in a way she could understand.

For a second Christina could barely speak and then, with tears stinging her eyes as she thought of all the childhood friends who, unlike herself, had not survived Hitler's Germany, she said, 'Yes. Yes Judith, I know lots. And I know lots of Jewish stories too. Would you like to hear one about a lady with the same name as yourself? A lady called Judith?'

Judith nodded, her eyes rounding. Her mummy had told her nursery rhymes but she hadn't told her stories. 'Can I call you auntie?' she asked as they began to cross the road. 'Can I call you Auntie Magic Lady?'

Zac strolled down Magnolia Hill towards Lewisham High Street, his thumbs hooked in the front pockets of his Levi's. He wasn't a bloke to brood over things, but he was brooding now. He knew, when he walked to freedom through Parkhurst Prison's high security gates, that he was going to have to play safe for a bit before haring off to New Zealand, but things were getting a little complicated. Not so complicated he was going to change his plans completely; he couldn't do that. New Zealand was where his share of the robbery he'd been jailed for was safely stashed. He had to go to New Zealand and, from all that his Kiwi mates had told him about it, once there he was going to want to stay.

The initial problem had always been how he was to get there, for there was certainly no point in getting there if the police were watching him in the hope he would lead them to unrecovered money. Whether they were suspicious that he knew where his share was waiting for him, or whether they believed him to be as ignorant of its whereabouts as they were themselves, he had no way of knowing. It was, however, a risk he had long ago decided he had no intention of running, which was why Jack Robson's offer of a billet and boxing work, all within spitting distance of the Thames, had fitted so well into his plans.

When he left Britain, he was going to do so inconspicuously, and the most inconspicuous way possible was as a deck-hand aboard a cargo boat. He already knew from conversations with Leon which were the docks used by boats from Australia and New Zealand, and he'd had dummy seaman's papers stowed in his wallet for over two weeks.

With springy athletic precision in his stride, he rounded the corner at the bottom of the hill, pondering the two hiccups in his plans, one of them minor, the other roaringly major. From the far side of the High Street, old Charlie called out a greeting to him and he grinned and waved in response, his thoughts still on the first of his problems. The last thing he wanted to do, before sailing down the Thames bound for the Southern Hemisphere, was to attract police attention. Yes, that was exactly what Jack's plans for him were likely to do, for the rozzers would love nothing better than to be able to nab him for taking part in a pirate fight.

Aware of a very interested gaze from an exceedingly nubile

young woman, he ignored it, frowning slightly. He didn't like letting Jack down. He liked Jack. And under other circumstances he'd have relished an illegit match. There was nothing like an illegit fight, with lots of his mates' money riding on his back, for generating an atmosphere of almost unbearable fizz and excitement. As it was, though . . . He crossed the road to the tiny traffic island dominated by Lewisham's clock tower. The risk of the fight being busted by the police was one he didn't want to take. Jack had been ashen with frustrated anger, but Jack's anger hadn't budged him from his decision. He had a whole new life waiting for him in New Zealand, and he wasn't going to put it at risk for the sake of making Jack, and Jack's mates, a bundle of money.

He paused for a second by the clock tower, traffic speeding past him on either side. His other problem wasn't one that could be so easily solved. Carrie was avoiding him like the plague. He looked over at the market stalls stretching from just across from where he was standing, all the way up the High Street in the direction of Catford. It wasn't because she wasn't as crazy about him as he was crazy about her, he knew that. Rather, it was because she *was* so crazy about him that she was going to every length possible not to be alone in his company. The trouble was, it was a ploy he couldn't allow her to carry on indefinitely. There simply wasn't the time for it, for when he left for New Zealand he wanted to do so knowing she would join him there, that travelling a more direct route than himself, she might even be there, waiting for him when he arrived.

With several female heads turning admiringly to watch him, he strolled across the road. The Jennings' fruit and veg stall was one place Carrie couldn't escape from him, and he visited it two, sometimes three times a day. 'I need lots of fresh fruit and veg to keep my strength up for the ring,' he said to her when she asked him what the heck he was playing at, buying enough fruit and veg every day to sink a ship.

His reasoning had cut no ice with her at all. 'Then bloomin' well buy them somewhere else!' she said, her hands thrust deep in her pinny pockets as if afraid he was going to seize hold of them. 'Nibbo sells fruit and veg. Why don't you buy it off him, for a change?'

'I'm not in love with Nibbo,' he said, laughter in his voice and undisguised heat in his eyes. 'But I am in love with you, and you're in love with me. Why try to pretend otherwise?'

She flushed scarlet and was saved from answering by a customer irately rattling an empty carrier bag and demanding to be served with a stone of potatoes.

'Hello there, Mr Hemingway,' Ruth Giles said pleasantly, crossing over from the market side of the High Street to the clock tower's traffic island. 'Have you seen the Coronation Day decorations the council have begun putting up everywhere? Lewisham is going to look very festive, isn't it?' Despite the light-heartedness of her words, she didn't look light-hearted. There were heavy shadows beneath her eyes and he suspected that, like many other Magnolia Square residents, she was worrying herself sick over the mystery of young Matthew Harvey's whereabouts.

'It's going to look smashing,' he said, wondering if he would still be in the country by the time Queen Elizabeth was crowned.

Ruth smiled and continued on her way, her pearl necklace, plum-coloured twin-set and plaid skirt looking oddly formal amongst the headscarves and cheap and cheerful get-ups of her fellow shoppers.

Zac negotiated his way between a box that had once held apples and a giant bag packed with onions. He was going to get Carrie into bed with him before the week was out if he had to throw her over his shoulder and stride off with her, cave-man fashion, in order to be able to do so. Grinning at the thought and looking forward to it exceedingly, he strolled to where she was captive behind a mountainous display of crisp, fresh produce.

The instant she saw him approaching she froze, but not in horror. He could practically see her heart beginning to pound and her blood beginning to race. His own heart was pounding with the same kind of intense excitement he felt when he stepped into the ring on a big fight night. He loved Carrie Collins. He loved her voluptuous curves, the wild tumble of her gypsy-dark hair, her totally unstriven-for sensuousness. Most of all he loved her blazing honesty and her warm, generously loving heart. He stepped towards her, noticing the bruised fruit she would never try to sell and that lay at her feet discarded. Something tightened within him. Carrie wouldn't have to stand amongst rotting fruit when they were in New Zealand. Once in New Zealand they would have money enough to live like royalty. In New Zealand, Carrie would never have to work again.

'Hello sweetheart,' he said, uncaring as to whether anyone was within earshot or not. 'Let's close the stall down and spend the day on the river. There's a lot I have to tell you and it's going to change your life. It's going to change it for ever.'

'I couldn't believe what I was hearing,' Jack said bitterly to Mavis. 'The match is all arranged and word of it is out. There's no way it can be called off.'

'And no way, without Hemingway fighting for you, that you can make on it?' Mavis asked, unable to bring herself to refer to Zac by his Christian name.

'Hell, no!' They were on the North Downs, sitting on grass at the edge of woodland, with a magnificent view of the Weald stretching before them, the Cadillac parked on a little-used country road some thirty yards away. 'I'm going to have to replace Zac with Big Jumbo and, as no one will expect Big Jumbo to win the fight anyway, there's no way money can be made by him throwing it.'

'And no way money can be made by him winning it?'

Jack plucked a long blade of grass. 'There's an outside chance, I suppose,' he said glumly, 'but the idea of the match was that we wouldn't be gambling on an outside chance. The idea was we'd be gambling on a certainty.'

Mavis slid down on to her side, resting her weight on one elbow, regarding him thoughtfully. 'And you still don't know who's going to be in the other corner?'

Jack chewed on the blade of grass, not looking towards her but gazing out over a heat-hazed view of small woods and fields and meandering streams. 'Nope,' he said, his thoughts too full of Christina for him to be overly concerned. 'That's the trouble with having a middle-man for illegit fights. You often have to go in to them blind.'

'Crikey!' Mavis said expressively, noting how springily his hair curled in the nape of his neck and how suntanned his skin was, so suntanned she ached to brush it with her lips. 'That's a bit of a risk, isn't it?'

With his hands loosely clasped around his knees, Jack looked towards her, saying wryly, 'It wouldn't be if Zac was fighting.'

Mavis thought of Zac's powerful physique and the way he hammered the speed-ball in the gym and, though she hated his guts for the way he was causing chaos in Carrie's life, she knew that Jack was right to have such confidence in his abilities. Any opponent of Zac Hemingway's would be swaying on his feet like a tree in high wind before the first round was even halfway over.

'What about the club?' she asked, changing the subject, her

fingertips burning with the need to reach out and touch him. 'Are we still opening Friday?'

With great difficulty, he thrust his thoughts of Christina to the rear of his mind. Wherever she was at the moment, she'd be back at her mother's by the time he and Mavis were back in London and, after he'd dropped Mavis off in Magnolia Square, he'd drive straight down to Greenwich to see her. For the moment, however, he was out in the countryside enjoying a breather he badly needed.

'We do, indeed, still open on Friday,' he said, his devil-damn-me grin back on his face, 'so I suggest that for the rest of the day we play, because there's not going to be many more chances to do so. What do you fancy, love? A pub lunch in Chevening or a picnic by the river at Edenbridge?'

'I fancy you,' Mavis said starkly, deciding to risk everything and go for broke. 'And I think it's high time I had a little of what I fancy, don't you?' And, her eyes holding his, she slowly and purposefully began undoing the buttons of her blouse.

Chapter Sixteen

Daisy sat morosely by the pond in Greenwich Park, waiting for Billy. The pond was their regular meeting place for, if Billy had simply wandered up the square and called for her at number four, the entire world would have known he was regularly doing so and that their relationship had undergone a radical change in character, and Daisy didn't want the entire world to know. She was an intensely private girl, and she didn't want the likes of Hettie Collins and Nellie Miller discussing the pros and cons of her and Billy becoming sweethearts, and she certainly didn't want Lettie Deakin chin-wagging about it to all and sundry in The Swan.

In her school uniform, her arms folded around her knees, she sat on the slightly rising ground on the south side of the pond, deep in unhappy thought. Over the last few weeks life had done nothing but grow more and more complicated. She and Billy ought to have been deliriously happy, but they weren't. How could they be, when the mystery of Matthew's disappearance grew deeper and deeper with each passing day? Tears stung the backs of her eyes. As if the agony of not knowing where Matthew was, and if he were safe or not, wasn't bad enough, worry over him had triggered off all sorts of other unexpected miseries. Her mum and dad, for instance. Her mum and dad never argued, or not that she'd ever been aware of. Her dad had the sunniest nature imaginable, and her mum was serenity itself. Now, however, her dad's lovely dusky face was crumpled with lines of worry and fatigue. He'd begun wondering if, having run away from St Osyth's, Matthew couldn't face the thought of returning home and confronting them; that, irrationally, he felt too ashamed to do so.

It was a line of reasoning Billy was unable to understand, but then Billy didn't know Matthew like she and her dad did. Ever since he was seven years old, Matthew had been a boarder at St Osyth's, and as a consequence no one in the square really knew him, not like they knew her and Luke and Jilly and Johnny. And what they didn't know was how sensitive Matthew was. It would be quite typical of Matthew to feel that his running away from school was behaviour that would have hurt his parents and, though even she couldn't quite understand why he should be hiding away for so long, stewing over it, it wasn't beyond the realms of possibility that that was exactly what he was doing.

It wasn't her dad's hope that this was the explanation that was causing so much added distress, though. Rather it was the inexplicable sense of tension that had suddenly sprung up between her mum and dad. As far as she and Luke could make out, it was all to do with their mum having gone down to St Osyth's to speak to Matthew's headmaster by herself, and without telling their dad that she was going to do so.

'Didn't you think I was capable of handling the situation?' he said to their mum with a bitterness in his voice none of them had ever heard before. 'Did you think it might be better if he could forget about Matthew having a half-caste West Indian for an adoptive dad?'

Neither she nor Luke were able to believe what they were hearing. Their dad's colour had never been an issue between their parents, yet their mum hadn't denied the allegation. All she had said was, 'I went on the spur of the moment after you had left for work, Leon. I went because I thought I was acting for the best,' and then, to both their horror and their dad's, she had covered her face with her hands, her shoulders shaking as sobs had convulsed her. Their dad had put his arms around her and comforted her, of course, but there had been something strange in the atmosphere ever since, an extra tension that was almost unbearable. And now, as if that weren't bad enough, there was a similar tension between herself and Billy.

'Why don't you want people to know I'm your boyfriend?' he asked, perplexed. 'Why does it matter if anyone sees me giving you a lift to and from school?'

'Because I'll get teased about you being a scrap-metal merchant,' she wanted to say and, because she didn't want to hurt his feelings, did not say. 'Because I'll get hassle from my teachers for not concentrating single-mindedly on my school-work.'

What would happen when she went to university? Would he be understanding about the number of years she would be away from Magnolia Square and about the long periods of time during which they wouldn't be able to see each other?

She hugged her knees a little tighter. She could well imagine what his response to the last little problem would be. He would take time off from his business and, if she was lucky enough to be at Somerville, would drive up to Somerville College, Oxford, in his scrap-metal lorry in order to see her. A light breeze ruffled her short bob of glossy black hair. She wouldn't feel ashamed of him – she couldn't feel ashamed of Billy, she simply wouldn't know how to – but she was honest enough to know that if such a scenario took place, she would feel self-conscious. Billy, amongst Oxford's dreaming spires, would be as out of place as . . . as . . . as her dad no doubt felt whenever he visited Matthew's snobby public school.

There came the sound of someone running down the slight

incline behind her, and she turned her head, her eyes meeting his.

'Hello, love,' he said breathlessly a few seconds later, flopping down beside her. 'Have you been here long? Did you get away from school early?'

'Last lesson was a free period. I'll do the work I should have done in it at home, tonight.'

His run down the slope had disarranged his artfully coiffured quiff and he took a comb from his jeans hip pocket in order to flick it back into shape.

'Yer should've told me and I'd have met you from school. I was over Blackheath picking up a load of old piping from the milk depot.' He put the comb back in his pocket and slid his arm around her shoulder, pulling her close, wishing he could kiss her but knowing it would only rile her if he attempted to do so. Kissing in public, when she was in school uniform, was a misdemeanour he'd never been able to persuade Daisy to commit.

'Do yer fancy coming with me to watch the fight next week?' he asked, not very hopefully. 'It was supposed to be Zac who was fighting, only now I think it's going to be Big Jumbo. Whoever it is, Jack'll be looking for support.'

Even though she tried not to, Daisy shuddered. Despite her dad's involvement with the Embassy Boxing Club, boxing was a sport she couldn't stomach.

'But your dad won medals galore for boxing when he was younger,' Billy had once said to her, mystified.

He had, and it made not the slightest difference. Though she thought her dad the most wonderful man in the world, she couldn't share his passion for boxing. To her, there was absolutely nothing edifying at all in two men climbing into a roped ring with the sole purpose of pounding each other unconscious.

'Thanks, but no thanks,' she said, wishing she didn't feel so low about everything; wishing Matthew were at home; wishing her mum and dad weren't at odds with each other; wishing her academic ambitions and her feelings for Billy didn't seem so incompatible. 'I really can't understand why you would want to watch Zac Hemingway or Big Jumbo fight, especially when it's not even a legitimate fight.'

'Hardly any good fight is,' Billy said, reasonably. 'And it isn't as if it's criminal, like burglary or fraud, is it? It's only against the law because someone *says* it's against the law. Your dad's as honest as they come, but I bet he'll be there. Or he would be if Matthew wasn't missing.'

Daisy was in no mood to argue against the rights and wrongs of pirate boxing matches. Like tax evasion, it seemed to be one of those things that a lot of otherwise law-abiding people perceived as being morally OK, even if it wasn't legally OK. 'I don't want to go,' she said with quiet firmness. 'I've masses of schoolwork to catch up on and—'

'Any old rags, bones or l . . . u . . . u . . . mber?' A couple of voices gigglingly cried out in imitative manner of a rag-and-bone man.

Billy's head whipped in the direction the voices were coming from. Two girls Daisy's age, and dressed like Daisy in Blackheath High uniform, were walking up the slope from the pond a half dozen yards or so away from them.

'Any old iron? Any junk? Any rubbish?' The girls were laughing so much they were hanging on to each other in an effort to remain upright and then, in case either Daisy or Billy hadn't realized they were the object of their ridicule, one of them called out, 'I thought you'd promised Miss Bumby you weren't going to be a street-totter's wife when you left school, Daisy Emmerson! I thought you were going to go to Oxford? Are you going to go on the back of your boyfriend's scrap-metal lorry? Is he going to park it outside the Bodleian?' Shrieking with laughter and clutching each other for support, they continued on up the slope. 'Any old iron?' Daisy and Billy could still hear even though the girls now had their backs towards them and the distance between them was growing. 'Any old junk? Any old l . . . u . . . u . . . mber?'

If the two girls had done nothing more than infer that being a scrap-metal dealer was little different from being a rag-and-bone man, Billy would have been unperturbed. He was used to being teased about his chosen line of business and, as it was a lucrative business, treated such derision with easy-going contempt.

The bit about Daisy having promised a teacher she wasn't going to become a street-totter's wife when she left school, though, was a different matter. Had Daisy had a conversation with a teacher about him? Was that why she didn't like him dropping her off at school, or meeting her at school, in his lorry? Because she'd promised the Miss Bumby person she wouldn't be seeing him again once she went to Oxford? He turned his head away from the girls' retreating backs and looked towards Daisy. She was so visibly upset he felt as if a fist had been punched hard into his chest. It *was* true! When she went away to university, she was going to do so without any intention of eventually marrying him. She intended marrying someone clever – a doctor or a lawyer or an architect. That was why she didn't want anyone seeing them together – Daisy, his Daisy, was ashamed of him!

'Jesus!' he said in a stunned voice, struggling to his feet and looking down at her with pain-filled incredulity. 'You '*ave* bin talking about me to yer teacher, 'aven't yer? Yer don't really think any different to yer two silly schoolmates, do yer?'

Daisy blinked. Her classmates' ridiculing of Billy made her feel so sick at heart she could hardly think straight. Wounded to the quick on his behalf, she stared at him bewilderedly. 'What do you mean, I don't think any differently to my two class-mates?' she said, struggling for understanding. 'Of course I think differently to them! How could I not do? They're nothing but ignorant idiots!' She began scrambling to her feet.

'But yer've talked about me to yer teacher, 'aven't yer?' If Daisy wasn't thinking straight, Billy wasn't listening straight. He felt as if he'd been hit by a bolt of lightning. Things he'd never been able to understand now seemed perfectly clear. Of course Daisy didn't want their friends and neighbours in Magnolia Square to know he thought she was his girlfriend! Not when she didn't intend anything serious coming of it!

The knowledge was so monstrous, he felt as if he was being crushed alive. He couldn't bear such pain and he certainly didn't know how he was going to live with it!

Daisy, striving to set things straight, said dazedly, 'Miss Bumby *did* speak to me about you dropping me off at the school-gates and . . .'

'No wonder you won't come with me to the fight! Your precious Miss Bumby wouldn't approve, would she? Going to a fight would be far too common for a girl who's going to go to Oxford and drink in posh pubs like the Bodleian!'

For Daisy, the conversation was becoming more and more surreal. 'The Bodleian isn't a pub,' she said, struggling for clarity, 'it's a library.'

'I don't care if it's a bleedin' pawnshop!' Billy knew if he stayed with her for even a second longer he'd be in tears. Jesus, but he'd never thought Daisy would look down on him just because he'd had the balls to get a business of his own off the ground! What did it matter if it was a scrap-metal business? There was money in scrap-metal. And when he made suffi-cient money he would branch out into something else. Like his idol, Jack Robson, he'd be an entrepreneur! And if Daisy wouldn't go with him to the fight, he'd take some other girl who wouldn't give a damn about being seen in the cab of his lorry!

'I'm off!' he said, his lean body so taut with tension he felt as if it was going to explode. 'Yer'd better get back to your schoolwork Daisy! Yer'll 'ave plenty of time for it now!' Fighting back the tears that were threatening to shame him at any moment, he spun on his heel, sprinting up the slope, heedless of the havoc being caused to his carefully combed quiff.

'Billy? Billy!' Daisy stood immobile for one stunned second and then broke into a run, trying to catch him up. It was impossible. Billy had had a lot of practice, when a youngster, of high-tailing it at speed from the clutches of irate adults and exasperated policemen. When Billy sprinted, he really sprinted.

Long before she crowned the summit of the steeply rising slope, she came to a defeated halt, tears streaking her face. What had her argument with Billy been *about*, for goodness sake? How could he even begin to think that she thought about him as her two classmates did? It didn't make any sense. Like a lot of other things in life at the moment, most especially Matthew's running away, it didn't make any sense at all.

'Course it makes sense,' Zac said to Carrie when, having asked one of her fellow stall-holders to keep an eye on the Jennings' fruit and veg stall until such time as Albert arrived to close up, promising him free entry to his next fight for his pains, he sat beside her on the upper deck of a steamer ploughing its way down the Thames to Southend. 'Everyone should have a day off every now and then. Your dad won't mind. If what your mother says is anything to go by, he's always sliding off and enjoying himself, isn't he?'

He was, but somehow Carrie didn't think the fact was going to count for much when he arrived to pack up the stall at five-thirty only to discover that she'd scarpered off several hours earlier with Zac Hemingway!

'And I need to talk to you and have you to myself for a bit,' he said, grinning at her as if virtually kidnapping her was the most normal behaviour in the world, 'and I can't do that when you're knee-deep in apples and pears in Lewisham market, can I?'

'It isn't the season for apples and pears.' With great difficulty Carrie tried to hold on to at least a shred of pretended outrage. 'It's all spring veg at the moment. Broccoli and broad beans and early lettuce.'

He shouted with laughter, his arm resting on the back of their shared seat, his hand clasping her shoulder. Why the devil were they discussing fruit and vegetables when they could at last kiss to their hearts' content? 'I'm crackers about you, Carrie Collins,' he said as, still chuckling, he cupped her chin with the thumb and forefinger of his free hand, tilting her face to his.

Reading the intent in his eyes, Carrie tried to push herself as far away from him as she was able. It wasn't far. It wasn't even a centimetre. 'No!' Her protest was a whispered croak. 'Please don't, Zac! I've made up my mind about us and—'

He, too, had made up his mind about them and the decision he had come to was one far different to hers. 'You're wasting time and effort on a losing battle, sweetheart.' His voice was thick with desire and supreme self-confidence. 'It's going to be just you and me, Carrie. You and me forever.'

It wasn't. Even as his mouth closed on hers and her lips melted burningly beneath his, Carrie knew that it could never be the two of them forever. Today, though, was different. Today it could be just the two of them; today it already was. It was as if, out of nowhere, a day had been conjured that had nothing to do with her real life. A day special and set apart. A stolen day. A magical day. A day she would lock in her heart and remember forever.

'Sarf end!' a voice aboard the steamer shouted as Southend and its mile-long pier and its funfair came into sight. 'An' don't miss your last boat back!'

In happy isolation from their fellow passengers, and not having seen an inch of the unspectacular scenery on their trip down-river, nearly all mud flats on the Essex side of the Thames and low, uninteresting hills on the Kent side, Zac and Carrie finally drew far enough apart to be able to grin at each other. Southend. There would be no one they knew in Southend, not on a week-day.

'We should have brought a picnic,' Carrie said as, arms around each other's waists, they disembarked. 'Fish-paste sandwiches and tomatoes and slices of home-made cake.'

'We don't need a picnic.' The heat of his hand on her rib-cage seared through the thin cotton of her dress. 'Not for the way we're going to spend the afternoon.'

A middle-aged woman behind them turned to her brow-beaten other half, saying acidly, 'Disgusting, that's what it is, behaving like that in public. They never left each other alone for a minute aboard the boat and now look at them! His hands are all over the place and she isn't a silly young girl not old enough to know better! If that ring on her finger is anything to go by, she's a married woman, but if the Tarzan she's with is her husband, I'll eat my hat!' Her other half wished she would. It would shut her up for a bit.

Oblivious of the malicious interest they were arousing, Zac and Carrie continued to walk, arms entwined around each other, not towards the amusement arcades and the funfair and the whelk and candyfloss stalls, but away from them all, heading out to the loneliness of scrubby dunes and ribbons of estuary sand and shingle.

'You said you had a lot to tell me,' she said, her head resting against his shoulders as, thigh to thigh, they walked out by the estuary, leaving the noise and carnival-like atmosphere of Southend far behind them.

He turned his head, his lips brushing her hair, not slackening his long, easy stride. 'I have,' he said, enjoying the freshness of the sea breeze against his face. 'And I will. Afterwards.'

She knew what he meant by the word 'afterwards' and, weak with longing for him, caution and conscience thrown to the winds for this one, never-to-be-repeated day, she didn't care. She wanted him just as he wanted her. In another lifetime, a lifetime that didn't already encompass Danny and, most of all, Rose, she would have been his her whole life long. 'I love you,' she said, knowing it was true; knowing he was her soulmate; that with Zac she would never feel unfulfilled, or dowdy or tediously ordinary.

His hand tightened on hers as he broke into a run. The dunes were now mounds of dark sand studded with tufts of sea-grass, and it was amongst these, in a small hollow, that he came to a halt, flopping down and tugging her down with him.

'People will be able to see us from the water,' she protested not very convincingly as he tugged his T-shirt over his head, revealing a muscled physique that would have tempted a nun from virtue.

'Let them.' As far as Zac was concerned, the boats ploughing in and out of the estuary were too far distant to be a source of concern. Their hollow was cosily sheltered from the breeze and only the keenest, binocular-slung voyeur was likely to espy them. He was undoing the buckle of his belt and as he did so Carrie's fingers began hastily fumbling with the buttons of her carnation-patterned dress. Despite the light breeze, it was getting hotter. Her fingers were trembling so much they wouldn't function.

'Here, let me . . .' his voice was hoarse, his body hard on hers as, imprisoning her beneath him, he unbuttoned her dress, revealing the heavy, lush curves of her breasts, her skin flawlessly pale in the bright afternoon light. 'Christ, Carrie! You're beautiful! So beautiful.'

Her nipples were darker than he had imagined, wine-red and silky. As he lowered his mouth to them she groaned, her legs curving round him, her skirt pushed high.

There was sand everywhere. It clung to their sweat-sheened skin, was between their toes, in their hair and then, as he entered her and she cried out beneath him, sand and sea-grass and the vast sky above them cartwheeled together, somersaulting and spinning in gaudy patterns of blurred, reflected light.

Later, as she lay in the curve of his arm, her head against his chest, her tumbled hair soft against his flesh, he said, 'And so I shall be leaving for New Zealand as soon as possible, sweetheart. When I've got mates and a job waiting for me there, it'd be daft not to, wouldn't it?' He hadn't told her about the money. She was so shiningly and transparently honest that when it came to doing so, he shied from telling her of his years in Parkhurst. Instead he emphasized the strong bond between himself and his Kiwi mates, mates who had returned to their homeland and wanted him to join them. The job was complete fiction. There would be time enough, when she was in New Zealand with him, to tell her that he had no need of a job, that he had money enough without one.

Carrie lay very still, glad that her face was against his naked chest and that he couldn't see her eyes. New Zealand. It was the other side of the world. So far away that, once he went there, she would never see him again. It was for the best, of course. There could never be anything else between them after today. Danny didn't set her heart on fire like Zac did; he wasn't the other part of her, as she was certain Zac was; but he'd been part of her life for as long as she could remember, and she couldn't cut him out of it. She and Danny were married. They would always be married. As for Rose . . . Even if circumstances were different between her and Danny, how could she leave Rose in order to build a new, fulfilling, exciting life in New Zealand with Zac? It wasn't possible. It could never be possible. New Zealand would suit Zac. There were blue-hazed mountains and glittering rivers and wide, open spaces there.

'That's wonderful for you,' she said, meaning every word, her throat so tight she could scarcely believe she had managed to speak.

He moved, shifting himself up on to an elbow and, with his free hand, hooked a thumb beneath her chin, turning her head to his. 'It's going to be wonderful for both of us.' His eyes held hers, daring her to correct him.

She couldn't do so. Not yet. She wanted to pretend for just a little longer. Just until the day was over. 'It's going to be wonderful for both of us,' she said, feasting on the sight of his corn-gold hair and hard-boned face, knowing she would never forget the sensuous, arousing curve of his mouth and the intriguing cleft in his chin. 'Make love to me again,' she said huskily, sliding her arms once more around the narrowness of his waist. 'Make love to me until it's dark, Zac. Make love to me until it's time for us to go.'

Mavis looked around The 21 with pride. Tomorrow was the official opening and she'd called in, alone, to give everything a last minute check. Mirrors shone, glasses gleamed, the bar was fully stocked. Jack Solomons had promised to pay the club a visit, which meant the equivalent of an official seal of approval where the boxing fraternity was concerned, and it was the boxing fraternity, with its show-business hangers-on, that Jack was intent on attracting. She walked over to the heavily draped windows and pulled a curtain aside, looking down into Dean Street. Gaudily lit neon signs winked and blinked, light spilling out from restaurant and club doorways. It was ten at night and Soho was alive and kicking, and would be until the wee small hours.

The 21 was only licensed as an afternoon drinking club, but neither she nor Jack anticipated such an irritation cramping their style. They weren't in the market to vie with strip clubs or jazz clubs. As long as they could succeed in breaking the gaming laws, their afternoon fight-game punters would give The 21 all the edge it needed.

She chewed the corner of her lip thoughtfully, debating with herself whether or not to try on again the tailored evening jacket that was hanging on the back of the ladies' powder-room door. She had bought it at Harrods that afternoon with money Jack had lavishly pressed upon her. 'Staff uniform,' he had said with his impudent grin. 'An absolutely legitimate business expense the Tax Man will find himself stumping up for.'

Whether the Tax Man would, one day, stump up for it, Mavis doubted very much. A sizzling midnight blue, and beautifully cut, it had sequin-studded revers and pockets, and would transform any one of her many pencil-straight skirts into a sumptuous outfit, especially when worn with sheer black stockings and dizzyingly high, stiletto-heeled shoes.

Her hand tightened on the curtain as a large black Humber eased into the busy street, slowing to a halt suspiciously near to The 21's narrow doorway. She knew from Jack exactly what kind of a car Archie Duke was driven around in, and her stomach muscles tensed. Why would Archie be visiting the club now, before it had officially opened? Intimidation needed an audience to be truly successful: punters who'd be scared off and who would spread the word that the club was too dodgy to risk patronizing.

That the Humber *was* Archie's was now beyond doubt, for he and four companions were spilling out of the car and on to the gas-lit pavement. She frowned, perplexed. If Archie wasn't visiting the club in order to raid it, why was he visiting it? Was he hoping to find Jack in it, and on his own? Was he hoping that another word with Jack might be enough to change Jack's mind where the question of protection money was concerned?

Angry with herself for not having the forethought to lock The 21's street entrance-door behind her, she let the curtain fall and walked swiftly in the direction of the stairs, intent on meeting Archie and his friends on them and fearlessly informing them that if they were looking for Jack, they'd have to look elsewhere.

Archie was most certainly not looking for Jack. He knew very well where Jack was, and that was in The Embassy. If he hadn't been, Archie would not now be about to turn his boys loose on a wrecking-spree in Jack's Soho spieler. Though not much of a thinking man, it had occurred to him quite some while ago that tangling with Jack, as he tangled with other recalcitrant benefactors, might not be to his advantage. For one thing, Jack was in the fight game and he, Archie, didn't particularly want to make enemies in that quarter – not when he was all set to make a wad of money backing Arnie in illegit pirate fights.

This decision made, the next had been obvious. He wouldn't wreck The 21 on its opening night, thereby causing Jack irreparable damage. Instead he'd wreck it before it opened, causing just enough damage to make Jack realize that his life would be easier if he toed the line a little. That way no one would be hurt, no punters would be involved and, in the aftermath, an accommodation satisfactory to both him and Jack would, no doubt, be reached.

The first indication that things weren't going to go quite as planned came when Ginger said tersely, 'The bleedin' door's off the latch! Robson must be in there!'

'Robson's safely stashed in his boxing gym doin' 'is nut 'cos one of 'is fighters, a new guy, is nowhere to be found,' Jemmy said flatly.

Archie rocked back on his heels, looking up at the second floor windows. A chink of light was clearly visible where the drawn curtains were not completely pulled together. Someone was up there, but it wasn't Robson. He'd seen Robson go into The Embassy with his own eyes and Robson couldn't have left it and driven into the West End, arriving before them. Not unless he had wings on his car instead of wheels.

'It'll be a cleaner,' he said, judiciously letting Ginger enter the building first. 'Lock her in a lav, Ginge, so she can't phone the rozzers.'

As Ginger and Arnie raced up the stairs, taking them two at a time, Mavis came flying down them.

'Where the bloody hell do you think you're going?' she demanded, coming to a sudden halt, her hands on her hips, her eyes blazing. 'We don't open till tomorrer, as if you didn't know!'

With their way so unexpectedly barred, Ginger and Arnie came to an abrupt halt. Archie, too corpulent to be nimble, careened into the back of them. Pongo and Jemmy, bringing up the rear, steadied themselves on the hand-rail that ran up the side of the left-hand wall.

'Some bleedin' cleaner!' Jemmy said, eyeing Mavis's sheer-stockinged legs and perilously high-heeled shoes.

'What the bugger are you waiting for?' Archie demanded,

regaining his balance and furious at having his dignity jeopardized. 'Lock her in the lav and get on with the job!'

Only then did Mavis realize that they weren't looking for Jack, but that they were out on a wrecking spree. 'Oh no you bloody well don't!' Bracing her hands on the walls either side of the stairs to give herself extra leverage, she kicked out at Ginger, hoping that by sending him flying backwards he would take the others down the stairs with him, like skittles.

It was a manoeuvre that, if it hadn't been for Arnie, would very likely have succeeded. As Ginger yelled and ducked to avoid the force of Mavis's stiletto-heeled foot, Arnie leapt forward, whipping Mavis's other leg from beneath her, twisting her over as she fell and doubling her arms up high behind her back.

Ginger, aware he'd come within a whisker of losing an eye, scrambled past the two of them. Stiletto-heeled shoes! They were more dangerous than bleedin' flick-knives!

'Lock her in the bloody lav!' Archie yelled again as Mavis struggled like a wild-cat against Arnie's overpowering strength, biting and spitting and kicking and hurling non-stop blasphemous abuse at the lot of them as she did so.

Arnie wasn't in the habit of taking shit from anyone, and especially not from a woman. With a violent wrench that had Pongo goggle-eyed with disbelief, he wrenched one of Mavis's arms out of its socket.

The pain was so severe Mavis couldn't even scream. With a deep, gasping moan, her knees buckled. 'Fucking bastard!' she whispered as Arnie began brutally manhandling her up the stairs and into the club's tiny entrance foyer. 'Bloody fucking ball-less bastard!'

Archie paused at the top of the stairs in order to regain his breath and brush a few specks of carpet dust from his trouser-legs. 'Put her where she can't do any more bloody damage!' he said irately and then, mindful of Mavis's identity and of her rumoured relationship with Jack Robson, 'and no funny business with her. Get your arse back out here and give Ginger and Pongo and Jemmy a hand.'

After what he'd just seen, Pongo didn't much relish the thought of Arnie giving him a hand in any shape, way or form. He couldn't, however, say so. Not now. Not with Archie rattled and everyone's nerves set on edge.

With all zest for the task lost, he followed Ginger and Jemmy into The 21's main drinking and gaming room, hoping Arnie would heed Archie's words and that Jack Robson's gutsy fancy-piece wouldn't have to take any more punishment at Arnie's hands.

As she heard the sound of mirrors being smashed and furniture wrecked, tears of anger, frustration and pain spilled down Mavis's face. Archie's mindless loons were wrecking her and Jack's beautiful club! How could she have been so stupid as to have left the door off the lock? How could she, when she had first seen Archie step out of the Humber and on to the pavement, not immediately have guessed his intentions and phoned for the police – and for Jack.

Pain screamed through her as Arnie slammed her against the mirrored wall in the ladies' powder-room. Jack. Jack would beat the living hell out of this mountainous cretin once he caught up with him.

'Bitch!' Arnie said, reaching for a drinking glass that had been thoughtfully provided for customers in a rack above the wash-basins, 'Ball-breaking tart and tramp!'

Over and above the physical pain Arnie had already inflicted on her, and the emotional pain of hearing the club being trashed to smithereens, Mavis faced a new horror. This good-looking loon now grinning so gloatingly at her wasn't an average run-of-the-mill villain. He was a basket-case. The kind of basket-case who gained pleasure from inflicting pain on women. As he smashed the glass into jagged shards on the porcelain and she read the intent in his eyes, she knew she was facing her worst nightmare. 'Not my face!' Her voice was hoarse, the pain in her chest where he had punched her with a bunched fist making it nearly impossible for her to breath. 'Sweet Christ! Not my face!'

Chapter Seventeen

∽

It was Danny who answered the telephone just after eleven o'clock in Jack's cubby-hole of an office at The Embassy, to be informed tersely by an unidentified caller that 'it might be best if someone gets down to The 21 as the blonde bint that was in there when Archie done it over is a bit hurt.'

Pongo didn't stay on the line long enough to be questioned and, even if he had done, Danny didn't need any more information. Slamming the receiver back on its rest he hared out of the office, yelling, 'Jack! Jack! Archie's boys have wrecked the club and Mavis was in it and is 'urt!'

When Beryl walked into the gym ten minutes later, hopeful of finding that Zac had at last turned up there and hopeful, also, that when he left he would suggest she left with him so that she wouldn't have to walk alone in the dark up Magnolia Hill, she found it empty save for a young man shoving a towel into a locker.

'Where is everyone?' she asked, bewildered. The gym rarely closed its doors before eleven-thirty at night, for both Jack and her Uncle Danny were night-birds.

The young man reddened. He'd only been coming to the gym for a few weeks but, as she called in there so often, her uncle being the manager, he knew her well by sight. He didn't think she knew him, though. He wasn't the sort of bloke girls noticed. 'There's a bit of a panic on, I think,' he said hesitantly, not quite sure what the panic had been and even if he should be talking about it. 'Your uncle took a phone message. Something about a chap called Archie and a club and someone in it having been hurt. Mr Robson was out of here in three seconds flat, and your uncle and Big Jumbo and a couple of the other boxers who were still here, went with them.' He didn't add that no one had asked him to go with them, and that no one ever did, rather hoping that she'd think he'd been left in charge of the gym.

Where he was concerned, Beryl didn't think anything. Disappointment settled inside her like lead. The name Archie meant absolutely nothing to her and, her mother not having told her an iota about The 21, neither did the young man's mention of a club.

'Did Zac go with them?' she asked, focusing on her one and only concern.

He reddened even further. There'd been a lot of angry words from Beryl's uncle that evening on the subject of Zac Hemingway. He hadn't shown for training and no one knew where the hell he was. 'No,' he said, knowing he was blushing and hating himself for it. 'Zac Hemingway hasn't been in the gym at all today.'

Beryl was too much of an innocent to be able to prevent the disappointment she was feeling from showing on her face. Presuming it was because she hadn't found her uncle in the gym, the young man said awkwardly, 'Were you hoping your uncle would walk you home up Magnolia Hill, because if you like I'll—'

Beryl shook her head, cutting his suggestion off even before he had finished making it. She didn't want to walk in the dark up Magnolia Hill with him. She didn't want to be walked home by anyone other than Zac. 'No. Thanks all the same. Goodnight.'

'Goodnight,' he said miserably, wondering why he never seemed to make any headway with girls. 'If I'm still here when your uncle gets back I'll tell him you called by.'

With her hands plunged deep in her coat pockets, Beryl walked desultorily out of the gym and down the creaking flight of uncarpeted stairs. Where was Zac? Where, come to that, was Billy and their Aunt Carrie? Daisy had been looking for Billy ever since tea-time. Though she hadn't said so to Beryl, Beryl was pretty sure that the two of them had had a quarrel and that Daisy was wanting to make it up. As for where her Aunt Carrie was, that was an even bigger mystery.

'She hasn't left a note,' Rose had said when she came round to number sixteen earlier in the evening, looking for her, 'and as Dad doesn't have a clue where she's got to, I thought your mum might know.'

Mavis, however, hadn't been home and, as this was quite a common occurrence, neither she nor Rose thought it odd or gave the matter a second thought. Now, to add to all these little mysteries, there was the mystery of where Jack and her Uncle Danny had hurried off to in such haste.

She trudged up Magnolia Hill towards the lamplit square, assuming it would have been to another boxing club, perhaps a club in Bermondsey or Deptford, or even one north of the river. Only when she entered the square did it occur to her to wonder as to the identity of the person who had been hurt. Whoever it was, it was obvious Jack and Danny knew them well, or they wouldn't have been so concerned. There wasn't much likelihood she would know them, though, and blissfully ignorant as to how very, very wrong this assumption would prove to be, she turned in at her gate, wondering if her mum were home from wherever she'd been gallivanting and if, perhaps, the kettle would be on so that they could share a cosy cup of tea.

*

Four hours later the shrill ringing of their telephone abruptly woke Ruth and Bob Giles.

'Oh dear,' Bob said heavily, fumbling in the dark for the switch on his table-lamp, 'it's bound to be bad news. News always is when it comes at this time of the morning.'

The lamp clicked on, filling the room with soft light, and Ruth pushed herself up against the pillows, blinking at the clock. It was five minutes after three. 'You weren't expecting to hear of a death, love, were you?' she asked as Bob swung his legs out of bed and reached for his dressing-gown.

He shook his head. At the present moment he didn't, mercifully, have any terminally ill parishioners. 'There may have been an accident,' he said, walking swiftly towards the bedroom door, adding hopefully, 'or it may be a wrong number.'

As he hurried downstairs to silence the ominous ringing, Ruth lay for a moment, debating whether it was worth trying to get back to sleep or whether she should instead go down to the kitchen to make a pot of tea.

The tone of Bob's voice in the seconds after he lifted up the telephone receiver decided the matter.

'What?' she heard him say in horrified incredulity, 'But how . . . ? Who . . . ? Which hospital is she in, Danny? Dear Lord, WHICH HOSPITAL?'

Ruth was out of bed in a flash, her heart slamming against her ribcage. Was it Carrie who had been injured? Was it Rose? As she ran down the stairs to join him at the telephone table in the hall her eyes urgently held his, but he was too shocked by what Danny was telling him for him to be able to mouth a name and put her out of her mental agony.

'Dear God,' he was saying, 'Jack did what? They've taken him where? St Thomas's? And Mavis is in Guy's and that's where you are? In Guy's Casualty Department?'

Ruth dug her nails into her palms. What in the name of God had happened? Had Jack and Danny, and Carrie or Rose, all been in Jack's car together and had the car been in a crash? Or perhaps it wasn't Carrie or Rose that Bob was referring to when he asked 'Which hospital was she in?' Perhaps it was Christina. Perhaps . . .

'It's Mavis,' he said to her in a cracked voice and then, to Danny, 'Yes, yes, of course I will. Straight away. And the police? Yes, yes, I understand.' His hand was shaking as he put the receiver back on its rest.

'What's happened?' Ruth never raised her voice or gave way to panic, but she could feel herself doing so now. 'Please, Bob! Was it a car accident? Is Mavis badly hurt? Is Jack hurt, too? And Danny?'

Dazedly Bob shook his head. As a vicar he was accustomed to hearing bad news, and to being the bearer of bad news, but this little lot was almost beyond belief. 'Mavis was in a club,' he said, wondering which home he should visit first, Mavis's, Danny's or Jack's. 'A club Jack owns in Soho. It isn't open yet and she was in it on her own . . . checking things over probably . . . Jack had asked her to run it for him . . .' There was no point in going down to Jack's, he thought, his mind racing. Christina wouldn't be there, she was living with her mother in Greenwich. 'Some thugs broke in – Archie Duke and his mob – and they . . . they . . .' His voice cracked again. Danny said they had dislocated her arm, broken three of her ribs and cut her face so badly with a broken drinking glass that it was doubtful if even Miriam would recognize her.

Try as he might, he couldn't put what had been done to Mavis into words. 'They beat her,' he said, knowing he'd have to break the news to Miriam and Albert, as well as to Ted. 'Badly.'

Ruth grasped hold of the banister rail. 'And Jack and Danny?

How were they hurt? You said Mavis was in the club on her own . . .'

Mindful of the many people he had to see and of the importance of seeing them all as quickly as possible, Bob forced himself out of his shocked stupor. He had to get dressed. Ted Lomax and Carrie Collins would be out of their minds with worry, wondering where their other halves were.

'An anonymous caller phoned the gym, telling Jack what had happened. He went straight down there and Danny and whoever else was in the gym at the time went with him . . .' He was already halfway back to the bedroom, Ruth at his heels, all thoughts of cups of tea forgotten. 'They called an ambulance for Mavis, and then Jack went immediately in search of Archie Duke,' he continued, pulling on trousers and socks, feverishly trying to locate his dog-collar.

'Dear God.' Ruth knew now what was to come. She sat down on the bed, weak-kneed. 'And he took Danny with him? He and Danny went to sort out Archie Duke and his mob and now they're so badly hurt they're both in hospital?'

Bob scrabbled under the wardrobe for a pair of shoes. He would speak to Ted first, then Carrie, and then he'd go down to Greenwich to speak to Christina. However unhappy the present situation between Jack and Christina, she needed to be told what had happened, especially as Jack's condition was obviously so grave. A knife wound, Danny had said, a knife wound close to his heart.

Telling Ruth only the good news, he said, 'Danny isn't badly hurt. He's on his way home now. Will you go round to Malcolm Lewis's for me and tell him I'm going to need his car and his help as a chauffeur?' He had his jacket on now and was again at the bedroom door. He was going to need transport if he were to get to Greenwich with all possible speed. Under the present circumstances, fifteen minutes spent walking there was going to be fifteen too long. Christina would need transport, too, to get to the hospital, as would Ted Lomax. Malcom Lewis, his scoutmaster and right-hand man, was going to be kept busy over the next few hours.

'If Malcolm wants to know where to find me, tell him I'm going to the Lomax's first, then to the Collins's.'

'And Charlie's,' Ruth said, knowing that Jack must have been badly hurt; that if he hadn't been, Bob would have told her. 'You'll have to let Charlie know what has happened.'

Bob blanched. Charlie was well in his eighties and Jack was his only son. It was going to be no fun waking Charlie with his news. 'Yes,' he agreed tersely. 'Tell Malcolm if he hasn't caught up with me by the time I've left Carrie's, I'll be at Charlie's.'

As he ran down the stairs, Ruth forced herself to her feet. She had to dress and go down to number eleven to wake Malcolm. Then she would come back home and put the kettle on for a pot of tea. Unless she was very much mistaken, she was going to have quite a few distressed callers over the next few hours.

Ted Lomax wasn't only distressed, he was beside himself with fury.

'If Jack knew Mavis had been hurt hours ago, why didn't he come round here and tell me? Why did he go racing up to the hospital with Danny, not me? I'm her husband, for Christ's sake! And it was down to me to sort Archie fucking Duke out, not him!'

Bob didn't turn a hair at Ted's language. He was accustomed to hearing people swear strongly when under stress, and Ted certainly had every reason to be stressed. He'd been sitting in an armchair, fully dressed, still waiting up for Mavis, when Bob knocked at the door and broke the news to him of what had happened. Now, refusing to wait for Malcolm to arrive, he was intent on making his own way up to Guy's Hospital.

Snatching up a jacket that was lying over the back of a chair in the untidy room, he said in a voice which was only a fraction away from breaking completely, 'I knew no good would come of her working in Jack's bleedin' club, but would she listen to me? Course she wouldn't! She was so happy about it you'd have thought all her Christmases had arrived at once . . .'

There came the sound of someone running anxiously down the stairs, and seconds later Billy, clad only in a pair of pyjama bottoms, burst into the room. At the unexpected sight of Bob Giles standing on the hearth-rug, he came to an abrupt halt, his eyes flying to his father's. 'What's 'appened?' he asked urgently. 'Is it Mum? Is it our Beryl? Has there bin an accident?'

'Your mum's been hurt,' Ted said tersely, striding past him out into the hallway. 'I'm going to see her now. You stay here with our Beryl.'

'Hurt?' Billy ran after him into the hallway. 'Hurt how? Dad? Dad!'

His only answer was the front door slamming shut as Ted set off with swift strides towards Magnolia Terrace and the shortest possible route up to London Bridge and Guy's.

Billy spun round to face Bob Giles. 'How 'as Mum bin 'urt?' he demanded, looking suddenly very young and very vulnerable, his hair tousled instead of being combed into a quiff, his baggy pyjama bottoms a stark contrast to his day-time trousers.

'I don't have all the details yet, Billy,' Bob said, mindful that he still had Carrie and Christina and Charlie to see and that Billy might not even know about The 21, much less his mother's involvement with it, and that explanations would take time. 'Your dad will be able to tell you how she is when he either rings the vicarage from the hospital, or gets back home.' He moved resolutely towards the front door, glad that Beryl hadn't woken up. Pacifying Beryl would have taken much, much longer. 'And as Beryl is still asleep, don't wake her,' he added. 'There's no point, not yet.' He opened the door, looking across the bottom corner of the square to number seventeen. The sitting-room light was on. Did that mean that Danny had already arrived home? Or was Carrie waiting up for him like Ted had been waiting up for Mavis?

'Mum's not going to . . . to die, is she, Vicar?' Billy asked, his face chalkily white.

Bob shook his head. Complete details he didn't have, but he did know that people didn't die from a dislocated shoulder, broken ribs and a ruined face. Though taking the last little item into the equation, they might very well want to. 'No,' he said, wondering how soon it would be before he, too, could reach Guy's to see Mavis. 'She isn't going to die, Billy.' He didn't add, 'But Jack very well might.' Billy didn't yet know about Jack and this wasn't the moment to tell him.

Heavy-heartedly he set off at a trot across the darkened square. Even if Danny hadn't yet returned home, he wasn't going to be able to spend much time with Carrie. He had to get down to Greenwich to see Christina, for if Jack's condition deteriorated before Christina was informed of what had happened and was able to reach his bedside . . . He winced, unable to bring the thought to its conclusion. Christina *would* get there. Malcolm would whizz her up to St Thomas's in his car in fifteen minutes or so. And Jack wasn't going to die. Not yet. Not, God willing, for another forty or fifty years.

When Carrie heard Bob Giles's knock, she put the mug she was drinking from down so suddenly that tea slopped over its rim and on to her kitchen table. The knock was the knock of authority. A doctor's knock, or a policeman's. What it most certainly was not, was Danny's knock. Not even if he had lost his door-key. Not even if he was paralytically drunk. Not that she thought he was out drinking. Ever since she had arrived home at just before midnight to find Rose in bed and not a sign of Danny, she was convinced he was trailing the streets, looking for her. How she felt about his reacting to her absence in this extreme manner, she didn't quite know. A part of her was pleased. Danny always took her so much for granted that it was a miracle he'd even noticed she wasn't home – though, of course, her not being there to cook his dinner would have helped bring her absence to his attention.

Another part of her was intensely annoyed at his stupidity. Why, whatever time it had been when he went out looking for her, hadn't he had the sense to realize that she would most certainly be home by now? And last but not least, she was in a fever of guilty apprehension. What was she going to tell him when he did come home? She couldn't tell him that she'd been in Southend with Zac – not without revealing the nature of her relationship with Zac. Yet she couldn't lie to Danny. She'd never lied to Danny.

Bob Giles's knock sent all her assumptions and mixed feelings flying. For the first time it occurred to her that the reason Danny was not home wasn't that he was out looking for her, but that he had fallen under a car or a bus – or even into the Thames. She sprinted to the door, yanking it open with such fierce force that Bob Giles took a hasty step backwards before she should fall on top of him.

'Oh my God!' Carrie stared, appalled, at the almost luminous whiteness of his dog-collar. 'There *has* been an accident! I should have known Danny wouldn't get himself in such a state looking for me! He's been hurt, hasn't he? Where is he, Mr Giles? How did it happen? When—'

Bob raised a hand in order to silence her frantic flow of

questions, bewildered as to why, at nearly half-three in the morning, she should think Danny was out looking for her. 'Danny's on his way home, Carrie,' he said in hasty reassurance. 'He telephoned the vicarage fifteen minutes or so ago. He and Jack met with trouble, and though Danny hasn't been seriously hurt, Jack has. I need to get down to Greenwich to break the news to Christina as soon as possible.' Before he could do so, though, he had to tell her about Mavis. 'There's something else, Carrie,' he said unwillingly. 'If I could just step inside for a minute . . .'

Icy fingers squeezed Carrie's heart. Had Bob Giles merely been preparing her for something far, far worse when he had said that Jack was seriously hurt? Was he now going to tell her that Jack was dead? And if he was, how on earth would Mavis cope with such news? Now that she knew what it was like to be helplessly, hopelessly, head-over-heels in love with a man not her husband, she felt a sympathy for Mavis's feelings for Jack that she had never felt before.

'It's Mavis, Carrie,' he said gently as she stepped back into the hallway and he crossed the threshold. 'She was by herself in a club Jack is opening in Soho, and some thugs broke in to smash it up and . . . and Mavis got hurt in the process.' Time enough for the hideous details later, he thought, when the first shock was over. 'She's been taken to Guy's and they're keeping her in. From what I could gather from Danny, she's likely to be there a few days.'

Carrie gave a choked cry, her pupils dilating so that her eyes appeared to be ink-black, not sea-green. Mavis hurt and in hospital, Jack hurt and in hospital and her Danny also hurt, though not as badly! How on earth had it all happened, and how was she to get up to Guy's to see Mavis if Danny was on his way home? She'd have to see Danny first. And she'd have to tell her mam and dad. And Ted, Ted would have to know.

'I've already told Ted,' Bob said, reading her chaotically whirling thoughts. 'And he's on his way to the hospital now. There's nothing you can do for the moment, Carrie, except wait for Danny to get in.'

She looked so dazed and distressed that he didn't like to leave her, but he had no option. Charlie still had to be told what had happened and, even more importantly, so did Christina. 'I have to be on my way,' he said reluctantly. 'I've still to speak to Christina. And Charlie.'

'Yes . . . yes, of course.' Bob Giles said that Jack had been seriously hurt. How seriously? And what was the club he had mentioned and why had Mavis been in it on her own? And if she had been in it on her own, where had her Danny and Jack been when they had been hurt?

'How—' she began as he turned to go, and got no further.

'I got your message, Vicar!' Malcolm Lewis was saying when he rounded the corner of her gate at a run. 'What do you want me to do first? Take Ted up to Guy's or give you a lift down to Greenwich?'

Bob strode to meet him, his relief vast. 'Ted's already on his way to Guy's. Would you go down to Christina's mother's for me, while I go across to Charlie's? She needs to be told that Jack's been taken to St Thomas's, and by the time you've done that, and she's dressed and is ready to leave, I'll have joined you.'

Even as they were talking, they were walking swiftly back down the pathway. 'A knifing,' Carrie heard Bob Giles say in answer to a question of Malcolm's, and then they were separating, Malcolm hurriedly wrenching his car door open, Bob Giles setting off at a swift lick up the square towards the house Charlie lived in, in the top right-hand corner, conveniently adjacent to the vicarage.

*

'A knifing!' Mr Nibbs said, horrified, as Daniel Collins broke the news to him the next morning. 'And your Danny with a cracked jaw and fifteen stitches in a cut over his eye? Dear, oh dear, what is the world coming to?'

They were standing on the pavement outside Nibbo's front gate, the carefully trimmed privets which flanked it such a solid mass of yellow that they resembled shields of dazzling brass. Daniel dragged his eyes away from their brightness. Today wasn't a day to be admiring the beauties of nature – not with Mavis lying with her face a mass of stitches and with the police coming down heavy-handedly on Jack and Danny for taking retribution for her injuries into their own hands.

'But why are the police going to prosecute Danny and Jack when it was Archie Duke's mob who beat up Mavis?' the bewildered Harriet Robson was asking Kate. 'It just doesn't make sense. Are Archie and his mobsters to be prosecuted as well? Can we perhaps give good character statements on Danny's and Jack's behalf?'

'I dunno why Archie Dook should be in the same ward as my Jack,' Charlie said in deep perplexity to Elisha Deakin, his collarless shirt of thick, striped flannel open at the throat, a pair of braces straining over his beer belly. 'It don't 'alf make visitin' awkward!'

'And you say Jack tried to break Archie Duke's neck?' Ellen Voigt, Kate's stepmother, asked Malcolm Lewis's mother, goggle-eyed. 'And that he would have done so if it hadn't been for one of Archie Duke's men knifing him in the chest?'

'It's a good job all Archie's boys weren't still with 'im when Jack caught up with 'im, or Jack would probably be dead,' Danny said flatly to Leon. 'As it was, I thought 'e was goin' to bleed to bloody death before I got 'im to the bloody 'ospital.'

'Christina is vith Jack now,' Christina's mother said to Ruth Giles. 'It vas so kind of the vicar to go up to the hospital vith her. I hope that now she and Jack will reconcile their differences, but who can say that they vill do so ven no one knows vat their differences are? It is all such a vorry, Mrs Giles. Such a very great vorry.'

Carrie, too, was worried, though not about explaining away yesterday's absence to Danny. With all Danny now had on his mind, she could have been in Timbuctoo with Clark Gable yesterday, not merely Southend with Zac. And her worry wasn't solely about Mavis, though as the doctors said, Mavis's facial scars were likely to be severe, and she *was* worried about Mavis. Nearly out of her mind with worry.

She stared at her reflection in the cracked bathroom mirror, another worry dominating her thoughts. How many hours ago had it been since she and Zac had made ecstatic love among the sand dunes? Eighteen? Twenty? Whatever the number, her just having been sick couldn't possibly have any connection to it.

Could it?

When she'd fallen pregnant with Rose and with the baby she had later miscarried, she had suffered with morning sickness before even missing her first period. It had been quite a joke between her and Doctor Roberts. But she couldn't, surely, be suffering with morning sickness after eighteen *hours*! 'You've been sick because you're in such a state of nerves worrying over Mavis,' she said aloud to herself, firmly. Her reflected eyes looked back at her, unconvinced. What if worry over Mavis wasn't the reason for her being sick and feeling so familiarly nauseous? What if she were pregnant? Pregnant with Zac's baby? What then, dear Lord? What then?

Chapter Eighteen

Dressed in a white silk shirt, black trousers, black ballerina pumps and with a yellow cashmere cardigan around her shoulders, Christina sat by Jack's bed, her eyes dark-shadowed by sleeplessness and stress. She had been home briefly since her first vigil at the hospital, for in her shocked response to Bob Giles's news, she hadn't thought to pack a bag with Jack's pyjamas or toilet things, and arrived at St Thomas's, just after four in the morning, completely empty-handed. Now, however, a small bag with everything he might need was stowed in his bedside locker, and Jack was propped up against pillows, looking like death.

'Your husband has had a lucky escape,' the surgeon said to her when, several hours previously, Jack was wheeled back into the ward after emergency surgery. 'Another half inch to the left, and the knife wound would have been fatal. The police are waiting to speak to him, but I've told them he's not yet fit to be questioned.'

She had flinched at the word 'knife' and, because she was an extremely beautiful woman and he was a man with a very healthy libido, he felt a pang of pity for her. She didn't look the sort of woman who could expect her husband to be half-killed in a sordid gangland knife fight. A fight that had been, if the information he had received was correct, over a woman other than herself. Mindful that the other person injured in the fight was lying behind screens only half a dozen beds away, he made a mental note to have Mr Duke removed to another ward at the first opportunity. He didn't want a fracas on the ward and, if Mr Robson and Mr Duke were too ill to cause one themselves, their respective visitors would not be. 'If you want to stay close by until your husband comes round from the anaesthetic, you can do so in the visitors' waiting-room,' he said, mystified as to why such a classy-looking woman should have married a Soho gambling-club villain. 'Visitors aren't allowed on the ward outside visiting hours, not even for cases such as your husband's.'

She thanked him, grateful that, as Malcolm Lewis had taken Bob Giles the short distance from St Thomas's to Guy's in order that he could check on Mavis's condition, she was at last on her own. She had plenty to think about, not least her reaction when, all the time Jack had been in the operating theatre, she was convinced he was going to die. She knew then that she didn't want to live her life without him – and that if he was in love with Mavis and a way of life that revolved around Soho and sleaze, that might very well be the future she was facing. She began to cry then, tears sliding down her face and dropping onto her hands. How had everything gone so very, very wrong between them? What other aspects of Jack's life, aspects such as the club Mavis had been involved in with him, did she know absolutely nothing about?

Later, for a few precious moments, she was allowed to sit by his bedside and, barely conscious, he reached for her hand, mumbling thickly, 'Tina? Is that you, love? Glad it's you, Teen. Ver glad . . .' His voice had tailed away as he slid again into unconsciousness, and the Ward Sister asked her to return to the waiting-room where, in lonely privacy, she wept even harder and longer.

Only when a deeply anxious Charlie arrived at the hospital

did she leave it, returning not to Greenwich, but to Magnolia Square where, within seconds, it became obvious to her that word of what had happened was rife, and had been for hours. 'Jack's going to be all right,' she said time and time again as people asked after him and, trying to hide prurient curiosity, asked also after Mavis. 'The wound isn't as critical as they first feared. I don't know anything about Mavis's condition other than that she was badly hurt. Mr Giles is at the hospital with her. He's the one who will have news.'

With intense relief, knowing very well that her enquirers and well-wishers were all wondering if there was, after all, some truth in the old rumours about the nature of Jack and Mavis's relationship, she closed her front door against everyone. Mavis. She still hadn't allowed herself to think too much about Mavis. She daren't think too much about Mavis and what had happened to her. The subject was too emotionally charged, too bound up with the fact that if it hadn't been for his reaction to Mavis's injuries, Jack would not have come so close to losing his life.

Instead of dwelling on thoughts she was unable to cope with, Christina scooped up Jack's razor and shaving brush from the bathroom shelf and plucked his toothbrush and toothpaste from the drinking glass on the wash-basin, tipping them into a toilet-bag. Then she stuffed the toilet-bag and two pairs of pyjamas into a capacious carry-all and hurried from the house, this time being waylaid only by Lettie and by Nellie.

Despite her fraught anxiety to get back to St Thomas's as swiftly as possible, she didn't catch a bus that would take her directly there, but cut across the heath, hurrying down Croom's Hill into Greenwich. It was a detour that would add fifteen minutes or so to her overall journey but, as she had reached an agreement with Madge Dracup that she would look after Judith every day, and, as her commitment to Judith was now total, it was an inconvenience she undertook gladly.

'Why can't I come in the hospital with you?' Judith asked her on the bus ride up to London Bridge. 'I'd be ever so good. I wouldn't make a squeak.'

For the first time that morning a shadow of a smile had touched Christina's mouth. She loved the feel of Judith's small hand in hers; of the trust in her eyes, eyes that were nearly the same astonishing amethyst colour as her own. 'Because children aren't allowed in the hospital,' she said truthfully. 'Not as visitors. You'll be able to wait for me in the gardens, though, and there'll be other children there. I won't be very long. The hospital doesn't allow even grown-up visitors to stay with patients for long.'

Now, allowed for a short period of time to sit by Jack's bed, she could see through the window to where, two floors below, Judith was playing marbles in the hospital gardens with another patiently waiting little girl.

'What are you thinking, love?' Jack asked thickly. Beneath his rarely worn pyjama jacket, his chest was bulkily bandaged and a saline drip was running into his left arm, just above the wrist.

Her eyes met his, her heart turning over with love and apprehension and deep, deep unhappiness. 'I was thinking about Mavis,' she said, her low voice betraying only the merest hint of an accent. 'I was wondering how long the two of you had been seeing so much of each other. I was wondering if, from now on, that was how you wanted things to be.'

Jack closed his eyes for a moment, his hold on her hand tightening. What had happened last night between himself and Archie had, in a way he couldn't understand, brought his and Christina's difficulties into sharp focus. It was impossible any longer to treat her leaving home to live with her mother and stepfather as if it were the outcome of an ordinary, run-of-the-mill domestic spat. Christina didn't indulge in needlessly dramatic domestic spats. Their marriage was at crisis point, and he didn't want it to be at crisis point. Christina was special – unique – so far removed in type from a rowdily jolly south-east London girl as to be a creature from another planet. If he lost her he would never find anyone like her ever again. And he wasn't going to lose her. No matter what the cost, he *wouldn't* lose her.

Fighting the fuzziness and nausea that were the after-effects of his anaesthesia, he said with raw truthfulness, knowing the issue could be fudged no longer, 'Things *have* been getting out of hand where me and Mavis are concerned, but I haven't wanted them to, Tina. God's honest truth, I haven't wanted them to.'

Christina could feel tears again burning the backs of her eyes. All her life she'd been so self-contained that she hardly ever cried and now, for a whole array of reasons, she couldn't seem to stop.

'It's you I love, Tina!' Jack's passionate fierceness drew the interested attention of the occupants of the beds at either side of him. 'If you don't believe anything else, you must believe that!'

She did believe it, but it still didn't make everything work-able again. 'The club,' she said, willing him to understand how she felt about him having such a dubious business in such a blatant red-light area. 'Have you other clubs in Soho, beside The 21? And is that what we've been living on? Money from . . . from—'

'The 21 isn't a strip club, love,' he said, guessing what it was she was trying, and couldn't bring herself, to say. He winced with pain when, unintentionally, he moved against his carefully arranged pillows.

Aware of his agonizing discomfort, she knew she should leave him in order that he could get some rest, but her relief that they were at last talking openly to each other was so vast, she couldn't bring herself to make the move.

Jack's eyes held hers, gold-flecked and intense. He didn't understand why she felt so strongly about the club but, as she did do, he was coming to a hard decision, one of the hardest he had ever made. 'Listen love,' he said, his hand still holding hers, 'How about if I hand over the club to Mavis and get myself a straight job? Will you move back home? Will you agree to our making a fresh start?'

Even white as a sheet from the after-effects of his operation, he still possessed more masculinity and charisma than any other man she'd ever met. They didn't have babies – would never have babies – but now that Judith had come into her life this was, perhaps, something she would one day be able to come to terms with. 'Yes,' she said, knowing that what he was offering was enough; that it was more than enough. From out of the corner of her eye she saw that the Ward Sister was heading their way and knew that her extra-concessionary visiting-time was coming to an end. 'Can you see out of the window, Jack?' she asked with sudden urgency. 'Can you see the little dark-haired girl playing marbles?' And ignoring the approaching swish of starched blue uniform, she began to tell him about Judith.

Later on in the day, when Danny came to visit him, Jack was still thinking over everything she had told him. 'Do you know anything about this kiddie Christina's taken up with?' he asked, battling agonizing discomfort and still finding speech an enormous effort.

Danny, looking like something out of a horror comic with his red hair sticking up at odd angles and his bruised and swollen face sporting a horrendous patchwork of stitches, stared at him blankly out of the only eye he could open. 'Blimey, Jack!

We've got more to worry about at the moment than your missus an' any kid she might be lookin' after! Mavis is in a right state an' ain't even allowed visitors, 'cept fer Ted and the vicar. Accordin' to Ted she doesn't remember us findin' her at the club or us gettin' 'er to 'ospital, an' she don't know yet about your run-in with Archie.'

Jack's mouth, already tight with pain, tightened even further. He might have nearly lost his life taking on Archie Duke with his bare fists, but it was an action he didn't regret. The only thing he did regret was that Archie's ginger-haired henchman had, by pulling a knife on him, put an end to the matter before he had put Archie out of commission not only temporarily, but for good.

'Ted says that despite the state of 'er face, Mavis's main worry is that if the rozzers 'ave bin called in, the club will lose its licence,' Danny added, his voice thick with worry.

Jack grunted. The problem of the police and The 21's drinking licence was one he'd been giving a lot of thought to, for it would certainly be lost if Mavis laid charges for Grievous Bodily Harm against Archie and his thugs and, likewise, if Archie and his thugs laid similar charges against himself and Danny. Not that it was likely Archie would do so. Tangling with the law, for any reason, was not in Archie's best interests.

As if reading his mind, Danny said, 'I 'ad an uncomfortable 'alf 'our with the rozzers earlier today, but I don't fink they're goin' to take fings any further, Jack. They've already questioned Archie and 'e ain't talkin'.' He grinned. 'Mind you, considerin' the condition you left Archie in, it'd be a miracle if 'e could talk even if 'e wanted to!'

Jack gave a passable imitation of a smile, grateful for the news. It certainly simplified things for him where his own pending statement to the police was concerned. With an effort, knowing Danny wouldn't be allowed to stay for much longer, he said, 'What about Monday night's pirate fight with Big Jumbo, Danny? Will you and Leon be able to cope?'

This time it was Danny's turn to grunt. The day he couldn't manage a pirate fight was the day he'd give up on life. 'Course we can,' he said, hoping his head would have stopped hurting by then. 'The only narking thing is, we still don't know who Big Jumbo's opponent is. The way these fights are fixed leaves a lot to be desired, Jack.'

Jack made a noise of agreement. He was flagging fast and knew it. What he needed was sleep. Lots of sleep. 'And without Zac, this particular fight is going to be pretty pointless,' he said, making no effort to hide the bitter disappointment he felt. Zac, and Zac alone, had been the reason the fight had been arranged. With Big Jumbo taking his place, there was no money to be made. Only money to be lost. Nor was that all. The professional fixer who arranged it had obviously been bombed out of his brain when he arranged the date for, as Leon had pointed out when they were first told of it, 'A lot of punters won't turn up, Jack. Not on the night before the coronation. Their wives will be wanting to spend the night up town, staking themselves a good place for a view of the procession.'

One thing was for sure. He wasn't going to get a good view of the coronation procession. Not unless a television was wheeled into the ward. He closed his eyes, wondering when he'd be given some more painkillers, wondering how Mavis was getting on; remembering again the scene from his bedside window as Christina had walked out of the hospital and across to where Judith was playing and Judith, seeing her, had run shining-eyed and open-armed towards her.

'I can't face the coronation,' Kate said bleakly to Leon as they walked a footpath close to Greenland Dock. 'I don't want to be amongst people all cheering and having the time of their lives. Not when I can't stop thinking about Matthew. Not when we still don't know if Matthew is alive or . . . or . . .'

She couldn't continue. She couldn't say the word 'dead', and nor did Leon want her to. His arm was around her shoulder and he clasped it tightly. As a waterman, he was well aware of how very many bodies were fished from the Thames in any one year. It had been seventy last year: most of them suicidal jumpers from Tower Bridge. If a waterman, or anyone else working on the river, fished one of them up, the going reward was seven shillings and sixpence. At the prospect of someone being paid seven shillings and sixpence for fishing up Matthew's body, Leon's chest constricted so tightly he had to fight for breath.

'What's the matter, darling?' Kate looked up at him sharply, fresh fear in her eyes.

'Nothing,' he lied, knowing he had to keep his worst fears to himself, that no good at all could come of his burdening her with them. With immense effort he forced himself to think, instead, of Queen Elizabeth's coronation. It would be a truly historic occasion, the kind of occasion that, no matter what the circumstances, Daisy and Luke, Jilly and Johnny, shouldn't be allowed to miss. 'Carrie and Rose will be going up town Monday night to save themselves places on the pavement in the Mall, won't they?' he asked, mindful that, as the long-arranged pirate fight was to take place on Monday evening, Danny wasn't likely to be accompanying them. 'How about suggesting to Daisy that she goes with them and that she takes the youngsters with her? The coronation is something they ought to see, and the adventure of sleeping out in the Mall will take their minds off Matthew for a bit.' His dark face, already gouged with lines of weariness and deep anxiety, took on an even more troubled expression. 'And Daisy, especially, needs something to take her mind off Matthew for a while. She's been trying to hide it, but she's spending most of her time crying.'

Kate remained silent. Daisy was making herself ill by worrying over Matthew, and he was certainly one of the reasons her eyes were so persistently red-rimmed from crying – but he wasn't the only reason. Though Leon wasn't aware that Daisy and Billy's relationship had become romantic, she was aware of it and she knew, too, that something had gone wrong with it. Where Daisy's tears for Matthew left off and her tears over Billy started, Kate didn't know. She was sure, though, that left to itself, the problem would sort itself out.

They were so close to the vast dock they were almost deafened by the noise of whistles and hooters as barges, tugs and ships vied for position at quays and loading bays. As crane drivers slung pallets and bales across the sky from ships' holds to barges, and dockers and stevedores went about their work shouting and swearing, Kate wondered how many times she and Leon had been down the Greenland together, showing Matthew's photograph to all and sundry, asking the same questions time and time again. 'Have you seen this boy? If you do see him, will you contact the River Police?'

Unlike on previous visits, the docks and dock-side now sported a garish array of Union Jacks and coronation bunting. Yesterday Jilly came home from school clutching a celebratory coronation mug she had been given. Harriet Robson was, she knew, baking sausage rolls and tarts on a mammoth scale, ready to feed all the neighbours who would be squeezing in to number two to watch the coronation on television. Elisha Deakin had already festooned the exterior of The Swan with giant-size flags, and the interior with red, white and blue paper streamers. The whole world, it seemed, was gearing itself up to enjoy the biggest visual spectacle of its life. But she and Leon weren't. Unless Matthew returned home safe and sound, she was sure she and Leon would never again joyfully celebrate anything.

Overcome by a despair impossible to control, she looked

away from the gaily fluttering flags and pressed her face against Leon's shoulder, beginning, once again, to weep.

'Mum and Dad have gone down to Greenland Dock,' Luke said to Deborah Harvey as she stepped imperiously into the house.

Deborah was unsurprised. Leon Emmerson was always searching some part of the river area for Matthew, and Kate often accompanied him. The anxiety she shared with the Emmersons had, as the days turned into weeks and there was still no news of Matthew, resulted in a grudging bond being formed between herself and them. As she said to Genevre that morning, 'Whatever the man's skin colour, there's no denying that Matthew's stepfather is as worried about him as the rest of us. The police, for reasons best known only to themselves, seem to have ceased looking for Matthew. If anyone is going to find him, I think it will be Leon Emmerson.'

And she no longer thought it strange to sit in a kitchen, for as she had also said to Genevre, 'The kitchens in Magnolia Square are remarkably roomy and, now it's nearly June, the Emmersons' kitchen is full of sunshine nearly all day long.' It was also, she saw when she sat down in the comfortable rocking-chair she always appropriated, full of flowers. On the deal kitchen table was a glazed brown teapot stuffed with fragrant carnations, and on the window-sill was a milk-jug crammed with pale pink, indigo-eyed phlox.

'You can give your mother a message for me, young man,' she said, beginning to ease lilac-coloured net gloves off arthritically gnarled fingers. 'Neither Genevre nor I relish the prospect of being in Kensington on Coronation Day. I don't know what sort of activities will be taking place in the grounds of Kensington Palace, but there's bound to be something, and it's bound to be noisy: guardsmen marching up and down and beating drums or some other such foolery. As I don't imagine for one minute that your parents will be in the mood to celebrate the Queen's crowning, I thought it might be a good idea if Genevre and I spent the day here, with them.'

It wasn't the real reason she wanted to spend Coronation Day in Magnolia Square, but it was the only one she felt prepared to give. The real reason was far too emotive for her to be able to put into words. Coronation Day was such a huge historical and symbolic landmark that it seemed impossible Matthew would not be home for it. If he were not . . . her crippled fingers tightened painfully together . . . if he were not, then she knew she would begin to lose all hope for his eventual safe return.

Luke shrugged, happily oblivious of Deborah Harvey's highly charged nervous tension. He'd long since ceased having any antipathetic feelings about her, and if she and Matthew's Aunt Genevre wanted to spend Coronation Day in Magnolia Square, it was all right by him.

With her message delivered, Deborah looked around the kitchen. It was a strange fact of life that, no matter how fraught her inner distress, she always experienced a comforting sense of ease whenever she was in Matthew's home. Was it, perhaps, because there was always so much of interest going on and always something for her to comment on or criticize? Take the strange collection of tiny articles set on top of the washing machine and all, apparently, sprouting grass.

'What are those strange little implements?' she asked, glad there was something which would divert her thoughts, for a little while at least, away from the distressing mystery of Matthew's whereabouts.

Luke sat down at the table and pulled the sketchpad he had been drawing on when she knocked at the door once again towards him. 'They're tiny saucepans belonging to Jilly's toy stove,' he said with a grin. 'Johnny's growing mustard and cress in them.'

Deborah felt a spurt of empathy. She, too, had grown mustard and cress as a child, though on a damp flannel, if her memory served her right. 'And what are you doing?' she asked in her brusque, no-nonsense way.

Luke, well accustomed to her manner and indifferent to it, slid his sketchpad around so that she could see what he was drawing. 'It's a building,' he said, in case she couldn't decipher it. 'A skyscraper-type building, like they have in New York and Chicago. They can't build them here,' he added knowledge-ably. 'It's a pity, isn't it?'

Deborah didn't agree with him. She was too taken aback. The drawing wasn't a drawing of a finished building. It was an elevation, a representation of the flat side of a building as an architect might have drawn it. And the building, multi-storied and quite obviously metal-framed, was like no building she had ever seen before.

'Such a building would never stand up,' she said, remem-bering all the hundreds and hundreds of building plans she had, as Deborah Harvey of the Harvey Construction Company, seen over the years. 'Where are the wall supports? Come to that, young man, where are the walls?'

Luke grinned. Matthew's great-aunt was a bad-tempered old bat, but she wasn't boring – or stupid. 'Skyscrapers are built on a very different principle to other buildings,' he said. 'That's what makes them so fascinating.' He pulled his chair away from the table and closer to hers, so that he could point out relevant parts of the drawing with the point of a pencil. 'See here? This glass exterior surface is known as a curtain-wall, but it doesn't support the building as old-fashioned walls of bricks and mortar do. The building is supported on the floors from within. It's clever, isn't it?'

It was clever, but it wasn't the cleverness of the construction technique that was rendering her speechless, it was the fact that it was Luke Emmerson who was explaining it to her. Luke Emmerson, a boy she had always been led to believe was not very bright and who was always in trouble at school for being inattentive; a mixed-race south-east London boy who she would have expected to have had no ambition other, perhaps, than that of becoming a Thames waterman, like his father.

The thought brought back a memory she had tried to suppress, a memory of the Emmersons telling her that it was Matthew – Matthew who was heir to an international construction company – who was interested in the River. She sucked in air, fighting for breath. And Luke, Leon Emmerson's son, was passionate about building!

Aware that she was winded, though not knowing why, Luke remembered that he hadn't yet made her a cup of tea. Regretfully he pushed his sketchpad to one side once again and rose to his feet. 'Would you like a cup of tea? A cup of Lapsang Souchong?'

Deborah nodded, grateful for the fact that Kate did at least keep a decent tea in her kitchen cupboard, even if it was only used for guests. She'd tried to convert Nellie to the pleasures of Lapsang Souchong and had failed. 'Cat's pee,' Nellie had pronounced, spluttering her first mouthful of it back into her cup. 'That's what it tastes like. Put some sugar an' condensed milk into it, that might perk it up a bit.'

'Is Architecture on your school syllabus?' she asked, unable to keep incredulity from her voice. A south-east London state school, a school that was not even a grammar school, with Architecture on its syllabus? It was surely unheard of. She doubted if even Matthew's public school taught so specialized a subject to eleven- and twelve-year-olds.

Luke shook his head as he filled the kettle at the sink, his thick mop of curly hair as luxuriant as a girl's. 'No,' he said, happy to talk to her, just as he was always happy to talk to Nellie. 'We do Art and Maths, but the two are never linked together. In Art all we ever do is mess about with clay, and in Maths it's all easy problems. How many apples six ounces each and costing one and threepence a pound you can buy for ten shillings and all that sort of boring stuff.'

Deborah stared again at his pencil-drawn elevation of a modern multi-storied building, not surprised that the lessons he had just described bored him, or that he was inattentive in them. 'Then who . . . ?' She waved a hand towards his drawing. 'How . . . ?'

Luke put the kettle on the electric hob and then took hold of a kitchen chair and straddled it, resting his folded arms on its bentwood back. 'My Grandad Voigt,' he said, adding, 'He's German,' just in case she didn't know.

Deborah shuddered. She knew very well that her nephew's maternal grandfather was a Hun. It was the initial reason her own father, Matthew's great-grandfather, had never wanted anything whatever to do with Matthew's mother or family.

Luke, happily unaware of the kind of dark memories he was disturbing, continued with his explanation. 'Grandad Voigt didn't want me to grow up thinking all Germans, apart from him, were bad Germans, and so he told me about Germans who are respected world-wide and who left Germany rather than live under Hitler. Germans like Mies van der Rohe, who used to be director of the Bauhaus.' He looked towards the kettle to see if it was beginning to puff steam yet, adding helpfully, 'The Bauhaus was in Weimar and was the world's—'

'Leading design centre,' Deborah finished for him testily, wondering if he realized just what the Harvey family business was. 'And I'm familiar with the name Mies.' But not, she thought frustratedly, *knowledgeable*. No German architects, not even

Nazi-hating ones, had ever served as role models for architects working for Harvey Construction International.

Luke's amber-brown eyes held hers with interest. Apart from his grandad, he'd never come across anyone who knew the name of any architect. 'I got a book from the library,' he said, rising to his feet in order to remove the now boiling kettle from the hob, 'and there were lots of photographs in it of Mies's work. Skyscrapers that were just . . . tremendous.' He poured a small amount of the boiling water into a teapot and swirled it round to warm it. 'They were all black steel and had curtain walls of clear glass, though I didn't know what a curtain wall was then, of course.' He emptied the water from the teapot into the sink and reached for the tea-caddy. 'Sometimes the glass was bronze-tinted!' There was awe in his voice and an expression of utter rapture on his dusky face. 'They look like something out of a science-fiction comic, but they're *real*.'

Deborah was beginning to feel that the conversation was far from real. If she were having it with Matthew it would, of course, have been a very different matter. But she wasn't having it with Matthew. Matthew wasn't remotely interested in any aspect of the construction industry, or of the vast company that would one day be a part of his inheritance. This boy, however, this very unlikely boy, was besotted with the beauty of buildings!

As Nellie would have said, it was a rum situation. A situation that needed a lot of thought. A lot of very careful thought.

'I've bin thinkin',' Nellie said ruminatively to Leah, 'about what's goin' to 'appen between your Mavis an' Jack when they come out of 'ospital. Do yer think they might move in with each other? They've obviously got a bit of a ding-dong goin', ain't they?'

If it were anyone else making such a remark, Leah would

have shot them down in flames. Nellie, however, was one of her oldest friends and, as she was also a friend she didn't see enough of, the bedroom stairs being too much of an obstacle for Nellie to tackle with any great regularity, she wasn't about to make a *tummel* by taking offence. 'Whatever kind of ding-dong Mavis and Jack are having, legitimate it's never going to be,' she said, yanking Boots a bit higher up the eiderdown so that, if Nellie should topple from her chair, she wouldn't fall on him and squash him flat. 'They're two of a kind, *bubee*, and that never works under one roof. Besides, Ted would never divorce Mavis. If he was the divorcing type, he'd have divorced her years ago!'

This was indubitably the truth, and something even Nellie couldn't argue with. 'P'rhaps it's for the best,' she said philo-sophically, 'especially as 'ow that monster Archie Duke cut up Mavis's face. It's bound to clip 'er wings, ain't it? I mean, she won't be able to gallivant now like she used to, will she?'

Leah's seamed mouth tightened so hard it nearly disappeared. She'd never had any patience with her eldest grand-daughter's good-time behaviour, but her face being cut with broken glass, she didn't deserve. *'Momzer!'* she said of the monster in ques-tion, glad that, if the rumours she and Nellie had heard were true, Jack had half-killed him. 'All these troubles! Mavis and Jack in hospital beds. No sight or sound of young Matthew Harvey. Billy and Daisy not speaking to each other, and Billy hanging around with one of Queenie Tillet's circus *artistes.*'

'Billy 'angin' around with *who*?' Nellie's eyes had nearly popped out of her head.

Leah raised her hands expressively. 'A circus *artiste*! I saw them the other night with my own eyes. And the clothes she wears! Black fishnet tights and high-heeled shoes, and when she got into that ramshackle lorry of his, she was wearing a man's tailcoat and was carrying a top-hat under her arm!'

'Blimey! Lion-tamers dress like that!' Nellie had always had a soft spot for Billy and, at the thought of him courting a lion-tamer, was vastly impressed. 'I don't suppose she'll be around for long, though,' she added, unable to hide the disappoint-ment accompanying this thought. 'The circus never stays in the area for more than a week or two at a time. Still, perhaps she'll be around long enough to teach Billy a few circus tricks, like fire-eatin' or trapeze-walkin'.'

Leah didn't respond to this remark. As far as she was concerned there were enough bizarre goings-on in Magnolia Square without young Billy Lomax adding to them by setting his quiff alight, fire-eating! The boxing chap who was lodging with Queenie for instance. Whenever Beryl came to visit her it was obvious she was still carrying a torch for him. Her plain, loveable face would be a picture of misery as she recounted how, no matter how many times she went to the gym, Zac Hemingway either wasn't there or, if he was, seemed unaware of her existence. 'He always asks after Aunt Carrie, though,' she had said guilelessly on her last lunch-time visit. 'Do you think he wants to see her so that he can ask her if I'm inter-ested in him? Do you think he's shy, Great-Gran? Do you think that's why he doesn't say anything to me himself?'

Leah thought Beryl was clutching at the frailest of straws. She'd seen Zac Hemingway lots of times from her bedroom window, and a man with his physique and looks and palpable self-confidence wasn't likely to be shy. What he was likely to be, though, was interested in a woman he had no business being interested in. A woman older than himself. A woman who was married. A woman who became as flustered as a schoolgirl every time his name was mentioned.

'*Oi vey*,' she said, this time not sharing her thoughts with her friend. '*Oi vey, oi vey*.' If Carrie was having an affair with Zac Hemingway, then there would be big trouble ahead.

'Stop frettin',' Nellie said comfortingly, thinking Leah was still dwelling on Billy and his bizarre new girlfriend. 'It'll blow over. Everythin' does – eventually.'

With long, easy strides Zac walked into the Hare and Billet. It was only just evening opening time, but he'd had an extremely satisfying day and was ready for a celebratory pint.

'You're early,' the landlord said, not remotely curious. 'What's it to be? The usual?'

Zac nodded. The thing he liked about the Hare and Billet was that he wasn't regarded there as a piece of public property, unlike at The Swan, where he was always plagued by ceaseless questions as to when he was going to fight in a fight that would put a bit of money in everyone's pocket.

As his pint of beer was being pulled, he reflected on his good fortune. 'The *Orion* will be arriving from Rio on Monday,' his contact down at the docks had said to him. 'She'll be in the Pool of London all day, unloading and then loading and then, because her captain doesn't want to get caught up in Tuesday's coronation razzmatazz, she'll be setting sail late that night.'

'And her captain will take me, no questions asked?' he had queried. 'And he'll take a woman passenger as well?'

His contact had grinned. 'Captain Juarez is so crooked that, for the right amount of money, he'd smuggle a couple of convicted murderers out of the country!'

The landlord passed his pint of beer across to him. 'Nasty news about the woman in Magnolia Square, isn't it? They say her face is badly glassed and that Jack Robson nearly killed the fellow responsible.'

He began wiping down the polished surface of the bar, glad of the opportunity to talk with someone who lived in Magnolia Square and who might have some more information on things.

'It's a miracle to me that Robson didn't finish him off good and proper,' he continued wryly. 'He's an ex-commando and those blokes are trained to kill with their bare hands.'

'Pity he didn't.' Zac's words were heartfelt. When, early that morning, he'd heard what had been done to Mavis, he'd wanted to throttle the bastard responsible. He'd also wanted to see Carrie, but, hard as he tried, he'd not been able to track her down. Assuming that this was because she was at Guy's, visiting Mavis, it was then that he decided to go down to the docks to see if there was any news of a suitable ship. He took a swallow of his beer, saying, 'Whatever Jack gave him, the bloke more than deserved.'

'No, he didn't,' a voice piped up from further down the bar. ''Cos it wasn't Archie what glassed 'er. It was Arnie what glassed 'er.'

Both Zac and the landlord turned and stared. Pongo shrugged. They could stare all they liked – what he was saying was the truth. Archie hadn't even told Arnie to rough up Jack Robson's blonde bint. All he'd told him to do was to lock her in the lav, out of the way.

'Say that again, mate,' Zac demanded.

'It wasn't Archie what glassed Jack Robson's bit of stuff,' Pongo said obligingly. 'It was Arnie, and Arnie was long gone by the time Jack Robson caught up with Archie.'

'Blimey!' the landlord said expressively. 'Robson isn't going to be very pleased with that little bit of information when he finally receives it!'

Zac eased himself away from the bar, tension in every line of his body. 'Arnie?' he said to Pongo. 'Arnie who?'

Pongo shrugged yet again. 'I dunno,' he said truthfully. 'Some pervert that boxes in pirate fights for Archie. He's fighting a bloke called Big Jumbo on Monday night, but I don't know where.'

Zac's hands were already balling into fists. 'I do,' he said grimly, knowing there'd be time for the fight before the *Orion* set sail; knowing that Big Jumbo wasn't going to mind if he took his place; knowing that as he'd soon be out of the country, it wouldn't even matter if he killed the bastard!

Chapter Nineteen

Carrie was in the kitchen, bathing Danny's patchwork quilt of facial stitches with tepid salt-water, when Zac strode into the house as if he owned it. Her reaction was one of such exhilarating, electrifying shock that she dropped the bowl she was holding, spilling water over Danny as well as the floor.

'Hey, steady on, pet! Don't bleedin' drown me!' Danny protested indignantly, and then, to Zac, 'She makes a rotten Florence Nightingale – it'd 'ave all bin the same if the water 'ad bin boilin'!'

Zac flashed Carrie a look of such heat and intimacy she had to grab hold of the sink to steady herself. What on earth was he doing walking in on her and Danny without so much as a by-your-leave or a knock on the door?

The possibility that he'd come to have a showdown with Danny stupefied her with panic, but then he was saying, 'It wasn't Archie who glassed Mavis, Danny. And it wasn't any of the cretins who were with him when you and Jack caught up with him. It was a geezer by the name of Arnie – the geezer Big Jumbo was all set to fight tomorrow night.'

'Christ all bleedin' mighty!' Danny gawped at him, trying to take on board that Jack had nearly killed, and swung for, the wrong bloke and that the bloke he *should* have nearly killed was walking around unscathed! Another thought occurred to his dazed brain. 'What do yer mean, *was* all set to fight? Does this

284

Arnie bloke know we've nobbled 'im, an' is 'e ducking out of the arrangement?'

'Nah.' Zac's usual ever-so-easy smile was grim. 'He doesn't have a clue we know it was him, and we don't want him to, otherwise he might not show.'

'But I thought yer said the fight was scuppered—'

'Nah.' There was a glint in Zac's eyes, a glint that had Carrie feeling she was racing down the biggest roller-coaster in the world. 'The fight's still on. But I want you to tell Jack it won't be Big Jumbo the bastard will be facing. It'll be me!'

'S'truth!' As realization as to what this would mean registered with him, Danny's freckled face was a picture of fierce satisfaction. Mavis's attacker would have his come-uppance – and he, and everyone else at the fight and in the know, would be quids in!

Thinking only of Mavis, the same fierce excitement gripped Carrie, as did another sensation.

'Blimey, pet,' her nearest and dearest said as she clapped a hand across her mouth and spun around to face the sink. 'Yer ain't bin eatin' my pickled gherkins, 'ave yer? That's the third time you've thrown up in an 'our!'

Carrie heaved, and brought up bile. She wasn't surprised. She'd been sick so often, there was nothing else left in her stomach to bring up!

'I'd better be gettin' down to St Thomas's to put Jack in the picture,' Danny said as she rinsed her mouth out with water. 'Then I'll 'ave a word with Big Jumbo – 'e's not goin' to mind bein' dropped from the fight. Not under the circumstances. An' I'll 'ave a word with Leon, as well – and old Charlie.'

'Danny!' Carrie was on her own private roller-coaster again. Danny couldn't leave now! Not right this very minute! Not leaving her and Zac alone in the house. 'Danny, hang on a minute—'

'I'll give Jack your love,' Danny said, already hurrying through the house towards the half-open front door. 'And you get dahn to the gym, Zac! I want you so fit yer could wipe the floor with Rocky bleedin' Marciano!'

Carrie ran after him, but before she could catch up with him he was down the path and out into the square. She stood on the front doorstep, struggling to regulate her racing heartbeat.

In the golden, early evening light, Pru Lewis, Malcolm Lewis's wife, was hanging a Union Jack out of a bedroom window in readiness for Tuesday's celebrations. Nellie was stomping her way across the square in the general direction of Kate and Leon's. Nibbo was trimming his hedge. Danny, heading for Lewisham High Street and a bus up to London Bridge, had already taken the corner into Magnolia Hill at a run and was lost to view.

Sucking in a steadying lungful of air, Carrie turned to re-enter her home and face Zac. He was leaning against the newel post at the bottom of the stairs, his thumbs hooked in the front pockets of his jeans, one leg crossing the other at the ankle. With a strong sense of *déjà vu*, she was reminded of the first time she had met him. He had been standing in her hallway, nonchalant and impudently at ease, just as he was now.

Now, though, they were lovers, and his being in her marital home, especially when Danny wasn't in it, disturbed her profoundly.

'I think you should leave . . .' she began through dry lips, the door still half-open behind her.

He grinned, his hair a dull gold in the shadowed hallway. 'We're both leaving,' he said, moving away from the newel post and towards her, 'immediately after tomorrow night's fight.' He caught hold of her wrists, pinioning them behind her back, drawing her so near to him she could feel his hardness through the thin cotton of her dress. 'I've got places for the two of us aboard a cargo ship sailing for New Zealand.'

She gave a gasp of disbelief. 'I can't leave tomorrow night!' Giddily she remembered that she wasn't going to leave at all; that she had vowed that yesterday, and only yesterday, was all the time they would ever have together.

The heat in his eyes deepened, turning his grey eyes almost black. 'Yes, you can,' he said in a honeyed voice of reason. 'It's easy. You just pack a small bag and step over the doorstep – and you don't turn around or look back.' His lips were brushing her temples, the curve of her cheek, the corner of her mouth.

'No, Zac!' Her voice was a croak. If she'd felt herself to be another person ever since she'd met him, she now felt herself disorientated almost to the point of disembodiment! Who was this woman contemplating, even for the briefest of seconds, leaving hearth and home, husband and child, friends and family – everything that was familiar, everything that made up the substance of her life – for a man she barely knew? It couldn't be her, Carrie Collins. It *couldn't* be. It was. As, with her arms still pinioned behind her, his mouth came down hot and sweet on hers, all she could think of was how dizzyingly wonderful it would be to be with him always: to be with him in a clean, quiet country of blue mountains and rushing rivers.

He lifted his head from hers and dazedly she opened her eyes, looking above his broad shoulders to the faded, familiar flower pattern of her hall wallpaper; the plaster head of an Alsatian dog that hung on the wall opposite the newel post and that Rose had brought back after a school day-trip to Margate; the worn stair carpet that had been nearly new when Danny filched it and, bringing it home while she was at the cinema with Kate, had laid straight away as a surprise for her.

'No,' she said again, her voice strangled. 'I can't, Zac. It's not possible. It's utterly *im*possible—'

There came the rat-a-tat-tat of Cuban-heeled shoes as someone slowed down at her gateway and then, seconds later, turned in at it.

Jerking free of Zac so suddenly that she stumbled, Carrie looked towards the open doorway and elderly Harriet Robson.

'I'm sorry, Carrie. I'll come back later,' Harriet said with stilted awkwardness, unsure of what it was she had seen.

'It's all right, Harriet! Don't go!' Circumnavigating Zac, Carrie stepped hastily towards her. 'I had something in my eye, but Zac's got it out. What was it you wanted?'

Ashamed of the suspicion that had, for a moment, crossed her mind, Harriet said hesitantly, 'I was wondering if Danny was home and if he could give Charlie a hand putting up the square's Coronation Day flags and bunting. I know Leon is at home, but I don't like to ask him – not under the circumstances.' She tucked a straying strand of silver hair back into her bun. 'To tell the truth, Carrie, I'm not sure we should be putting up decorations, not when Matthew is still missing and Mavis and Jack are lying in hospital. Charlie doesn't agree with me. He says both Mavis and Jack would want whatever show was going on, to still go on, and that Coronation Day might just be the attraction to bring young Matthew home, and that if he does come home on Coronation Day, it would be a sorry state of affairs if there were no flags or bunting up.'

Carrie struggled to think straight. With Zac still only mere inches away from her, the task wasn't easy. 'Danny isn't in, Harriet,' she said, trying to come to grips with the fact that the coronation was nearly upon them and that, as yet, she'd hardly given it a thought. 'He's gone up to St Thomas's to visit Jack.'

'Then I wonder, Mr Hemingway, if you might be able to give my husband a hand?' Harriet said queryingly to Zac. 'Mr Nibbs is already helping him, but he hasn't a head for heights

and the bunting needs to be strung from the top of one lamp-
post to the top of another.'

Zac, mindful that the evening before a fight was too late for
a heavy training session to make much of a difference to the
outcome, shrugged away Danny's advice to get immediately
down to the gym, saying with easy good humour, 'I'm at your
disposal. Lead the way and I'll have Magnolia Square a sea of
red, white and blue in no time at all.'

Harriet beamed. She still thought him a rather disconcerting
young man, but at least he was obliging. As she led the way
back down Carrie's front path, the obliging Mr Hemingway
looked back towards Carrie, and winked. Scarlet-faced, Carrie
whipped the door shut and then leaned exhaustedly against it.
What on earth was happening to her nice, ordered, *safe* world?

Mavis was in hospital with her face cut to ribbons, though
Zac was going to give royal punishment to the bastard responsible. Zac was also leaving the country immediately after the
fight and, though not obviously certifiably insane, must be,
seeing as he expected her to go with him! As if that weren't
enough, she was certain she was pregnant – and Zac didn't
know and neither did Danny. There was, as well, the little fact
of her doctor, years ago, telling her she should never risk a
pregnancy again.

If only she could go to Kate and have a no-nonsense heart-
to-heart and receive a bit of straight advice, but how could she?
Kate had more than enough on her mind worrying about
Matthew. The last thing her best friend needed right now was
to be burdened with more problems. 'You're going to have to
soft it all out for yourself, Carrie girl,' she said grimly as, with
immense effort, she heaved herself away from the door. 'And
what you need before you start, is a cup of tea. Several cups
of tea!'

*

'The tea in here is like dishwater,' Jack said the minute Danny sat down beside his bed.

'Never mind yer tea!' Danny retorted, still breathless from his hurried journey. 'Yer goin' to choke on it anyway when yer 'ear what I 'ave to tell yer!'

'You mean I've put Archie Duke into a neck-collar and brace and all for nothing?' Jack was saying in incredulity five minutes later.

Danny nodded, anxiously aware that, as it was now five minutes into evening visiting time, Christina would soon be arriving and that when she did, there'd be no further conversation with Jack about Archie and Arnie. 'And the bastard yer should 'ave bin 'ammering to 'ell is walkin' around with a grin on 'is face.'

Jack's hands clenched until the knuckles showed white. 'He won't be when Zac's finished with him,' he said fiercely. 'My God, what wouldn't I give to be at the ringside tomorrow night!'

'I 'spect Mavis will feel the same, when I tell her.'

Mavis. At the thought of Mavis, and of what had been done to her, both men were silent for a moment and then Jack said, 'I want you to talk to Mavis for me, Danny. I want you to tell her that, if she wants it, The 21 is hers – and make sure she knows about tomorrow night's fight. When the bastard who ruined her face is being beaten to a pulp, I want her to *know* he's being beaten to a pulp. Understand?'

Danny understood perfectly. Before he could say so, however, the expression on Jack's face changed and Danny knew, even though he was seated with his back towards the ward doors, that Christina had arrived. Marvelling that a bloke as tough as Jack could be so soppy about a woman – especially a woman he was married to – Danny rose to his feet and turned to greet her.

Wearing beige linen slacks, a cream shirt, sandals, and a white silk blazer, her shoulder-length hair held away from her face by ivory combs, she looked exquisite. Tall and delicate and, Danny supposed, elegant and sexy. She didn't look sexy to him, though. She looked as remote and as untouchable as the moon.

''Lo, Christina,' he said affably, wondering just what the situation was going to be between her and Mavis, when Mavis got out of hospital. 'Jack tells me you're regularly lookin' after someone's nipper for 'em. Keepin' yer busy, is it?'

'Yes.' With an acknowledging smile, the smile that Jack always referred to as her *Mona Lisa* smile, Christina sat down in the chair he had just vacated.

Danny stared at her. There was a glow about her he'd never seen before. A glow that didn't make sense when you considered that Jack was laid up with a knife wound in his chest. He shrugged. Christina had always taken a lot of fathoming. Maybe the new spring in her step was because Jack had decided to off-load The 21. Remembering that he was going over to Guy's to ask Mavis how she felt about taking The 21 on, he said a speedy goodbye. He didn't want to find, by the time he got to Guy's, that visiting was over.

'Even if visiting had been over, the Ward Sister would still have you let in to see me,' Mavis said, her dislocated shoulder back in its socket, her broken ribs strapped, the only thing familiar about her swollen and heavily stitched face the defiant light in her cat-green eyes. 'She and me are mates. She's going to come down to The 21 when we open.'

Danny pulled a chair up to the side of her bed and sat down, grateful that, for the moment at least, Ted wasn't around. 'Jack's plans 'ave changed where The 21 is concerned,' he said bluntly, seeing no sense in argey-bargeying around. ''E wants to off-load the ownership. 'E 'asn't said so, but I reckon 'e's tryin' to keep Christina 'appy.'

Mavis gasped, her eyes shooting wide.

''E wants to know if you'll take it on,' Danny added speedily before there should be any misunderstanding. ''E says it's yours if yer want it.'

Still Mavis didn't speak. At the thought of Jack 'keeping Christina happy', she couldn't speak.

Mistaking the reason for her shocked silence, Danny said, ''Course, if yer don't think yer goin' to want to be out an' about in future, owin' to yer face an' everythin'—'

Mavis uttered a word that made even Danny flinch.

'Hey, steady on, pet,' he said defensively, 'I only thought that as—'

'I know bloomin' well what you thought!' Mavis was as spitting mad as her condition allowed. 'You thought the same as Ted! That now I've had broken glass pitched in my face, I'm suddenly going to begin living like a bloomin' nun! Well you've both thought wrong! When I get some pancake make-up on the top of this little lot, I'll be as good as new!'

Danny was glad to hear it. 'And the club . . . ?' he ventured, knowing that if she did accept Jack's offer it would cause bloody ructions between her and Ted. 'I doubt if Archie Duke will ever give you trouble again, but—'

'*No one* will ever give me trouble again!' Mavis fumed, her eyes flashing fire. 'As for the bastard who put me in here . . .'

Danny's grin, thanks to his stitches, was macabre. 'Don't you worry abaht 'im, pet,' he said, and told her how that little matter was going to be taken care of.

Later, when he had gone, Mavis laid back against her pillows, her eyes bleak. So . . . Jack wanted out of The 21, did he? They wouldn't, after all, be working together and seeing each other every day. That little dream was over, as was the blissful interlude of the two of them being lovers as well as friends. Tears pricked her eyes and she blinked them fiercely away. Tears falling on the raw cuts on her face would make them hurt more than ever, and, besides, tears where Jack was concerned would be an admission of defeat.

'And I'm not defeated yet!' she said aloud, noticing that her scarlet nail varnish had been removed for her operation and that her nails were in dire need of a little jazzing up. 'Christina may have won this particular match but she hasn't won the game. Not yet. Not by a bleedin' long chalk!'

Daisy was seated on the low wall that fronted number four's garden. Still in school uniform, a bulging satchel of books at her feet, she was gazing miserably across the square to where Billy and one of Queenie Tillet's lodgers were talking together on Queenie's doorstep. The lodger was young and female and startlingly exotic. At least Daisy thought that was the word for her. How else could a get-up of a tightly belted trench-coat, black fishnet tights and teeteringly high, red-sequinned ankle-strapped shoes, be described? She was probably a dancer, Daisy thought, acutely aware of the childishness of the ankle socks and lace-up shoes that were an obligatory part of Blackheath High uniform. Queenie took in a lot of dancers as lodgers. *Artistes*, she called them. Rumour had it that some of them were strippers, an accusation that Queenie, mindful of the importance of being seen to be respectable, always vehemently denied. Circus folk sometimes stayed with her, though, and Queenie never made any attempt to hide the nature of *their* work. 'I've got an elephant-trainer with me this week,' she would say proudly to Hettie or Miriam or Nellie. 'His caravan is full to the gunnels with visiting family and so he's bed-and-breakfasting with me for a few days.' Sometimes it wasn't an elephant-trainer. Sometimes it was a circus strong-man or a clown or a trapeze artist.

With a hurting heart, Daisy wondered if perhaps the girl talking to Billy wasn't a dancer, but was from a circus. As a youngster, Billy had been fascinated by the circuses that visited the heath and, when they moved on to their next pitch, regularly ran away from home to go with them. Whoever the girl was, it was obvious Billy wasn't going to call her over so that the two of them could be introduced. Though he would have had to be blind not to see her, he hadn't acknowledged her presence in any way whatsoever.

The girl on Queenie's doorstep threw back her head, laughing, her hands plunged deep in the pockets of her trench-coat. Even from a distance Daisy could see that extravagant flicks of black eyeliner had been applied to the outer corners of her eyes to give her a doe-eyed look, and that her eyebrows were high and arched, her lips a bright pink.

Despairingly, Daisy knew there was no way she could compete with such glamour. She'd lost Billy and all over a stupid misunderstanding that, because he was no longer speaking to her, she couldn't even begin to put right. As the girl laughed again and Billy began walking her down Queenie's path towards his parked lorry, she reached down for her schoolbag, tears scalding her eyes, her misery total.

Carrie was seated at her kitchen table, alone, her hands hugging a mug of tea. It could have been her fourth mug of tea, or her fifth or sixth. She didn't know, for she'd long since lost count. The sun was beginning to set and the light spilling through the window was a deep copper-gold. Very faintly she could hear the whirr of a lawnmower being trundled up and down and the sound of someone calling in a playing child. No doubt if she were seated at the same table ten, fifteen, twenty years from now, the sounds drifting in through the half-open window would be very similar. She wouldn't know about them, though. Not if she were in New Zealand.

But she wouldn't be in New Zealand. She couldn't be.

She looked around the cheerfully cluttered room. There were pots of mint on the window-sill; gaily coloured rag-rugs on the red-tiled floor. That it was even possible that after tomorrow night she might never sit at the dearly familiar table ever again, was nearly beyond her imagination. That it was even likely was so dumbfounding as to seem like science fiction. And yet what would happen to her if she didn't leave the country with Zac? She'd lose her home, anyway, for there was no way she could pass the baby off as Danny's. She simply wasn't capable of a deceit so terrible and so prolonged. As she wondered if her mother would be likely to take her and the baby in, hysteria bubbled in her throat. Living two doors away, at her mother's, would be little different to her remaining at home! And then there were Rose's feelings to consider – not to mention Danny's.

Fear engulfed her. She'd never had to make a decision like this before; a decision on which her entire future, and the future of those she loved, depended. If she went with Zac – and oh, there was a part of her, the part of her that had only come alive since she had known him, that yearned to go with him – then Rose would be devastated. She would be more than devastated. She would be heartbroken. For that reason alone, she couldn't possibly go to New Zealand. She stared down into her now cold tea. Rose was fourteen. In another five years it might very well be Rose who would be wanting to start a new life in Australia or Canada – or New Zealand. All it took for an assisted passage was ten pounds.

If Rose emigrated, she would be separated from her anyway. The difference would be, though, that she, Carrie, wouldn't be with Zac. Instead she would be working on the fruit and veg stall in Lewisham High Street; going to the cinema in Catford for an occasional treat; having a drink now and then in The Swan. And the man who made her laugh and made her feel desirable and made her feel alive, the man whose baby she was in all probability carrying, would be thousands and thousands of miles away, out of her life forever.

In anguish she pushed the mug of cold tea away. It was nearly dark now and Danny would be home at any moment. With Zac leaving the country tomorrow night, it wasn't possible for her to keep things secret from him any longer. She had to tell him that she was in love with another man, and she had to tell him that she thought she was pregnant. The very thought had beads of sweat standing out on her forehead. His pride was going to be terribly, terribly hurt, and she didn't want to hurt Danny. She didn't want to hurt him in any way whatsoever. She loved him. She'd loved him all her life. She wasn't *in* love with him, though, not the way she was in love with Zac. She'd never been in love with him that way.

There came the sound of the front door being opened and she covered her face with her hands. 'Oh dear God,' she whispered devoutly, knowing she was about to live through the worst few moments she had ever lived through. 'Oh Christ! Oh *hell*!'

Chapter Twenty

'What the bleedin' 'ell are yer doin' sittin' at the table starin' into space?' Danny asked, stopping short in shock the instant he entered the kitchen. 'Why isn't the oven on? Where's my grub?'

He looked around, bewildered, to see if there was a plate being kept warm somewhere. There was nothing. Not even a dish of something cooked and waiting to be re-heated. Not even a jar of pickles signifying cold meat under the larder net. 'Bleedin' 'ell, Carrie!' he exploded, running a hand through his already spiky hair. 'Don't yer know I need to be in and out in a couple of jiffs? Zac'll be dahn the gym waitin' fer me to put 'im through a workout. Ternight's the only real time we've got before 'e takes this Arnie geezer on!'

'I need to talk to you, Danny.' Carrie's heart was beating like a sledgehammer. She felt sick again, but she couldn't be sick just yet. She had to get the words that had to be said out and over with. Crazily it occurred to her that, apart from knowing his pride would be devastated, she didn't have a clue what his reaction was going to be. She drew in a ragged breath.

'Danny, I—'

'An' I come back from seein' Jack an' there's nothin' on the bleedin' table!' Danny continued, annoyance turning into real anger. 'Christ Almighty, Carrie! It ain't as if you've bin knocking yourself out with work this last few days, is it? Yer dad still doesn't know where yer scarpered off to when yer left the stall the other day, and come to that, neither do I—'

'I'm not knocked out with work,' she said, fighting a rising surge of hysteria at his choice of words. 'I'm knocked up, Danny. I've been seeing someone . . . I've been having an affair. And though I haven't missed a period yet, I know I'm pregnant . . .' She couldn't go on. There was no need for her to go on. Everything that had to be said, she'd said. Everything was out and in the open now. Tangible. Real. There could be no going back to the way things had been a few seconds ago. Between herself and Danny, things were never going to be the same ever again. They couldn't be. Their lives were always going to be divided up into 'before' and into 'after'.

'What did yer say?' Danny didn't move from where he had come to a halt, just inside the kitchen door. Even if he'd been paid a million quid to move, he couldn't have done.

Carrie didn't move either. Still seated at the table, her hands clasped tightly in her lap, her tortured eyes holding his, she said, 'I've been seeing someone . . . someone I've fallen in love with. He's going away and he wants me to go with him . . . and . . . and . . . and I think I might go with him, Danny. I think I might.' The tears she had battled against for so long were now streaming down her face. 'I'm sorry, Danny. So sorry. Truly I am.'

'Yer've bin . . . yer've bin 'aving an affair?' Danny's face was a picture of dazed, disbelieving incredulity. 'But you ain't . . . you ain't—'

'The type?' Despite her distress, there was an edge in Carrie's voice. Was it because Danny had never thought her 'the type', by which he meant glamorous and, in the eyes of other men, desirable, that she had fallen so swiftly and irrevocably for a man who did think her glamorous and desirable?

The edge in her voice was lost on him. He was staring around the kitchen as if he no longer knew where he was and was trying to find something familiar to orientate himself by. 'But yer can't . . . yer can't be goin' to leave us?' he said at last as, failing in his task, his eyes came back to hers. 'Not me an' Rose!'

Tears were falling onto Carrie's clasped hands. This wasn't how she had thought it would be. It was worse. Much worse. She had thought Danny's first demand would have been the name of the person she was having the affair with. Instead it was a question that didn't seem to have occurred to him. Was that because he had taken it for granted that the man would be someone he didn't know? That it was beyond his imagination that she might be having an affair with someone he knew, someone he might even think of as being a friend?

It was then she knew she couldn't possibly tell him it was Zac. Not when he and Zac needed to be in close mental unity ready for tomorrow night's fight. When the fight was over, then she would tell him. She would have to. And for now she would struggle to answer the question he had asked. 'It's just . . .' She came to a halt, unable to find the right words. Panic bubbled up into her throat. If she couldn't find the right words to explain to Danny, how in God's name was she going to explain to Rose? And to her mum and dad and gran? And Mavis? And Kate? Feeling as if she were struggling in quicksand, she said, 'I'm in love with him. I don't know him very well, but I'm in love with him. I can't help it. And I'm expecting his baby—'

'Yer can't be!' Danny swayed on his feet. 'Yer not to 'ave any more babies! The doctor said so when you 'ad your miscarriage!'

The feeling of being in quicksand was getting worse. Why wasn't he giving vent to his hurt pride in raging, roaring anger? Why wasn't he lifting his hand to her, demanding to know how long she'd been seeing her fancy-man? Where she had been seeing him? Where it was she intended going with him? Why, when she had told him about the baby, was his first reaction to think of *her*? To be worried about *her*?

He passed a hand across his eyes. 'Whoever this bloke is . . . I don't want yer to go away with 'im, Carrie. I don't want . . . want . . .'

'Danny? *Danny?*' There was as much disbelief and incredulity in her voice as there had been, mere seconds ago, in his. He was crying. Her bumptious, hard-as-nails, know-it-all, smart-alecky Danny was crying! With her feeling of panic now full-blown, Carrie was on her feet and rounding the table towards him.

In a few simple words, he stopped her dead in her tracks. Stopped her from breathing. 'I know yer wouldn't want to get rid of it, Carrie, but this bloke won't know how dodgy a pregnancy could be for yer. He mightn't look after yer properly. If yer'll stay – an' I want yer to stay,' his voice cracked and broke, 'I don't know what I'll do if yer don't stay, Carrie, but if yer *do* stay, then I'll take the nipper on as mine. No one need ever know any different. Not Rose. Not my mum and dad, or your mum and dad.'

Carrie tried to speak, but the words wouldn't come. There was a ringing noise in her ears and the floor was threatening to shelve away at her feet.

'But . . . why?' How she forced the words out, when there was no air in her lungs, she never knew.

He looked at her in pathetic bewilderment, unable to even begin to understand why she would ask such a question. 'Because I love yer, Carrie,' he said, as if the fact were far too obvious to need putting into words. 'I've always loved yer. I think yer beautiful.'

*

'Christ!' It was next morning and Jack was staring at Danny, wondering just how many more of Danny's visits he could survive. Yesterday he'd knocked him sidewise telling him it wasn't Archie who'd glassed Mavis – and now this!

'No one else'll ever know, but I had to tell someone.' Against his sheet-white face, Danny's freckles were a sickly orange. 'I still don't know what she's goin' to do, yer see.'

Never in his life had Jack seen a bloke with so much stuffing knocked out of him. Danny didn't merely look like a shadow of his former self, he looked like another bloke entirely.

'When I told 'er I'd take the nipper she's expectin' on as mine, she just started to cry. She went ter bed an' locked the door and I fink she cried all night.'

'Christ!' It was the second time Jack had blasphemed in as many minutes, but no other exclamation seemed remotely adequate. If Carrie was having a baby, then he knew damn well who the father was – but Danny obviously didn't! He passed a hand unsteadily across his eyes, deeply grateful that, when it came to revealing the father's name, Carrie's courage had failed her. If it hadn't . . . He thought of the fight that was to take place that night and blanched. For Mavis's sake, it was vital the fight took place, and a mammoth set-to between Danny and Zac would have very likely scuppered it.

'I don't know what I'll do if Carrie goes away with this fella,' Danny was saying, his voice raw with pain at the very thought. 'I love her, yer see? She's just . . . she's just *Carrie.*' It wasn't a very articulate way of putting his feelings into words, but it was effective.

Jack, thinking of Carrie's vibrancy and sizzling liveliness and sunny good nature, knew exactly what he meant. He also knew that, as he was the only person Danny had taken into his confidence, he was the only person who could give him some straight advice. Or a word of warning. 'I can imagine how you feel, mate,' he began tactfully. And stopped. He couldn't imagine how Danny felt. The mere thought of Christina being pregnant to another man made him feel as if he would explode. 'You can't do it, Danny mate!' he erupted harshly. 'You can't take on another bloke's kid as if it's your own!'

Danny blinked, his faded red hair so grizzled with grey, he looked to be in his forties, not his mid-thirties. 'What do yer mean?' he asked, bewildered. 'A kiddie's a kiddie. It don't matter who its real dad is, not if you're the one carin' fer it an' bringin' it up.' He rose to his feet. 'I 'ave ter get back to the square, Jack. I 'ave ter make sure Zac is sorted fer tonight's fight – an' I 'ave to be with Carrie. I 'ave to know what it is she's goin' ter do. I 'ave ter know if she's goin' ter stay with me or . . . or not.'

Jack made no response. As Danny walked from the ward in abject misery, his hands plunged deep in his trouser pockets, Jack simply stared after him, feeling as Saint Paul must have felt on the road to Damascus. How could he have been so blind for so long to something that was, to Danny, so obvious? And not only to Danny. He thought of Leon's attitude towards Matthew and Daisy. Leon loved Matthew and Daisy just as much as he did Luke, Jilly and Johnny. Like Danny, Leon knew that when it came to kiddies, it was the caring and cherishing that mattered, and nothing else. He thought of Christina walking out into the hospital gardens and Judith running shining-eyed towards her, and excitement began to surge deep in the pit of his stomach. Judith looked so like Tina, and though Jewishness was passed down through the female line, Judith's father being Jewish surely made her half-Jewish; in his eyes, this was exactly what any child of his and Christina's would have been. And Judith's mother was dead and her father had abandoned her.

He clenched his knuckles, his excitement so fierce he could

hardly contain it. Would Judith's aunt allow him and Tina to foster Judith? Even as the thought occurred to him, he was certain of the answer. Of course she would. From what Tina had told him, Madge Dracup never wanted to look after Judith in the first place, and would be only too happy to off-load responsibility for her. Together, he and Tina and Judith could be a family. The kind of family Tina had yearned for, for so long – and that he, in blind stupidity, had refused to consider.

'Nurse!' He pressed the buzzer by the side of his bed. He needed to get a message to Tina now. Immediately. He'd wasted enough time – years of it – and he wasn't going to waste so much as another minute!

'If we are to spend tomorrow with the Emmersons, I think it would be good manners if you were introduced to them today,' Deborah was saying to a dazed Genevre. 'Not that we shall be doing any celebrating tomorrow, of course. I've already told Nellie not to expect us to join her at the Robsons'—'

'Nellie?' Genevre asked faintly, wondering if there was something wrong with her hearing. Spend Coronation Day with the Emmersons? Finally, after all these years, to meet Matthew's mother? And his adoptive father? His *black* father? Surely she couldn't be hearing right! And who was Nellie? Her aunt never referred to people by their Christian names; not unless they were family.

'Nellie is the . . .' Deborah began, impatient with Genevre's dim-wittedness, and then stopped. She had been about to say 'lady', but if Nellie ever knew she'd been referred to as a lady, she would cackle herself into a coma. 'Nellie is the individual who came to my aid the day Adams was taken ill and the Emmersons were not home.'

'And the Robsons?' Now that she knew she hadn't completely misunderstood what Deborah was saying to her, Genevre was aware of a feeling of anticipation so intense, it hurt. Ever since her brother first fell in love with Kate, she had wanted to meet her. Then Toby was killed at Dunkirk and, after Kate had met and married Leon Emmerson, it seemed as if a meeting between herself and Kate would never take place. Now Deborah was suggesting not only that they visit Kate's home in Magnolia Square, but that they spend all of Coronation Day there!

'The Robsons?' Deborah frowned. If her fifty-five-year-old niece were to be taken aback when introduced to Nellie, she was going to be a hospital case when introduced to Charlie. It was possible, of course, that his eminently presentable wife would coerce him into a collar and tie on Coronation Day morning. Possible, but doubtful. 'The Robsons are the only people in the square, apart from Charlie Robson's son and his wife, who possess a television set,' she said, deciding that Genevre would just have to take the more working-class elements of Magnolia Square in her stride. 'Nellie will be watching the Queen's crowning on it as, I expect, will lots of their friends and neighbours.'

Genevre's jaw dropped when she realized that not only was she going to meet Matthew's south-east London family, but that there was also the chance she might be invited into a neighbouring home to watch the coronation in the most wonderfully vulgar way imaginable. On television!

'I know I said I wouldn't dream of watching the coronation on the Robsons' television when we could, instead, be up in town, watching the procession for real,' Ruth Giles said to Bob as she disturbed his weekly sermon preparation by setting a mid-morning tray of tea and biscuits down on his desk. 'But I've changed my mind.'

Bob blinked, struggling to re-focus his thoughts. They hadn't been centred on next Sunday's sermon, as they should have been. Though he would never dream of admitting as much to Ruth, he had been thinking, instead, of the illegal boxing match that was to take place that evening in a deserted warehouse, somewhere down near the river. He wasn't, of course, supposed to know about it and, as a vicar, he certainly wasn't supposed to be approving of it. Not that he was approving of it. But he didn't report the matter to the police and nor was he going to.

'Why, love?' he asked, perplexed, as she waited for a response from him.

'Because without going up to town tonight, to stake out a good place to see everything from, it won't be worth it,' she said, trim and neat in a green-and-maroon plaid skirt and a lavender-hued Fair Isle twin-set. 'We'll be at the back of the crowd and won't be able to see very much.'

'Yes, love,' he agreed patiently, his perplexity growing. 'But as we are going up to town tonight—'

'I'm not.' From where she was standing, at the far side of his desk, Ruth's eyes held his. To the best of her knowledge, she had never, since their first meeting, ever done or said anything that would shock or offend him. She knew, though, that she was about to do so now. 'I'm not going,' she said quietly and firmly. 'I'm not going, Bob, because I'm going to the boxing match that I know you're not supposed to know about, but that you do know about.'

'You're going to go to an illegitimate boxing match?' He stared at her in stunned, goggle-eyed stupefaction. She might as well have said she was going to go down to Soho and strip in a clip-joint! 'You can't, Ruth!' He forced himself to his feet, wondering if she had the faintest idea as to what such a fight would be like. 'People get hurt, love, in pirate fights. You'll hate every minute of it and—'

'Mavis got hurt.' Ruth's voice was as taut as a bow-string. 'And even if the police brought charges against the villain who scarred her for life, he wouldn't get much of a sentence, would he? Ted said that when the police interviewed Mavis they seemed to think that, as she was in a Soho club when it happened, it really wasn't such a big deal. They didn't *say* they thought she was a prostitute who'd been done over by her pimp, but Ted said it was obvious that was what they thought. Though why it should make any difference even if she were a prostitute, I don't understand.'

Swiftly, aware of the depth of her distress, he rounded his desk, taking her in his arms.

Her small-boned hands clenched into fists against his chest. 'And so that's why I'm going to the fight tonight,' she said with a fierceness that shocked him inexpressibly. 'I want the villain who took a broken drinking glass to Mavis's face to receive some kind of punishment for what he did – and Zac is the only person who's going to be able to give that punishment.'

'If anyone should be knocking that bastard into the middle of next week, it's me, not Zac Hemingway!' Ted Lomax said explosively to Leon. It was lunchtime and they were standing on the pavement opposite St Mark's church, Leon on his way to the gym, Ted on his way tip-town, to visit Mavis.

Leon, who had boxed in the Navy and helped train more fighters than he could remember, regarded Ted's narrow physique with something approaching despair. Ted had the bravery – and a war medal to prove his bravery – but he didn't have the build to go into a boxing ring. Especially not against an opponent he knew would be built like a brick out-house.

'Everyone understands how you feel, Ted,' he said sympathetically, 'but Zac has the opportunity to paste the bloke in question, and you don't.'

The skin tightened over Ted's high cheekbones. 'And we all

know who is giving him the opportunity and who set it all up. It was Jack. You can't pretend it wasn't. And I've had a bellyful of Jack pitching in where my Mavis is concerned.'

Leon regarded him unhappily. He could quite understand Ted being prickly where Jack was concerned. The rumours that were flying around Magnolia Square about Jack and Mavis were enough to make the steadiest head spin. Christina, however, didn't seem to be setting much store by them. When he'd left home only minutes ago, she was helping Kate peg out washing, radiant with the news that she and Jack were, at last, about to foster a child.

Hoping to ease Ted's tortured mind a little, he said, 'Jack didn't know who his fighter was going to be up against tonight, Ted. Not until yesterday. And when he did find out, he didn't ask Zac to take Big Jumbo's place. That was Zac's own decision. And as for anything else . . . it's hardly likely Jack would be playing away from home when he and Christina are all set to foster a kiddie.'

'Foster a kid? Jack?' Ted was so startled, he forgot that he was also furiously angry. 'I think you've made a mistake, Leon. Jack's never held with fostering and adopting—'

'He might not have once upon a time, Ted, but he's thinking differently now. Christina says he wants the two of them to foster the little girl she's been looking after. He's dead keen, apparently. And she's over the moon about it.'

'Blimey!' Ted pondered Leon's information. If Jack really was all set to foster a kiddie, it was hardly likely there'd been anything serious going on between him and Mavis. 'Blimey,' he said again and scratched the back of his head. 'My Beryl told me Hemingway wasn't fighting tonight because Jack had told him to. She said he was doing it for her, but I couldn't see it at the time.'

Leon didn't see it either. He wondered if he'd somehow

missed an important part of the conversation. 'Beryl? I'm sorry, Ted. I don't quite understand.'

Ted gave a glimmer of a smile. 'He and Beryl are apparently smitten with each other,' he said wryly. 'The minute she heard he was stepping into the ring tonight instead of Big Jumbo, she said that he was doing it on her account. She's been in a terrible state ever since her mum was . . . was . . .' He couldn't bring himself to say the word 'glassed'. Instead he said, 'She's up at Guy's now. The Ward Sister is good about visiting. She lets Billy and Beryl see Mavis no matter what time of day it is.'

'Good.' Leon meant it. It certainly wasn't so easy getting in to see Jack outside of visiting hours. The only person able to manage it was Danny, presumably because, with his face a sea of stitches, Jack's Ward Sister thought he was a patient, not a visitor.

'Give Mavis my best,' he said, glad to know he'd eased Ted's mind a little.

'And give Zac Hemingway *my* best.' Ted was all fierce grimness again. 'Tell him I'll be at the ringside tonight. He'll know just where, because he'll be able to hear me. By hell he'll be able to hear me!'

It was early afternoon and Kate was standing on her back step, watching her laundry fluttering in the breeze. Christina had left an hour or so ago, hurrying down into Greenwich to meet Judith before taking the child with her up to St Thomas's. She also intended doing some hospital visiting later on in the afternoon. She had already been up to Guy's once to see Mavis, and Mavis had asked her, on her next visit, to take her in a bottle of fire-engine red nail varnish. Despite the agonizing heaviness of her heart, a shadow of a smile touched the corners of Kate's full-lipped mouth. In boxing terms, Mavis was down, but she was very far from being out. Jack was handing The 21 over to her lock, stock and barrel and it was a business opportunity Mavis was quite determined to seize with both hands.

'The make-up will be a bit heavier in the future, Kate,' she had said, managing a defiant wink despite the horrendous soreness of her bruised and battered face, 'but the style will still be the same!'

Kate's admiration for her was boundless. Mavis would never let things get her down. No matter what life threw at her, she would survive – and would survive with panache.

From where she was standing, she could see that Nibbo had tied clusters of red, white and blue balloons to his magnolia tree. The slight smile that had touched her mouth died. There were red, white and blue trimmings everywhere one looked. Lewisham clock-tower was decked out like a Christmas tree, and the narrow streets of Blackheath Village were a riot of flags and bunting.

Nibbo was sheepish about his own efforts to get into the coronation spirit. 'It isn't that I've forgotten Matthew is still missing,' he said to her and Leon before putting the balloons in his tree. 'It's just that, as Charlie says, if Matthew were to be found and returned home and there were no decorations up, well, it would be a sorry state of affairs, wouldn't it?'

Nibbo wasn't the only person who seemed to think that Matthew would have to be found by Coronation Day morning. Harriet said much the same thing, as did Hettie. Was it because, in some strange way, they saw the coronation as a dividing line? That Matthew would either be found by the time it took place, or would never be found?

At the thought of Matthew never being found, Kate felt as if she were going to die. She loved all her children, but Matthew held a very special place in her heart. She had given birth to him months after his father was killed, flying a Spitfire over the beaches of Dunkirk. He was the child she had carried through months of agonizing heartache, the child who bonded her not only to her first love, but also to Leon, for it was Leon, in the chaotic aftermath of an air-raid, who had delivered him.

The balloons continued to toss gaily in the summer breeze. Nibbo had put them up in the hope Matthew would be home to see them. Suddenly she knew what it was she was going to do. She was going to behave exactly as if it were a certainty that Matthew would be home for the coronation. She was going to bake his favourite cake, make his favourite trifle. She was going to *will* Matthew home!

'So how are we going to get to the warehouse where the fight's being held?' Hettie asked Miriam as the latter, aware that it was nearly four-thirty and that Rose would soon be calling in on her way home from school, spread mashed sardine onto great slabs of bread. 'It's down near the docks, isn't it?'

'Albert's givin' you, me and Daniel a lift in the fruit and veg cart,' Miriam said, slapping one slice of bread down on top of another. 'It won't be as uncomfy as it sounds, because he's slung a couple of old armchairs on the back.'

'And what about Nellie?' Under other circumstances Hettie would have died rather than be seen sitting in an old armchair on the back of a fruit and vegetable cart. She couldn't be fussy tonight, though. Not if she wanted to see Zac Hemingway give Mavis's attacker a taste of his own medicine. 'Nellie'll need a lift and she can hardly walk, let alone climb onto the back of a lorry!'

'Malcolm Lewis is takin' 'er in 'is car.'

'Crikey!' The fake cherries on Hettie's black straw hat wobbled alarmingly. 'His scoutmaster days will be over if old Baden-Powell gets to hear he's been giving old ladies lifts to dodgy boxing matches!'

'Baden-what's-is-name is dead,' Miriam said, wiping her fingers on her floral, wrap-around pinafore. 'An' even if 'e wasn't, I don't expect 'e'd object to tonight's fight. Not if he knew what that Arnie beast did to my Mavis.'

Hettie shuddered. She hadn't seen Mavis's face for herself, but if it was even an eighth as bad as her Danny's, she didn't need to. Danny's scars were going to make him look like a south-London mobster for the rest of his life. What Mavis was going to look like didn't bear thinking about.

'What will we do when the fight's over?' she asked, hoping the smell of sardine wasn't going to cling to her hair and her hat. 'Go straight up to the Mall to stake out a place to watch things from tomorrow?'

Miriam nodded. 'I've got a ground-sheet Malcolm's lent me, and an old rug. Rose will be sleepin' out on the pavement with us and she's borrowed a couple of collapsible stools from 'er school's Art department. They'll be useful for tomorrow while we're waiting for things to start. We're going to need as many flasks of tea as we can carry. And sandwiches. We're goin' to need lots of sandwiches.'

'Is your Carrie coming up with us?' Hettie averted her eyes from the mammoth sardine doorsteps, determining to make plenty of civilized-sized sandwiches for herself and Daniel. 'I've hardly seen your Carrie this last day or two, and when I have done she's looked as if she was in another world.'

'She's taken what 'appened to Mavis very badly,' Miriam said, not about to admit even to her best friend that Carrie was not so much in another world these days as on another planet. 'She's only got to think of what that Arnie bastard did to our Mavis's face and she throws up somethin' shockin'.'

Carrie rested her head in her hands, her elbows on the rim of the lavatory bowl. Why morning sickness was called morning sickness beat her. Where she was concerned, it went on all bloomin' day.

'Are you sure you ain't expectin' an 'appy event?' a fellow market trader asked when, a few minutes later, they stood side by side at the wash-basins.

With immense effort, Carrie gave the woman a friendly grin and, letting it serve as a reply that could have meant anything, walked out of the public loos into welcoming fresh air. For the last couple of days, she'd spent far more time being sick than she had minding the stall. Today, being the day before the coronation, hadn't mattered so much. Shoppers were more intent on buying in party food than they were on shopping for fresh fruit and veg.

'You want to get whatever's wrong with you seen to, love,' the neighbouring stall-holder, who had been looking after things for her, said. 'I'm spending more time sellin' your spuds and lettuces than I am my own!'

Again Carrie summoned up a smile, though the effort nearly killed her. How she was going through the motions of being normal to people, she couldn't for the life of her imagine. Zac had been down at the stall an hour or so earlier, looking as relaxed and at ease as if he had no more on his mind than whether to opt for a couple of pounds of apples or oranges.

'Just bring one bag with you tonight,' he said, uncaring of the strange look the customer she was serving gave him. 'It'll be easier, travelling light.' Then, his jacket held by his thumb and slung nonchalantly over his shoulder, he shot her a look that had nearly undone her there and then and strolled off, head and shoulders above the High Street crowds, heading back to the gym presumably.

Now, as she began making a start on packing up the stall, her stomach was knotted with nerves. As if the thought of the cargo boat – already, no doubt, at dock and waiting for them

to board her – wasn't enough to unhinge anyone's mind, the
fight between Zac and Arnie was all set to begin in just over
two hours' time. She would be at the ringside, of course. For
Mavis's sake alone, how could she not be? But she would be
there for more reasons than the primeval desire to see Mavis's
sadistic attacker get his come-uppance. She would be there
because Zac expected her to be there. She would be there because
it would be the very last time she would ever be anywhere with
Zac and with her family and friends as well.

''Ow are yer doin' Blossom?' her dad asked, his braces at
full stretch over his paunch as he arrived to take over the task
of dismantling the stall. 'There's no need to be lookin' so peaky.
Not when ternight's goin' to be so bloomin' memorable!'

Chapter Twenty-One

Zac lay face down on the massage bench in the improvised dressing-room down at the warehouse where the fight was to take place. He was first on the card and, as there was only an hour and a half or so to go now, Leon was expertly kneading and pummelling his muscles in order to get them into a nicely loosened condition.

'Word this is going to be a very special grudge match hasn't reached Archie Duke's lot, thank goodness,' Leon said, a sheen of sweat on his own well-muscled arms and shoulders as he continued to give Zac the very best massage he was capable of. 'There's a squad of Archie's boys here already and, according to Danny, they're full of just what Arnie is going to do to the tiddler in Jack Robson's pond.'

'And they think I'm the tiddler?' Zac asked with a wry grin.

'You or Big Jumbo. Either way they don't think Jack's going to be putting up any fighter worth his salt tonight.' This time it was Leon who grinned. Since Matthew's disappearance it was something he did very rarely. 'They've got a bit of a surprise coming to them, haven't they? Shame is, it doesn't look as if Archie's going to be here to see it happen. Word is he's been discharged from hospital but is lying low.'

'His money won't be.' Zac was indifferent as to whether Archie Duke was at the ringside or not. His beef wasn't with Archie. It was with Arnie. 'You can bet your sweet life that

Archie will have a packet of money riding on the outcome.' He chuckled as Leon began hand-chopping the backs
of his legs. 'And he's going to lose it all. Every last penny of
it.'

Leon was glad Zac was so very confident, because there was
one little thing that was worrying him – and that was that
neither he, Danny nor Jack had actually seen Zac at full belt
in a boxing ring. All they had seen were his fairly low-key workouts with Big Jumbo. What if Zac really wasn't up to this Arnie
bloke's standard? How were Mavis's family going to feel if,
instead of meting out raw punishment to the sicko who had
ruined Mavis's face, he was, instead, on the receiving end of a
thrashing?

'Is Carrie here yet?' Zac asked, breaking in on Leon's anxious
thoughts.

'Not that I know of.' Leon didn't think it at all strange that
Zac should be enquiring as to whether or not members of
Mavis's family had arrived.

Normally the vast majority of Magnolia Square's women-
folk, apart from Mavis and, occasionally, Queenie Tillet, never
turned up to watch fights, illegitimate or legitimate. Tonight,
though, was going to be very different. Kate had told him that
not only did Carrie intend coming to it, but that Miriam and
Hettie and Nellie were coming as well. 'And Ruth is going to
go,' she said, leaving him gasping for air with disbelief. 'And
so is Pru Lewis.'

He was left wondering whether, if it hadn't been for her
reluctance to leave the house in case there was word of Matthew,
Kate wouldn't have been at the ringside as well! Christina, of
course, wouldn't be there. He wasn't sure, but he thought it
highly likely that Christina was the only person in Magnolia
Square unaware that a fight was taking place.

'Billy is here, though,' he said as Danny walked into the

cramped little room, 'And Elisha Deakin. Word has it he's closed The Swan's doors for the night.'

''E's 'ad to as Lettie wouldn't mind fings for 'im,' Danny said, the knife-edge of tension he was on palpable. 'She's already nabbed one of the best ringside seats. The landlord from The 'Are and Billet is 'ere as well, though 'ow 'e got to 'ear about it, Gawd only knows.'

Leon gave Zac a light slap on his rump. 'It's time to have your hands wrapped. Who do you want to do it? Me or Danny?'

'You might as well do it,' Zac said easily, pushing himself up into a sitting position on the edge of the massage bench, not remotely embarrassed by Danny's presence.

Danny, happily unaware that there were circumstances which made Zac's manner towards him quite remarkable, threw the two rolls of gauze and the roll of tape he had been carrying across to Leon. 'Money's changin' 'ands out there like it's goin' out of style. Even the Vicar's scoutmaster is backin' yer to the 'ilt.'

As Leon set to work bandaging his hands, devoting as much care to the task as a surgeon performing an operation, Zac grinned. He'd taken the fight on, not, as everyone assumed, for Mavis's sake, but for Carrie's. He'd known how much she would want Mavis's attacker to be given the hiding of his life and so, despite the risk that the fight might be raided by the police and that, if it were, he'd be spending his last night in England dodging the law, he'd decided he was going to do his damnedest to give him it.

Now, however, as pre-fight adrenalin hit his system, he knew he was also fighting for the sheer hell of it. Big money bets were being made. In more ways than one, a lot was riding on the outcome. The knowledge gave him a high like no other; not even the high of robbing a bank. As Leon continued to take immense care with every turn of the adhesive white tape, transforming his hands into lethal weapons, he felt power surge into them. When it came to fighting he had the killer instinct – a fact he was well aware Leon and Danny could only trust he had.

He grinned reassuringly at them, the blonde stubble on his chin evidence that, as was traditional before a fight, he hadn't shaved that day.

'Stop looking so nervous, you two, and don't hope for an early knockout. I'm going to batter this bastard through nine long rounds.'

'I wish I 'ad the same ice-water in my veins you 'ave,' Danny said, beads of sweat visible on his forehead. 'Now remember, keep nice and tight for the opening rounds. Operate behind a solid left jab and focus it on 'is left shoulder as much as yer can. That way, 'is deltoid won't 'ave the strength fer a knock-out punch.'

Danny was so whole-heartedly for him that Zac experienced an emotion utterly foreign to him. A shaft of conscience. What was the poor bugger going to feel tomorrow when he realized that Carrie had left him, and that she'd left with him – Zac? He remembered a probation officer once saying about him that he was the most likeable, amoral young man he'd ever met. He'd never been quite sure what amoral meant, but if it meant breezing through life and not getting too upset about things, then he supposed the description was pretty apt. As a kid, he'd never had anything and he'd forced himself not to care too much. It was a habit that had stuck.

'How long have we got?' Leon was asking. 'Thirty minutes? Thirty-five?'

'Thirty.' Danny was as tense as a coiled spring. He wished Jack was in the building. The temporary seating that had been put up around the ring was, of necessity, limited. For the majority of the punters it was going to be standing room only, though the warehouse catwalk would give those with a head for heights a great bird's-eye-view. Without Jack by his side he was acutely aware that crowd control was going to be more a matter of luck than management. The vast majority of the punters now surging into the makeshift venue were villains, or border-line villains. And seated in their midst, taking pride of place at the ringside, were his ma and pa, his ma-in-law and pa-in-law, his sister-in-law's husband, his nephew and, very probably, his niece. Not to mention the fact that though she hadn't said so – for she'd said hardly anything to him all day – his wife would probably be there as well. And he knew that Jack's eighty-year-old dad was there, because he'd seen him shamble in, accompanied by Pru and Malcolm Lewis – and if that wasn't enough, Nellie had been with them, as had the vicar's wife!

'Hell's bells, Jack,' he said beneath his breath as he checked that Zac was suitably oiled and greased and that his protective cup and boxing gloves were to hand. 'I could do with yer 'ere tonight, mate. I really bleedin' could!'

''Ere pet, 'ave an aniseed ball,' Charlie, having to shout to make himself heard above the mayhem around them, proffered a paper sweetie bag in Ruth Giles's direction.

Ruth, who was struggling hard to acclimatize herself to an atmosphere so alien she felt almost numbed by it, shook her head.

'Robson's fighter's goin' to be fuckin' down in five fuckin' minutes!' a man somewhere to the rear of her shouted glee-fully to his companion. 'Arnie could knock a bleedin' building down!'

Ruth looked down at her white-gloved hands. She wouldn't listen to the swearing every man in the building seemed to be indulging in. It didn't matter. All that mattered was that the mobster who had rammed a broken drinking glass into Mavis's face would, in just another few minutes, step all unsuspecting into the ring to face Zac.

'There ain't any punch that 'urts like a hook to the liver.' Nellie, who didn't believe in short rations no matter where she was, was happily tucking into the top layer of a box of Milk Tray as she gave Charlie the benefit of her opinion. 'An' that's what Zac'll do to 'im straight off, you mark my words.'

'Who's Jack Robson puttin' in the ring against Arnie, then?' a slick-suited gent was yelling down from the catwalk to where Albert and Miriam were seated on a long bench by the ring-side. 'One of the boy scouts that's always milling about his gym?'

There was a roar of laughter from everyone within earshot.

'Mebbe it isn't a boy scout! Mebbe it's a kid from the Boys' Brigade!' another joker pitched in.

Albert, uncaring of the gales of laughter, smiled grimly. He knew who'd be having the last laugh, by crikey he did!

Hettie, seated at the far end of the bench in question, was ear-wigging in to each and every conversation going on around her. All she wanted was to hear someone boast of having been the person who had laid into her Danny and she'd have the hat-pin out of her black straw titfer and straight in his big, fat, you-know-what in two shakes of a lamb's tail!

'Of course Zac Hemingway's going to prove to be a destructive fighter,' Daniel Collins was saying a little exasperatedly to middle-aged Harold Miller, Nellie's nephew.

Harold, one of life's pessimists, wasn't too sure. He wanted to make a bet on Zac Hemingway but, as no one, not even Daniel's son, Danny, who was supposed to be Zac's trainer, had seen Zac fight in a pukka match, he couldn't quite bring himself to take the risk.

'You beat style!' a know-all stood in the middle of the standing crush behind the benches could be heard shouting. 'The other guy's style! That's how you win fights!'

'I've put all next week's housekeeping on Zac Hemingway,' Pru Lewis was saying nervously to Beryl. 'I've never made a bet on anything before, not ever. He will win, won't he? If he doesn't, I don't know how I'm going to explain to Malcolm!'

Beryl was too racked with nerves to even answer her. All these horrible, horrible people crowing that Zac was going to be knocked out in the first round! Tears stung the backs of her eyes. What if he were? What if the Arnie person hurt him? What if he mutilated him, as he'd mutilated her mother? What if he *killed* Zac?

'Arnie'll bleedin' kill 'im,' Billy could hear someone saying a little to the left of him. 'He'll take 'im out in the first round with a right upper-cut and a straight left 'and.'

Standing a little apart from the Magnolia Square contingent, Billy clenched his fists, a nerve ticking at the corner of his lean jaw. When he thought of what the bastard being talked about had done to his mum's face, he wanted to take him on himself. There was no way he could do so, though. Not without ending up in jail, and his mum wouldn't want that. It'd rile her something rotten! He sucked in his breath so sharply he nearly swallowed the gum he was chewing. There, on her own and pushing her way with difficulty through the crowd, obviously looking for a familiar face, was Daisy! His heart felt as if it were somersaulting in his chest. She looked so neat and clean and shiningly pure! A lout wearing a gangster-style trilby put his big paw on her shoulder, obviously making a pass at her. Billy saw her colour and shake her head and then he didn't see anything because he was too busy pushing and shoving a way through to her.

'C'm on! C'm on! C'm on!' a tout was hollering. 'Time's runnin' out! Place your bets!'

'He'll be down in less time than it takes to boil an egg,' someone else was yelling, but whether they were referring to Arnie or to Zac, Billy didn't know.

'Daisy! Daisy!' He side-stepped a big bloke he'd once seen box somewhere. He had to get to Daisy before the fight started. He had to get her out of the warehouse before the opening bell sounded. 'DAISY!'

She heard his voice, turned her head towards him, the relief on her delicately boned face so vast he could hardly breathe, his throat was so tight. At last he was by her side, and the bloke with the gangster-style trilby shrugged, turning away to talk to his mates.

'What the heck are you doing here, Daisy?' He seized hold of her arm, steadying her as they were both jostled by those around them trying to get a better view of the ring. 'Who brought you down 'ere? Who . . . ?'

'I came to see you! I have to talk to you, Billy!' She was wearing a mustard-coloured corduroy pinafore dress and snowy-white blouse with a Peter Pan collar, and looked like a Sunday school teacher. A heavily made-up young woman, the kind who liked to be seen with the kind of monied men who attended fights, squeezed past them. 'If you don't want to see me any more because . . . because you like someone else better, then I'll understand.' Her voice throbbed emotionally. 'But I can't bear it if you don't want to see me because of something you think is my fault, and that isn't my fault at all!'

A recorded trumpet voluntary deafened them. Daisy clapped

her hands over her ears. Billy kept hold of her elbow. He'd never manage to get her out of the building once the fight started, and it was only brief minutes away from doing so. 'This way . . .' He began pushing a way through to the back of the dense crowd, pulling her with him.

The trumpet voluntary came to a brief end, obviously only a practise run. The big arc lights that had been erected over the ring clicked full on.

Daisy was oblivious. 'Whatever those girls from my class may have led you to believe, I've never been ashamed of you,' she was saying to him fiercely. 'I've always known it would be difficult, me being away at university whilst you were here, working, but I've never been ashamed of you because of what you do. I couldn't be. I'm proud of you, Billy. I'm proud of the way you're running a business of your own at twenty-one. And I know that your business won't always be scrap-metal. I know that one day you'll be a . . . a . . .'

'A business magnate?' Billy finished for her, happiness fizzing through him till he thought he was going to burst with it.

Time seemed to stop and stand still for Daisy. Was it going to be all right? Was Billy not, after all, in love with his exotic companion of the last few days?

'The girl I've kept seeing you with . . .' she said hesitantly. 'The one who is lodging with Queenie—'

'Perdita?' Billy's grin was splitting his face. What fool would want a girl as exotic as Perdita on his arm when he could have Daisy instead?

'Is she . . . ? Was she . . . ?'

'Nah.' Billy knew what it was she was trying to put into words. 'Course she wasn't. She's far too bossy. Comes of 'er bein' a lion-tamer, I expect.'

There was a crackling of static indicating that the recorded trumpet voluntary was about to once again blast their eardrums.

'Come on,' he said, continuing to battle a way through to the nearest exit. 'Let's get out of 'ere.'

'But the fight? Don't you want to stay and watch it for your mum's sake?'

Billy hauled her past a couple of muscle-men who were doing duty as doormen, and out into the blue-spangled light of late evening. Ten minutes ago he would have thought nothing in the world could tempt him away from seeing Zac pound his mother's attacker into a quivering heap. Now, however, he knew differently. He wasn't going to expose Daisy to the kind of catcalls and language that would soon be raising the warehouse roof.

'Nah. I don't need to see it to know what kind of a performance Zac's goin' to turn in.' He tucked her hand into the crook of his arm. It felt wonderfully right there, and it was going to feel wonderfully right there for as long as he lived. 'Let's go up to Guy's,' he said. 'Visiting will be over, but they'll still let us in.'

As she smiled sunnily up at him, her neat bob of blue-black hair shining like satin, he hoped the jeweller's they would have to walk past to reach the hospital would have its lights on. There was something in the window he wanted to show her; something he intended buying for her; something she would be able to wear on the fourth finger of her left hand and that would, when she went away to university, remind her of the future they were going to share.

Ted wasn't aware that Billy was no longer in the crowd. He was in such a state of acute tension, he was barely aware of anything other than that the bastard who had beaten Mavis was, any second, going to be in the ring only yards away from him. His hands bunched into fists. How he was going to prevent himself from vaulting over the ropes and smashing his fist into the bastard's face, he truly didn't know.

'Move over a bit, Ted,' Nibbo's familiar voice shouted over the din. 'Let me and my lady-friend squeeze in next to you.'

The word 'lady-friend' caught even Ted's attention. Nibbo didn't have a reputation as a lady's man. The last time he'd been known to indulge in a spot of courting was during the war, and it had come to a speedy conclusion when his lady-friend's husband came home unexpectedly from Tobruk. He dragged his eyes away from the still empty ring, looking across at Nibbo's companion.

'Good evening, Mr Lomax,' Mavis's Ward Sister said with a naughty smile. 'This makes a rare old change from going to the cinema on my night off!'

The trumpet voluntary was blasting everyone's eardrums, the arc lights were blazing down at full force, the Master of Ceremonies was in the centre of the ring, bawling details of the evening's card through a megaphone as Carrie pushed and squirmed and squeezed her way through to where the rest of her family were sitting and standing.

'I thought you weren't goin' to make it, pet!' her dad bawled at her, a bottle of stout in one hand, a Coronation Day flag in the other.

'IN THE RIGHT-HAND CORNER WE HAVE *ARNIE*!' the Master of Ceremonies was hollering as the crowd parted beyond the right-hand side of the ring to allow a giant-sized, fist-punching, silk dressing-gowned figure through to the ring apron. 'AND IN THE LEFT-HAND CORNER . . .'

'Oh my God,' Carrie said through parched lips, 'Oh my *dear* God!'

'Here he comes!' Queenie Tillet screamed in her ear. 'Ain't

he just gorgeous? Ain't he the most beautiful-looking guy you've ever seen?'

'I suppose the fight will be getting under way now,' Harriet Robson said, as, seated in a wicker chair next to Leah's bed, she changed her knitting needles over from one hand to the other. 'I must say, I'll be glad when this evening is over and Charlie is safely back home. He's getting a little old for galli- vanting in a deserted dockside warehouse, especially when those he'll be gallivanting with will, for the most part, be south- London criminals or East End mobsters.'

Leah forbore to point out that, considering Charlie's own criminal past, he would be more at home than most in such company. Harriet hadn't been married to Charlie when he had been known as the most efficient safe-blower south of the Thames and, in her ex-headmistress-like manner, was always trying to present him as being far more respectable than he really was.

'You want there should be boy scouts and Sunday school teachers at a pirate fight?' she asked, shifting Boots's weight from off her legs, where he had been lying for far too long.

Harriet watched the waddling Pekinese reposition himself at Leah's feet. Presumably he would serve more as a hot-water bottle there than a dead-weight. 'As Malcolm Lewis and your Beryl are among those who have gone to watch it, scouts and Sunday school teachers will most certainly be represented,' she said dryly, flicking bilberry-coloured wool around her flashing needles.

'Beryl's there because she thinks she owes it to her mum to be there.' That wasn't the whole truth and Leah knew it, but she wasn't about to start telling Harriet about Beryl's crush on Zac Hemingway. 'And I know you don't approve of what's takin' place tonight, Harriet, and that you've never much approved of Mavis and her goings-on, but she didn't deserve what happened to her. It was a sin and a shame, and I hope that *goy* boxer of Jack's pulverizes the *meshuggener* responsible.'

It was a sentiment Harriet couldn't help agreeing with, even though she had no intention of putting it into words. She came to the end of a row and switched needles. 'Mavis has so much personality, I doubt if it will register on people that her face has been scarred,' she said, hoping to be reassuring and praying her words would prove prophetic. 'And she certainly won't let what has happened prevent her from enjoying life to the hilt, just as she's always done. I was her headmistress, Leah. Believe me, I know!'

Kate was seated in one of St Mark's Church front pews, her head bowed as if the weight of her burnished-gold plait of hair was too heavy for her to bear. Although neither Leon nor Daisy were at home, she had no need to find a babysitter in order to leave the house for a little while. Deborah and Genevre Harvey had descended on number four late in the afternoon, and were still there; Deborah, for reasons Kate couldn't begin to understand, focusing most of her attention on Luke; Genevre happily engrossed in playing Ludo with Jilly and Johnny.

When St Mark's heavy oak door creaked open, she was too deep in her silent pleas to God that Matthew would be returned to her, to take any notice.

Stiffly, aided by the silver-knobbed walking-cane she had begun, of late, to favour, Deborah Harvey made her way down between the rows of empty pews. She had done a lot of thinking in the last few days and she, too, needed to commune with her Maker. She already knew that, when she did so, she was also going to have a long, long conversation with the Emmersons; that no matter what the outcome of Matthew's disappearance, she was going to suggest that, at her expense, Luke Emmerson receive the kind of education that would best fit him for a future as an architect.

With the scent of her distinctive lavender cologne making Kate draw her breath in sharply, she seated herself next to her, her near ankle-length purple coat brushing Kate's floral-patterned, cotton skirt. Kate didn't raise her head or open her eyes. She had a prayer to finish and she wasn't going to be detracted from it by anyone – not even Deborah Harvey.

Deborah, too, bowed her head, her toque hat wobbling ever so slightly. The other decision she had made, and which she still had to communicate to the Emmersons, she now communicated to God: if Matthew was found, safe and sound, he would have her blessing to follow whatever profession it was his choice to follow. And if that meant becoming a Thames waterman like his adoptive father, she would, if necessary, go with him to Waterman's Hall to see him indentured.

When at last Kate raised her head, Deborah reached out and laid a mauve-gloved, arthritic hand over Kate's still clasped hands. It was a gesture that would, a mere week or so ago, have been inconceivable to both of them. Without speaking, knowing everything that was being silently said to her, Kate unclasped her hands, her fingers sliding between Deborah's. For both of them, reaching the new relationship that now existed between them had been a long, painful process. All they needed now, to make it complete, was Matthew.

Chapter Twenty-Two

As the recorded trumpet voluntary sounded, Zac strolled out of his dressing-room, Danny and Leon in his wake, and as the crowd parted to make way for them, he padded into the makeshift spotlight as casually as if he were on a morning shopping trip in Lewisham market. Without a robe or socks, wearing plain black trunks and boots laced high above the instep, he crossed the ring apron and, as the Magnolia Square contingent roared themselves hoarse, climbed the corner steps and ducked under the top rope, a no-frills gladiator, oiled and greased and with a mission to accomplish.

'ON MY RIGHT,' the compère was shouting authoritatively into the megaphone, 'WE HAVE *ARNIE*, HEIGHT SIX FEET THREE INCHES AND WEIGHING IN AT FIF-TEEN STONE EIGHT POUNDS . . .'

'Where's Big Jumbo?' someone yelled from the floor. 'I thought Arnie was fighting Big Jumbo?'

So did Arnie. In narrow-eyed perplexity, he glared across at Zac's corner. He'd been told he'd be either up against Big Jumbo, who he'd been assured was, in boxing slang, nothing more than dogmeat, or another of the tiddlers in The Embassy's pathetic little pond. The guy now being gloved up in the oppos-ite corner looked nothing like dogmeat, and he certainly wasn't a tiddler.

'Who the fuck is he?' he snapped to Ginger, who was acting

as his second. 'I thought you said Robson's fighters were nothing more than glorified boy scouts.'

Ginger eyed Zac. Whoever he was, he most certainly wasn't a boy scout. He was, though, utterly without nerves, betraying none of the restless movements most boxers were unable to control once in their corners, waiting for the bell. 'He must be the geezer Pongo told us about,' he said, beginning, for the first time, to doubt Arnie's chances. 'Just because he looks the part doesn't mean he can deliver the goods, though, does it?'

'. . . AND ON MY LEFT,' the compère continued at the top of his lungs, 'WE HAVE ZAC HEMINGWAY WEIGHING IN AT FIFTEEN STONE TWO POUNDS!'

Ginger's eyes glazed. He'd heard of a geezer by the name of Hemingway on one of his visits to a mate in Parkhurst nick. 'Every time 'e 'its yer, yer see a flash of light,' his mate, who worked out regularly in the prison sports hall, had said. 'Yer either grab 'im or yer move back, because if 'e 'its yer twice, you're gone.' Ginger could see the fat wad of money he'd bet on Arnie going as well. Going right down the Swanee River! When he thought of the amount Archie had riding on Arnie's back, small black dots danced before his eyes. There was going to be murder done if Arnie went down.

'If he comes this way at you, go that way,' he snapped back at Arnie, aware it was advice that left a lot to be desired.

'THE FIGHT'S LISTED AS BEING BETWEEN ANYONE ARCHIE DUKE CHOOSES TO PUT UP AGAINST ANYONE FROM THE EMBASSY BOXING CLUB,' the compère was reminding the vociferous section of the crowd who knew that already, but who hadn't expected The Embassy to produce such a nasty surprise.

As Arnie and Zac walked out into the centre of the ring to face each other, everyone, even those standing on beer crates at the back of the crowd, could see Zac's grin. It wasn't a pleasant grin. And what those nearer, by the ringside, heard him say, wasn't pleasant either.

'The compère may think I'm fighting for Jack, you lily-livered pile of shit, but I'm not. I'm fighting because you're the swine who shoved a broken glass into my girlfriend's sister's face. When I deck you tonight, I'll be decking you for Mavis.'

Leon, in his corner as his chief second, merely thought Zac had meant to say 'in my girlfriend's mother's face'. As did Ted and Beryl and nearly everyone else from Magnolia Square, sitting or standing near them. Lettie Deakin knew differently, though. And so did Danny. He wasn't in the ring, as Leon was. He was standing close up to the ringside, at Zac's corner, and he stumbled against it, dropping the water bottle he had been carrying, his face ashen.

'Blimey,' Nellie said to Charlie, chewing on a chocolate caramel, 'Danny needs ter steady 'is nerves a bit. The fight ain't started yet!'

'SECONDS OUT!' the compère yelled as Zac and Arnie returned to their corners, Arnie blaspheming viciously, Zac cucumber-cool.

'Don't be too over-confident,' Leon said urgently to Zac as, in the seconds before the bell went, he popped a rubber gumshield into Zac's mouth. 'He looks like he has both power and speed. Be defensive till you get his measure!'

The bell went, and the split second it did so, Arnie was across the ring and on Zac like a human torpedo.

Beryl screamed, and buried her head in her grandad's shoulder. Nellie choked on her caramel and had to be pounded on her back by a man from a north-of-the-river boxing club, who was standing behind her.

Carrie's nails dug so hard into her palms they drew blood.

'He's got big legs and thick ankles!' a voice she didn't recognize was yelling close by her. 'It's a great foundation.'

She knew he was talking about Arnie, not Zac.

'Hit! Don't get hit!' Someone else was yelling, this time to Zac as Arnie leaned on him, holding him round the neck with his left arm while he punched away at Zac's ribs and stomach with his right.

'Referee! REFEREE!' Leon yelled, trying to draw the referee's attention to this flouting of the rules and knowing, even as he did so, that he was wasting his time. In an illegitimate fight, the niceties of the rule-book went out of the window.

Arnie was now thumping Zac with the butt and edge of his glove and Danny, jerked out of his torpor of shock by sheer professionalism, began yelling at the referee with as much, if not more, outraged indignation as Leon. Until the fight was over, it was going to be as if he had never heard what Zac had said to Arnie. It had to be that way. Any other way of reacting would be to risk scuppering Zac's chances of winning – and if Zac didn't win, both Mavis and Jack would be shamefully let down. Afterwards, however . . . Afterwards would be a very different matter.

'For Christ's sake, ref! Open yer bleedin' eyes!' he yelled to the referee and, to Zac, 'Drive 'im back across the ring! Otherwise the fight's goin' to be over before it's bleedin' well started!'

The warehouse was in uproar, Arnie's supporters raising the roof because they were now sure Zac was a turkey and that their bets were, after all, going to be made good, Zac's supporters howling outrage at the dirty play going unreprimanded.

'I fink you've said goodbye to yer 'ousekeeping money,' a man standing behind Pru Lewis shouted gleefully in her ear. 'It's goin' to be bread and jam for the old man next week – an' mebbe not much jam!'

'That's it, Zac! Show him what you're made of!' Nibbo suddenly shouted, and Beryl opened her eyes to see Zac's opponent staggering backwards under the force of a blow that had taken him completely by surprise.

A second later, Arnie was delivering a left-right combination of punches so vicious that Zac was again sent skittering back against the ropes.

Beryl screamed and buried her head once again against Albert's shoulder. 'Please God, let it soon be over!' she prayed, tears soaking Albert's well-worn jacket as whistles, cheers, boos and catcalls rained in her ears. 'Please don't let Zac be hurt! Even if it means he doesn't win, please don't let Zac be hurt!'

When the bell rang to signal the end of the round, the only person in Zac's camp not stunned with horror at the way things were shaping was Zac himself.

'Yer got to stagger 'im and drop 'im with a quick left 'ook,' Danny instructed urgently as at lightning speed Leon cleaned Zac off and wiped his gloves and greased him. 'Yer not goin' to be able to play around with this geezer . . . 'e's the one who's playin' with you!'

Zac spat out his gumshield. 'You think so?' he said in what to Leon seemed almost like amusement.

'Christ all-bleedin'-mighty! 'E nearly 'ad you down in the first five fuckin' seconds!' Danny exploded, thinking of all the hopes Jack had had; knowing that Mavis was lying in her hospital bed, thinking of nothing but the fight and its outcome.

Zac took a swig of water from the bottle Leon raised to his lips, winked at Leon and, as the opening bell for the second round rang, sprang to his feet and was out of the corner like a bullet from a gun.

'Is your girlfriend a tart like her sister?' Arnie taunted, as he lashed out with a left hook. The words were muffled by his gumshield but, as Zac ducked the blow, perfectly audible. The word that Zac spat back at him was also perfectly audible. And obscene. Vaguely surprised that Zac avoided the blow he hooked at him, Arnie hooked at him again. Still his fist didn't contact with muscle or bone.

There were hoarse cries of encouragement from the ringside, but who for, Arnie and Zac neither knew nor cared. Arnie followed three more blows up in quick succession. Zac ducked them all.

'Oh, YES!' Daniel Collins exulted as he avoided being knocked in the eye by the decorative cherries on his wife's hat. 'This is style Zac's showing! This is the ticket!'

Ginger thought so, too. The fleet-footed way Zac was now avoiding every blow Arnie tried to plant, showed very clearly he wasn't the dummy he seemed to be in the previous round. And if Mavis Lomax was his girlfriend's sister, then he wasn't in the ring for money. He was out to give Arnie the kind of pasting even he had to admit Arnie deserved. 'This is goin' to be a bugger of a fight, Archie,' he said grimly as if Archie were by his side to hear him. 'And if we're not careful, we're going to lose a shocking amount of ready cash!'

Pongo, who had positioned himself well away from the ringside, up on the warehouse catwalk, grinned. He knew exactly how much ready cash Archie stood to lose if Zac Hemingway won the fight. His grin deepened. He felt no allegiance now to Archie. None whatsoever. And where money was concerned, his was on Hemingway!

In the final second before the bell for the end of round two sounded, Zac unleashed a ripping left to Arnie's body. 'Tart, did you say?' he snarled as Arnie gasped with shock and pain. 'Is that what you called Mavis when you got your jollies by marking her for life?'

333

As he headed gratefully for his corner, Arnie, who had never before been seriously hurt in a boxing ring, or anywhere else for that matter, continued to gasp for air like a beached fish. 'I'll fucking crucify Duke for setting this one up!' he panted to Ginger as Ginger did his stuff as his chief-second. 'And who the hell let slip to this goon it was me that glassed Robson's bird's face?'

'How the bleeding hell do I know?' As Ginger worked with sponge and grease it was a question he, also, would have liked the answer to. 'But if you'd kept your mitts to yourself when we did Robson's club, this wouldn't have happened, would it? You'd be facing dogmeat Big Jumbo and we'd all be quids in!'

'Oh dear Lord! Here we go again,' Hettie said to anyone who cared to listen as the bell for round three clanged, and Zac and Arnie loped from their corners.

'Deck him, Arnie!' one of Archie's crowd, with a lot of cash at stake, bellowed.

'Make mincemeat of him, Zac!' Nibbo exploded. 'Give him a bit of what we gave old Hitler!'

Carrie didn't utter a word. She was beyond speech. Her hands were deep in her coat pockets, knuckled into fists, her eyes fixed on Zac, not moving from him for a second.

'Oh my giddy aunt! He's got him!' Queenie Tillet shrieked, jumping up and down and clapping her hands as Zac drove Arnie across the ring and into the ropes.

Danny's desire that Zac should stagger Arnie was now amply fulfilled. He didn't only stagger, he tottered. As he did so, Zac followed his advantage up with a quick left hook that dropped Arnie in a heap on the deck.

There was a sharp intake of breath from the crowd. From the Magnolia Square contingent, shouts of excitement went up and then, even before the referee's count really got underway, Arnie was on his feet again, and though the pandemonium was such that no one, not even the chief-seconds, could hear what was being said, everyone could tell that Zac was not only fighting Arnie, but was giving him plenty of verbal as well.

'So you enjoy beating up women, do you?' he demanded as he drove the mountainously muscular Arnie backwards again, this time with three vicious lefts to the body and three simultaneous rights to the jaw. 'Well now you're going to pay for your enjoyment!' As the warehouse roof practically lifted, he beat Arnie down on to one knee.

'Finish 'im, Zac!' Danny bawled. 'This ain't no time for stringin' fings out!'

Whether Zac would have taken his advice or not, he never knew, for the bell sounded, saving Arnie's bacon.

'I think Archie Duke's camp have got the message,' Leon said gleefully as he pushed Zac's sweat-soaked blond hair away from his eyes and sponged his face. 'They look sick as horses.'

'Yer'd like to be somewhere else now, wouldn't yer, yer bastard!' Miriam Jennings was shouting at Arnie from where she was sitting. 'It was my daughter yer carved with glass an' I 'ope Zac punctures yer bleedin' kidneys fer yer!'

'Blimey,' Nellie said to Hettie, impressed, 'Miriam ain't 'alf got 'er gander up, ain't she?'

'I've had enough of this,' Arnie gasped tersely to Ginger. 'I want out!'

'I dare say you do, but the only way out before the final bell is to KO Hemingway or throw in the towel,' Ginger said, granite-eyed. 'And if you throw in the towel there's an awful lot of mean people who aren't going to be at all pleased. It isn't only our mob who have money riding on you. The biggest gang in the East End is here, and so is half of north London's Enterprise Boxing Club and The Langham.'

The bell sounded. Wishing he'd never heard of Archie Duke, wishing he'd never gone with Archie to do over The 21, and certainly wishing he'd never laid a hand on Jack Robson's tart, he propelled himself once more into the centre of the ring where Zac was already waiting for him.

'It's only round four,' Leon said to Danny as Zac jabbed and hooked and feinted Arnie into knots. 'What kind of a state do you reckon Arnie's going to be in by round eight? Or ten?'

'I doubt it'll go that far.' Danny was so lost in admiration as a swift left-right combination by Zac nearly had Arnie not only down, but almost out of the ring, that he almost forgot Zac was the man trying to take Carrie away from him. 'It's certainly not goin' to go the full fifteen, no matter 'ow much Zac might want it to.'

'Crikey, I wish Mavis was 'ere to see this!' Miriam said in high satisfaction, her beefy arms folded across her roll-top desk of a chest.

'She'll know exactly how it's gone, round for round, before she goes to sleep tonight,' Nibbo's companion promised, accepting the offer of a peppermint from Albert.

Ted, standing close by her, was too intent on what was taking place in the ring to even notice Albert's offer of a peppermint. Zac Hemingway was meting out to Arnie exactly the kind of punishment he'd hoped he would mete out to him. All Arnie's dirty tricks – the elbowing, the thumb in the eye, the head butts, were falling on stony ground. Zac seemed impervious to them. Relentlessly he worked in close to Arnie's body, not letting him back away, not giving him breathing room. And all the time, he was talking. Ted couldn't hear what he was saying, but he could guess. That this phenomenally powerful young man was enamoured of his Beryl was still pretty hard for him to grasp, but why else would he be in the ring instead of Big Jumbo? As Zac bombarded Arnie with a rain of crucifying blows, he shook his head in wonderment. And he'd thought Beryl was trotting off to The Embassy to meet a boy scout!

By the end of the round, Zac was nailing Arnie with every jab he threw, and was absorbing Arnie's blows without any noticeable effect.

'I ain't never seen nuffink like it,' Charlie said to Nellie, a bottle of milk stout in one hand, a bag of sugar-coated shredded coconut in the other. ''E should be fightin' for the 'Eavyweight Championship of the World! 'E could take on Rocky Marciano with one 'and tied behind 'is back and still win!'

'Is it over yet, Grandad? Oh, please, is it over yet?' Beryl pleaded into Albert's tear-sodden jacket.

Albert, standing with his legs apart, the better to balance the weight of his paunch or, as he preferred to call it, his 'corporation', patted her shoulder. 'Yer shouldn't 'ave come, pet. Rose and Daisy aren't 'ere, are they?'

'It wasn't their mum he hurt,' Beryl responded with a sudden surge of fierceness. 'It was my mum, and Zac's doing this for me, remember?'

Albert didn't remember. He'd been under the impression Zac was fighting for Jack, and why Beryl should think any differently was a mystery to him. It wasn't, however, a mystery he intended mulling over. Not now the bell sounded for round five.

Arnie could hardly walk right. His hands hurt. His body hurt. He hated the human cannonball who was giving him such a public humiliation and hiding. He hated Archie Duke, because if it weren't for Archie he wouldn't be in the ring at all. He hated all Archie's mates who had put money on him and who wouldn't take kindly to losing it. He hated the overweight woman seated at the side of the ring who said she was Jack Robson's bird's mother and who kept hollering insults at him. He hated all south-Londoners, and the sooner he could put some distance between himself and them the better he would like it.

'This isn't as easy as smashin' a broken glass into a woman's

337

face, is it?' Zac was spitting at him as, using both his right hand and his left hand to equal effect, he bombarded him with blows, punching and swinging, hacking and chopping.

Arnie wanted the referee to stop the fight, but as the fight wasn't a legit one, knew there wasn't a hope in hell that the referee would do so. He wanted to throw in the towel, but, because of the number of mobsters who would be out for his blood if he did so, didn't dare. He wished he'd never set eyes on Mavis Lomax. He wished himself a million miles away.

'And this . . .' Zac snarled, 'is for all the other women you've cut and hurt!' The blow sent Arnie spinning glassy-eyed back against the ropes.

'Zac ain't goin' to be able to make this last for much longer,' Danny yelled to Leon above the roar of the shouting, stamping crowd. 'And I don't fink 'e needs to. I fink 'e's made 'is point, don't you?'

Arnie spat out his mouthpiece – was slithering out of the ring, beneath the bottom rope. Amongst utter pandemonium, Miriam rushed across to where he lay sprawled on the ring apron and clouted him around his head with her handbag.

'Churchill should have had Miriam in his War Cabinet,' Daniel said admiringly to Hettie. 'The war would have been over by 1941!'

There was a commotion to the rear of the warehouse almost as noisy as the commotion taking place around the ring. 'POLICE!' an authoritative voice bellowed. 'Remain where you're standing!'

'Rozzers!' went up the cry of a hundred or so people who had no intention of remaining anywhere any longer. 'Scarper!'

Danny's and Leon's reactions were of exasperated irritation more than real alarm. Pirate fights got busted all the time, the adrenalin-charged risk of a police raid being part and parcel of their attraction. The worst that would happen was that they'd have to take a day off work to appear in court and that they'd be slapped with a fine. A fine Jack would pay.

'The fight was over, anyway,' Leon said to Danny with a grin. 'Arnie couldn't crawl to his knees now, let alone his feet.'

As the police began arresting anyone who stayed still long enough for them to be able to do so, Zac ducked under the top rope and sprang down to the ring-apron. A police raid might be neither here nor there for Leon and Danny and the punters, but it was a matter of grave concern to himself. Once under arrest, he'd stand no chance of leaving the country aboard the *Orion* – and with his past record there was no telling what cock-and-bull charges the rozzers might drum up against him.

As people rushed for the doors in the hope of avoiding having the long arm of the law laid on their sleeves, he yelled to Carrie above a sea of heads. 'The Greenland! Pier 25!' and then, with an indecent amount of spring in his legs for a man who had just fought like he had fought, he was dodging anyone in blue and haring towards the rear of the ring and the room that had served as his dressing-room. There was a window in it that led out into a back alley. He'd have to grab his clothes from wherever Leon had stowed them and dress on the hoof if necessary. Running half-naked, wearing only a pair of black satin boxing trunks, was not how he'd imagined setting off for the docks, but it was better than not setting off for them at all. And Carrie wouldn't have trouble leaving the warehouse and joining him at the pier. The chances of a woman being arrested were surely pretty slim.

'Yer can't arrest a woman!' Charlie was saying in outrage to two overly keen young coppers as they laid hands on Ruth Giles. 'An' especially not this woman! She's a vicar's wife!'

'And I'm Kublai Khan,' one of the coppers said grimly. 'Come on, sweetheart. Down the station with you.'

'Blimey, this is a bit of all right, ain't it?' Nellie said gleefully to Hettie. 'If we play our cards right, we'll get a lift in a Black Maria! And a Black Maria'll be far comfier than Albert's fruit and veg lorry!'

'Carrie! CARRIE!' Danny bawled as, the towel around his neck proclaiming him one of the seconds and perhaps one of the fight organizers, the police made a bee-line for him. 'I got to talk to yer!'

For one split second, Carrie hesitated. To begin forcing a way through the mayhem to Danny's side would mean being almost instantly apprehended by a policeman. No matter how utterly dreadful it made her feel, it was a risk she couldn't take. Aware that she was now at absolute crisis point, feeling as if her heart were being wrenched from her chest, she began, instead, to push and pummel her way to the nearest exit.

'The Greenland,' she said breathlessly to the cabby who, once she had sprinted clear of the warren of cobbled streets around the warehouse, swerved to stop for her.

'There ain't a pub I know of by that name,' he said helpfully as she scrambled into the rear of the cab. 'Only a bleedin' great dock.'

'I want the dock. I want the dock entrance.'

He looked at her through his driving mirror, his eyebrows rising. 'Blimey, everyone else in London is makin' for the Mall and Whitehall, and you want a bleedin' dock! What do you know that no one else knows? Is the Coronation Procession goin' to be sailing down the Thames?'

Incredibly, despite the almost unbearable state of nervous and emotional tension she was in, a grin twitched at the corner of Carrie's mouth. She'd forgotten completely about tomorrow being Coronation Day. As the cab veered off the main road and into cobbled streets similar to those that surrounded the warehouse, she was aware of the unusual number of people making their way to the centre of the city on foot. Most of them were carrying blankets or picnic rugs, intent, once they had found a suitable pitch from which they would be able to get a good view of things, on keeping warm throughout the night. Her mother and Hettie would no doubt soon be joining their ranks. Or they would if they didn't end up spending the night in a police station.

The cab swerved round a sharp corner on which a red-white-and-blue-festooned pub stood.

'There'll be fireworks down by the river soon, I shouldn't wonder,' the cab-driver said chattily. 'You'll get a good view of them from the Greenland.'

Fireworks were the very last thing on Carrie's mind. She sat back on the cracked leather seat, aware of the smell of stale exhaust fumes and Capstan full-strength tobacco. Her dad smoked Capstan full-strength. The smell was redolent of home, as was the familiar smell of the Thames when she opened the window. She couldn't even begin to imagine what the scents and smells of New Zealand would be like.

'You're here, love,' the cabby said, skidding to a halt with a screech of brakes. 'But are you sure you want to be? The docks are no place for a woman, especially when it's as black as pitch.'

Carrie fumbled in the pocket of her swing-back coat for her purse. 'I'm fine,' she lied. 'Really I am.'

The cabby shrugged. He'd given a word of warning, he couldn't do more. 'Take care,' he said as she stepped out of the cab and proffered him his fare through his open window, adding for no real reason except that it was a piece of advice most people could do with, 'And don't do anything you might regret!'

Chapter Twenty-Three

꩜

It had been drizzling and the cobbles were sheened with damp. Pier 25. How on earth, in an area as vast as the Greenland, was she going to find pier 25? Panic bubbled up in her throat. What if the *Orion* sailed before she found it? What if she never saw Zac again?

'Pier 25?' a night-time dock-worker said in answer to her frantic query. 'You're nearly on top of it, Missis. You see that big black hulk over there? That's the ship that's just limped in. Engine trouble, I believe. It'll be lucky to be unloaded now before Wednesday.'

Carrie began to run. She wasn't familiar with the docks and she didn't like them. They were too vast; too lonely; too dark. Jumping over a pile of rope, narrowly avoiding a pile of barely visible crates, she neared the enormous cargo-ship, seeing with vast relief the name *Orion* on its prow.

The gangplank was down and there were people about. '*Vamos a tomar un trago, hombre,*' she heard a sailor who had obviously just disembarked saying wearily to his companion. She didn't know what he was saying, and didn't care. All that mattered was that she'd found the boat and that she was, surely, only seconds away from finding Zac.

'Carrie!' He was striding away from the knot of sailors standing at the far side of the gangplank, his hair as pale as barley in the moonlight.

343

Somehow, between leaving the warehouse and arriving at the ship, he had managed to dress. His sweat-marked T-shirt was stretched across his magnificent chest and his American jeans were snug on his hips. He was at her side, his arms around her, his lips hard and hot on hers. She clung to him as if she were clinging to a life-raft in a stormy sea. She loved him. He'd walked into her life without the slightest warning and the chaos he had caused in it would reverberate life-long.

'Carrie?' He lifted his head from hers and was looking down at where she was standing. 'Where's your bag? Did you have to leave it behind at the warehouse?'

'*Si, esa es una buena idea,*' someone was saying close by them.

'No.' She shook her head, drinking in the sight of him and the male scent of him so that she would be able to remember it forever. 'I didn't pack a bag, Zac. I'm not going, you see.' Tears were streaming down her face. 'I can't go. I can't leave Rose . . . or Danny. He loves me, even though he has a funny way of showing it at times. And he needs me—'

'*I need you!*'

Carrie felt as if she was literally fighting for breath. The gangplank was only a couple of feet away. Two steps, that was all that it would take. She didn't see the young boy at the top of the gangplank; didn't see him begin to stumble down it, relief and trepidation in every line of his body.

'I love you, Carrie!' Zac said with a ferocity that robbed her legs of all strength. 'I love you as you *ought* to be loved! There's a life waiting for us in New Zealand that you can't even begin to imagine. I have mates there, money—'

The slight figure stepped from the bottom of the gangplank on to the dockside. 'Aunt Carrie?' Matthew's voice was filled with dazed disbelief. 'Is that you, Aunt Carrie? How did you know I was on the *Orion?* Do Mum and Dad know as well? Are they here? Are—'

'MATTHEW!' Carrie spun to face him as if shot. 'Matthew! It's you? Really you?' She darted towards him, seizing hold of him, sure she must be hallucinating.

'Why are you here, Aunt Carrie?' Matthew asked again, aware, now, that his mum and dad weren't with her. That no one was with her except a man he had never seen before. 'How did you know I was on the *Orion* if Mum and Dad didn't know?'

'Oh, *Matthew*!' Carrie hugged him close. 'I didn't know you were on the *Orion*! No one did! Did you stow away? Your mum and dad have been frantic—'

'I didn't stow away.' His face was wan with tiredness and stress. 'It was all an accident, Aunt Carrie. Mum and Dad will believe me, won't they? Are we going to go home now? Are we going to go home together?'

With her arm still clasping his shoulders, Carrie lifted her head, her eyes holding Zac's. 'Yes,' she said quietly. 'Yes, Matthew, we're going home together.'

There was utter finality in her voice. Looking at her, as she stood with her coal-dark hair a drizzle-damp tangle of curls, her raspberry-pink coat almost luminous in the darkness, Zac knew that nothing he could now say would change her mind. For the moment, he was beaten. But he wasn't beaten for good. Once in New Zealand, and with the money waiting there for him safely in his possession, the world would be his oyster. He stepped towards her and, uncaring of Matthew Harvey's presence, kissed her long and hard.

'I shall be back for you, Carrie Collins,' he said hoarsely when at last he raised his head from hers. 'It isn't over between us. By crikey it isn't!'

Carrie didn't speak. Couldn't speak. With her arm still hugging Matthew's shoulder, she turned and began walking away from him. Away from the ship. Away from the dock. She hadn't said the word 'goodbye'. It had been beyond her. And she hadn't told him about the baby she was certain she was carrying. To have done so would have made what she was now doing impossible. And what she was now doing was walking back towards Magnolia Square, to everything that made up the fabric of her life – Rose, Danny, her mum and dad, her friends.

'Look, Aunt Carrie!' Matthew said suddenly. 'Fireworks!'

They blazed across the sky, cascading down over the Thames in a huge, golden shower. Carrie came to a halt for a moment, looking up at them. Somewhere, distantly, a civic clock began chiming midnight. It was Coronation Day and their families were waiting for them.

'Let's run, Matthew!' she said with sudden urgency, letting go of his shoulder and seizing hold of his hand. 'Let's run all the way up Greenwich Hill and over the heath! Let's run and run until we're home!'

Chapter Twenty-Four

'She's run off,' Danny was saying in a cracked voice as he stood in stupefied anguish on the colourful rag-rug that graced the centre of the Emmersons' roomy kitchen. 'My Carrie's left me. She's gone off with that bastard 'Emingway and she ain't never comin' back. I know she ain't.' His voice broke completely, tears streaking his freckled face. 'What am I goin' ter do?' His plea was addressed to Leon, his desperation total. 'What are me and Rose goin' ter do if Carrie don't come 'ome?'

Leon stared at his friend, too appalled for speech. It was after midnight and the two of them had not long returned from Greenwich police station where they had both been released on bail. Bob Giles was still down there, for Ruth was so outraged at the way she had been manhandled into a Black Maria, she was refusing to allow him to pay bail for her, declaring that she had every intention of remaining in a police cell until she received a written apology.

'She'll wait till Doomsday,' Miriam said as, let off with a caution, she'd barrelled out of the police station, Hettie and Nellie on either side of her. 'An her Fair Isle sweater'll never be the same again,' she added sagely, 'not now it's bin snagged to 'igh 'eaven by 'andcuffs!'

Now, as if it wasn't enough that Leon had to tell Kate that Ruth was still in a cell at Greenwich nick, Danny was now telling them all that Carrie had run off with Zac Hemingway!

It was too preposterous to be true – though Danny obviously didn't think it so. Danny looked like a man whose world had come to a very unexpected, cataclysmic end.

'Just because Carrie isn't home, and Zac isn't at his digs, doesn't mean . . .' Leon began inadequately.

'Is Mr Hemingway the gentleman who won the fight?' Genevre Harvey interrupted with bright interest. 'Because if he is, perhaps he's being held in a police station? If his opponent is still being held in a police station somewhere, and if—'

'The ape that glassed my mother is in 'ospital, not nick,' Billy put in from where he was standing, leaning against the sink, one arm around Daisy's shoulders.

Leon groaned. Why the Harvey aunts were still in his home, privy to this domestic mayhem, he didn't for the life of him know.

'They want to spend Coronation Day in Magnolia Square,' Kate said to him when he had arrived home from the police station to find them installed in the kitchen. 'They're going to stay the night in a local hotel. Or they are if the hotel is still open,' she added, looking at the clock. 'They've been too interested in everything that's been going on to want to leave. First Lettie called by, telling us of how the fight had been raided, and then Queenie called in, full of how you, Danny, Nellie, Hettie, Ruth and goodness only knows who else, had been arrested.'

'And Matthew's Aunt Deborah and Nellie are friends,' Jilly had said from where she was sitting on a pouffe in her dressing-gown and slippers, a bowl of warm, milky cornflakes on her knee. 'And so she wasn't going to leave, Daddy. Not until we heard if everyone was to be released from the police station for Coronation Day.'

Aware of Jilly's continuing presence, Leon groaned again. How was he going to explain away Danny's announcement that Carrie had run off with Zac Hemingway? How, come to that, was he going to explain it to Luke and Johnny, both of whom had been woken by all the comings and goings and were sitting at the kitchen table in their pyjamas, Johnny still sleepy and not understanding too much; Luke understanding everything.

'I'll come home with you mate, and wait with you till Carrie shows up,' he said now to Danny. 'I'm sure things aren't as bad as you think they are and—'

'I love 'er, yer see.' Danny ran a hand despairingly through spiky hair that had once been carrot-red and was now peppered with grey. 'I've never ever loved anyone else. Only Carrie.'

He looked so totally despairing, so bewildered and dazed, that even Deborah Harvey was moved to pity. 'You must pull yourself together, young man,' she said gruffly from the rocking-chair she had, as usual, appropriated. 'There's no sense in giving way before you're even certain of the facts.'

Johnny turned towards Kate, tugging at her skirt. 'Wassermatter, Mummy?' he asked plaintively, his speech blurred by sleepiness. 'Where's Auntie Cawwie? Why has she gone away?' Aware that something was very wrong, even though he didn't understand what, he began to cry. 'Want Aunt Cawwie back,' he hiccuped through his tears. 'Don't want her gone away. Want her back.'

'Sssh, sweetheart,' Kate said comfortingly, hugging him close. 'Everything is going to be all right.' Even to her own ears, her words lacked conviction. If Carrie had indeed run off with Zac Hemingway, then nothing would be all right ever again. At the knowledge that Carrie must have needed to confide in her for weeks past and, not wanting to burden her with even more worries, hadn't done so, Kate felt so sick at heart that she couldn't imagine ever feeling happy again. If Carrie were to disappear out of her life . . . She couldn't bring the thought to a conclusion. It was too dreadful, too utterly unthinkable. Danny had to be wrong in his assumption that Carrie had run off with Zac Hemingway, because if he wasn't . . . if he wasn't, then life in Magnolia Square would never be the same again.

'I think I should get Danny home,' Leon said to her, not wanting there to be any further revelations about Carrie and Zac in front of the children.

Kate nodded. There was, after all, nothing else anyone could do. As Leon compassionately took hold of Danny's arm and began steering him out of the kitchen, she looked towards the clock. It was nearly one in the morning. Deborah and Genevre Harvey would never gain admittance to their hotel now. If Luke slept in Matthew's room, and Johnny slept toe-to-toe with Jilly, then Deborah and Genevre could share Luke and Johnny's twin-bedded room.

Wondering if she had the energy to put fresh sheets on the beds, she followed Leon and Danny down the hallway, her family trailing in her wake. Somewhere, as Leon opened the front door and he and Danny stepped out into the rain-damp air, a church clock chimed the hour.

'It's an hour into Coronation Day,' Daisy said to Billy as light from the open doorway spilled down the garden path, 'and none of us are going to want to celebrate, are we? We don't know where Matthew is, and now we don't know where Carrie is, either.'

Johnny who, unlike Jilly and Luke, had no dressing-gown on over his pyjamas, began shivering, and Billy hoisted him up into his arms. What his mum was going to say when she heard about Carrie's disappearance, he dreaded to think. She'd been quite chipper when he and Daisy said good night to her at the hospital a few hours earlier. He remembered that his mum didn't like Zac Hemingway overmuch, and wondered if it was because she knew there was something going on between him and Carrie.

'I wonder if . . .' he began to say to Daisy as Deborah and Genevre Harvey joined them on the doorstep and Leon began walking Danny down the short flight of steps that led to the path. It was a sentence he never finished.

From the direction of Magnolia Terrace and the heath, there came the sound of running feet. More than one pair of feet. And one of the pairs sounded to be wearing high heels. Everyone stood still. Whoever the runners were, they would be in the square within another few seconds. A drizzle of rain misted the moonlight, and on Nibbo's magnolia tree coronation flags and balloons bobbed and swayed, milkily pale. The runners rounded the corner. Though it was too dark to distinguish them clearly, it was obvious that one was a woman and that the other was a boy. A boy of about twelve years old.

'Oh my God!' Kate sucked in her breath. 'Oh my DEAR God!' Before realization had dawned on anyone else, she began running down the steps, pushing past Danny and Leon, sprinting for the gate.

'Mum!' Matthew shouted, running as he'd never run in his life before, 'MUM!' He cut the vicarage corner, making a bee-line across it for number four. He saw the flags and balloons. He saw his family crowded on his doorstep, all of them bathed in golden light; Billy Lomax standing close to Daisy, Johnny in his arms; Jilly and Luke and, incredibly, his Aunt Genevre and Great-Aunt Deborah! His dad was standing on the pathway with Danny Collins, and his mum . . . his mum was racing towards him as if she had wings on her heels.

'Mum! Mum!' With a strangled sob, he covered the rapidly diminishing distance between them, flying into her arms like an arrow entering the gold. He was home! *Home!*

'I only ran away from school, Mum!' he gasped as she hugged

and hugged him, and his dad, and his brothers and sisters, and even his Aunt Genevre and his elderly Great-Aunt Deborah, ran towards them. Only Danny Collins remained stock-still. 'I never ran away from home! Honest I didn't.'

'Carrie?' Still Danny didn't move. Couldn't move. He stared past the joyful, moonlit reunion scene to where Carrie, winded and breathless by her long run, had slowed to a walk as she crossed the dark square towards him. 'You 'aven't left me?' he asked hoarsely as, at last, she stepped onto the rain-slicked pavement. 'You're not goin' ter leave me? You're not goin' ter run off with 'Emingway?'

Carrie paused at the Emmersons' gateway. In the long years she and Danny had been together, she had known him in many different moods and tempers, but she had never known him like this before. She had never known him to be frightened. 'No,' she said with quiet finality from where she was standing and then, gently, 'We're married, remember?'

A slow, wide, sizzling grin split his snub-nosed face. 'Course we are.' His voice was raw with emotion. 'An' we're 'avin' another kiddie, ain't we?'

Carrie nodded, tears glittering on her eyelashes. In his own, inimitable way, he was telling her all she needed to know. Together with Rose, they and the new baby were going to be a family – were already a family. He walked towards her with a measure of his old jauntiness. 'It's bin a funny old summer, ain't it?' he said with mammoth understatement as she stepped into the circle of his arms. 'A coronation summer – an' they don't come round very often, thank Gawd. With a bit o' luck, you and me'll never 'ave another.'

She blinked away the tears that threatened to fall. Her coronation summer had been the most memorable, most special summer of her life – and Danny was right, there wouldn't be another. There would, though, be a baby. A baby that was going to fill her life with joy and purpose.

'Let's go home, love,' she said, suddenly wanting to be home more than she wanted anything else in the world.

'There's nuffink I'd like better,' he said with fervent sincerity, 'an' when we get indoors I'll make yer a nice cup o' scaldin' 'ot tea.'

She smiled lovingly up into his dearly familiar face. A cup of tea at her own kitchen table. Rose sleeping peacefully in the little bedroom next to theirs. Coronation morning to look forward to. 'That sounds smashing,' she said, her head resting against his shoulder, his arm around her waist, as they began walking homewards across the moonlit square.

A Season of Secrets

**the latest novel by bestselling author
Margaret Pemberton is out now.**

Sweeping from the Great War, through the Jazz Age to the
1940s, this story follows the entwined lives of the Fentons, an
aristocratic family from Yorkshire.

Thea, the eldest daughter of Viscount Gilbert Fenton, flouts
the unwritten rules of her class by embarking on a love affair
with Hal, the fiercely socialist son of one of her father's tenant
farmers. Carrie, her close childhood friend and granddaughter
of the Viscount's nanny, has always been expected to marry Hal
– but when she goes into service she finds herself longing for
the one person she can never hope to marry.

Olivia, the middle Fenton sister, follows a more conventional
path, forging friendships with the British royal family and
attending a finishing school in Germany. Her relationship with
Count von der Schulenburg does not raise eyebrows, but as the
mid-1930s approach, she finds herself in a country experiencing
rapid, radical and dangerous social change. Violet, the youngest
of the Fenton sisters, is also the most reckless. She dreams of
becoming an actress in Hollywood, unaware her life will be filled
with more drama than any part she will ever play.

And then there is Rozalind, their American cousin, who is
secretly in love with a married US senator. Her ambitions to
become a photojournalist will also take her into the heart of
Hitler's Germany.

Set against the rich backdrop of the first half of the twentieth
century, *A Season of Secrets* is an unforgettable tale of passion
and betrayal, love and war.

The first chapter follows here.

Chapter One

৩৩

AUGUST 1915

It was early morning and eight-year-old Carrie Thornton sat on a sheep-studded hillside, her arms hugging her knees, her face wet with tears. Below her, in one of the loveliest valleys North Yorkshire possessed, a river curved. On its far bank, beyond an ancient three-arched stone bridge, lay a Georgian mansion sheltered by trees.

With blurred vision and deeply apprehensive, Carrie stared down at it. Gorton Hall was the home of the Fenton family. Carrie was familiar with stories about the Fentons, for when Viscount Fenton had been a child, her granny had been his nanny. Not only that, but when her widowed father had marched off to war, a little over a year ago, his company commander had been Lord Fenton, and Lord Fenton had still been his senior commanding officer when, three short weeks ago at the battle of Hooge, German shellfire had ended his life.

The tears Carrie was now shedding were for the father, who had been loving and kind and had always had time for her. The apprehension she felt was because of the letter Lord Fenton had written to his wife, suggesting it might help the grand-daughter of his old nanny get over her grief if, for the remainder of the summer, she were to spend a little time each day at

357

Gorton with their daughters, two of whom were close to Carrie in age.

Ever since her mother had died of diphtheria her granny had said that when she was old enough – twelve or thirteen – there could be no better training for her than to be taken on as a tweeny at Gorton, and when the news of Lord Fenton's suggestion had been broken to her, Carrie had said, not under-standing, 'But I'm too young to be a tweeny, Granny.'

Her granny had hugged her close to her ample bosom. 'You're not going there to work, silly-billy – and won't be doing so for a long time yet. You're going there to be company for Miss Thea and Miss Olivia.'

Carrie had frowned, still deeply puzzled. She had known Thea and Olivia ever since she could remember, for whenever the family were at Gorton, and not at their London town house, Lady Fenton would call on her husband's nanny for a cosy chat, a cup of tea and a slice of home-made ginger cake. When she did so she nearly always brought Thea and Olivia, and sometimes their younger sister, Violet, with her. Not only that, but the Fentons' current nanny often walked Thea and Olivia into the village so that they could spend their pocket-money on butterscotch at the village shop.

'But why do I have to be company for them at the big house?' she'd asked, not liking the way it would set her apart from her friends. 'Why can't they come down to Outhwaite to play?'

'Because that wouldn't be at all proper,' her granny had said briskly. 'Now stop asking questions and just think what a lucky little girl you are, being invited to play in such a wonderful house.'

Not feeling at all lucky, Carrie wiped the last of her tears away, pushed wheat-coloured plaits back over her shoulders and rose glumly to her feet. Until now, she had never set foot inside the house and had never expected to until the day when, if she fulfilled her granny's plans for her, she would begin working there.

Hal was a year older than Carrie, and his father, who was one of Lord Fenton's tenant farmers, had told her quite bluntly what he thought of her being invited to Gorton to be a play-mate for Thea and Olivia. 'It's going to muck things up,' he'd said grimly, wiping his nose on the sleeve of a shabby jacket. 'How can you spend time wi' them and still spend time wi' me? You can't. You're not going to be able to do any bilberry-picking, and you're not going to be able to watch the vole pups take to the water – and seein' as how it's August, it'll be the last litter this year.'

'Perhaps Miss Thea and Miss Olivia will want to bilberry-pick and see the vole pups as well,' she'd said.

Hal had laughed so much he'd had to hug his tummy. 'Not in a million years, daft idiot!' Suddenly he'd straightened up. Pushing a tumble of coal-black curls away from his forehead, he'd said fiercely, 'And if you're playmates, don't call them *Miss* Thea and *Miss* Olivia. Not unless they call you *Miss* Caroline.' And at this unlikelihood he'd begun laughing again, this time so hard that Carrie had thought he was going to be sick.

'Hello, Carrie,' Blanche Fenton's voice was low-pitched and full of reassurance as, still holding her granny's hand, Carrie faced her in the intimidating surroundings of a room stuffed with gilt-framed paintings, silver-framed photographs and small tables crammed with ornaments. 'Thea and Olivia are very much looking forward to you spending time with them.'

Despite her nervousness, Carrie was glad to discover that Lady Fenton was just as nice and approachable within the walls of her home as she had always seemed to be outside it. She had a cloud of dark hair that she wore caught in a loose knot on the top of her head and, wherever she went, she carried the faint scent of roses with her. Though she seemed old to Carrie, her granny had told her that Lady Fenton was only twenty-nine, which, she had said, wasn't old at all.

'And Gilbert is only thirty,' she had added, forgetting her rule always to refer to her former charge as either 'Lord Fenton' or 'his lordship'. 'They were scarcely old enough to be out in society when they married, and neither of them has any side whatsoever.'

Carrie had been mystified by the word 'side' until her granny had explained it meant that Lord and Lady Fenton weren't pretentious. 'Which means they behave in exactly the same way to absolutely everyone, no matter who they are,' she had added when Carrie had continued to look bewildered.

'Please don't worry about anything, Nanny Thornton,' Blanche Fenton said now. 'I'm sure this arrangement is going to work beautifully.' She took hold of Carrie's free hand. 'Jim Crosby will collect Carrie every morning in the pony-trap and bring her home in it every teatime.'

Carrie felt a flash of alarm. As well as being the general handyman at Gorton Hall, Jim Crosby was Hal's uncle, and Carrie didn't think he'd take kindly to ferrying her back and forth every day. He'd think she was getting ideas far above her station in life – as would her friends in the village when they got to hear about it.

Foreseeing all kinds of difficulties ahead, she said a reluctant goodbye to her granny and allowed herself to be led from the room.

'Thea and Olivia are in the playroom,' Blanche said encouragingly. 'Violet doesn't visit it much, as she is still in the nursery and spends most of her time with Nanny Eskdale.'

They were walking down a royal-blue carpeted corridor lined with marble busts set on fluted pedestals. Through an open doorway Carrie saw a maid busily dusting. The room looked to be a smaller version of the room they had just left and she wondered how many other such rooms there were, and how the Fentons decided which room it was they wanted to spend time in.

Another maid, a smart black dress skimming neat buttoned boots and wearing a snowy lace apron and cap, walked down the corridor towards them. She stood to one side as they passed, giving Blanche a respectful little bob and shooting Carrie a look of curiosity.

Together, Blanche and Carrie turned a corner and began climbing a balustraded staircase carpeted in the same dazzling blue. At the top, on a spacious landing, it divided into two.

'This is the main staircase of the house,' Blanche said. 'I'm taking you this way so that we can look at a few family portraits together.'

The portrait looking down on them as they approached the landing was of a robust-looking gentleman with a shock of silver hair.

'This portrait is of Samuel George Fenton, Lord Fenton's grandfather,' Blanche said as they came to a halt in front of it. 'He was a Yorkshire wool baron, a Member of Parliament and the first Viscount Fenton.'

They turned and began to mount the left-hand flight of stairs.

'This portrait,' she said, referring to the first painting they came to, 'is of his wife, Isabella May.'

Isabella May's stout figure was encased in purple silk. She was heavy-featured and stern-faced, her thin lips set in a line as tight as a trap. Carrie didn't like the look of her, but knew it would be bad manners to say so.

There were several more portraits. One was of the present viscount's late father who, Blanche told her, had spent his early years in India, an officer in the British Army. Carrie liked the dashing red of his uniform and the wonderful sword at his side.

By the time they reached the next landing, where the royal-blue carpet gave way to carpeting a lot less dazzling, Carrie knew that, where Lady Fenton was concerned, she had never met any adult she thought more wonderful.

'The playroom is up here on the third floor, so that noisy games can be played without the rest of the house being disturbed,' Blanche said. 'The schoolroom is on the second floor of the east wing and easier to get to.'

'The schoolroom?' Carrie had never before given any thought as to how Thea and Olivia were educated. All she knew was that they certainly didn't go to Outhwaite elementary school where, clutching slates and chalk, everyone sat in rows on uncomfortable benches and only their teacher, Miss Calvert, had a desk.

They were outside the playroom door now, but Blanche didn't open it. Until now she had never had any doubt that inviting Carrie to spend time with Thea and Olivia was, under the circumstances, the right thing to do. It wasn't as if Carrie was just any village child. As Gilbert's nanny, Ivy Thornton had played an important part in his childhood and his affection for her was deep. When he had outgrown the nursery, Ivy had become nanny to one of his young cousins and then, later, nanny to a whole string of his nieces and nephews. Now in her seventies and comfortably pensioned off by him, she lived rent-free in one of Gorton's tied cottages.

Knowing her husband as she did, Blanche was certain that, like her, he would have assumed any grandchild of Ivy's would be reasonably well-educated. Now, seeing how startled Carrie was by the word 'schoolroom', she was no longer so sure.

'Can you read and write, Carrie?' she asked, trying not to let her concern show in her voice.

Carrie looked even more surprised at this.

'Yes.' She tried not to show how affronted she was by the question. 'My granny taught me to read and write – and how to do numbers – long before I went to school.'

Blanche breathed a sigh of relief. If Carrie could read and write, it made things easier. She would feel less awkward with Thea and Olivia and might even be able to join them in their lessons when Miss Cumberbatch, their governess, returned from her summer leave.

Hoping that Thea and Olivia would be immediately friendly towards Carrie – especially as she had explained to them the manner in which Carrie had been orphaned – Blanche opened the playroom door.

With butterflies dancing in her tummy, Carrie followed her into the room. What she had been expecting she didn't quite know, but certainly it wasn't the sight of Thea garbed in a trailing cloak of gold-coloured velvet, a cardboard crow crammed on a waterfall of glossy chestnut ringlets.

'I'm King Cophetua,' she said, looking exceedingly cross. 'Olivia is supposed to be the beggar-maid, only she refuses to take off her shoes and stockings and she won't wear anything raggedy out of the dressing-up box.'

Olivia, her marmalade-coloured hair held away from her face by a floppy brown bow, skipped up to them, unrepentant. 'That's because Thea always takes the grand parts and never lets me wear the crown. Would you like to be the beggar-maid, Carrie? Or have we to play at being pirates instead?'

Blanche, grateful that Ivy Thornton wouldn't now have to be told by Carrie that on her first day at Gorton she'd been asked to dress in rags, said, 'Being pirates sounds far more interesting than being King Cophetua and his beggar-maid.'

Thea, still trailing a river of gold-coloured velvet behind her, came over to stand next to Olivia. Blanche, aware that her daughters were patiently waiting for her to go, blew them a kiss and, certain they would now take good care of Carrie, closed the door behind her.

Thea swept her late grandmother's opera cloak up and over her shoulder, toga-like. 'What is it like to be an orphan?' she asked bluntly as the sound of her mother's footsteps receded. 'Is it very hideous?'

'Yes.' Carrie felt it was a stupid question, but as she hadn't yet got the measure of Thea, didn't tell her so. 'And I'm only an orphan because my father was killed fighting in Flanders. How would you feel if it had been your father?'

Thea, who was a year older than Carrie and Olivia, regarded her with eyes that were very narrow, very green and very bright. She'd been happy at the thought of having Carrie as a temporary playmate and was quite prepared to be condescendingly nice to her, but she wasn't happy about a village girl being uppity with her.

As she tried to think of a suitably crushing retort, Olivia took hold of Carrie's hand and began leading her towards a huge wicker hamper that was the dressing-up box. 'Papa isn't going to be killed. Mama gave him a little silver crucifix that used to hang on one of her necklace chains, and he carries it with him all the time.'

There was such happy trust in Olivia's voice that Carrie hadn't the heart to express doubt as to whether the crucifix would stop bullets, bayonets and murderous shellfire.

'Are you wearing a black pinafore dress because you're in mourning?' Olivia asked. 'I saw you in a pretty red gingham dress once. We don't have any gingham dresses. All our dresses have pin-tucked bodices and big sashes that are always coming undone.'

'Yes,' Carrie said to the question. 'And the red gingham is my Sunday-best dress. Granny made it.'

The flowered linen smocks Thea and Olivia were wearing now were far from being either pin-tucked or sashed and were not the kind of clothes Carrie had expected them to be wearing. Thea even had a hole in one of her white stockings. That she was so obviously unembarrassed by it impressed Carrie. Aiming for self-confidence herself, she liked to see it in other people.

Thea, aware that the moment for saying something crushing to Carrie had passed, said impatiently, 'If we're going to be pirates, let's find something pirate-like to wear.'

Energetically she began rummaging in the hamper, tossing things in Olivia's direction. Carrie didn't help in the search. Instead she looked around her.

The room was large and packed with things she itched to take a closer look at. There was a huge rocking horse with flaring nostrils and a long swishy mane and tail in one corner. In another was the largest doll's house she had ever seen. There was a long shelf stacked higgledy-piggledy with books, includ-ing one she recognized because she had been given the same book, *The Wind in the Willows*, as a present two Christmases ago. On other shelves there were jigsaw puzzles and board games and on the bottom shelf was a row of beautifully dressed dolls. Beneath the dolls was a gaily painted wooden box crammed with toys. Spilling out of it were a train, a spinning top, a musical box and a monkey-up-a-stick.

Just as she was about to go and have a closer look at the monkey-up-a-stick, Thea said, 'I think we have enough stuff now to be going on with, but as I could only find one pair of breeches, you and Olivia will have to be lady pirates.' She stuffed a pile of garments into Carrie's arms. 'There's a red-spotted scarf you can tie around your head like a bandana, a striped shirt, a fringed orange sash for tying round your waist and an eye-patch that belonged to Mama's Uncle Walter.'

Olivia was already clambering into an outlandish selection

of garments, and Carrie, beginning to get into the spirit of the thing, pulled the man's shirt over her head, anchoring it around her waist with the sash.

Olivia giggled. 'You look first-rate, Carrie. All you need now is a big black moustache. There's a stick of burnt cork somewhere. Let's see if we can find it.'

'So we drew moustaches on our faces with the burnt cork,' she said to Hal, much later in the day. 'And we had enormous fun jumping from the table onto a chair and then onto other chairs, pretending the floor was the sea and that we would drown if we touched it.'

Hal made the kind of sound in his throat that he always made when he wasn't impressed. 'Doesn't sound like much of a game ter me.' He scowled so hard his eyebrows almost met in the middle. He was herding his father's cows in for their evening milking and bad-temperedly switched the rump of the animal nearest to him. 'Aren't you going to do 'owt else this summer but go ter Gorton? The vole pups were out this afternoon, but it weren't much fun watching 'em all on me own.'

Carrie tried to feel sorry about not having been with him, but she'd enjoyed herself so much she couldn't quite manage it.

'Before I came home Lady Fenton introduced me to Mr Heaton,' she said as the cows headed up the narrow tree-lined track towards the farm buildings and the summer sky now smoked to dusk. 'Mr Heaton is the butler. She told him I was Miss Caroline Thornton, that I was a guest of Miss Thea and Miss Olivia and that I would be at Gorton Hall every day until mid-September.'

Instead of being impressed, Hal forgot about his bad mood and hooted with laughter.

Carrie punched his shoulder. 'What's so funny?' she

demanded hotly. 'Mr Heaton was very nice to me. *Everyone* was very nice to me – apart from Thea, but that was only in the beginning. And Lady Fenton is like the Good Queen in a fairy story. She's . . .' Carrie struggled to find words that would do Blanche Fenton justice. 'She smells of roses, and she talked to me as if I was a grown-up. Apart from Granny, I think she's the most special person in the whole wide world.'

'You're barmy.' Still chuckling, Hal fastened a rusting iron gate behind them so that if the cows decided to head back to the meadow they wouldn't get very far. 'And you're not the only one. My Uncle Jim says Lady Fenton isn't right in the head, and that her having you up at Gorton every day is proof of it. I know you don't want to go there, getting above your-self, because you told me you didn't.'

It was true. She had. But that had been yesterday. It had been before she'd fallen under Lady Fenton's spell, and before she'd known she was going to be best friends with Olivia and possibly a friend of Thea's, too. It had been before she'd sensed that, where the Fenton family was concerned, she had started on a long and very special journey.

At Bello, we believe in the timeless power of books, and our extensive list of classic fiction has something for everyone. Whether you want to indulge in a heart-warming tale of life in the Hebrides from Lillian Beckwith's *The Hills is Lonely*, read a classic Yorkshire saga from award-winning author Brenda Jagger, or escape to the scandalous world of Renaissance Italy in Sarah Bower's *The Sins of the House of Borgia*, we've got the book for you.

BELL◎

panmacmillan.com/bello

@bellobooks   bellobooks

It's time to relax with your next good book

THEWINDOWSEAT.CO.UK

If you've enjoyed this book, but don't know what
to read next, then we can help. The Window Seat is
a site that's all about making it easier to discover your
next good book. We feature recommendations,
behind-the-scenes tales from the world of publishing,
creative writing tips, competitions, and, if we're honest,
quite a lot of lists based on our favourite reads.

You'll find stories and features
by authors including Lucinda Riley, Karen Swan,
Diane Chamberlain, Jane Green, Lucy Diamond
and many more. We showcase brand-new talent
as well as classic favourites, so you'll never be
stuck for what to read again.

We'd love to know what you think of the site, our books,
and what you'd like us to feature, so do let us know.

@panmacmillan.com

facebook.com/panmacmillan

WWW.THEWINDOWSEAT.CO.UK